Legacy

By Vince Pinkerton

Copyright © 2024 by Vince E. Pinkerton

This is a work of fiction. Unless otherwise indicated, all the names, characters, businesses, places, events and incidents in this book are either the product of the author's imagination or used in a fictitious manner. Any resemblance to actual persons, living or dead, or actual events is purely coincidental.

*Dedicated to
Harrison and Vicki*

*Very special thanks to
Carra Smith-Gross MSPAS, PA-C
For her help with all my medical questions.*

OTHER BOOKS BY THE AUTHOR

The Devil Plays Six Strings
The Devil and the Dance Hall Girl

Foreword

A few years ago, following a lunch meeting with a business associate, our conversation turned to movies, specifically horror movies. We discussed the elements that made a good horror movie, and he told me about his idea for a possible film. Always up for a challenge, I took his idea and set out to write a film script based on it.

I failed miserably.

But that attempt at screenwriting reawakened an urge deep inside of me to start writing again. I had done some short-story and journalism-style writing in college, and during my days chasing dreams of being the next great rock-n-roll bass player, I wrote many songs for the bands I was a part of. In my day job as a television producer, I had written more commercial and promotional scripts than I could remember. But I had never written anything long form, and my gut was telling me that it was time to try.

I set my eye on a shorter piece; I just needed a challenge. The idea came to me to write something where the main character spoke only in Bible verses- not preaching- but speaking the verses conversationally. I figured if I could pull that off, then I was on the right track.

That challenge turned into an argument between an old, blind black man and his son. When I finished it, I showed it to my wife (my toughest critic and most trusted advisor). She said it was interesting. A little weird, but good.

Success!

Now what?

I reread what I had written, and questions began to pop up. Who was this old black man, why was he blind, and why was he only speaking in Bible verses?

Turns out his name was Elijah Parker and he had sold his soul to the devil. That story morphed into *The Devil Plays Six Strings*, my first novel. Six months later came its sister novel, *The Devil and the Dance Hall Girl*.

I had been bitten by the writing bug, and after *Dance Hall Girl* was published, I dove straight into *The Devil and the Disciple*, the third book in what I have come to think of as my Devil Stories, but there was a problem. I had a good beginning for the book, but I wasn't sure yet where it was going. I needed to step away from that series and do something different.

Also, the story idea my associate had presented to me would not leave me alone, so maybe it was time to try again. It took me over a year to write, and I've strayed far from the original concept, but *Legacy* is what I came up with. I hope you enjoy reading it as much as I enjoyed writing it.

Vince

Legacy

Chapter One

March 5, 1870
Animas Forks, Colorado

A cold wind blew out of the mountains and down through the small mining town of Animas Forks, Colorado, causing Curtis to shiver as he stepped out onto the porch of Miss Ellen's boarding house. The crisp, early morning sunlight warmed his face but did little to relieve the chill.

A sign advertising *10 Cents a Dance* hung on the wall in Miss Ellen's parlor, but everyone knew what that really meant, especially as there was no piano, music box, or Victrola to be found, but the ladies—Marlene, Becca, June, and Prissy—danced all night, most every night. In that part of the world, you did what you had to do to survive.

The boarding house was quiet now, but echoes of the night before still rang in Curtis's ears. He had been living at Miss Ellen's for the last two months since an avalanche had taken his home and blacksmith shop.

It had also taken the lives of his wife and son. He had to fight hardest on mornings like this, to keep from getting lost in their memories. He could see their smiling, laughing faces in the early morning sun and hear their voices in the wind that swept down from the mountain. On mornings like this, he just wanted to stay inside and remember, but this was hard country and out here life had a way of forcing you to move on, even if that was the last thing you wanted to do.

He had re-opened the blacksmith shop temporarily in the stables of the Colorado Mining Company's home base. The company foreman, old man Hinkle, was charging him two bits a week for a stall and a lean-to for the forge. At that rate, Curtis wouldn't stay in business long, so every morning he rose with the sun to spend a few hours trying to rebuild his business, and his life, from the wreckage the avalanche had left behind.

His boots broke through the crust of frozen mud that served as the town's main street. The cold cut through his too-thin coat, and he pulled its collar tighter around his neck as he started walking toward the opposite end of town.

"You're looking mighty cold out there this morning, Curtis. Why don't you come back inside and let me warm you up?"

Prissy, the newest of the four *ladies* that Miss Ellen currently had on hand to entertain the men from the eight active mines surrounding Animas Forks, waved to him from the upstairs window of the boarding house. She couldn't have been more than fifteen years old. The first night he spent in the boarding house, Prissy told him that her parents had hired her out to Miss Ellen for enough money to keep their farm in South Georgia up and running. Once she had earned enough to pay Miss Ellen back, she would start making the same as the other girls. Curtis had the unique pleasure of calling the room next to Prissy's, *home*, and from the noises he heard coming from it each night, he guessed that she was well on her way to paying off that debt.

There had been *five* ladies at Miss Ellen's, but one of the mine workers, filled with Christmas cheer—courtesy of the holiday whiskey special at the Sagebrush Saloon—had created a vacancy. Miss Ellen couldn't get a new girl until the spring thaw opened the lower pass, so until then, she had agreed to rent the empty room to Curtis.

"I'm plenty warm, Prissy," Curtis called, waving back at her. "But thanks for the offer."

"Oh well," she said with a laugh as she started to close the window. "If you change your mind, you know where to find me."

In another life, in another town, Prissy would have made some man a good wife, but hard times and her parents' bad decisions had landed her there, not any fault of her own.

Since the avalanche, he had been able to rebuild the basic frame of the blacksmith shop, and today, he would start putting on the roof. The owner of the Cavalry Mine had provided him with lumber in exchange for future work, and a mine wagon had delivered a load of roughhewn boards the day before. He had been able to salvage a hammer and some nails form the wreckage. Today, he would climb to the top of the new framing and hope that the sun would keep him warm enough to do what needed to be done.

He nailed the first board in place, then flexed his fingers to try and loosen his cold, stiff hands. A strange noise echoed down from the high pass—low and mournful, like a mother wolf who had lost her pups. He scanned the horizon but saw nothing. The high pass wouldn't be clear of snow till mid-summer, and then only the bravest or most stupid traveler would try his luck. For most, the high pass was a death march.

The second board was in place, and he was about to nail it down when the mournful cry came again. A shiver ran down his spine, causing the hairs on the back of his neck to stand on end.

The high-pass road led away from town and into the shadows cast by the mountain. He stared into the darkness, waiting, expecting to see something move out of their depths and into the morning sun.

Nothing did.

Curtis shook his head and chuckled, feeling foolish. He was tired, and his mind was playing tricks on him.

He went back to work but couldn't stop thinking about what could be lurking in the darkness at the base of the mountain. Distracted, he missed the nail he was holding and hit his thumb.

"Damn it!" He shook his hand in the cold air, hoping to fling away the pain. His voice echoed against the walls of the sleeping town and came back to him on the cold morning air.

He thrust his hand under his arm, closed his eyes hard, and gritted his teeth against the pain. His thumb throbbed with every heartbeat.

The wailing from the mountain came again as if in answer to his own cry. It was closer this time and so loud that Curtis ignored the pain and covered his ears to try and block the sound. It didn't do any good.

A feeling of absolute despair flooded over him and thoughts of his wife and son exploded into his mind. He was frantically wiping the snow from his son's face. The boy's skin was blue, and a thin coating of ice covered his open eyes. He pulled his wife from beneath a mound of snow, her face frozen in a look of shock and terror.

The memory was so vivid, so real, that Curtis cried out. His foot slipped off the rafter he was perched on, and he tumbled from the roof, landing flat on his back on the hard frozen earth.

Another memory assaulted him as he lay there trying to catch his breath. The bodies of his wife and son, wrapped in white cloth and arranged like cord wood, alongside the bodies of the mine worker that had killed Miss Ellen's special girl, of Mr. Brighton, the town drunk who had fallen asleep in a snowbank, and the special girl herself who had just turned eighteen the week before Christmas. They were all stored in an old smokehouse outside of town and would lay there frozen until the ground thawed enough for them to be buried.

Something came between him and the sun. He opened his eyes and fear rushed over him like the avalanche that had killed his family. He struggled to his feet, still short of breath from the fall.

A black undulating mass floated above him, the desperate cry came again, echoing from deep within it, and an overwhelming feeling of hopelessness and misery replaced his fear. He gasped for breath, fought back tears, and crab-crawled backward to get away. Panic raced through him. He turned and tried to run, but his feet froze in place before he could make the first stride.

The cold swiftly traveled up the length of his body. His vision blurred as a thin sheet of ice formed over his eyes. He tried to scream, but his tongue was frozen to the roof of his mouth. A wave of cold entered his brain, and he lifted up a desperate, silent prayer,

Dear God! Save Me!

If God answered, Curtis never heard Him.

Chapter Two

December 10, 2008
Springfield, Illinois

Streamers and noisemakers filled the air with a rainbow of color and sound. James had done it; it had taken sixteen years and more loans than he could ever hope to repay, but he was a doctor. Not just any doctor, a surgeon, it said so in black and white on his diploma.

How many times had he wished that he could just quit and walk away? Sleepless nights in pre-med and medical school, picking up shifts as a waiter and bartender just to make ends meet. Reading and studying after work until his vision blurred and he fell asleep on a pile of books. Then residency at the local VA Hospital, working with doctors that couldn't get a job anywhere else. But no matter how bad he wanted to quit, he hadn't. He had stayed the course and now it had all paid off, he was officially *Doctor* James Michael Hughes.

"Congratulations, son, you did it!" Dr. David Carroll, Dean of Medicine and James' mentor, shook his hand and slapped him on the back.

"Thank you, sir," James said, beaming with pride.

On his rare nights off, he and Dr. Carroll would drink and discuss the ethics and morality of surgery and what it really meant to be a doctor. He would never forget the nights he spent listening to Dr. Carroll drunkenly sermonizing about how so many surgeons left medical school with dollar signs in their eyes to go directly into private practice.

"All they care about is fixing the bulbous noses and sagging breasts of the ridiculously wealthy. And for what?" he would ask to the crowd that would inevitably gather around. "Only to end up years later rich, but empty. That's what. Having never really accomplished anything with their lives, they try to fill the void with cars, boats, trophy wives, and drugs. But it's never enough."

Dr. Carroll would lecture James night after night, saying that a true doctor lived to serve - not himself but those most in need. "There are more than enough tight butts and perky boobies in the world, James." That was his favorite line. "But there are never enough real doctors!"

It wouldn't be long after that when James would pour Dr. Carroll into his beat-up '95 Ford Bronco and take him home.

Today, Dr. Carroll was fresh, sober, and beaming with pride. That morning, he had presided over the small, mid-year graduation ceremony. Now, he was host to the fifteen graduates and their families in his modest home across the street from the university.

James had lost his parents in a car accident during his first year in Med School. Dr. Carroll must have sensed his discomfort at being the only graduate without family at the gathering and had made it a point to stay close.

"I know your parents would have been so proud of you today," he said, then looked around the room at the clusters of smiling families. "They would have even been *more proud* that you have decided to work at the VA."

James smiled and nodded, his decision to become a surgeon and work at that Veterans Association hospital had not been an easy one. He had made that decision after a particularly grueling night during his residency. A night that would change his life in more ways than one.

The night had started out like most every night at the VA. He had been sent to prep a recently discharged veteran that had been wounded in the leg during one of the never-ending Middle East conflicts for surgery. The treatment the man had received in a European military hospital had at first seemed successful, but now, a month later, he had taken a turn for the worst, leaving him with no feeling below the knee. He was scheduled for exploratory surgery to determine the extent of the problem and to set a course for treatment.

"I got to tell you, Doc, I'm a little nervous about this," he said.

"Nothing to worry about Mr...." James checked the chart. "I'm sorry, Private Duboski, we are just going to check under the hood, change the oil, and send you on your way."

"Yeah, right." Duboski chuckled.

"All kidding aside, we are just going to go in, see what's causing your problem, and figure out how to get you back on your feet again." James followed that with a wink and a confident smile.

"If you say so, Doc. Are *you* doing the surgery?"

"Nope, I'm just the junior mechanic." He checked the chart again. "You will be in the capable hands of Dr. Fredrick Kemple."

"Is that good?"

"Well, I don't know him personally. I'm still new here but he's been with the VA a long time," James answered. "So, he must be pretty good."

"If you trust him, then so do I." Duboski smiled and seemed a little less worried.

The anesthesiologist came into the room, checked Duboski's chart and wristband, then proceeded to inject a shot of propofol into the IV.

"That's the good stuff." James smiled down at Duboski, whose faraway look indicated he was already starting to feel the effects of the drug. "Nighty night, I'll see you when you wake up."

Duboski tried to wave, but sleep was overtaking him. James watched as the attendants rolled him out of the room and toward the operating theaters.

Half an hour later, he was working on a chart at the nurses' station when shouting and the sound of breaking glass came from the surgery wing. James ran down the hall, rounded the corner, and stopped short. A fat, old doctor in scrubs was leaning headfirst against the wall, covered in so much blood that it ran off him and puddled at his feet.

James started down the hallway toward the doctor. "Don't you start on me!" the man yelled. A spray of blood few from his lips. He spat and wiped his mouth on the arm of his scrubs. "You all think you are so high and mighty. You don't know! You don't know anything..." he trailed off as he began to sob and seemed to slump.

"What happened?" James managed to ask.

The doctor looked him straight in the eye, then he raised his right hand. Blood ran down his extended middle finger. Then with a little chuckle, the doctor lowered his eyes, turned, and made his way down the hall. A trail of bloody footprints marked his departure.

"Somebody help me!"

The scream came from inside the operating theater, and James rushed in without giving it a second thought.

Blood was everywhere. A nurse was bent over the table, trying to hold pressure on the patient's leg. She screamed as blood fountained up through her fingers. James grabbed some towels from a cart at the side of the door and hurried over to try and help stop the bleeding. His foot hit a pool of blood, and he slid, slamming his hip against the corner of the table. Ignoring the pain, he reached across and added pressure to the wound.

"What happened in here?" he asked the nurse.

"That bastard, Kemple, that's what happened."

Raised voices came from the hallway. James shifted his weight to add more pressure to the still-bleeding leg.

"He was drunk *again*," the nurse continued. "He just came in muttering something about a golf game and picked up the scalpel." She started crying, and her tears left trails in the blood spattered on her face. "I told him he needed to wait for the rest of the team, and the next thing I knew, there was blood everywhere."

James risked a look under the towel at the open wound. "He must have severed the femoral artery."

People started coming into the room, and he heard a mix of cursing and sobbing from the growing crowd. The head of surgery burst through the doors, surveyed the situation, then told James and the nurse to leave the room and get cleaned up.

The next few hours were a blur of questions from the hospital administrators and the police. During that time, he got the news that Duboski had bled to death on the table.

"I can't believe it happened again."

He turned and looked across the room at two of the nurses who had come to clean up the mess Kemple had made. They spoke in whispers, but he easily overheard them.

"Maybe this time they finally have enough to get rid of him."

"I don't know, drunk or not, his family are still big supporters of the hospital. I guess a big enough check can make anything disappear."

James left the holding area to get a drink of water. "Well, he's finally killed one." He overheard one of the administrators say. "Now maybe we can force him to retire."

Duboski's death had been ruled unavoidable, and he was buried with full military honors. James was the only one from the hospital to attend the funeral. A month later, the hospital hosted a retirement party for Kemple that James did *not* attend.

Chapter Three

March 5, 1870
Animas Forks, Colorado

Doc Mitchell was just finishing his morning coffee in his office across the street from the Sagebrush Saloon when someone screamed.

He rushed to the door and out onto the uneven boards of the sidewalk. "What the...?" He rubbed his eyes, then raised his hand to help block the rays of the morning sun. The light had to be playing tricks on him—or maybe what he saw came from the bottle of whiskey he had made friends with the night before. The road at the other end of town seemed to disappear into a thick black haze, like a massive swarm of bees was making its way through Animas Forks. Bodies were littered along the sides of the street, lying in the mud like discarded wooden planks.

He started in their direction, but something grabbed his shoulder and stopped him. A freezing dagger of pain shot down the length of his body from neck to ankle. He tried to pull away, but another bright flash of intense pain coursed through him. He was suddenly pulled backward, he tripped over the edge of the sidewalk, and landed on his rear with his back against his office door. For the first time, he saw his attacker. Curtis Bello, the town blacksmith.

"My God, Curtis. What the devil has…?"

The blacksmith reached out, grabbed the lapels of his coat, and yanked him back to his feet. The blacksmith's eyes darted frantically left and right underneath a thin coating of ice, but the rest of his face showed no sign of panic or fear.

"You are the white healer." Chips of ice fell from Curtis's lips when he spoke. The words came from his mouth, but the voice wasn't his. This voice was deep and guttural, and the words sounded broken and forced.

"Curtis, you know who I am. It's me, Doc Mitchell. I'm the one who—"

"You are the white healer!" The statement came again, this time with frightening force.

He hesitated, fearing that his life might depend on his answer. "Yes, I'm the town physician."

Curtis threw him into the street like an angry child tossing away a broken toy. He landed in the icy mud, looking up at the man who used to be his friend. Curtis tilted his head just enough to look down at him, causing the ice that surrounded his throat to break and fall away.

"YOU ARE THE WHITE HEALER!" Loud as thunder the proclamation came again.

"Yes! Yes!" Doc Mitchell screamed. "I am the white healer! I am, I am the healer!"

Tears ran down his face as he lost what little composure he had managed to maintain. A wave of misery washed over him and cold invaded every part of his being. He looked away as great sobs escaped him, his hot tears releasing little ringlets of steam as they traveled down his cheeks. When he dared to lift his head again, the blacksmith was gone.

The darkness that had been hovering near the edge of town was moving toward him. The bodies that had been lying in the street now flanked the dark cloud, all walking in match step. He could see *them* clearly but still couldn't make out the thing that they were obviously leading his way.

Crawling through the mud, he made it back onto the sidewalk and used the wall of his office for support to get back on his feet. He couldn't drag his eyes away from the spectacle of the townspeople, his friends, his patients, escorting the hulking darkness like they would a casket on its way to the grave.

The group drew ever closer, and his ears began to fill with the sound of millions of buzzing insects. He frantically felt behind himself for the doorknob that would let him back into his office and provide a needed escape from this insanity. If he could just get inside and have a wall between him and this nightmare, he felt sure that the incessant thrumming would come to an end, and he would be able to think. He grabbed the doorknob, then jerked his hand away. It was cold, so cold that it *burned*. He managed to tear his eyes from the approaching crowd and looked down at the red welts that had formed on his fingertips, and the traces of ice that circled their edges.

The black form suddenly towered over him. No more than six feet separated him from its hulking mass, but he still couldn't make out what it was. Seven people surrounded it. Four men, two women, and little Marcie Miller who was holding her mother's hand. He almost cried out when he saw that those hands were frozen together by a thick coating of ice.

"Healer," the townspeople began chanting in unison. "Healer, healer, healer."

Curtis stepped out from behind the black undulating mass, carrying a limp and lifeless body. The chant continued as Curtis walked past him and entered the office. A moment later, he returned to the sidewalk, and without saying a word, turned and looked through the office window at the body he had just placed on the examination table. The remaining members of the party joined him at the window. They stood like statues and stared into the office.

"I, I don't understand," Doc Mitchell said to whomever would listen. "What do you want me to do?"

"Healer," came the guttural reply.

"But I don't know what to—"

The black mass began to change, undulating, shimmering, and stretching until it loomed over him at least twelve feet high.

Something began to move inside the massive form as it churned and pulsed. Waves formed on its surface, rippling up to its peak before flowing back down. Again, from deep inside the quivering mass, came the cry of a mighty eagle. It was so loud that he ducked and covered his head in fear that a massive bird would fly out of the darkness to attack him. The cry stopped abruptly, leaving a deafening silence in its wake.

He lowered his hands; a regal white horse was now standing in front of him. Its mane and skin were stippled with red mud. Where its eyes should have been, were two bottomless, black holes. Steam poured from the animal's nostrils with every breath, and it pawed relentlessly at the ground, leaving deep gashes in the mud.

Atop the stallion sat a mighty warrior silhouetted by the morning sun. The man had to be at least seven feet tall. His ribs were plainly visible through the dark-tanned skin of his chest. He wore a loin cloth, and the painted markings of a warrior covered his body. On his head was the skull of a large wolf. Silently, he dismounted.

A cold sadness washed over Doc Mitchell again, and he wanted to die. He felt broken and violated as if his tortured soul had been ripped from his body and replaced with mounds of ice.

The warrior leaned down, coming face to face with him, his eyes cold blue in contrast with his deep-red skin.

The warrior opened its mouth and began to scream. Its breath smelled of rot and disease, and the air flowing from its lungs assaulted him and made him want to gag. The warrior's mouth grew ever larger, its lips first drawing tight across its teeth, before beginning to crack and split open.

Blood burst from the wounds and splattered Doc Mitchell's face, still he couldn't look away. Dark black fluid gathered in the corners of the warrior's eyes, then spilled down its cheeks, causing the skin there to melt and flow into its ever-widening mouth, yet the war cry continued.

The sound of the warrior's cry rang in Doc Mitchell's ears, its horrid breath filled his mouth and nose. He could feel his sanity unraveling, and he wanted nothing more than to scream along with the warrior, scream until he could scream no more.

Then silence.

Chapter Four

December 10, 2008

"Thank you again for coming." Dr. Carroll smiled as the last of his guests left the house. "That boy of yours has a great future ahead of him, you mark my words!" He closed the door. "A great future washing dishes," he murmured to himself.

"That wasn't very nice," James said from where he was seated on the doctor's old, faded leather sofa.

Dr. Carroll finished off the scotch he was holding and placed the glass on the bar trolley. "When you get to be my age, the compulsion *for* and the ability *to* be nice seems to lessen." He smiled and rolled his eyes. "I stand by my position." He slumped into an overstuffed chair, then leaned forward and slapped James on the knee. "So, what now Dr. James Michael Hughes? How do you plan to fill the six weeks before you begin your reformation of the esteemed VA Hospital?"

"You know, Doc, you have a way of making a very difficult decision seem about as important as picking out socks." James shook his head with a smirk. "I would say that I'm going to go on some great adventure, but that takes money, and money is one thing I *do not* have. So, I guess I'm just going to wait and see what life has in store for me."

"All decisions are hard decisions, young James." Dr. Carroll stood and took his orator's stance. "And all decisions carry equal weight in this existence that we call life. A great philosopher once said that if you choose not to decide, you still have made a choice."

"You're drunk," James interrupted.

"Is that your learned medical opinion?" He made his way back to the bar trolley, picked up a mostly empty bottle of Glenlivet and looked at the label, closing one eye to make it come into focus.

"Don't you think you've had enough?"

"Enough what?" He shook the bottle gently, testing how much scotch remained. "Teaching? Probably. Scotch? Never." He attempted to lift the bottle to his lips but only managed to drop it. When he bent over to pick it up, he banged his head on the edge of the trolley hard enough that black spots appeared in his vision.

Next thing he knew, James was putting his arms around his shoulders to steady him. "Okay, Doc, I think it's time for bed."

"Perhaps you're right, I am a bit tired." He straightened up and cleared his throat in an attempt to appear dignified.

"A bit," James agreed.

* * *

Dr. Carroll's bedroom was dimly lit and bore all the marks of a lifelong bachelor. The bed was unmade, and clothes were scattered about the room. A large collection of water bottles of various brands and sizes sat half drunk on the nightstand, along with a few glasses in dire need of washing.

James steered Dr. Carroll to the bed and the old man sat down heavily, the ancient wooden frame squeaking under his weight.

He knelt in front of his mentor and began to untie his shoes. "Let's just get these shoes off so you—" A knock at the front door interrupted him.

"Who could that be?" Dr. Carroll tried to stand, nearly stepping on James' fingers in the process.

"Someone must have forgotten something. Don't try to get up, Doc. I'll be right back."

He made his way to the front door and flipped the wall switch that turned on the porch light. Through the peephole, he could see that the porch and front yard were empty. He opened the door, and there was a small package wrapped in brown paper and covered in tape sitting on the step. He took a moment to survey the yard, hoping to get a look at whoever had left the package, before picking it up and taking it inside.

His name was printed in simple block letters on the top. Other than that, there was no postage, no return address, or any indication of where it had originated. The unmistakable sound of someone vomiting came from the bedroom. James placed the package on the coffee table and went back to help Dr. Carroll get into bed.

Chapter Five

December 11, 2008

Morning sun annoyingly poured through the living room windows as Dr. Carroll shuffled out of his bedroom, still wearing his clothes from the previous night. He lifted his hand to try to keep the sun from blinding him. The scotch he drank the night before had coated his tongue, and he cleared his throat in a futile attempt to force some moisture into his mouth.

"Good morning, Doc," James said with halfhearted enthusiasm as he stretched and sat up on the couch.

He stopped and turned back into the living room at the sound of James' voice. Squinting, he tried blinking James into focus, then realized that he was not wearing his glasses.

"Looking for these?" James picked the glasses up off the table by the couch and held them out to him.

He snatched them out of his hand and put them on. "What the devil are you doing here so early?"

"It's not so early." James checked his watch. "It's after nine."

He sat down and twisted James' wrist so that he could see the watch.

"So, it is," he agreed. "That still doesn't explain your presence in my home."

The young man stood and stretched again.

"After you closed down the bar last night," James said, "this package was dropped off at your front door." He sat back down and handed him the box.

"So, you took it upon yourself to open it?" he said, allowing his hangover to make him grumpy. "So much for my privacy."

"It was actually addressed to me." James turned the packaged over in his hand and pointed to his name written there.

Dr. Carroll examined all six sides. "No address, no postage, no return address. What did the person who delivered it have to say?"

James shook his head. "No delivery person either. By the time I got to the door, they were gone, and the package was just sitting there."

James placed the shoebox-sized package back on the coffee table. For a moment, they just stared at it as if expecting it to spill out all its secrets.

"Well..." Dr. Carroll broke the silence. "Are you going to tell me what's in it, or are we going to just keep gawking at it like a couple of idiots?"

"I'll show you," James replied. "But we may still both feel like idiots once I do."

From inside the box, he removed a small, leather messenger's pouch and laid it on the table. He opened it gently and removed a rolled, oilcloth bundle. It was tied with a piece of leather the size and thickness of a shoestring. The bundle made a metallic *clink* as he placed it on the table.

"What is it?"

"Wait, that's not all." James reached back inside and pulled out a small stack of yellowed papers and placed them beside the cloth bundle.

"That's it." James moved the empty box to the floor at his feet. "I spent most of the night looking through these, and then decided to wait for you. I was hoping you could shed some light on them."

Dr. Carroll picked up the bundle. The once-white, oiled cloth was covered in brown stains and remnants of old fingerprints. The soft clink of metal-striking-metal came again when he lifted it. It was heavier than he expected. He gently placed it back on the table, untied the leather strap and unrolled it. Inside, he found more brown stains on the flap of material that covered its contents. Carefully, using both hands, he lifted the flap and let it fall back onto the table. Underneath was a row of bone-handled surgical tools, each in its own sewn compartment. Next to them, in a larger section, he found a pair of forceps and a small wooden-handled saw.

"It's a surgical kit," he explained. "But I guess you figured that out already. From the looks of them, I would say they are Civil War era." He began to inspect each tool, turning them over in his hands, feeling their weight and balance, then replacing them with care.

"Looks like three scalpels of various lengths, one double-sided. A pair of forceps, a metacarpal saw, three suture needles attached to a piece of buckskin, and this thin piece of metal with the ivory tip." He held the delicate-looking instrument up to get a better look at it. "I believe this is a bullet probe. It would have been used to locate the bullet inside the wound before cutting. Helped to keep the surgical damage to a minimum." He rolled the tools back up and handed the bundle to James. "Looks like someone has gifted you a complete mid-eighteen-hundreds surgical kit. Was there a note or anything to indicate who it was?"

"Nothing, except those newspaper clippings."

Dr. Carroll spread them out on the table and began to go through them.

"Let me save you some time," James said. "They are all articles or death notices about doctors who, during their lifetime, miraculously saved patients or performed surgeries that were thought impossible." He reached down and pulled a very yellowed piece of paper from the pile and handed it to him.

"This appears to be the oldest. It's from *The Kansas City Star*. It's a death notice about a Dr. Melvin Mitchell. The latest is from 1987 about a surgeon named McKissell who created a surgical technique that researchers at the time felt could lead to the first successful full-face transplant."

Dr. Carroll quickly went through the rest of the stack, then started over again with the first.

"I know what you're thinking," James continued." I spent most of the night on your computer searching the web. All the clippings are from *actual* newspapers, but for the life of me I can't find any connection between the doctors, except for the fact that they are all surgeons."

Dr. Carroll continued to sort through the clippings, about eight in all, and arranged them on the table by date. "The length of time between articles appears to be between fifteen and forty-five years." He picked up the most recent clipping. "I met this man McKissell once. Would have been back in the late '70s."

"Really? Was it at some kind of awards ceremony or celebration of his work?" James asked.

"No in fact, quite the opposite." He shook his head and chuckled, finding the memory funny. "He was interviewing for a position in the general surgery department at the hospital where I was working at the time. We didn't hire him."

"Why not?" James picked up the article. "Says here he was a brilliant and inventive surgeon."

"You wouldn't have known it at the time. During the initial interview, he was so nervous that his hands shook like someone suffering from Parkinson's, and he stumbled over his answers to the most basic of medical-knowledge questions. We never gave him a second look."

"I guess people change." James returned the clipping to the table.

"Not in my experience." Dr. Carroll rubbed his temples, trying to remember anything about McKissell that they could have missed during that interview. "No, someone as unsure of himself as McKissell would never have been able to overcome his insecurities to do the detailed work it takes to do what this article describes. It's just not possible."

"Yet there it is in black and white."

"So, it is." He gathered up the clippings, carefully returned them to the pouch, and handed it back to James. "This is quite the mystery." He got to his feet. "I do know one thing. I need coffee and lots of it before I can start playing detective. You look as if you could use a little pick-me-up as well."

James placed all the items back in their box, then stretched. "After spending the night on your couch, you're right. But what do we do about these?"

"Let's take them with us. I may know someone who can give us a little insight."

Chapter Six

March 5, 1870

Shrouded in bright, white light, Doc Mitchell began to hear birds singing in the distance, then the sounds of children playing and laughing cut through the fog, along with the sound of women singing. He smelled wood smoke and cooking meat. The misery he had been feeling melted away, replaced with a feeling of uncommon joy.

The light slowly faded, and he found himself on a high mountain pass looking down on an Indian village. Cook fires spotted the valley below, and children laughed as they ran from tent to tent. The last of the winter snow was melting in patches and the sun shone bright overhead. To his right, a group of hunters on horseback were making their way toward the camp. They carried a large buck strapped between two of their horses, while another set brought a young fawn. The hunt had been successful, and the tribe would eat well for many days.

A rumbling came from his left, and a cloud of dust appeared on the horizon. Four covered wagons moved out of the mountain's shadow and headed across the plain. This wasn't an unusual sight. Many families had begun to make their way west in search of fertile farmland and in hopes of making a life for themselves in the uncharted West. What Doc Mitchell found unusual was for a wagon train to dare get this close to an Indian encampment. Migrants were always told of villages like these and were warned to keep their distance. Those that didn't listen often found their trek westward cut short.

The world around him seemed to shift and spin. He found himself in the midst of the Indian village. None of the Natives noticed him, and he felt no fear as he walked, like a ghost, among them.

A nervous energy radiated through the village. The camp sentries had seen the wagons. Women and children were hurried into their tents. Fires were doused and the few remaining men in camp took a defensive stance at its perimeter.

An old Indian emerged from the largest tent in the village. He was not dressed as a warrior but carried himself like a person of great importance. He walked with confidence up to the line of warriors. A headdress of pitch-black raven's feathers sat on his head, underneath which the skin of his dark cheeks bore scars that had been painted a glowing white. He was nude to the waist, his chest and back bore a latticework of painted scars as well. Rawhide pants were gathered around his waist with a belt made of woven leather strips, and numerous pouches and carved totems hung from it.

Silently, he watched as the wagons drew closer to the village. He turned from the warriors and started toward his tent where a low fire burned inside a circle of rocks. Without hesitation, he stepped barefoot into the midst of the flames.

Doc Mitchell had heard stories of Indian Medicine Men doing that type of ritual. It was said that the prayers they lifted to their gods kept them from feeling the pain, and that the flames didn't burn them.

The old man began moving around rhythmically in the fire, kicking up sparks and ashes, and singing an intricate song that had very little melody. He pulled a bone-handled knife from his belt and drew it across the skin of his neck and chest. It released a flow of blood that soon covered his upper body and saturated the front of his rawhide britches.

His chanting grew louder as one of the wagons broke ranks and headed in the direction of the hunting party. The shaman's feet began to blacken and blister. Blood from his cuts hissed as it fell onto the coals.

The three remaining wagons stopped in a line about two hundred yards from the camp. The birds fell silent, leaving no sound except that of the shaman's song as it carried over the plain.

A noise like thunder rumbled across the plain. War cries were followed by more thunder, then silence. The medicine man abruptly stopped chanting and stood motionless in the fire.

The wagons began to move again. The warriors remained in their position as the only safeguard of the camp. They notched arrows and took aim. Once close enough, the arrows would be loosed as a warning to stay away. Before they had crossed that line, the wagons stopped again.

The shaman knelt in the fire, filled his hands with burning coals, and began to hoot like an owl. He raised the glowing embers over his head. Smoke rose from his outstretched hands and floated into the clear sky.

Dark clouds began to form high above him. The shaman returned to his chanting. He extended his arms even higher, causing the clouds above him to darken as thunder rumbled through the sky. Wind whistled across the plains, bringing with it a cold and stinging rain.

The fourth wagon returned and took its place at the end of the formation. The drivers climbed down off their seats and moved into the back of the wagons.

A shrill whistle cut through the wind, and all hell was loosed on the small Indian village. With practiced precision, all four wagons' covers were ripped away, revealing the Gatling guns mounted in the back of each. The drivers stood behind the massive machines of war, cranking their handles as fast as they could. Hundreds of rounds poured from the guns, their discarded casings littering the prairie floor and piling up around the wagon's wheels.

Within seconds, the warriors who had stood as the camp's only protectors lay in bloody heaps on the ground, their bodies flayed open and ripped apart by the barrage. The hail of bullets continued, tearing into the tents, shredding them along with those unlucky enough to be inside. Screams of women and children filled the air only to be drowned out by the deluge of more rounds being fired.

The shaman gave a mighty howl, brought his coal-filled hands down from the sky, and pressed them against his bare chest. Lightning burst from the storm overhead and struck the wagon train. Flames immediately engulfed two of the wagons. Undaunted, the two that remained continued firing. The shaman took a bullet to the shoulder and a second round grazed his cheek. He fell into the fire and began to convulse.

The guns stopped firing.

The shaman stopped moving.

Doc Mitchell stared in awe at the devastation all around him. His heart ached for the dead, and fury raged deep inside of him toward the men that had done this. He understood that the Indians had to be kept in line, had to be taught how to be civilized, but these had been peaceful Natives, and this attack had been unprovoked. He couldn't understand why he was being forced to witness this inhumanity.

A few weak cries of pain and sorrow escaped from beneath the wreckage of the tents. He longed to help the people inside, but he was a ghost and unable to do anything but watch.

A haze of gun smoke lingered between the wagons and the ruins of the camp. From within it, a lone figure appeared. He was a tall, lean man wearing a faded, black bowler hat low on his head. Its brim tipped forward, obscuring his eyes. He wore a revolver holstered on his right side; a slim-bladed sword hung from the gun belt on his left. The butt of a single-shot pistol stuck out of the pocket of his scarred leather vest. He carried a large earthen jug in his right hand, in his left was a burning torch that left a trail of acrid black smoke as he walked toward the camp. He set the jug down long enough to pull a hand-rolled cigarette from his shirt pocket and lit it with the torch.

The cowboy smiled as he surveyed the damage that his Gatling guns had done, then retrieved the jug and made his way into the camp. Mud created by his victims' blood spread underneath his feet and collected on the tips of his worn boots. He stopped at the first tent just long enough to pour a bit of liquid from the jug onto the pile of rubble and set his torch to it. It went up like a pile of dead leaves. Methodically, he made his way tent to tent finishing the job his guns had started.

Doc Mitchell couldn't believe the pure evil he was witnessing at the hands of this man, this cowboy, this *demon*. He tried to turn away, but whatever had brought him there controlled what he could see, and it wanted him to witness this horror.

The cowboy stopped beside the bodies of the fallen warriors. For a moment, he stood still and took in the sight of the carnage spread out before him. He smiled again, then reached up and took the cigarette from between his cracked lips. He tapped its ashes onto the remains of the nearest warrior and flicked away the butt. He whistled quietly as he splashed the liquid from the jug on the bodies of the fallen warriors. He touched the torch to them. The flames engulfed the bodies, burning away the warrior's traditional leather pants and decorative leggings. The bodies flailed in the mud as their dead muscles reacted to the touch of the fire.

A woman screamed and ran into the clearing, carrying a spear. She hurled it with practiced precision toward the cowboy's head.

His hand, moving quicker than should have been possible, grabbed the spear in midair. He never flinched, even when the point stopped just inches from his face.

The woman fell to the ground, weeping, having failed at her attempt to kill the invader.

The cowboy crossed the compound and looked down at her. He showed no concern for his own safety, no fear that the woman might have another weapon concealed in the folds of her clothing. He just stood there, waiting.

Agonizing seconds passed as Doc Mitchell watched all that was happening around him, unable to look away or intervene. The woman's weeping grew louder. If the cowboy noticed, he showed no sign, he merely stood with her huddled at his feet.

Suddenly, she struck. With snake-like speed, she uncoiled, holding a knife at the ready. She swung at the cowboy's throat. He pivoted away with equal speed, and the knife missed its target by a hair's width.

The cowboy dropped the torch and drew his sword. As the power of the woman's swing carried her on around, he separated her head from her shoulders with a single stroke. Her dead body hit the ground and lay still. The cowboy sheathed his word, retrieved the torch, tipped his jug over her, and touched the flame to the liquid that spilled out. A moment later, he did the same to her head which had rolled to a stop next to the shaman lying motionless in the fire pit.

The shaman rose from behind the smoke from the burning head. His body charred and blistered, but not burned. His old hands were filled with burning coals, again he raised them to the sky and began to chant. The dark clouds returned, but this time they reacted differently to the shaman's calls. They became angry. They formed quickly and cast the small village into a darkness more like midnight than morning.

The cowboy looked up at the clouds, and Doc Mitchell followed his gaze. They watched as the clouds formed together into a tight, dark mass. The same dark mass he had seen only moments before, coming down the street in Animas Forks.

The undulating darkness settled just above the ground and floated toward the camp. It passed the two remaining wagons, and they became instantly encased in ice, the men frozen in place behind their guns.

Just as it had in town, it began to shimmer and ripple—its shape coming together in the form of the mounted warrior.

Doc Mitchell heard the unmistakable sound of a revolver's hammer locking into place. While he had been watching the cloud warrior's arrival, the cowboy had unholstered his pistol and was pointing it directly at the old medicine man. Without hesitation, he fired a round directly into the old man's chest. The medicine man stopped chanting and stood perfectly still. The cowboy looked back over his shoulder at the warrior, who continued his advance toward the camp.

The shaman began to hoot again. The cowboy turned back around, and the old man struck him with one of the rocks that surrounded the fire. Its jagged edge caught him on the crest of his forehead and traveled downward at an angle, splitting his eyelid in two, destroying the eyeball beneath it. It shattered the bridge of his nose before tearing open his upper lip to expose a mouth full of rotting teeth and black gums.

The cowboy never uttered a sound, never lowered his gun. His second round entered the shaman's chest just above the first. It lifted the old man off his feet and dropped him into the fire. Coolly, the cowboy walked around the fire pit and stood above the fallen shaman. He stared down into the old man's unblinking eyes. Blood dripping from his wounds fell like rain onto the old man, turning his creased and aged features red before running into the coals where it hissed like a den of snakes. The cowboy smiled, took aim, and fired his remaining rounds into the shaman's chest.

The warrior arrived at the edge of the village. When his horse's hooves touched the ground, a sheet of solid ice shot out toward the cowboy with the speed of a flooding river. It passed beneath Doc Mitchell's feet, and when it reached the shaman and cowboy, they instantly froze in place. The intense cold even froze the flames of the shaman's fire.

The warrior dismounted and knelt at the old man's side. He carefully broke the ice from around him, and with a gentle reverence, took the shaman into his arms and lifted the stiff and frozen body to the sky as if offering it to the gods.

The cowboy remained encased in a coffin of ice. His eyes were open, and his gun was still extended toward the now-empty, frozen fire.

From atop his horse, the warrior began to chant. He still cradled the old medicine man's body in his arms as the darkness reformed around them. An eagle's cry came from deep inside the dark mass. The wagons, along with their guns and the men frozen behind them, shattered into pieces and fell to the ground. The clouds parted, and the dark mass became lost in the sunshine that poured through the gap.

A muffled cry came from the midst of the rubble. Doc Mitchell turned to see two young women crawl from beneath the only destroyed tent that had not been met with the cowboy's torch. The girls appeared to be identical. One's long, black hair and brown skin the mirror image of the other. They held hands and wept as they looked around at the destruction leveled on their village.

The world around Doc Mitchell softened and glowed with an iridescent white. His view of the two girls was lost to the mist as the sound of the warrior's cry again filled his ears. He chanced another look at the cowboy, but the man had vanished. Only a hollow shell of ice remained. The white overtook Doc Mitchell, and when the world came back into focus, he was again in Animas Forks.

The cloud warrior raised a pointed finger at the office. The door opened under its own power, and the warrior took a step forward, forcing the doctor to retreat inside. The Indian's massive body filled the door frame and blocked any chance of escape.

"Healer, healer, healer."

The droning chant came again from the voices of the town's dead as they stood guard outside his office. He looked at their dead faces staring at him through the window, then at the body of the medicine man. The old man's chest rose and fell with a shuddering breath.

The chanting stopped. The townspeople turned away from the window. The cloud warrior turned his back but continued to stand guard in the door.

Blood, ice, and water dripped off the exam table, making little splat sounds as it wet the tops of his boots and the floor around them. The noise loud in the now silent exam room. The shaman's eyes were closed but his chest continued to rise and fall with each shallow, irregular breath. He had six red, angry-looking wounds in his chest, one dead center, and the others in a tight pattern above and to the left of the first. The round from the Gatling gun had destroyed the old man's shoulder, and a second had creased his cheek and torn off part of his ear. The old man was managing to breathe, but there was no way that he could survive.

Doc Mitchell looked back over his shoulder at the warrior blocking his office door. A wave of cold passed through him, and he shivered. It occurred to him that if he didn't at least try and save the old man, he could end up as dead as the poor souls standing with their backs to his window.

He fought to steady his trembling hands as he unrolled his surgical kit on the stand next to the exam table and removed a bullet probe. The probe sank over an inch deep into the center hole, far enough that he knew that the bullet had entered the old man's heart. The shaman's chest rose and fell evenly, taking in a portion of the probe's length then revealing it again.

"This just don't make sense," he told the old Indian. "By all rights and measures you should be dead." He looked down into his face as if expecting him to agree.

A trickle of blood leaked from the hole as he removed the probe. Still, the old man's chest rose and fell in a slow, but steady, rhythm. He placed a piece of cotton bandage over the exposed hole and held pressure on it. Blood immediately soaked through and pooled between his fingers.

The medicine man took a deep hitching breath, causing more blood to flow from his wounds and pool on the table. The old man's eyes fluttered open. He took another shallow breath, raised a shaking hand, and placed it on top of Doc Mitchell's. He tried to lift his head but didn't have the strength. His lips began to move in a whispered chant. The old Indian's eyelids fluttered, and a wheezing sound accompanied his singing.

"Oh, no you don't," Doc Mitchell told the old man. "I don't

know how you have managed to stay alive this long, but you are not going to die on me now."

He returned to his surgical kit and removed the double-bladed scalpel. His hand now steady, he used the blade to widen the second bullet hole. He placed the bloody scalpel on the shaman's chest, then pulled the forceps from the kit. Using them, he reached into the wound to retrieve the bullet.

The old man reached up and took hold of the scalpel. Doc Mitchell released the forceps and grabbed the old man's hand, fearing that the shaman wanted to take another soul with him to the great hereafter.

He could not believe the strength in the old Indian's hands as he tried to pull the scalpel loose.

The shaman's lips parted and began to move. The whispered words were like a soft breeze blowing through dried leaves. Doc Mitchell felt the medicine man's hand grow warm inside his. He tried again to loosen the man's hold on the scalpel, but his grip was like iron.

"Your spirit is strong," the Indian whispered in halting, but completely understandable, English.

Shocked, Doc Mitchell stopped wrestling for control of the scalpel but didn't turn it loose. He looked down into the withered face of the shaman.

"You have done your best, more than many of your kind would." The pink tip of the old man's tongue darted out and ran along his chapped, crusty lips. "I have spoken your name to the Great One and His blessing is upon you and your sons." Again, his tongue traveled slowly across his lips.

The shaman took a deep breath, his chest rose, then fell and didn't rise again.

The old man's grip on the scalpel loosened. Doc Mitchell took it from him and slowly pulled his hand away, buying time to try and figure out what he was going to do next.

Suddenly, the shaman's eyes flew open. He sucked in a deep breath and grabbed the hand holding the scalpel.

A surge of power passed through the old man into Doc Mitchell's hand, and into the scalpel which turned bright red, then white with heat. Pain shot through his hand like lightning through the night sky, forcing him to drop the smoldering scalpel. It fell to the floor where it sizzled in the water, and blood pooled there. Doc Mitchell looked down at the scalpel-shaped burn on his palm, then clutched his throbbing hand to his chest.

The shaman shuddered and stopped moving.

The warrior approached the table. Doc Mitchell rounded it, placing the old Indian's body between himself and the giant.

"Now wait a minute," he said, raising his hands. "You saw it. I did everything I could possibly do to try and save him."

The warrior took the old man's body into his arms. He looked into the shaman's face, then lifted his eyes to Doc Mitchell.

"I'm sorry," Doc Mitchell said, locking eyes with him.

The warrior nodded slightly, then opened his mouth. A dark mist flowed out of him, encircling them before filling the room. Doc Mitchell used his sleeve to cover his mouth. The eagle's cry filled the room, then, as if a mighty wind had blown through the building, the mist flowed out the door, leaving the doctor standing alone next to the exam table.

A scream came from outside the office. Doc Mitchell looked up, still expecting to see all the townspeople staring in at him. Instead, he saw that his once dead friends were now gathered in a circle outside the office looking down at something in the street.

He rushed outside. The first person he came to was Stan Walters, the mine agent. He grabbed him by the shoulder and spun him around. "Stan, are you okay?"

"Sure, Doc," he said. "But what in God's name happened to *him*?"

Stan moved to the side, giving Doc Mitchell a clear view of the street. He took a staggering step forward and fell to his knees. Curtis Bello was lying in the mud, his body broken into a thousand pieces like a shattered pane of glass. Except, unlike glass, these broken, human shards were melting.

Chapter Seven

December 11, 2008

Dr. Carroll sipped a steaming cup of coffee as he and James sat in a waiting room that looked like it had been taken from a 1950s copy of *Doctors' Quarterly*. The walls were home to a collection of diplomas as well as antique ads for cocaine toothache drops, Dr. Williams Pink Pills, and Asthma Cigarettes. James took a drink from his iced coffee and looked around the room, trying to take it all in.

"We really have come a long way, haven't we?" he said, half to himself.

Dr. Carroll looked up from the *Life* magazine he was reading. The cover featured a picture of actress Vivian Blaine. James had no clue who she was.

"Not really," the doctor answered. "A hundred years from now, doctors will look back at us with amazement at the archaic way we practiced medicine. Every generation thinks they have all the answers, only for the next generation to come along and change the questions."

James pondered that for a minute, but before he could ask Dr. Carroll what he meant, a door opened and a small group of about seven people filed into the lobby. A pudgy little man wearing the traditional doctor's white lab coat and an old-fashioned reflector attached to a cloth strip around his head followed them.

"Thank you, s-s-s-so much for coming by and remember to t-t-t-tell your friends!" the man cheerfully said as he took off his glasses and polished them with the tail of his coat.

The crowd returned their thanks, and James noticed that a few of them slipped the man a tip as they were leaving.

"All right, next group please s-s-s-step up," the man said absent-mindedly. "Welcome to—" His eyes widened in surprise, and he stopped mid-sentence. "W-W-W-Well, David Carroll as I live and breathe! How long has it been? Tw-Tw-Tw-twenty years? I thought you were dead."

"Not dead, just teaching." Dr. Carroll extended his hand to the man who shook it thoroughly.

"It's good to see you, Calvin," Dr. Carroll said, his voice jittery from all the handshaking. He managed to free his hand and placed it on James' shoulder. "Calvin Coolidge, I would like to introduce my protégé, Dr. James Michael Hughes."

"Did you say Calvin Coolidge?" James gave Dr. Carroll a strange look.

Calvin took James' hand and started shaking it as thoroughly as he had Dr. Carroll's.

"That's right, I am C-C-C-Calvin C-C-C-Coolidge." He pulled James closer and leaned in "M-M-M-My parents had an odd s-s-sense of humor," he added and gave him a quick wink.

"Well, all right then," he said, still shaking Calvin's hand. "It's a pleasure."

"Oh, m-m-m-mine too, m-m-mine too." Calvin finally released his hand, then stood back and took a good look at the two of them. "So, what brings you to my l-l-l-little museum?"

"Museum?" James echoed.

"James," Dr. Carroll said, "Calvin is the nation's foremost authority on medical ephemera. He—"

"If it kills, cuts, sutures, staples, or s-s-s-sterilizes, we have it here at the C-C-C-Coolidge Museum of Medical Knowledge," Calvin excitedly interrupted.

"And that is why we are here, Calvin. Dr. Hughes—"

"Please, call me James," James interrupted.

"Right," Dr. Carroll continued. "Calvin, *Dr. Hughes* was mysteriously gifted an antique surgical kit for his graduation. I thought perhaps you could give us some insight into its history."

"If anyone can, it's m-m-m-me," Calvin said. "J-J-J-Just let me close up for lunch, and we'll take a little look."

James watched the curious little man lock the outer door, then remove the lab coat and reflector. He turned a full circle, obviously looking for a place to put them, before deciding on a 1960s weight-loss machine, the type with the belt that vibrated the pounds away.

"Let's go b-b-b-back in here where the light's b-b-b-better." Calvin motioned for them to follow.

They walked through a few rooms filled floor to ceiling with old machines, medical displays, and shelves of unidentifiable things floating in murky liquid.

James stopped to look at what appeared to be a mummified finger nailed to a piece of wood. Dr. Carroll turned back to him and glanced at the finger. "You don't want to know."

The next room they entered was a replica of a surgical suite. Calvin reached up and turned on a grouping of lights mounted above the operating table.

"All right boys, sh-sh-sh-show me what you've got."

James set the box on the table and carefully emptied its contents out under the lights.

Chapter Eight

March 6, 1870

Doc Mitchell removed the shingle that had hung beside his office door for the last ten years and walked away from medicine for good.

* * *

By the eleventh of March, Doc Mitchell had sold all his equipment and property. That afternoon, he boarded the eastbound stage, not caring where it took him as long as it had busy streets, crowded walkways, and no Indians.

The one bag he had with him contained his clothes, a Bible his mother had given him when he went west for the first time, a comb, and shaving kit. He had started to leave his surgical tools behind, but at the last minute, tossed them—along with four cigars—into a small, leather messenger's pouch that he would keep with him inside the stage.

* * *

The stagecoach had been heading northeast for almost twenty-four hours, and Doc Mitchell figured that they must be nearing the Wyoming border. Their first scheduled stop was for fresh horses at the stage stables just across the state line. The drivers had warned them not to expect much, but said that it was a good place to stretch their legs and do their necessaries.

When he boarded the stage outside Animas Forks, there had been only one other passenger. She was tall with long, black hair that she wore down, underneath a black lace-and-tulle hat. She wore a simple black frock over shoes made of dark leather with a low heel, and she had her arm through the strap of a small bag that she kept close to her side.

He tipped his hat to her as he boarded the stage, then took a seat across from her in the opposite corner. She dipped her chin to him once in return, otherwise she gave him little regard.

They rode in silence for hours, and he slept fitfully, sitting up in the rough-riding stage. At one point in the night, he awoke and saw the woman looking out the window at the moonlit prairie.

"It's beautiful out here at night, isn't it?" he asked, hoping to strike up a conversation.

"To some, perhaps," she tersely replied.

For the rest of the night, he kept his eyes closed and pretended to be asleep.

The stage came to a stop alongside a small creek, just after sunup. The driver unhitched the horses to let them drink, while the shotgun messenger stayed on top of the stage keeping watch. The driver made a small fire and placed a coffee pot over it. As the coffee was boiling, he offered Doc Mitchell and the woman some hard tack and cold bacon. She refused the food but accepted a cup of strong, black coffee.

A short time later, the driver took a shovel and dug a shallow hole behind a large bush on the creek bank. He explained its use, and the woman excused herself to take advantage of it.

"I usually hate it when we have women on these long trips," the driver said while tending the fire. "Makes for extra work. When it's just men, all I have to do is *point* at the bush."

Doc Mitchell chuckled at the man's remark, then finished his coffee.

"In her case," the man went on, "I don't mind as much, seeing as who she is and all." He dumped the remainder of the coffee over the hot coals, then kicked dirt over them with his boot.

"I don't understand," Doc Mitchell said. "Who is she?"

"You don't know?" The driver continued to stomp around on top of the covered fire to make sure it was out. "Her husband was the military commander at Cove Fort over in Utah. Back two months or so, redskins attacked it. The soldiers finally run 'em off, but not before they had snatched Mrs. Gattis, her husband, and a wagon-mounted Gatling gun. Word is that before the soldiers found them, she had to watch what they did to her husband."

"What did they do?" he asked, not really sure that he wanted to know the answer.

"Story goes that the platoon leader heard her hollering for help. They followed the sound of her voice to the camp. She was hogtied next to her husband. Them dirty redskins had done run off but not before they had scalped him. He was still alive when the soldiers showed up. Can you imagine, being skint like a rabbit while you was still alive to feel it? He died before they could get him back to the fort."

Doc Mitchell handed his empty cup to the driver. He had seen a lot of brutality in his time in the West, but if what the man was saying was the truth, then nothing he had experienced could come close to it.

"What about her?" He tilted his head in the direction Mrs. Gattis had gone.

"Don't know. They said she didn't seem hurt, but I can't imagine that them savages would have done what they did to the colonel and not have touched her."

They both turned at the sound of rustling leaves indicating that Mrs. Gattis was returning. She appeared from the bushes a moment later and climbed into the stage without speaking.

"Better load up, Doc," the driver said. "We've been stopped too long already. It's best to keep moving out here."

They rode in silence for a few more hours, but Doc Mitchell had the feeling that Mrs. Gattis had something on her mind. She was constantly shifting positions in her seat, crossing, and uncrossing her arms. He watched the endless prairie pass outside the window and did his best to ignore it.

"It's not true," she said flatly.

He turned to face her, surprised by the foreign sound of a voice inside the stage. "What's that, ma'am?"

"That story the driver told you while I was indisposed." She looked out her window as she spoke. "It's not true, but no one will believe me when I tell them."

"Tell them what exactly?"

She finally turned from the window and looked across the stage at him. She wore a hard expression, and dark shadows had formed around her eyes. "That it wasn't Natives that raided the fort and killed my husband."

"If it wasn't them, then who was it?"

"It was a mixture of white men and Mexicans. They had rubbed red clay on their skin, they were dressed in animal hides, and rode their horses bareback to make it look like they were Natives. I don't think they intended to take anyone hostage, but my husband and I were outside the front gate looking at the moon over the prairie when they came up to the fort. They were after the Gatling gun, but when they saw us, and we saw them, they didn't have a choice. I guess they could have killed us right there, but that would have alerted the camp.

"They threw a bag over Joseph's head, then one of them hit him with the butt of a revolver to keep him quiet. Another man had his hand over my mouth and my arms pinned to my side. They snuck in through the gate we had left open and took the gun and its ammunition."

She stopped talking and looked back out the window, her hands opening and closing slowly in her lap. Doc Mitchell could only imagine how it must have been paining her to retell the story.

"It's okay, ma'am, you don't—"

Mrs. Gattis shook her head, then reached into her purse and retrieved a handkerchief. She gently touched it to the corner of each eye before facing him again.

"I've cried so many tears since that night that I think surely someday I'll run out." She made a fist around the handkerchief, and he saw her hand shake with the effort. "But yet they still come."

"Crying's healthy," he said with a slight nod. "It helps clear the mind and aids in the healing process."

"If that's the case, then I should be nearly good as new." She smiled for the first time since they had been together, and Doc Mitchell got a glimpse of the beauty that had been hiding behind her sorrow. She returned the delicate cloth to her bag and took a deep breath.

"They threw Joseph over the rump of one of their horses," she continued. "When they tried to put me there beside him, I grabbed the gun of the man holding me. I managed to fire two rounds before he hit me, and I passed out as well.

"I woke up in a camp inside of a box canyon. My husband and I were bound together at the wrists with our feet tied as well. Joseph was struggling beside me, trying to loosen the ropes. I saw a man without red clay on his face enter the camp. I whispered to Joseph to hold still. It was obvious that this man was their leader. I could feel the evil radiating off him. It was also obvious that all the other men feared him. They were having a heated discussion, all of them talking at the same time except for him. He never said a word. He only stood there in their midst looking at us."

She swallowed hard, and Doc Mitchell suspected that she was again fighting back tears. This time, he offered his handkerchief to her, but she refused it with a slight shake of her head.

"After a few minutes," she went on, "their leader broke from the crowd and came over to where we were. He was a tall, thin man. Dressed like a working cowboy with a scarred leather vest and rough-hewn trousers and shirt. I couldn't see his face clearly, as the bowler hat he was wearing cast a shadow over his features."

A cowboy in a leather vest and bowler hat... Doc Mitchell's thoughts flashed back to the man that he watched decimate the Indian village in the warrior's vision. The man whose face was split open by the old shaman. The man that somehow vanished after the warrior had arrived to save the old medicine man.

"I'm sorry to interrupt, ma'am, but this cowboy—did he wear a revolver hanging off one side of his belt and a sword on the other?"

"So, you know him?" she asked.

"No, uh, no, ma'am, but I've heard stories."

"Then you can imagine what happened next. He motioned for one of his men to untie me from my husband, then with me out of the way, that evil man removed the sword you heard about and used it to remove the skin from my husband's head." She stopped talking, and this time when he offered, she accepted his handkerchief and patted her eyes dry. "A woman should never have to hear her husband scream, Dr. Mitchell."

The stage lurched, and they were both nearly tossed into the floor. The driver began shouting at the horses, then three shots from a rifle rang out.

"Get down in there!" the shotgun messenger shouted.

Doc Mitchell pulled Mrs. Gattis onto the floor of the cabin and positioned himself in a protective position over her. More shots were fired. He could hear the leather straps of the bridle slapping against the horses' backs urging them to run faster.

An arrow adorned with hawk feathers zipped past his ear and buried itself into the back of the seat where he had been sitting.

"Stay down!" he shouted. Pulling a revolver from beneath his jacket, he positioned himself below one of the open windows, then risked raising up just enough to look out.

A pack of Natives on horseback were running alongside the coach. He steadied himself against the wall, took aim, and shot into the pack. He had only ever fired his gun at old medicine bottles for target practice, and his novice abilities combined with the jostling coach caused his shot to go wild. He fired again with the same result, then continued until all six chambers were spent. From what he could tell, he never so much as grazed one of the attackers.

He dropped back to reload and was surprised to see Mrs. Gattis standing behind him with a gun in her hand.

"Get down woman!" he bellowed. "Before you get your fool head shot—"

She fired before he could finish his sentence. He looked out the window and with each shot she fired, one of the raiding party fell to the hard prairie soil below.

One of the raiders notched an arrow and let it fly toward the front of the stagecoach. The driver fell from his seat. A split-second later, the coach's rear wheels bumped over his body. Without the snap of the reins on their rumps, the exhausted horses slowed, then stopped.

The raiding party surrounded the stagecoach.

"Come out!" one of the Natives shouted. He was a tall, muscular man with skin the color of dark, red clay and his deep rugged voice cut through the silence.

Doc Mitchell opened the door and eased out into the midday sun. He closed it behind him, hoping that the men wouldn't see Mrs. Gattis who had returned to her hiding place on the floor. He held his hands high in the air in a gesture of surrender, praying that they would take him and the stage's strong box without looking inside the cabin. It wasn't likely, but it was all he could think to do to try and protect the lady hiding inside.

A scream came from behind him as Mrs. Gattis was dragged, kicking and shouting, around the side of the stage and dropped in the dust at Doc Mitchell's feet. Her captor then stood guard over them as the others began to go through the stagecoach, tossing anything of value out onto the prairie floor. Once they had completed their work, they packed everything they had discovered onto their horses and re-mounted.

The raiding party then formed a semicircle in front of them. As one, they raised their bows, notched arrows, and took aim.

Doc Mitchell felt a small trembling hand touch his, and he helped Mrs. Gattis to her feet.

"You've taken everything we have, why don't you just leave us be?" he asked. "What good would it do for you to kill us? Or do you just want to prove that you are the inhumane savages that all white men believe you to be?"

Doc Mitchell stepped in front of Mrs. Gattis, placing himself between her and the arrows that were pointed at them.

The leader of the raiding party lowered his bow, handed it to the brave nearest him, and dismounted.

"You have a big mouth for such a little old man," he said and slapped Doc Mitchell across the face.

The blow rocked him, causing his head to spin, but he felt Mrs. Gattis tighten her grip on his hand and managed to stay on his feet. The Native smiled, nodded, and began to laugh. He looked to his men, and they all laughed along with him. When he turned back to Doc. Mitchell, he held a long-bladed knife in his hand.

"We will see how brave you are when you have no scalp, and your blood runs down the face of your woman." His free hand shot out. He grabbed Doc Mitchell's thinning hair as he raised the knife over his head.

A clap of thunder sounded in the cloudless sky. The men's horses began nervously whinnying and pawing at the earth. A single cloud suddenly formed above their heads, casting a shadow over the raiding party in the shape of a giant eagle. The thunder pealed again, and lightning struck the blade of the knife. The man holding it was instantly reduced to a smoldering black scar on the prairie floor. The other raiders dropped their bows and tried to get their mounts under control. It did no good. The frightened horses turned and ran from the stagecoach, taking their riders with them.

The lightning had also knocked Doc Mitchell and Mrs. Gattis to the ground. Stunned, he got to his feet, then looked up just as the last wisps of the cloud melted away, leaving the sky a perfect, uninterrupted blue. He offered his hand to Mrs. Gattis and helped her up. She looked as if she was about to say something, but before she could, he turned his back on her and went to check on the shotgun messenger.

Chapter Nine

December 11, 2008

"Well, this is v-v-v-very interesting," Calvin said. "Y-Y-Yes, yes, very interesting."

James wanted to ask him what was so interesting about it but wasn't sure whether he should. Calvin was bent down so low over the surgical tools that James was surprised he wasn't pushing them around the table with his nose.

Dr. Carroll seemed willing to wait for Calvin to give them his opinion in his own time, so he decided to do the same.

"Hmmmmm, yes." Calvin lifted the scalpel and raised it up closer to the cluster of lights. The sharpened metal reflected the light onto his face as he rotated the blade in his fingers, causing little rainbows to appear in the lenses of his thick glasses.

He then repeated the process with each tool in the set. Finally, he straightened up, removed his glasses, and began nervously cleaning them with the tail of his shirt. "Where d-d-d-did you say you g-g-g-got these instruments?"

"They were a gift. I got them yesterday after our graduation party at Dr. Carroll's house."

"Yes, yes, yes." Calvin was still cleaning the lenses of his glasses. "I understand that, but who g-g-g-gave them to you?"

"I have no idea."

Calvin returned his glasses to his nose, then looked up at Dr. Carroll. "Maybe I should be asking you these questions, David. Y-Y-Y-Young Dr. Hughes here seems q-q-q-quite confused."

"To be honest, Calvin we both are. James is telling you the truth. This surgical kit was delivered anonymously to my home last night. It was covered in brown butcher paper with only James' name written on it. No address for delivery or return, just his full name, James Michael Hughes."

"How did they know that he w-w-w-would be at your home? O-O-O-Or anywhere for that matter w-w-w-with no address?"

Dr. Carroll shrugged and gave his friend a bewildered look. "That is only one of many unanswerable questions concerning this gift. We thought that if you could shed some light on its origins, then we might work backward to find some answers."

James set the leather pouch containing the newspaper clippings beside the surgical tools. "This was also in the package. They appear to be just a random assortment of newspaper articles from the last hundred years or so."

Calvin meticulously emptied the contents onto the table, then quickly glanced at the clippings before turning his attention to the pouch itself. He ran his fingers over the seams and the rudimentary clasp that held the flap closed. Next, he turned his attention to the edges of the pouch's opening. At each side, he found a small place where the old leather was torn.

"Very interesting," Calvin said again as he reached up and began to feel around the top of his head. "I seem to have m-m-m-misplaced my reflector." He looked at James and Dr. Carroll as if they might have it.

"I believe you left it out in the lobby," James told him. "I'll go get it."

"Oh, d-d-d-don't bother." Calvin set the pouch down and started running his hands up and down the length of his upper body. "I keep an extra here in the pocket of my lab coat..." He looked down at himself them back up at them. "I seem to have m-m-m-misplaced my lab coat as well."

"Also in the lobby," James said. "I'll be right back." He left the mock operating room and wound his way back to the lobby. The lab coat and reflector were where Calvin had left them on the weight-loss machine.

A shadow crossed the wall in front of him and came to rest with its shape surrounding the door back into the museum. James stopped and looked out the window behind him to see who had cast it. There was no one there. When he looked back toward the door, the shadow remained. It appeared to be the shadow of a large man wearing a hat with a narrow brim.

He looked out the window again, this time checking up and down the street to see if someone was standing there out of sight, but the street was empty. He placed his back to the window and looked again at the wall. The shadow remained, but now, *his* shadow, smaller and darker, joined it. He raised his hands, one empty and one holding the jacket, and his shadow did likewise. He moved his arms up and down, causing his shadow to take on the appearance of some oddly shaped bird. As he did so, the other shadow began to fade and disappear. Another glance out the window still showed nothing but the empty street.

He returned to the other room to find Calvin and Dr. Carroll laughing.

"Oh, there you are J-J-J-James." Calvin sounded like he was surprised to see him. "David and I were just talking about our days at the university, and this l-l-l-lovely young woman who had a pet snake that she kept u-u-u-under her bed. You see, if you whistled when you were about to—"

"I don't think James needs to hear about all that," Dr. Carroll interrupted him.

James would have sworn that Dr. Carroll was blushing, but before he could comment on it, Calvin reached out and took the coat and reflector from him.

"Oh, I see you have my c-c-c-coat and reflector. I was just l-l-l-looking for those." Calvin put on the coat and slipped the strap of the reflector over his head, then picked up the pouch. "Yes, yes, yes, just as I thought, v-v-v-very interesting," he said, adjusting the reflector so it would direct more light from the overhead lamps deep into the pouch's opening.

This time James couldn't hold back. "What's very interesting, Mr. Coolidge?"

Calvin looked up at him as if he were seeing him for the very first time. "P-P-P-Please, c-c-c-c-call me Calvin," he said cheerfully, then went back to looking at the inside of the pouch. "Yes, yes, yes, very interesting."

"Have you discovered something, Calvin?" Dr. Carroll cut his eyes over at James. "Something maybe *we* should know about?"

"Oh, oh, oh, yes." Calvin looked up from the bag and smiled. "Yes, I have."

He gently turned the pouch inside out enough that James and Dr. Carroll could see the area at the bottom. Just above the seam, a name had been carefully burned into the leather:

M. Mitchell MD

Chapter Ten

March 14, 1870

For a day and a half, Doc Mitchell drove the stagecoach. He followed the only tracks he could see and stopped only long enough to get a couple of hours sleep while Mrs. Gattis stood guard. Now, as the sun was setting on the second day, those tracks had disappeared.

He stood and strained his eyes, scanning the prairie, hoping to spot the trail or any other indication that another coach had passed through the area. He saw nothing but the sun above and the scrub grass that seemed to endlessly surround them.

Haven't we been through enough already? he thought to himself and sat down heavy on the hard, wooden driver's seat. *What do we do now?*

The events of the last few days played out in his mind.

Images of the shotgun messenger hanging off the platform with an arrow through his neck haunted him—along with how the man's boot had caught under the very plank he was now seated on. How the poor man had bled out down the side of the stage. It had taken some work to get him loose. Once he did, the body had fallen to the prairie floor with a soft thud.

He had been impressed by the way Mrs. Gattis had gently tended to the driver until he had gotten there. There was no need to examine the driver's body. By the way the man was lying there twisted and broken on the trail, he knew that he was dead.

They'd spent the next hour digging two graves with the small shovel that had most recently been used to dig a makeshift latrine. Mrs. Gattis had read some appropriate verses from the Bible his mother had given him, then they had taken to the driver's area and continued on their way.

It crossed his mind that *if* there was a bright side to the whole ordeal, it was that the Indians had not harmed the horses. They were tired from being driven so hard during the chase but were otherwise fine.

Now, as he looked into the setting sun, out at the trackless prairie, he didn't know what to do. He was a doctor, not a navigator. Some men could look up at the night sky and determine which direction to take, but he wasn't one of those gifted few.

Earlier, Mrs. Gattis had left him for the modest comforts of the coach. Now that they had stopped, she opened the door and stepped out. Her black mourning dress had been exchanged for a pair of men's pants and a cotton shirt. Doc Mitchell couldn't help but notice how the buttons of the shirt struggled to stay in place across her breasts or how the pants accentuated her hips.

"I found the drivers' spare clothes and a few other things hidden in a space underneath the seats," she said by way of explanation. "I figured that if we were going to be forced into playing the part of coach drivers, then I should probably dress for the job."

"I guess you're right about that." He laughed and used his handkerchief to wipe sweat and dust from his face. "But I doubt anyone would ever mistake you for a coach jockey."

She came forward and scratched the lead horse behind the ears as she looked out at what lay ahead of them. The horse snorted and shook its head.

"I don't see any tracks."

"There aren't any, they just faded away into the rough."

"So, what do we do now, Dr. Mitchell? Turn back and look for another trail, or forge ahead into the great unknown?"

"Well, first off, I wish you would call me Mel. I think we've been through enough together to drop the formality."

Mrs. Gattis smiled and walked back to the coach. "Then you shall call me Ella, short for Eloise. That's what my husband called me."

"Good enough, Ella. Now that we have the introductions out of the way, I think we should camp here for the night and make our decision about how to proceed in the morning when we can see better."

"That's a fine idea. I believe there is a little of that hard tack left, and I can make a fire for coffee."

Doc Mitchell dropped down off the stage and winced as his knees absorbed the shock. He stretched, and his back caught, then gave way with a pop like a child's toy rifle.

"We can definitely eat the hard tack, but I think we best forgo the fire. We don't know what could be prowling around out here after dark, and we don't want the fire to get its attention."

Ella nodded and removed the small shovel from its place hanging on the side of the stagecoach's seat.

"What do ya need that for?"

"Well..." She held up the short-handled shovel and pointed it toward him. "If there are no bodies to bury, and no fire to dampen, then I guess that only leaves one thing."

His cheeks heated in embarrassment as she headed for a small copse of trees a few yards away.

By the time she returned, he had unhitched the team. They were grazing on tall prairie grass as he wiped them down with a towel he had found under the driver's seat. She secured the shovel back in its appointed place, then reached into the stagecoach's cabin and brought out the hard tack and a canteen of water.

"We will need to share *that* with the horses." He pointed at the canteen. "They need it more that we do."

Ella shook the canteen and listened to the water sloshing around inside. "Probably just enough for them." She handed the canteen over to him. "Let them have it, and I'll go back and see if there's another canteen hidden somewhere inside the coach."

He poured a small amount of water into his hand and offered it to the nearest horse. The animal lapped at it, and he grimaced at the feel of its tongue desperately searching his palm for more. He realized that his hands were not going to be an effective way to water the animals and returned to the stage, hoping to find something more suitable for the job. Before he could begin searching, Ella emerged from the coach holding her mourning hat in one hand and a mostly full bottle of whiskey in the other. She exchanged the bottle for the canteen.

She proceeded to fill the hat with water, then held it up to the first horse, enabling it to drink deeply. When the hat was empty, she filled it again with the remaining water and did the same for the second animal.

"I guess I won't be wearing this hat again," she laughed. "I never have understood why, in order to be considered a proper widow, you must always wear a black hat." She turned the hat over in her hand and looked at its damaged interior. "My husband's been dead for almost three months now. I miss him, but I must be realistic and get on with my life. If there is anything I have learned from what's happened to me over the last few months, it is that life is too short to be wasted." She crumpled the remains of the hat into a ball and tossed it out into the open prairie.

"Is a proper widow allowed to share a drink with a man unaccompanied?" he asked as he motioned to her with the bottle and smiled.

"Gracious, *no*!" She touched her fingers to her lips in mock offence. "But what the hell." She took the bottle from him and used her teeth to pull the stopper free. "Here's to propriety!" She turned the bottle up and took a deep drink of the amber liquid before handing it back to him. "The first thing you learn being a soldier's wife is how to drink."

Ella sat on the ground and leaned back against the coach's wheel, and he joined her there.

"I want to thank you for what you did for me yesterday," she said. "You don't know me from Adam, but you protected me. First in the coach, then from those Natives. That's the first time I've felt safe since—well."

"Think nothing of it, I'm just an old soldier, that's what we do. It's in our blood." He took the bottle and raised it to his lips, hoping to put an end to the conversation. He had never been comfortable with praise or with women, truth be known. His formative years had been spent in military service, moving from camp to camp. He had never had time for relationships. By the time he left the service, he was older, and female companionship for more than one night seemed like too much trouble.

"No," she said and placed her hand on the bottle, moving it away from his lips before he had taken a drink. "I think it's more than that. If there's one thing I know, it's soldiers. Chivalry in the line of duty is one thing, but to stand up and risk your life for a woman you just met is quite another."

Doc Mitchell looked over at her, and their eyes met. She smiled, reached up, and placed her hand on his cheek. She left it there for a few seconds before letting it fall away.

"I'm done with mourning, Mel." She pulled her knees up to her chest, wrapped her arms around them, and looked up at the rising moon. "I had decided that when we reached Kansas City that I was going to shed my widow's clothes and begin my life over again. I loved my husband, and I will miss him. But he's dead, not me."

She took another drink before handing the bottle back to him.

"It's cold out tonight." She shivered. "What about you Mel? What does Kansas City hold for you?"

He had never put his thoughts on his future into words, and he struggled for a moment. "Well," he said, "I guess I'm looking for a new beginning myself. I'm too old to soldier, and medicine has lost its allure. So, I'm looking for a new path to follow. I have to admit, I didn't think that path would start by me getting us lost out here on the prairie. But I guess we will just have to wait and see what fate has in store for us."

He smiled down at her, then lifted the bottle in a toast. "Here's to fate!" He took a deep drink. The liquor burned his throat and made him cough.

Ella giggled. "What are you, some kind of lightweight?"

"I'll have you know, young lady, that I was drinking rotgut whiskey long before *you* were born." He took another pull off the bottle. This time the liquor went down smooth as silk, and he let out a deep, satisfied sigh. "That's one way to stay warm on a cold, prairie night."

"A few more drinks of this…" She took the bottle from him and upended it again, then wiped her mouth on her sleeve. "…and a few other ways might come to mind." She winked and passed the bottle back to him.

Chapter Eleven

December 11, 2008

James climbed the cracked and decaying concrete steps leading up to the door of an old, four-story brick apartment building. A rusted metal box was mounted to the wall beside the door. A row of buttons lined the front panel, and next to each one was a strip of brightly colored plastic with the residents' names pressed into it. He pushed the button next to a red strip that read *N. Cousins* and only had to wait a moment before there was a burst of static followed by a thump as the electronic lock retracted.

He leaned in and gave the door a hard pull, having learned early on that it often stuck. The entry way was dimly lit, cold, and damp. There was a door to each side of him and a stairwell rose on his left, casting its shadow over a row of scarred and battered mailboxes built into the opposite wall. The exterior door snapped shut behind him. Before he could set foot on the first step, the door to apartment A-1 opened slightly.

"Who is it?" Mrs. Rosenbloom whispered in a cracked voice.

He stopped, smiled, and shook his head. "It's just me, Mrs. Rosenbloom."

"Me, who?"

"James Hughes," he said with a laugh. This exchange happened every time he came in. "I'm Nancy's boyfriend."

Mrs. Rosenbloom flung the door open wide and leaned against the frame. She was dressed in her usual lime-green housecoat, fuzzy slippers, and well-worn black wig. A lit Virginia Slims Menthol cigarette was tucked between the middle and ring finger of her left hand which she held against her chest.

"James, why didn't you say so?" Her voice was low and raspy from years of smoking. She brought the cigarette up to her lips and took a deep drag which caused her housecoat to fall open and present him with a view of her calf and thigh that he could have done without. "That Nancy, she's a lucky girl!" She exhaled a plume of stale-smelling gray smoke, then pointed the cigarette at him. "If you ever get tired of her company, you know where to find *me*!" She started to laugh but it turned into a rasping, wet cough.

"That I do, Mrs. Rosenbloom." He gave her a polite smile. "But for now, I best get upstairs, and you need to close up the front of your housecoat before you catch cold."

She looked down at her exposed leg, then slowly raised her eyes up to his. "You may be a doctor..." She straightened up and let her housecoat fall closed. "But you don't know what you're missing!" She stuck the cigarette in her mouth and gave him a quick wink before going back inside her apartment, leaving a cloud of smoke in her wake.

James waited till he heard her throw the deadbolt, then started up the stairs to Nancy's fourth-floor apartment. Meeting Nancy at the VA was the only good that had come from the Duboski incident. She had unfortunately been the nurse scheduled to assist Dr. Kemple.

Weeks of hearings and depositions had followed Duboski's death, and they had often been called to appear for questioning at the same time. Small talk in waiting rooms had turned to deeper conversations over coffee. He smiled, thinking back on that one afternoon when he got up the nerve to offer to walk her home. That evening on the doorstep, she had kissed him goodnight, and they had been together ever since. James kept his sad little one-room apartment near campus, but he preferred to spend most nights at Nancy's slightly nicer, three-room walk-up.

He made it to the fourth floor where Nancy was waiting in the doorway. He stopped at the head of the stairs, stunned by the sight of her. In stark contrast to Mrs. Rosenbloom's green housecoat and wig, Nancy was wearing a large, black Ace of Base concert t-shirt that hung down just low enough, but still left plenty of her shapely legs exposed. Her naturally curly brown hair framed her face and tumbled over her shoulders.

"It's about time you came home, stranger. Like what you see?" She spun around and walked back into the apartment, causing her shirt to lift just enough to give him a glimpse of the red panties she had on underneath. The door started to close, but before it could, he ran after her and into the apartment.

Nancy was sitting on the secondhand love seat that took up most of the small living room, and James settled in beside her. She leaned over and kissed him gently.

"Sorry I couldn't make the party last night," she said and snuggled up close.

"Don't sweat it, you had to work. Elegant digs like this don't come cheap."

"Bite me." She giggled and slapped playfully at him. "Not all of us can afford a palatial doctor's estate like yours."

They had yet to say the actual words, but he knew she loved him, and he loved her as well.

"So," she continued, "it must have been a heck of a bash if you had to babysit Dr. Carroll all night."

"He was pretty ripped, but that's not the reason I stayed." He noticed the questioning look on her face. "Right after I put him to bed, someone delivered a package addressed to me, at his place. Weirdest thing, it was an old surgical kit and a bunch of ancient newspaper clippings. It was all inside a box that had been taped together and wrapped in brown paper. I knew you would be sleeping all day after your shift, so when the doc woke up, we went to see a friend of his that has a medical museum. Ready for this?" He looked over at her, and she nodded. "His name is *Calvin Coolidge*."

"As in President Coolidge?"

"Yep, says his parents had a sense of humor."

"Ha, ha," she said sarcastically, and rolled her eyes.

"Anyway, Calvin says it is a perfectly preserved Civil War era kit. Says he's never seen a complete one before."

"Well, that's pretty cool. Who sent it to you?"

"I have no idea. There was no note, no return address. Just a box with my name on it."

"That is weird." She patted his knee, then stood up, giving him another quick glimpse of the red cotton hiding underneath her shirt. "I just got up, and I'm hungry. Want some eggs?" She didn't wait for an answer, just turned and walked into the kitchen.

"I've got an idea," he said as he followed her.

"What's that?" Her voice sounded muffled.

When he stepped into the overcrowded, tiny kitchen he saw why. She was bent over at the waist with her head inside the refrigerator, gathering the things she needed to cook. He got more than a quick glance of her red panties this time, and he had a feeling that she was doing it on purpose. She looked back, gave him a wink, and wiggled her hips.

Feelings confirmed.

"Now what were you saying? Something about an idea?" She closed the refrigerator and brought the eggs over to the stove where a skillet was heating up.

"I...uh..." he muttered, trying to remember what he had been thinking before she put all sorts of other ideas in his head. "Oh yeah, now I remember! I've got two weeks before I have to report to the VA, and I was thinking that we should take a road trip, just get away for a while."

"Sounds good to me." Nancy cracked an egg into the hot skillet. "I've got some vacation time built up, so I'll see if I can get a rush approval."

"What would you think if we went to the mountains, maybe up in Nevada or Colorado?"

"That sounds fun." She cracked another egg into the skillet, then dusted them with salt and pepper. "But no tourist traps. If we're going to the mountains, then I want to see the mountains—not just a bunch of cheesy, crap-filled stores."

"Fair enough, then that's the plan. Mountains *yes*, crap *no*!"

Nancy turned and ran her fingers through his hair, sending shivers down his spine. "I like it when you take charge." She looked up into his eyes and suggestively bit her lower lip. "Have you got any other big plans?" Her fingers slowly fell from his hair and left a trail across his chest as she walked past him toward the bedroom.

James followed her with his eyes. As she approached the bedroom door, she pulled the Ace of Base shirt off over her head and let it fall to the floor.

"But...but, what about your eggs?"

The bedsprings squeaked in the other room. A second later, a pair of red panties flew through the bedroom door and landed on the loveseat.

Screw the eggs! He shoved the skillet off the hot eye, turned the knob below it to off, then sprinted across the living room and through the open bedroom door.

Chapter Twelve

March 15, 1870

Something struck the sole of Doc Mitchell's boot and jolted him awake. He opened his eyes, and the morning sun immediately blinded him. He tried to raise his arm to block some the light, but it lay trapped underneath Ella who was snoring softly beside him.

"Hey, mister, is you alive?"

He blinked a few times and slowly his vision cleared. A young boy wearing overalls and a floppy hat was standing in front of him. He looked to be around nine years old.

A donkey brayed somewhere off in the distance. Doc Mitchell started to look in that the direction, but the boy kicked the bottom of his boot again.

"Stop doing that!" he snapped, then felt bad about it when the boy looked frightened and took a step back.

His head pounded, and his throat was dry. He remembered Ella watering the horses with her hat, then they had a few drinks from a bottle of whiskey, then...then...oh yes, then they had—

"Hey, mister!"

"Yes, son, sorry. I didn't mean to snap. Just give me minute to get my wits about me."

What was I thinking? She's half my age, and then to fall asleep out here in the middle of nowhere, anything could have happened. Wild animals, another raiding party, and there we'd sit, passed out drunk like we didn't have care in the world. Stupid, stupid...

"Um..." The boy cleared his throat.

"What? What is it, boy? Speak up! What can be so important that you can't—?"

The boy pointed down at Ella. He followed the line of the boy's finger and looked down at her for the first time, only to realize that her shirt was open and one of her breasts was fully exposed. He quickly reached over and pulled her shirt closed before starting to jostle her, trying to get her to wake up.

"Ella! Ella, wake up."

Her eyes fluttered open. "Good morning, Mel." She beamed, her cheeks flushed with color, and she smiled broadly up at him. "I thought after last night that you might—"

He vigorously shook his head, then indicated the boy with a nod.

"Oh." She gasped and sat up, causing her shirt to fall open again. "Oh!" She grabbed at it and managed to stand at the same time. The unbuttoned, oversized men's trousers she was wearing started to slide down off her hips, and she snatched them with her free hand before throwing herself into the coach and slamming the door.

Doc Mitchell gripped a spoke of the stage wheel he was leaning against and used it to pull himself up, then turned his back to the boy long enough to button his britches and tuck his shirt in.

"Now that you've gotten an eyeful," he started, hoping that his voice didn't betray the embarrassment he felt, "why don't you tell me where you came from."

The boy snickered, then pointed to his right, past the donkey and the stand of trees where Ella had done her business the night before. "I come from over yonder."

Doc Mitchell moved closer to the boy and looked in the direction he was pointing. Sure enough, in the light of the morning sun, he could just make out the shape of a small building on the horizon. "So, you do." He started rubbing at the stubble of hair on his chin. "How did you happen to stumble upon us?"

"Pa sent me to fetch my ma and sister some washin' water from the crick, so I hitched up old Braveheart over there." He pointed at the mule, and Doc Mitchell noticed for the first time that the animal was tethered to a travois loaded with two large wooden buckets. "The crick's just over thata way." He motioned to the area behind him with his thumb. "I heard your horses a whinnyin' and come to see why somebody stopped out here 'stead of comin' on up to the house. When I seen you all spread out with that lady layin' on top of you, I figured you was dead."

"Yes, well, thank you for coming to our rescue." He felt the blood rush into his cheeks and hastily changed the subject. "What's your name, son?"

"It's Gene, after my pa's daddy."

"Ok, Gene, do you think it would be possible for my companion and I to follow you back to your home? I'm hoping your father can give us directions to the nearest settlement."

"I don't see why not, all the other stages stop there. Pa gives 'um fresh horses, and Ma feeds 'um dinner."

"Wonderful, well then, I best get the horses—"

"But I gotta get the water first, or Pa'll tan my hide."

"Of course, you do." Doc Mitchell pulled a handkerchief out of his back pocket and ran it across his face, wincing at the smell of whiskey in his sweat. "You go do that, and by the time you come back, I'll have the team hitched to the stage and be ready to follow you."

Gene seemed to think about that for a second, then without saying a word he went over to Braveheart, and they were on their way.

The stagecoach door opened with a creak. Ella had changed out of the men's clothes and into her more formal mourning dress. "I heard you two talking and figured that I best make myself more presentable before we go calling on the neighbors."

"You look beautiful." He reached out and took her hands in his. "About last night—"

She stopped him with a shake of her head. "Don't talk about it, just let it be what it was." She smiled and caressed his cheek. "You need a shave."

He ran his fingers across the skin on his cheeks. "I guess I do at that. Maybe Gene will let me borrow enough *crick* water to get in a quick one before we go. For now, I best tend to the horses."

* * *

Doc Mitchell had the horses hitched to the stage and was changing into a clean shirt when a distant whistle cut through the quiet of the late morning.

"Did you hear that?" he asked Ella.

"I'm sorry..." She leaned out of the open coach window. "Did you say something?"

"Never mind." He shook his head and went back to buttoning his shirt.

"The raiders made quite a mess in here," she told him through the open window. "I've done my best to tidy up and repack what's left of our things, which isn't much." She stepped down out of the stage and handed him a string tie. "That was underneath the rug."

"Thanks." He took the tie and slipped it over his head.

The whistle came again, this time slightly louder.

"Did you hear that?" Ella asked him, and he answered her with a look of frustration.

"Over there, look." She pointed toward a dark figure traveling slowly past them. "Is that Gene?"

"I guess it could be, but he was—" The whistle came for the third time and was followed by the unmistakable *hee-haw* from Braveheart, the donkey. "That's him."

He quickly tightened the clasp on the tie, then handed his bag to Ella before climbing up onto the driver's seat. Braveheart was moving slow under the weight of the water barrels and within minutes, they caught up with them.

It took the better part of an hour for the heavy-laden mule to travel the distance to Gene's house, which turned out to be a stage relay station.

"I wondered what happened to y'all," Gene's father said after the initial introductions had been made. He had come out of the station when their little party arrived and introduced himself as Edward Turnbull. Doc Mitchell shook his hand, then introduced Ella.

"It's okay, Constance, y'all can come out now!" Edward called out toward the house.

Constance, Edward's wife, was a petite woman, but Doc Mitchell could tell with one look that she was not a woman to be trifled with. A young girl followed her out of the station and shyly peeked from behind her mother's dress. When he smiled at her, she *humphed* and went back inside.

"Marie, that's rude!" Constance chided her, then turned her attention back to their new arrivals. "You will have to excuse Marie, she's at that age. I'm afraid she may have a little schoolgirl crush on Mr. Clement, your driver." She looked around him and Ella. "Where is Mr. Clement?"

Doc Mitchell lowered his eyes. "He's buried along with the shotgun messenger about fifty miles back the way we came. We were attacked by an Indian raiding party. Mrs. Gattis and I barely escaped with our lives." He decided it best to leave out the odd happening that saved them and hoped that Mrs. Turnbull would just accept his story as he told it.

"I'm sorry to hear that, I truly am." She took a deep breath and let it out. "It is a hard land we are living in, and the sooner we can tame it, the better. Why don't the two of you come on inside and let me feed you some breakfast while Edward sees to your horses?" She didn't wait for a reply.

"You go ahead, *Mrs. Gattis*," Doc Mitchell said as he motioned her toward the door. "I'll be in momentarily."

Ella did as she was told, and he watched her as she walked away. When the door closed, he stepped closer to Edward. "Should we be concerned about that raiding party returning and attacking the station?" He made a point to keep his voice low.

"I don't think so," Edward assured him. "We've been here seven years, and the only Indians we've encountered have been peaceful. Constance doesn't like it when they come around, but it's been my experience that if you treat them with respect, they'll do the same to you. After all, this was their land long before we set foot on it."

"I see..." Doc Mitchell absentmindedly ran his hands across the whiskers on his chin. "We left Animas Forks, Colorado a few days ago. We never had much trouble there either, but the mines have been operating in the mountains surrounding the town for a few years now, so the Natives have learned to keep their distance."

"Those were probably Ute's you ran afoul of. There's been rumors of a group of whites roaming around destroying the Indian camps across three different territories. It's got a lot of the tribes up in arms. They didn't really trust us to start with, and now they think every man in a bowler hat is a direct threat."

"Did you say a bowler hat?"

"Yeah," Edward chuckled. "Word is that the band of marauders have a leader who's a cowboy that wears a bowler hat."

"Mr. Mitchell." Constance stood in the doorway with a frying pan in her hand. "How do you like your eggs?"

"Tell her scrambled," Edward whispered. "Woman never has figured out how to fry a proper egg."

"Scrambled would be perfect, Mrs. Turnbull." He looked back at Edward who was smiling as he led the horses around the station to the stables in back. "Is there a place I can wash up before our meal?"

Chapter Thirteen

December 14, 2008

James and Nancy huddled together, trying to stay warm as a cold wind blew down the street in front of The Coolidge Museum of Medical Knowledge. Calvin had called earlier that morning asking for him and Dr. Carroll to stop by at noon so he could tell them what he had discovered about the surgical kit and clippings.

James rang the bell that hung next to the museum's old-fashioned screen door for the third time. It was now five minutes after twelve, and the door was locked.

"I really shouldn't be here," Nancy said, shivering around her words. "If we are going to leave for our trip in the morning, I should really be home, packing."

"You're just saying that 'cause you're cold."

"Yes, that's exactly why I'm saying it." She pushed in tighter against James, and he could feel her chin quivering against his chest.

"I'm sorry, if had known he was going to keep us waiting out here on the street, I never would have suggested you come along. It's just that he is such a character, I really wanted you to meet him."

"Hey, you kids, get a room!"

James immediately recognized Dr. Carroll's voice. "Don't tempt us."

Nancy giggled and slapped his chest.

Dr. Carroll was bundled up inside an ankle-length wool coat with a colorful rainbow scarf wrapped around his neck. He held three cups of coffee with steam pouring out from under their plastic lids. "I thought something like this might happen, so I came prepared." He handed a cup to James and one to Nancy. "Wonderful to see you again, Nancy. Glad you could join us."

"Now that you're here, I'm glad I did." She took the coffee from him, then playfully stuck her tongue out at James before taking a sip. She gasped and started coughing.

"What's wrong, is it too hot?" James looked over at her, worried, as she got herself under control.

"Oh, I think I know what happened." Dr. Carroll reached out and tried to exchange cups with Nancy. "I put a little something extra in mine. I'm sorry, Nancy. I must have gotten them mixed up."

"Oh no you don't, Doc." She stepped back and held the cup out of his reach. "This is the first time I've felt warm since we got here. You *gave* this to me, and I'm keeping it."

"But Nancy, I—"

The inner door to the museum opened with a creak, and Calvin started wrestling with the screen door. "Blasted thing, n-n-n-never wants to open." He shook it, kicked at it, then shook it some more. "Oh, there it is!"

Nancy looked up at James wide-eyed.

"What did I tell you?" He winked at her and smiled.

"Come in, c-c-c-come in." Calvin pushed open the screen door and moved back out of the way. "You must be freezing. I wasn't expecting you till n-n-n-noon, good thing I happened to walk past the window and saw you s-s-s-standing out there."

Dr. Carroll was the last inside and closed the door behind himself. "Calvin, it's twelve-fifteen."

"What?" Calvin looked at each one of them in turn, then up at the clock hanging above the reception desk. The clock was mounted inside a painted porcelain sign that featured a doctor with a reflector on his forehead and a stethoscope in his hand. *There's no bad time for a checkup* was etched into the clock's porcelain base. "Well, s-s-s-so it is. Then it's you who are late. Y-Y-Y-You know it's very rude to keep people waiting. I would have thought you would have been excited over my news. Y-Y-Y-You know it's not often—" He stopped and looked at them again, then extended his hand to Nancy. "I don't believe we've m-m-m-met. I'm Calvin Coolidge."

"Oh." Nancy appeared bewildered by his mannerisms and hesitated before taking his hand. "I'm Nancy Cousins, I'm James's, um, girlfriend?" She looked over at him, wide-eyed.

Calvin looked up at James as well, all the while holding Nancy's hand.

"Sorry, Calvin," James said. "I'm being rude. This is my *girlfriend*, Nancy Cousins."

"It's a p-p-p-pleasure to meet you, Nancy." Calvin started vigorously shaking her hand. "Any f-f-f-friend of James is a f-f-f-friend of mine. You are a lucky, lucky girl. Oh, yes you are. You know James here b-b-b-brought me the most interesting thing a few days ago, it was a—"

Dr. Carroll reached out and put his hand on top of theirs, stopping the relentless pumping. "Calvin, didn't you have something you wanted to show us?"

"I did?" Calvin released Nancy's hand and looked up at Dr. Carroll. "Oh yes, I-I-I-I did!" He turned abruptly and left the room.

With a shrug, Dr. Carroll motioned for them to take the lead as they followed Calvin deeper into the museum.

Inside the mock operating theater, Calvin had arranged all the clippings on the table and was fussing over them. They looked at one another questioningly as they waited for Calvin to realize they were there. After a full minute had passed, James cleared his throat.

"Humph." Calvin looked up at them and seemed somewhat surprised to see them there. "Oh, yes." He looked at each of them in turn before returning to the clippings. "I have arranged the c-c-c-clippings in order from earliest to m-m-m-most recent, and there does not seem to be any p-p-p-pattern other than the obvious." He looked up again.

No one said anything.

"The earliest clipping," he went on, "is from the *K-K-K-Kansas City Evening Star* and is dated December 20, eh-eh-eh-1875. It is an obituary for a Dr. M-M-M-Melvin Mitchell, age seventy-two. It states, *Dr. Mitchell, a former surgeon, came out of retirement to perform a lifesaving operation on a young Jedidiah Walkins, age six, who had been shot five times during a gunfight at the Gray's Saloon where he was enjoying a birthday sarsaparilla with his father, Jedidiah Walkins Sr. Mister Walkins was killed in the skirmish. The surgery was a complete success and young Jed is resting peacefully at home and expected to make a full recovery.*" Calvin stopped reading, removed his glasses, and began to furiously clean them with the hem of his lab coat.

"There's no way he could have done that," James observed. He also noticed that Calvin didn't stutter while he was reading the clipping. He made a mental note to do some research on stuttering when he had a chance. "It would be almost impossible now, much less in the 1870s."

"Yes," Calvin agreed. "Especially n-n-n-not using a set of tools like th-th-th-these." He pointed at the surgical kit that had been delivered with the clippings.

"So, he was this M. Mitchell MD?" James picked up the messenger bag and looked again at the initials burned on the inside seam.

"I-I-I-It appears so," Calvin answered. "The clip goes on to say that D-D-D-Dr. Mitchell was found dead from a head injury a few d-d-d-days later in the lot behind his residence. It says that he left a w-w-w-widow, Eloise, and a five-year-old son n-n-n-named Melvin Mitchell Jr."

"That's so sad." Nancy looked up at James, and he could see tears forming in her eyes. He reached out and pulled her close.

"Q-Q-Q-Quite," Calvin said as he picked up the next clipping in the line. "Next is from the *Calvary Dispatch*, d-d-d-dated March 15,

1907. This appears to b-b-b-be the company newsletter for the multiple mines in the area owned b-b-b-by the Calvary Mine Company. It reports that they are l-l-l-looking for a replacement company doctor after the m-m-m-mysterious death of their physician M-M-M-Melvin Mitchell Jr., whose body was d-d-d-discovered inside one of the m-m-m-main m-m-m-mine entrances m-m-m-missing all its appendages. The m-m-m-mine owner reported it to police as an animal attack." He lifted the article. "*Dr. Mitchell Jr. left behind a widow, Julia, who was expecting their first child. The mine company has set up a special fund to help the widow relocate.*"

"I guess it's not too far-fetched that Dr. Mitchell Sr. and Jr. both met with questionable deaths, considering the time period." Dr. Carroll looked over at them, and Nancy nodded.

"I-I-I-If-If that was all," Calvin said, "then I might agree with you." He picked up the third clipping. "From the *Nashville Banner*, August 20, n-n-n-1952. *Funeral services were held today for renowned Nashville heart surgeon, Christopher Elgin Linton. In attendance was his wife of six years, Karen, who is eight months pregnant with their first child, Linton's mother, Francis, other family members, and close friends. The funeral comes three days after Linton's body was discovered in an alley behind Mid-State Baptist Hospital. Police reports say that the hands had been severed from the body causing death from blood loss.*"

"It's a horrible story, but what's the connection?" James asked. "It was forty years later."

Calvin held up a finger to get his attention. "The c-c-c-clipping c-c-c-continues, *Dr. Linton was buried along with his prized possession. A Civil War era surgical kit given to him for his medical school graduation by his grandmother, Minnie Mitchell-Combes.*"

They all stared at Calvin in silence while he cleaned his glasses.

"Next..." He placed his glasses back on his nose and picked up another clipping from the table. "From the *Nashville Banner*, August t-t-t-23, 1952. *Nashville Police are reporting that the grave of recently deceased, Dr. Christopher Elgin Linton was desecrated last night in the*

Nashville City Cemetery. The grave was opened, and the body was discovered sitting against a nearby pine tree. The coffin's lining was shredded and strewn over the nearby graves. The deceased's prized Civil War surgical kit, a gift from his grandmother, was not found at the scene."

Nancy swooned against James, and he grabbed a nearby stool for her to sit on. Her face was pale, and she looked worried.

"You need to get rid of it," she whispered. "It's cursed."

"Cursed, that's a v-v-v-very good word for it." Calvin looked over at her, nodding excitedly. "B-B-B-Bedeviled, b-b-b- blighted, unholy. I agree with young N-N-N-Nancy here, you need to be r-r-r-rid of it."

"Wait just a minute, now," Dr. Carroll interrupted. "This is ridiculous, there is no such thing as a curse. That's just silly superstition." He turned to Calvin. "This could be the crown jewel of your museum. You said just the other day that you had never seen a complete surgical kit from that era, and now you're telling them to throw it in the trash?"

"Oh n-n-n-no, I never said that." Calvin violently shook his head. "That wouldn't w-w-w-work, if it is truly c-c-c-cursed, it would just find its way back to James. This k-k-k-kit needs to be destroyed, but if I were a b-b-b-betting man, and I'm not, I would b-b-b-bet that the kit will not let itself be d-d-d-destroyed."

"That's crazy, Calvin, even for you."

"Oh, n-n-n-no." Calvin shook his head. "There are m-m-m-many stories of c-c-c-cursed or h-h-h-haunted items following family lines."

"Are you saying that you think that our James here is a descendant of this Dr. Melvin Mitchell?"

"That's exactly what I-I-I-I'm saying. There were th-th-th-three more clippings in the p-p-p-package. One is about a dental surgeon in C-C-C-Cleveland in the mid-seventies that created a n-n-n-new type of dental implant that m-m-m-modernized the way dentures are worn. He m-m-m-mentioned at an awards dinner that his good luck ch-ch-ch-charm was a Civil War surgical kit that he r-r-r-received from a distant relative. He even s-s-s-stated that his first models were carved using its s-s-s-scalpel. He d-d-d-died in a horrendous single car accident during a rainstorm. Hit a t-t-t-tree after swerving off the road and was impaled by a-a-a-a low-hanging limb." Calvin picked up another clipping. "Th-Th-Th-The next time the surgical kit appeared was in n-n-n-1984. A man claimed th-th-th-that he had received it in the mail. He t-t-t-tried to pawn it at a shop outside Estelline, Texas. While he was there, a t-t-t-tornado t-t-t-touched down on top of the shop, destroying it and k-k-k-killing the man and the shop owner. He was identified as Ch-Ch-Ch-Charlie Kelly—wanted for the robbery and murder of a Dr. Alvin Hughes."

"Hughes?" James clutched Nancy's hand. "Did you say Hughes?"

"Yes, I did." Calvin handed James the last clipping. "D-D-D-Dr. Hughes lived in Modesto, C-C-C-California where he worked as a n-n-n-neo-natal surgeon. He was known w-w-w-worldwide for his advances in surgical techniques on n-n-n-newborn infants with atrial septal defects. W-W-W-Was he any relation?"

"I don't know." James gently placed the clipping back on the table in line with the others. "I guess it's possible. My dad never knew his family. His mother and father were never married, and he and Grandma moved around a lot, so I guess, maybe?"

"There is a phone out in the l-l-l-lobby. I suggest you g-g-g-give him a call. Perhaps he would remember the name."

"That won't work, Calvin," Dr. Carroll cut in. "James' parents were killed in a car accident six years ago."

"Oh, I'm sorry." Calvin began cleaning his glasses again, then abruptly stopped and looked over at James. "Was your father in th-th-th-the medical profession?"

"He drove a city bus, and Mom was an accountant."

Calvin scratched his forehead, then put his glasses back in place. "The final c-c-c-clipping is about a Dr. McKissell—"

"I knew him," Dr. Carroll interrupted. "Remember, James, we talked about him? He was the one who was so nervous when we interviewed him for a staff position that the committee felt he would be useless as a surgeon."

"Yes." Calvin laid the clipping back on the table. "I knew him, as well. I-I-I-I attended his funeral, closed-casket as I recall. If memory serves me c-c-c-correctly, he was involved in a murder-suicide with another s-s-s-surgeon. Police found Dr. McKissell had been s-s-s-stabbed repeatedly in the chest with a double-edged scalpel and his th-th-th-throat had been slit. His partner at the surgical center had s-s-s-severed the arteries in both of his own ankles before using a scalpel to slit his wrists. The papers mentioned something about p-p-p-professional jealousy."

"But nothing about the cursed surgical kit?" Nancy asked.

"No, but I think it is a fair assumption that M-M-M-McKissell was the recipient of it much like our James here." Calvin raised his eyebrows at James, then circled the table, leaned against it, and crossed his arms. "So, from the c-c-c-circumstantial evidence that we can gather from these c-c-c-clippings, there are a few conclusions that I feel we can draw. S-S-S-Somehow, the surgical kit only goes to the m-m-m-male heirs of Dr. Melvin M-M-M-Mitchell Sr. who have become physicians. Once in their p-p-p-possession, these same heirs become top men in their field, often inventing some new p-p-p-procedure or gadget that brings them great reward and notoriety. Finally, they all d-d-d-die in horrible ways. Interesting."

"It's not interesting." Dr. Carroll's voice carried a tone of disbelief and irritation. "It's ludicrous. We are all adults here and were acting like snot-nosed teenagers huddled around a Ouija board. Come on, let's be serious here. That..." He pointed at the surgical kit sitting at the edge of the table. "Is just an antique piece of medical equipment. It's not cursed, haunted, or otherwise possessed with the ability to track down the blood relatives of its original owner and gift them mystical abilities to—"

The surgical kit loudly clattered onto the hard, cement floor of the mock operating room, interrupting him mid-thought. They all stared silently at the scattered surgical tools.

"I'll get them." Dr. Carroll started to move in the direction of the tools.

"No!" James barked, louder than he had meant to. "Better let me." He moved behind Nancy and Dr. Carroll to gather up the pieces and place them back inside their holder.

Calvin held up his hand and stopped him from placing them back on the table, then turned and pulled the box they had been shipped in off a nearby shelf. James placed the kit in the box as Calvin gathered up the clippings and slipped them into it as well.

"I think it's best if you take those home with you, James."

Chapter Fourteen

March 15, 1870

Doc Mitchell used a small piece of biscuit to push the last of his scrambled eggs onto his fork. He placed them in his mouth and chewed thoroughly, then washed it down with the remaining drops of coffee in his cup. Marie watched him, seemingly entranced by his movements, and she laughed when a little burp escaped him.

"Momma says burping is rude."

Gene was sitting next to him and made a loud, fake burping sound, then began to laugh.

"That is enough!" Constance had her back to the table, but Doc Mitchell could tell that the children knew she meant business just by the tone of her voice. Gene stopped laughing mid-cackle. "We have guests." She turned from the wash tub that she kept next to the fire and came back to the table. "Please excuse our children, Doctor. I'm afraid growing up out here on the prairie has not been the best thing for their manners."

"Think nothing of it." He brushed a few biscuit crumbs off the front of his shirt and winked at Gene.

"May I help with the dishes?" Ella started to pick up a plate and cup, but Constance stopped her with a look, then took them from her. "No, ma'am, you may not. You are a guest in my home, and I will not have you acting like some darkie slave."

"Ain't no more of them," Edward said, speaking for the first time since dinner was served. "Never understood why some folks figured it was okay to own other folks just 'cause their skin was a different color."

"I know there aren't slaves anymore." Constance slapped at him with the dish rag she had over her arm. "It was just a figure of speech. Now, why don't you take our guests outside for some air, while the children and I gather up the dinner dishes?"

"Aw, Maw, have I gotta?" Gene whined.

"*I'll* help you, Momma." Marie jumped to her feet and started gathering dishes.

"Thank you, Marie." Constance smiled and gently touched her daughter's hair as she passed by carrying an armload of plates. "And since you are too good to help with the dishes, young man, you may empty the chamber pot in the bedroom, and then place the extra one in the loft above the barn."

"That's our cue to leave." Edward stood and held the chair for Ella as she scooted away from the table. "What say you folks come with me out front? Doc, I have some fresh tobacco that come in on the last stage if you'd like to smoke a bowl."

"Don't mind if I do." He reached inside his coat and pulled out his pipe.

The full moon bathed the prairie in cold, blue light. Edward allowed Doc Mitchell to fill his pipe first before filling his own. He struck a match off the door frame and lifted it to the bowl. It took two hard puffs to get the dried leaves burning. Once his pipe was lit, he held the match out for Edward. Soon the night air was filled with the comforting aroma of pipe tobacco.

"Would you care for a smoke, Mrs. Gattis?" Edward offered her the pouch of tobacco. "I understand that pipe smoking has become something that some modern ladies feel is their right to do these days." He placed his pipe back in his mouth, and Doc Mitchell could tell he was trying to hide his disapproval.

"No thank you, Mr. Turnbull." She smiled and took a few steps away from the smoke. "But being that I am one of those modern ladies you spoke of, I do appreciate the offer."

Edward choked on the smoke and coughed. "Yes, ma'am." He turned his attention to Doc Mitchell. "I expect the next stage to come through sometime around midday tomorrow. They'll take you on into Lawrence, Kansas, and from there it's less than a day's ride to Kansas City, so you should be there within a week. As for tonight, Constance says I should bunk with you out in the hayloft over the barn, and Mrs. Gattis here can sleep with her in our bed. We don't usually have overnight guests, and I'm afraid we just aren't set up for it."

"That won't be necessary, Mr. Turnbull," Ella spoke up. "I am perfectly capable of sleeping in the stage we came in on, and I will not be responsible for keeping you from your bed."

"I, I don't know about that, Mrs. Gattis." Edward sounded concerned. "Constance won't be too happy about it, and I'm just not sure it will be safe out here for a lady to be sleeping in a stage all alone."

"How dangerous could it be? You have pulled the stage into the corral between the house where you will be sleeping with your wife and children, and the barn where Dr. Mitchell will be sleeping."

Edward rubbed at the beard stubble on his chin. "I—"

"I can see you are concerned that your wife will not be as accepting of the idea as you are." Ella walked past them to the door of the house. "Don't concern yourself with that. I'll speak to her about it myself." She opened the door and went inside.

"I, uh," Edward stammered and looked over at Doc Mitchell who was fighting hard to suppress a laugh. "I don't suppose I could interest you in a little nip of whiskey before bed, could I, Doc? It's purely medicinal."

"As a man of medicine..." He tapped his pipe on the heel of his boot to empty it of any remaining ash. "I believe after the whooping you just got, a little nip would surely help heal your wounds."

An hour later, the house and lot were quiet. Doc Mitchell looked out from the hayloft and watched a shadowy figure slip out of the coach and cross the short distance to the barn. A moment later, Ella shimmied up the wooden ladder from the stables below and into his waiting arms.

Chapter Fifteen

December 15, 2008

The sun was just peeking over the horizon as James and Nancy pulled away from the curb outside her apartment. The frost-covered trees with the early morning sun glinting off their thin coating of ice made the deserted streets seem like an enchanted fairyland. She could not have asked for a more perfect way to start their first adventure together. *The first of many,* she thought before turning her face into the bright rays of the morning sun.

"It's a little chilly out this morning," James said, as he adjusted the heat. "But it's going to be a lot colder than this where we're headed, I'm afraid."

"That's why I packed us heavy coats and sweaters. If we're still cold after that, then we will just have to brew us up a pot of Dr. Carroll's magic coffee."

"The only thing magic about *that* coffee comes from a flask."

She turned to look at him. He smiled, and her heart melted. "I love ya, you know."

"WHAT?" James eyes grew wide with make-believe shock. "Are you talking to me?" He whipped his head from side to side, looking around the car. "You must be talking to me, there's nobody else in here."

"Bite me! Twice!" She punched him on the shoulder and pretended to pout.

"I love you, too." His words were like music in her ears. She already knew that he loved her, but hearing him say it for the first time was magical.

"Do you, *really*?" She knew she was blushing, but now that they had told each other how they felt, she couldn't accept it. She had been in a few previous relationships, even said those words before, but for the first time, she really believed that she meant it, and she needed to know that he meant it, too.

James didn't answer. Instead, he whipped the car into the parking lot of a convenience store, threw it into park, and rushed inside. *Why?* Was he sick, or angry that she needed reassurance? Had she pushed too hard?

A few minutes later, James ran back to the car, holding a brown paper bag. He slid in behind the wheel and turned to face her.

"Here." He pulled a banana out of the bag and handed it to her.

"What?"

James held up his hand to stop her question, then reached into the bag again and pulled out a single, Hershey's kiss. He unwrapped it and motioned for her to open her mouth, then popped the chocolate in it. He used his fingers to gently press up on her chin and close her mouth before going back into the bag. Next, he brought out a single red rose still wrapped in clear cellophane with a $1.99 price tag attached. He handed that to her, and she took it with the hand not holding the banana.

"Hmmmm, it's still not quite right." James leaned back against the door and started rubbing his chin. He studied her for another few seconds, then snapped his fingers. "Got it!"

He reached back in the bag and made a show out of rummaging around inside it. What was he up to, and why was she eating chocolate while holding a rose in one hand and a banana in the other? He brought his hand out of the bag, and this time he was holding a small, felt box.

With a trembling hand he opened the box and showed her the diamond ring inside.

"Yes, really."

Nancy couldn't breathe, she hadn't known what he was up to, but she never expected this. Tears tingled in the corners of her eyes, and her lips began to quiver.

"This wasn't how I had planned to ask you to marry me. I had intended to wait till we were high above a perfect little mountain village on top of a perfect mountain, with perfect snowflakes drifting down around us. You know, the ultimate romantic gesture." He looked around the car and smiled. "It's no mountain, but I guess the inside of a '95 Ford Bronco with two hundred and fifty thousand miles and a hole in the muffler is the next best thing, isn't it?"

Nancy looked at him, then back at the ring and said the first thing that came into her mind. "You're an idiot!" Then she couldn't hold back any longer. She started laughing and crying all at the same time. "You are an absolute idiot, and I guess I am, too, 'cause I'm going to marry you!"

"You are?" He fumbled to get the ring out of the box, then took the rose from her left hand and slipped the ring on her finger.

"Yes! Yes, I am!" She leaned in, kissed him, then whispered, "Why am I holding a banana?"

"Oh, that." James took the banana from her, peeled it, and took a big bite. "Because proposing really makes me hungry!"

"Why, you!" She took the rest of the banana from him and threatened to shove it in his face, then took a big bite and kissed him again.

The hours they spent on the road that day seemed to fly by, filled with talk of the future, the wedding, family, and a new home that they could call their own. There was laughter mixed with comfortable silences, followed by more laughter. As the sun sank behind the low foothills that had begun appearing on the horizon, James yawned and took his hands off the wheel long enough to stretch.

"I think you need a night's rest in a comfy hotel bed." Nancy reached over and gently rubbed his shoulder.

"Only if you promise to do that some more once we get there."

"I think that can be arranged. Why don't we pull off at the next exit and see what we can find?"

He answered her with another yawn.

They drove on for another forty miles before they came to an exit. The sign read:

> Exit 157
> Sweet Springs
> One Mile

"Sweet Springs, that sounds like the ideal place for a newly engaged couple to spend their first night together."

James looked over at her and raised an eyebrow.

"Well, first night as an engaged couple." She laughed, then pointed out the front window. "Watch where you're going, smart guy, or we won't make it to a hotel."

James eased the Bronco off the interstate and onto a dimly lit street. Two gas stations sat on opposite sides of the off ramp. They were closed, but the harsh fluorescent light over the pumps caused them to glow like a neon oasis in the night.

"Ummmm," she groaned and rolled her head around on her shoulders. "Let's find a resort with a king-size bed, a jacuzzi tub, fluffy down pillows, and a mattress so soft you can dig your toes into it."

James pulled the car into the parking lot of a Knights Inn and stopped. A sign hanging from the brick wall beside the dirty glass lobby doors blinked *Va ncy*. With every blink the two missing letters would light up and others would be off.

V ancy - Vaca y - V ca cy - Vacancy

"Oh look, they have a vacancy!" James said, pointing at the sign.

She looked back at the two closed gas stations, then at the dark empty expanse on either side of them. "Well, it ain't the Ritz, but I guess we don't have much of a choice."

"We can try the next exit down," James offered.

"That could be another forty miles." She took a deep breath and smiled. "Nope, you're tired, and I'm ready to stop for the night. This place will be fine." She leaned over and kissed him on the cheek. "As long as I'm with you."

"Great, I'll go get us checked in."

* * *

The front doors of the hotel were locked, but there was a little button glowing in the shadows of the entryway. James pulled his Motorola Razr out of his pocket—a gift from the VA so that he could always be on call—and flipped it open. The glow from the screen revealed a small hand-lettered sign that said *After Hours.*

The doors were coated with grime from years of neglect. All he could make out inside were the blurry shapes of a counter and a couple of chairs. He pushed the button, and a bell rang somewhere deep inside the dark lobby. He looked back at Nancy, she shrugged, then made a pointing gesture; James nodded and rang the bell again.

Dim light filled the lobby as a door off the far wall opened. A large, vaguely male figure moved through it and started in his direction. As it approached the door it waved for him to step back, then with a loud rattling of keys, it unlocked the door and pushed it open.

"What?" the man towering above him said in a gruff, sleep-thickened voice.

The giant was wearing a pair of striped boxers and a strap t-shirt that strained to cover his massive belly. He had flip-flops on his feet—one red and one green—and was smoking a cigar that would have choked a normal-sized man.

"Sorry to bother you," James sputtered. "We've been driving all day and were hoping we could get a room." He hated how weak his voice sounded.

"Humph," the man grunted and walked back into the lobby.

James hesitated, then took a deep steadying breath and followed him in.

"Room's twenty-nine fifty and checkout is at eleven," the man told him as he made his way behind the counter. He had to duck down to get through the door, and once inside the little room that served as the front desk area, his hair scraped the ceiling.

"Great." James gave the man his most winning smile.

"Humph."

He handed James a piece of paper from a drawer and crossed his arms, waiting for him to fill out. The ink had smeared when it was taken off the printer, but he could still make out the usual questions: name, address, make and model of the car, and a line for a signature at the bottom. He quickly filled in all the spaces and returned it to the man along with two bills, a twenty and a ten.

"Cash drawers locked. I can't make change."

"Oh, no problem. Just keep it, please."

"Humph." He slid James a key attached to a large, blue plastic triangle with the number *Sixteen* written on it in scratched gold ink.

James looked up to thank the man just in time to see the door off the lobby close with a loud thud. Immediately uncomfortable at being all alone in the deserted room, he crossed to the door in two long strides and went outside. The door closed behind him, and he heard the unmistakable sound of the lock snapping into place.

Room *Sixteen* was near the end of the building and there was an open parking space directly in front of it. Not such a big deal considering that there was only one other vehicle in the parking lot on that side. It was an old beat-up pickup truck sitting on a jack with one of the rear tires removed.

James wrestled with the key for a moment before the lock surrendered and allowed him to open the door. He reached in and flipped the light switch on the wall next to the door just as Nancy came up behind him carrying one of their bags.

"Wow," she said, looking over his shoulder.

Pressed-wood paneling stained to resemble cedar covered the walls. The reddish color of the wood clashed with the lime-green shag carpet. A lamp with a dingy white shade hung over the head of the bed from a chain attached to the ceiling.

"Home sweet home." He looked over at Nancy and smiled.

She nodded, then pushed past him. "It's not that bad." She shrugged. He could tell from the sound of her voice that she was trying to make the best of it, but her disappointment was hard to miss. "At least it's clean." She dropped their bag on the bed, and then stepped back to avoid the cloud of dust that rose off the worn, red comforter. "We'll just take that off before we go to bed."

"Right, I'll go get the other bag." He started back to the car and came face to face with a man wearing a floppy hat and a blue jean jacket. James stepped back into the room, and the man came forward enough that his features could be seen in the glow from the lamp. He had dark skin, but he wasn't black. James thought he must be Native American, especially seeing how his long, braided black hair was hanging down at each side of his face. He wore jeans that matched his jacket and scarred, leather pointed-toe boots.

"Can I help you?" James sputtered as Nancy stepped up beside him.

"Yeah, I think you can." The man spoke slowly, his voice low and rough. "Or maybe it's me that can help you." He pulled a pack of Marlboro Reds from the jacket's inner pocket, took one for himself, and offered the pack to James.

"No, thank you." He waved him off, and the man offered the pack to Nancy who just smiled and shook her head. "Look, we just checked in. We've been driving all day and we're tired, so can you just cut to the chase?"

"No." The man pushed past them and entered their room. "Nice place." He looked around, then pointed to the lamp hanging from the ceiling. "Mom has one just like that back home."

"That's great, man, but really, you got to go." James started toward him, thinking that he would push him out, then call the cops if things got physical.

"Franklin," the man said and extended his hand.

"Excuse me?"

"My name is Franklin." He reached out, took James' hand, and shook it. "Did you get a package in the last week or so, one filled with newspaper clippings and an old surgical kit?"

"How did you know that?" Nancy's voice now sounded more curious than concerned.

"That's what I thought," Franklin said and took another drag off the cigarette. The ash grew long and dangled perilously at the end.

"How *did* you know about that?" James asked him. "About the package, I mean."

"That's an interesting story." Franklin sat on the bed, then leaned over and picked up a small metal trashcan from beside the wall. He placed it on the floor between his feet. Using his middle finger, he knocked the ash into the waste basket, then took another deep drag. "I'm a descendant of a powerful medicine man called Floating Feather, just as you are a descendant of a great man of medicine called Melvin Mitchell. Because their lives were intertwined, so are ours."

Franklin held the cigarette over the waste can, spit on the hot end, then pinched off the smoldering section. "I left New Mexico yesterday to try and find you, but I had a flat on my truck this morning and had to stop here. I planned to get it patched tomorrow and move on, but the Great Spirit brought you to me instead. So now, we can travel together, like brothers." Franklin dropped the cigarette into the can, then intertwined his fingers and pulled to show they were inseparable. "That is why I am here."

"Wait." James' head was starting to spin. "*What*, is why you're here?"

"To help you return the tools to where they belong." He stood up and looked James in the eyes. "Before they get you killed."

Chapter Sixteen

March 16, 1870

The sun was directly overhead, and not a shadow could be seen when the stage to Kansas City stopped for fresh horses at the Turnbull's station. The driver jumped down and helped the passengers out of the hot coach and inside for a cool drink of water and bite to eat.

"I've got two more for you Turk," Edward Turnbull said. He was busy unhooking the team, but not so busy that he missed the scowl that appeared on the driver's face. "Just you simmer down now, they are—"

"I don't care what they are. You know full well that we can't take on extra passengers out here in the middle of nowhere."

Edward mopped the sweat off his forehead with the sleeve of his shirt. "Carter Clement and the boy that was riding shotgun for him are dead. Some kind of ambush, a few miles west of here. My boy, Gene, found their passengers asleep in the field over there yesterday morning. Carter's stage is out back by the barn. On your next trip through, maybe you can bring another driver to take it back to where it come from."

"Carter and Mick are dead?" Turk removed his hat and held it to his chest as a sign of respect. "They're dead, but the passengers are still alive? How did that happen?"

"I don't know, and I didn't ask, but they seem to be good people. They've been stuck here overnight, so I would appreciate it if you could see past the rules and take them back with you."

Turk seemed to be considering his options. "All right. Lucky for them, I've only got two of my own, so there's room. I'm short on supplies, though. Got enough for two, but not four, so you're gonna have to kick in with some fatback and biscuits."

"Fine."

"And don't think I'm paying for 'em either. You want to get paid, you gotta take that up with the stage company next time you're in Kansas City."

"I wouldn't dream of it," Edward said sarcastically, then went back to tending the horses. What he really wanted to do was smack Turk across the face and tell him what he could do with his free supplies. He knew full well that the stages carried extra rations for emergencies, Turk was just trying to get a little extra for himself. Something he could sell to the next wagon train they came across, or trade to the Natives for blankets or hides.

* * *

Turk went inside to get some grub and meet his new passengers. He found them all sitting around the Turnbull's table. Mrs. Turnbull had laid out a plate of sliced meat and some biscuits and honey.

"Well, I see you folks have met each other." He stopped at the end of the table and looked down at them. "Pastor Jacobs, Mr. Shay, these folks will be joining us for the rest of the trip. It'll be a mite snug, but my understanding from Edward out there," he motioned to the door with his thumb, "is that they have had a hard go of it. So, on behalf of the Kansas City Stage Company, I feel it's only right that we help them to finish their journey."

"That's mighty kind of you." An older man sporting what looked like a four-day growth of white whiskers pushed his chair away from the table, stood, and offered Turk his hand. "I'm Dr. Melvin Mitchell, and this is my traveling companion, Mrs. Eloise Gattis." The woman that nodded to him was plain but pretty and looked considerably younger than the doctor. Turk wasn't sure if she was his wife or his daughter.

"Dr. Mitchell was just telling us about their run-in with the raiding party." Pastor Jacobs' voice was weak and quivering. "Is that something we should be concerned about between here and Kansas City?"

Turk had picked up the reverend a few days earlier, and the elderly man's nervous nature had made him immediately uncomfortable. It became especially apparent when Turk informed him that they would be traveling without a shotgun rider due to his other passenger's need to get to Kansas City in a hurry. He cracked a smile and looked down at the old man. They couldn't eat before he blessed the food, and they couldn't sleep until he prayed for their souls in case something happened before sunrise. Now, thanks to the doc, he had something else to worry about.

"No, Pastor, it's nothing to concern yourself with. Raiding parties are few and far between out here. In fact, this is the first one I've heard about in well over a year."

"Oh, that's good, that's good." Pastor Jacobs reached inside his coat and pulled out the silver cross that he wore around his neck on a chain. "I'll pray for us, all the same."

Mr. Shay reached over and laid a hand on the trembling pastor's shoulder. "You do that, Padre." He stood and started for the door. "How much longer, driver? I've got business to attend to that won't wait."

"Just as soon as Mr. Turnbull gets the new team hitched and ready to go. Shouldn't be long now."

Mr. Shay gave him a curt nod and went outside. He was the reason they were traveling without a shotgun messenger to serve as lookout. He was a man of means and had bribed the stage line manager with a twenty-dollar gold piece to ensure that there would be no delays in getting him to St. Louis. Turk had argued that going out with a single driver was dangerous and stupid. He had lost that argument.

Constance started clearing the dishes. "He's not a very pleasant man, is he?"

"Gambler," Turk said to no one in particular. "Headed to a game in St. Louis."

"Figures." She reached for another plate. "A man like that travels around acting all high and mighty while folks like us have to break our backs for what little we have."

"Let me help you with that." Mrs. Gattis took the plate from her and picked up another. "It's the least I can do for your hospitality."

The station door burst open, and Mr. Shay leaned in. "You better get out here, Doc. Turnbull's hurt."

Dr. Mitchell rushed outside with Constance and Mrs. Gattis close behind him. As Turk started past him, Mr. Shay caught him by the sleeve of his shirt.

"I won't be late to my appointment," he whispered through gritted teeth. "If this is going to slow us down, then you best leave that doctor and his *traveling companion* behind to tend to Turnbull. Do I make myself clear?"

Turk looked into his eyes and didn't like what he saw there. "Yeah, I understand."

"Good." He let go of his sleeve. "Padre, I think they might could use a little of what you got to offer out here as well."

The old man used the back of a chair for balance as he got to his feet. Mr. Shay offered him a steadying arm as he made his way down the short step from the station, out to the dusty yard where Mr. Turnbull was sitting cross-legged with his hand curled in his lap.

* * *

"Let me see." Doc Mitchell knelt beside Edward. He could tell that the strong, proud man was on the verge of passing out from the pain.

"It's bad, Doc. I don't know if I can."

"It's all right. I'll help." He looked toward the house and saw Marie and Gene come out. Gene was bouncing nervously from foot to foot while Marie kept her distance. He could see the fear in her face. "Gene, do you know where your daddy keeps his medicinal?"

"I'm sorry, Doctor," Constance said from behind him. "There's no whiskey here. We don't—"

"I'll get it!" Gene ran around the house toward the barn.

"Sorry, Constance," Edward whispered through gritted teeth.

"It doesn't matter. We can discuss it later." Constance laid her hand on her husband's lowered head and gently stroked his hair. A moment later, Gene returned with an earthen jug and handed it to Doc Mitchell.

"Drink this, Edward." He held the mouth of the jug to Edward's lips and tilted it so that the contents poured liberally into his mouth. Edward swallowed, choked, and turned his head away.

"That's not enough. This is going to hurt, and I need you as calm and numb as possible." Edward nodded and let him pour more into his mouth.

"That's going to have to do. Now Edward, listen to me, I want you to turn you head and keep your eyes closed. I've got to get your hand open enough to see how bad it is."

Edward did as he was instructed, but when Doc Mitchell touched his hand, the big man screamed.

"Jesus, God almighty," Pastor Jacobs began praying.

Constance gasped and turned away, burying her face in Ella's shoulder.

"Marie!" Doc Mitchell shouted to the scared little girl. "Get my bag. Inside of it is a rolled bundle, it's my surgical kit. Unroll it on the table, then get some water from the rain barrel and put it in a pot over the fire. I'm going to need a lot, and it has to be boiling hot."

Marie gave a single nod and rushed back into the house.

"Edward, I *have to* have a closer look. Take a deep breath and turn away." He watched Edward turn his head to the side and waited for his chest to rise, then forced his hand open wider. It was a mess of blood, torn skin, and muscle—split halfway down the palm between his middle and ring finger.

"I was trying to get the horses tethered to the wagon when somethin' spooked 'em," Edward told him through gritted teeth. His breath was coming in short bursts, his chest rising and falling rapidly. "They jumped and caught my hand between the yoke and the harness chain."

Doc Mitchell knew the signs of a man on the verge of panic. If he didn't get the bleeding under control, and Edward calmed down, he could lose him before he ever got a chance to try and save his hand.

"Ella, go get me all the rags you can find. I've got to keep pressure on this wound till we can get him inside."

"There's a piece of raw cloth on the foot of our bed that I ordered to make Marie a new dress," Constance said. "Just get that." She had pulled herself together and was kneeling next to Edward. "It's going to be all right, Ed. Dr. Mitchell's going to fix you right up, good as new."

I'm not so sure that I'm going to be able to live up to that promise. He shook his head at the thought. *The kit does have a small bone saw in it, so maybe I can save his life if not his hand.*

"Constance, give him another shot of that rotgut, this is gonna hurt like the devil when we move him inside."

Constance nodded and poured a generous amount of whiskey into her husband's mouth.

* * *

Ella had spent enough time around soldiers to know a life-threatening wound when she saw one. She ran the short distance from the stage to the house and burst inside. Mr. Shay was standing at the table with his back to her. He startled when she came in, knocking the black medical bag off the table, dumping the surgical tools and its other contents across the floor. Marie had been carrying a dipperful of water from the rain barrel to a cast-iron pot on the stove and spilled most of *it* on the floor as well at the sound of the crash.

"For God's sake!" Ella shouted. "We have a badly hurt man lying out there on the ground, and all you can think to do is rifle through my husband's things?"

The word, husband, had slipped out before she had thought about what she was saying. It felt comfortable. She would have to think long and hard about that, but now wasn't the time. "Pick all that up, and you better pray you didn't damage anything, then go help that girl get some water on to boil."

She rushed past him and into the small bedroom. The piece of cloth was right where Constance had said it would be. When she got back to the main room, Mel's bag was back on the table, and Mr. Shay was pouring water from a small pan into the larger one on the stove.

"That's enough water," she told him. "Now why don't you come out here and see if you can make yourself useful?"

She rushed over to Mel and showed him the cloth.

"That will have to do," he said. "Tear it into long strips and start handing them to me as fast as you can. He's losing a lot of blood."

She tore off each strip and watched as he rapidly bound Edward's hand. Blood still leaked out around the bandages, but it appeared that Mel was satisfied with the results.

"Shay!" Mel called out. "Help me get Edward inside!"

Chapter Seventeen

December 16, 2008

The waitress at the Sweet Springs grocery and café pointed James, Nancy, and Franklin to a booth next to a large plate-glass window that looked out over a field of scrub grass and bull thistle. James had managed to convince Franklin that they needed get some sleep and would be in a better state of mind to listen to his story over breakfast.

James was still tired and was not looking forward to dealing with the crazy Indian, but what choice was there? Franklin must have been waiting outside the door to their room, because as soon as they started moving around, he had started knocking.

After Franklin left, they had showered and crawled into bed together. Nancy had cuddled up to him and fallen asleep almost immediately. He had just laid there listening to her steady breathing and soft snores, thinking about everything Franklin had said.

A few things had become very apparent as the night had worn on; Franklin knew that the surgical kit James received had once belonged to Dr. Melvin Mitchell and that James had it in his possession. Franklin told them that Dr. Mitchell had used it to try and save the life of his forefather, Floating Feather, a shaman of a remote tribe of Plains Indians. He also believed that the ghost of the man who dealt the injuries to Floating Feather, that had ultimately taken his life, still followed the kit and caused the death of all that came in contact with it. That put James next in line, and without Franklin's help, James would suffer a similar fate.

No wonder I couldn't sleep.

"What can I get you folks?" the waitress asked, walking up to their table.

"Coffee and some toast for me," James absently replied, then looked up at her. A faded nametag was attached to her uniform. *Kellie* had been neatly printed on it in purple magic marker. Kellie was a heavyset, older woman with gray roots that blended unevenly into a head full of pumpkin-orange hair. She was straight out of an old movie—complete with pink uniform, white apron, hair net, and sensible shoes. She looked tired and vigorously chewed a piece of gum as she took their order.

"What about you, young lady?"

"Coffee and toast sounds good." Nancy stifled a yawn. "And maybe a little grape jelly if you have it."

Kellie made a note on her order pad and turned to Franklin who was looking through a bunch of old receipts and other papers in his wallet. From the look on his face, James assumed that there was no money in the billfold. He reached over and covered it with his hand. "Breakfast is on me."

"Thank you." Franklin carefully folded the worn leather wallet and slid it back into his pants pocket. "I'll have three eggs over easy, a steak medium, toast, and coffee with extra cream."

Kellie cut her eyes over at James, and he reluctantly nodded.

"Will that be *all*, sir?"

James could hear the cynicism in her voice, but if Franklin had picked up on it, he didn't let it show.

"Maybe a couple of those donuts over there." Franklin pointed to a glass cloche sitting on the counter filled with pastries. "You guys want donuts?" He waited, wide-eyed, for an answer. When one didn't come, he turned back to the waitress. "Two donuts."

"And two donuts." She raised her eyebrows at Franklin. "Got it." She flipped the order pad closed and dropped it in her apron.

A short time later, Kellie returned to the table with a steaming pot of coffee and three cups. She filled the cups almost to the rim, then took two plastic containers of creamer from her apron and dropped them next to Franklin's.

"*Extra* cream, please." Franklin looked up at her and smiled.

Kellie found three more creamers in her apron, along with three sets of silverware neatly rolled inside of white paper napkins, and placed them on the end of the table.

She gave Franklin a questioning look.

"Perfect." Franklin winked at her. "Thank you."

He began to carefully open each little cup of creamer. As he added them to his coffee, the dark, black liquid changed to a light shade of beige. James watched in amazement as he gave each creamer a gentle shake, making sure to get every drop. The last one fell into the cup and the ripples it caused on the coffee's surface threatened to spill over the rim. After a moment's consideration, Franklin pulled a straw from a basket at the end of the table and tore off the paper covering. With a steady hand, he inserted the tip of the straw into the coffee and took a few tentative sips before letting it slide all the way into the cup.

"Coffee's not very hot." He wrinkled his nose. "Really strong, too."

"Now that we've had some sleep and some coffee to get us going..." Nancy paused and blew across the surface of her coffee, then took a sip. From the look on her face, James knew that it was still too hot to drink. "Why don't you try again to help us understand what you were talking about last night."

"Excuse me!" Franklin raised his hand.

Kellie had just come out of the kitchen and rolled her eyes when she looked over at their table. She stopped where she was, took a deep breath, and came back. "Yes, sir?"

"Could I have a Coke, please?"

She cut her eyes over at Nancy, then back to Franklin. "Of course. Are you *finished* with your coffee?"

"Yes. Thank you."

Her smile faded as she reached down and picked up the cup. It immediately spilled, sending coffee running over her hand and down onto the table.

"I'm sorry," she said through pursed lips. "I'll be right back to clean that up."

"Don't forget the Coke." Franklin smiled up at her and winked again.

James could see in the waitress's expression that Franklin was about one word away from having his overly strong, beige coffee thrown in his face. He mouthed the words *I'm sorry* to her. She gave him a curt nod and made her way back to the counter, leaving a trail of spilled coffee behind her.

"Now, about last night—" James said, hoping to get the conversation back on track.

"I am a tenth-generation shaman of the Abodoni tribe that my ancestor, Floating Feather, gave his life to protect," Franklin cut in. "As shaman, it is my duty to try and—"

Kellie set a clear plastic glass filled with ice and cola in front of Franklin and began wiping up the spilled coffee. "Y'all's food should be ready shortly."

Franklin waited until she had left the table, then took a sip of his drink. His upper lip curled back, and his nose wrinkled in disgust. "Diet." He shook his head violently, then started to raise his hand to get Kellie's attention again.

Nancy put her hand over his to stop him. "Let's let her wait on a few other folks before we make her come back over here again."

Franklin nodded and pushed the glass of soda away.

"How many current members are there in the Abodoni tribe that you are shaman of?" James asked.

Franklin seemed to be considering his answer as he reached out, picked up the glass of soda, and took another sip. "Just me."

"Really?" James looked over at Nancy who raised an eyebrow in a quizzical manner. "If you're the shaman, then who do you shaman to?"

Franklin pushed the soda to the side again and leaned in. "I, like my ancestors, worship at the feet of the Great Spirit. As long as one of us survives, the Great Spirit will continue to watch over our land. When I die, if I have not brought a child into this world to take my place, then the Great Spirit will abandon it, and mankind will suffer at the hands of the other until the world falls into the depths of the eternal fire."

The hairs on the back of James' neck stood at attention, and when Nancy placed her hand on his leg, he knew she felt the tension as well. "What *other*?"

"The Abodoni never gave it a name, as naming it would only give it strength. Instead, our forefathers chose to be ever watchful and remain silent, knowing that if it did come upon our people, that the warrior who guards the throne of the Great Spirit would protect us."

"Are you talking about the devil?" Nancy asked just above a whisper—as if saying the word aloud would cause a portal to hell to open under their table.

"Your people have named *it* and given *it* power, now look and see where your world is. Our people lived in peace, fighting only when our lives or land were threatened. Your people fight first, then divide the ruins among themselves and call it victory. Your people do *its* bidding willingly."

"So, your father also was a shaman of the Great Spirit?" James asked.

"As was his father and his father's father—"

"All the way back to Floating Feather." Nancy finished his sentence for him, and Franklin nodded slow and ominously in agreement.

"The Great Spirit imparted a blessing on our tribe when He-dow, the mate of the tribe's greatest warrior Wirasuap, gave birth to twin girls. Wirasuap presented the girls to Floating Feather to be used in service to the Great Spirit. Twins in our culture are rare, and it was believed at the time that if they were gifted to the shaman and they bore his children, that the tribe would grow and prosper. Keegsquaw and Nijlon were raised by He-dow until their first blood, then they were moved into Floating Feather's residence. The two girls cooked and cared for Floating Feather. They saw to his every need. Soon Keegsquaw was with child. The tribe planned a celebration that would include a great feast and a blessing of the unborn."

"Okay, I've got three eggs over easy, a steak medium, toast, and two donuts."

James and Nancy both jumped at the sound of Kellie's voice. They had become so caught up in Franklin's story that they hadn't heard her come to the table.

"Settle down, folks, your toast is on here, too." Kellie laughed. The last thing off her tray was a large platter filled with eggs and a steak big enough to choke a trucker. "I think that's everything."

Franklin held up his glass. "This is diet."

"With all that food I just set down in front of you, do ya really think you need a fully leaded one?" Her hands were balled into fists and planted firmly on her wide hips. The look she was giving Franklin should have melted his face.

"Yes, please." Wink.

Kellie took the glass from him, and Franklin started in on his eggs. He cut them into small pieces, then added salt, pepper, and a healthy dose of tomato ketchup.

"She's probably gonna spit in that glass before she brings it back," Nancy whispered.

James pictured their waitress standing behind the bar and hocking up a loogie to spit in Franklin's Coke and laughed before he could stop himself.

"What's so funny?" Franklin asked around a mouthful of egg. "What did I miss?"

"Oh, nothing." Nancy waved him off and started buttering her toast. "So, you were telling us about the twins?"

"Keegsquaw and Nijlon." Franklin cut off a big hunk of steak and stuffed it in his mouth. "Yeah, so the tribe had planned this great celebration, and as was the custom, most of the warriors went off to hunt. They needed a large deer to eat and a fawn to offer as a sacrifice to the

Great Spirit. Wirasuap and his two fiercest warriors stayed behind to guard the camp."

Kellie returned with Franklin's soda and stood watching until he had taken a drink. "Good enough?"

"Yes, thank you." He raised the glass in her direction in a form of salute.

Kellie looked down at James. "I expect a big tip."

"Yes'm." He nodded.

"She does deserve a big tip." Franklin took a long drink of his soda. "She's been very helpful."

"Yes, she has," Nancy agreed and kicked James' leg under the table. "So did they have the feast?"

"No. The warriors left the camp to hunt, and while they were gone, Keegsquaw and Nijlon stayed in their tent to prepare for the celebration. There were certain expectations of how Keegsquaw should look, and the women of the tribe had spent many days collecting all the correct feathers and flowers that were to be woven into her hair, and fashioning the outfit that she was expected to wear. While they were in the tent, the girls began to hear thunder echoing through the valley, and they were afraid that the rains would come and ruin the celebration.

"Suddenly, something tore through their tent, barely missing Keegsquaw. The tent fell on them, and the girls cowered together underneath the heavy leather and wood. They listened as their sisters screamed and babies cried. They heard Floating Feather begin to chant and sing in a way they had never heard before. Soon the camp grew quiet, except for a low whistling sound."

Franklin stopped talking long enough to break one of the donuts in half and use it to soak up the leftover egg yolk on his plate. He popped the half donut in his mouth, then washed it down.

"Pala, the tribe's mightiest woman, lived in the trees behind Floating Feather's tent. The girls heard her scream as she ran past their tent, then she began to weep. Nijlon wanted to try and push away the wreckage so she could see what could cause such a brave and mighty woman to cry, but Keegsquaw pulled her back and begged her to remain still. Floating Feather began to chant again. They heard gunfire, and he fell silent. The story goes on that they heard the cry of a mighty eagle, followed by more gunfire. It was then that a fierce wind rushed through the camp, pushing ahead of it a wave of cold air, and the sisters had to huddle together for warmth. When they finally climbed from the remains of their tent, they found everyone they had ever known dead, and Floating Feather, missing."

Franklin belched loudly, whispered an "Excuse me," and began slathering butter on a piece of toast.

"That's it?" Nancy looked over at James who just shrugged. She sighed and sank back against the torn cushion on the back of the booth. "Well, it's a good story, I'll give you that. But what does it have to do with our situation?"

"Yeah," James agreed. "Where does Melvin Mitchell come into this?"

"Oh, that..." Franklin licked at some stray jam that was dribbling down the side of his hand.

Chapter Eighteen

March 16, 1870

With Mr. Shay's help, Doc Mitchell got Edward up on the table where just moments before they had all shared a meal. He was growing concerned over the amount of blood Edward had lost and how pale his complexion had become. If he didn't get the bleeding stopped, losing a hand would be the least of Edward's worries.

"More whiskey!"

Constance lifted Edward's head up enough to pour some of the whiskey into his mouth. He coughed and sputtered but managed to swallow most of it.

Doc Mitchell looked over at Mr. Shay. He didn't like the man. In the few minutes that he had known him, Shay had proved himself to be a self-centered, uncaring coward. His soul focus was seeing that he got his way and everything else be damned.

Shay had stayed close to the door and was using a monogrammed silk handkerchief to rub at a spot of blood on his coat. Turk and Pastor Jacobs came in, and Shay grabbed Turk by the sleeve and whispered something to him. The driver snatched his arm free of Shay's grasp and had a few choice words of his own for the gambler.

Doc Mitchell had seen enough. If he didn't have some help, Edward was going to die.

"Turk, Shay, stop that foolishness and get over here. I'm going to need you to hold him down while I do this."

Turk glared at Shay, then went to the table. "Where do you need me, Doc?"

"Go down there and hold his legs, lay on them if you have to. If he moves while I'm trying to sew him up, it could mean him losing his hand."

Turk nodded and took his position at the end of the table.

"Shay, you—" He looked around the room, but the gambler was nowhere to be seen. "Shay!"

"Don't worry about him, Mel, he's not worth it," Ella said, stepping up beside him. "Tell me what you need, and I'll do it."

He glanced over at the door, then nodded. "Take his good arm, stretch it straight out, and hold it there. Put your other hand on his shoulder and hold him down. If he tries to struggle, press down on his arm. The pain will make him stop."

Ella took a deep breath and got into position.

"Marie, did you get that water hot like I asked you to?"

"Yes, sir." Marie's voice floated across the room from the cook stove. She sounded scared.

"Good girl, I need you to grab that stool by the door and pull it over here, then put a pan full of that hot water on it. Can you do that?"

"Yes, sir." This time her voice sounded stronger, and in no time, a cracked, white porcelain bowl of steaming water was sitting next to him.

"Now open my surgical kit and carefully drop each tool into the water. Be careful not to cut yourself, they're sharp."

The cabin door flew open, and Gene ran inside. "Hey, why is that big man out there messing with the horses?"

"That son of a bitch. I'll kill him!" Turk started for the door.

"Turk, stop!" Doc Mitchell yelled at the driver. "Let him go. Edward's hand is more important. Now get back where I told you to be."

"Keep an eye on him, kid." Turk pointed Gene back outside. "But don't get in his way."

Marie delicately placed each of Doc Mitchell's tools in the steaming water.

He looked down into the girl's dark brown eyes and saw determination there, he also saw fear. "Your daddy's gonna be okay, understand?" Marie nodded. "Good, now I need you to do one more thing for me. Go find your momma's mending and get me some thread—black if there is any."

"You know where I keep it, Marie. In the bedroom next to the rocking chair," Constance reminded her, then went back to gently stroking Edward's thinning hair.

"You go in there and find that thread," Doc Mitchell told her. "Then I need you to take one of those needles from my kit and thread it with the longest piece you can find. You gotta be careful because those aren't like regular sewing needles, they're flat and have sharp edges. When you get it ready, put it and the thread in the bowl as well."

Marie nodded and ran into the next room.

"More whiskey, Constance. Keep giving it to him."

Marie quickly came back and managed to thread one of his suture needles on the first try.

"Thank you, Marie. That's perfect. Now, I think you best go outside and make sure your little brother stays out of trouble. Can you do that?"

Marie looked over at her mother, and Constance gave her a nod. "Yes, sir," Marie said and ran outside.

"Constance, give him one more swig, and I'll get started."

Constance poured another shot of whiskey into Edward's mouth. He swallowed, then his head lolled to one side, and his eyes closed.

"That'll have to do. Ella, Turk, hold him down." Doc Mitchell reached into the scalding hot water and picked up his doubled-edged scalpel, then pushed open Edward's hand, fully exposing the damage.

* * *

Marie found Gene standing with his hands on his hips, watching as Mr. Shay leapt onto the back of one of the horses. She thought he looked silly sitting on the horse bareback, but he didn't seem concerned. Shay raised a hand, saluted them, and gave the horse a kick in the side. It reared up on its hind legs, then took off in a hard gallop.

The noise of the horse's hooves striking the dry prairie soil was drowned out by the sound of her father's screams.

Chapter Nineteen

December 16, 2008

Franklin sat on the tailgate of his rusty, old pickup truck, smoking. He swung his legs back and forth, letting the soles of his shoes scratch softly on the packed dirt of the hotel parking lot. He blew out a plume of gray smoke and seemed mystified as he watched the cool morning breeze carry it away.

James paced behind Nancy who stood just far enough away from Franklin that the smoke and his swinging legs couldn't reach her. He was struggling to make sense of everything Franklin had told them. Did this man, who they had met just twelve hours before, really expect him to believe that his great, great, *whatever* had been forced by a giant Indian spirit to try and save the life of an old medicine man after a crazy cowboy had destroyed their village, and then just disappeared? It was just too much to fathom that any of that could be true.

"So, which one of the twins was your great-great grandmother?"

James stopped pacing when he heard Nancy ask the question. Surely, she wasn't buying into all this.

"*Four* greats." Franklin wiggled four of the fingers on the hand not holding the cigarette. "My great-great-great-great grandmother was

Keegsquaw." Franklin flicked the butt of his cigarette onto the pavement. James stomped on it before it could blow across the parking lot and out into the dry weeds of the scrub field. "After their camp was destroyed, the sisters began walking and were soon captured by a neighboring tribe. Nijlon became the property of the tribe's shaman who served the unnamed. Keegsquaw was claimed by the tribe's strongest warrior, a man named Calian. Calian took Keegsquaw's son as his own, and he loved Keegsquaw and her son. When a year had passed, and Nijlon was unable to provide the shaman with a son of his own, he sacrificed her to the other, underneath the full, blood moon."

"So, this story has been passed down through the generations of your ancestors, like some kind of oral history?" James asked.

Franklin looked up from peeling the cellophane off a fresh pack of Marlboro Reds and laughed. "Oh no, man, I never knew my dad or my grandfather. About two weeks ago I ran into this old Native while I was poking around in the woods outside the reservation. He said his name was Randy, and we shared in the ancient greeting ritual of smoking peyote from a pipe carved from a ram's horn. That was when the Great Spirit revealed our history to me and told me that my quest was to help you return the tools to their rightful owner and put an end to the carnage." He slapped the top of the pack against his hand, then peeled back the silver paper cover, revealing the tightly packed cigarettes underneath. He eased one out and put it between his lips.

"Wait a minute." James held his hand up to Franklin. "Are you telling me that you only found all this out a couple of weeks ago when you were gorked out of your skull on mescaline?"

Franklin lit the cigarette and gave him a slow nod. "Peyote is *very* powerful. It opens the doors between the past and present."

"Come on, Nancy." James took her arm and started leading her away toward their room. "We have wasted enough of our vacation on this craziness."

"Wait." Franklin stood up and flicked his cigarette out into the weeds. "It also showed me other things, things that you need to know.

Please, come back and let me finish. If you want me to leave then, I will. I promise."

"Quit pulling at me!" Nancy jerked her arm away. "I don't believe him either," she whispered, "but I think we need to hear him out. He seems to believe what he's telling us is the truth."

"I don't care what he believes. I believe he's nuts, and that's all I need to know." He raised a hand to Franklin. "Good luck with your tire!" James stormed across the parking lot and back to their room. He stopped just inside the door. "Are you coming?" he called back to Nancy.

Nancy waved to Franklin as well, then followed James inside and closed the door.

* * *

James stomped around the room, packing their things and mumbling to himself about *crazy Indians* and *great way to start a vacation*. Nancy wrapped her arms around him from behind, nuzzled her hair against the back of his neck, and planted a kiss on his shoulder. When she felt his tension start to fade, she led him to the bed, sat down beside him, and placed her head on his shoulder.

"Stupid Indian," James whispered.

All the tension and anxiety that had been building up inside of her all morning desperately needed a release. She started to laugh. It was just a giggle at first, but before she could stop herself, she had tears running down her cheeks, and she was braying like a mule. It wasn't long until James was braying right along with her, and they fell back on the bed in a tangle of arms and legs.

He reached out and wiped the tears from her cheek, and she kissed him. She didn't feel like laughing anymore, she thought there was a different kind of release that would work better. She rolled over on top of him. Their kissing became more passionate, stopping only long enough to breathe and for her to unbutton her blouse. She had just reached in between them to unbuckle his belt when someone began banging on their door. She snatched her hand back, and they both looked at the door, like two teenagers who had been caught when their parents came home early.

"Go away!" James shouted at the closed door.

Silence. She looked down at him, and with a giggle, went back to work on his belt.

The banging came again, this time harder.

"Damn it!" Nancy stopped what she was doing, rolled off James, and started buttoning her shirt.

"If that's Franklin, I'm gonna kick his peyote-smoking ass." James rolled off the bed and tightened his belt. He stormed across the room and snatched open the door. "I thought I made it clear that we—"

Franklin stood in the doorway with a cigarette hanging out of his mouth and a massive gash running up his arm from his wrist almost to his elbow. Blood dripped off his arm, ran down the front of his pants, and pooled on the top of his boots.

"Jesus." James grabbed Franklin's arm and raised it above his heart to try and slow the bleeding. "Nancy, grab some clean towels."

Her eyes widened as she gaped at Franklin's arm.

"Nancy, now!" James shouted.

She jumped from the bed and grabbed the towels from a shelf outside the bathroom door.

"I was trying to get my jack out of the truck when I slipped and landed on some scrap metal I was going to take to the dump." Franklin winced when she wrapped a towel tightly around his arm. "You gotta do something, James."

"Call 911. Get an ambulance out here," James said, taking over holding the towel.

Franklin reached out with his good hand and grabbed Nancy's arm. "There's no time for that. Nearest hospital is ninety miles away." He turned to James. "You're a doctor, you sew me up."

"I can't do that, not here. You need an ambulance and a hospital." He pulled Nancy free of Franklin's grip. "Call 911 now and tell them it's an emergency."

Nancy ran to the phone and typed in the three numbers.

***

Franklin wrenched his arm away and shook off the towel.

"What do you think you're doing?" James picked the towel up off the warn carpet and started to rewrap Franklin's arm. "That needs to stay—"

Franklin yanked a knife from a sheath on his belt, using his *good* hand, and stabbed it to the hilt into the thickest part of his thigh. His eyes rolled back, and he fell over onto the bed.

"Shit!" James grabbed another towel from the stack Nancy had left beside the bed and packed it around the knife. It immediately became saturated with blood.

"My God, what happened?" Nancy looked over his shoulder at Franklin splayed out on the bed, now with two bleedings wounds.

"I don't know!" James removed the blood-soaked towel and replaced it with a clean one. "I told him that I wasn't going to sew him up and that we could wait for the ambulance. Next thing I know, he's done this to himself."

"He was right about the ambulance. It won't get here for at least ninety minutes." She wrapped a fresh towel around Franklin's arm and held it tight. "We've got to do something now, or else he's gonna bleed out."

"What are we supposed to do? We've got no instruments, nothing to sterilize the wounds. We'll just have to keep pressure on them till the ambulance gets here and hope for the best."

"Maybe not. Here, hold this." Nancy placed James' free hand on the towel she had been holding closed, then reached around him, unbuckled his belt, and pulled it loose. "We can use your belt as a tourniquet to slow the bleeding." She wrapped the belt around Franklin's upper thigh and pulled it tight. It was made of a woven material, so she was able to push the tongue of the buckle through at any place in the belt to keep it secure. Her overnight bag was sitting on the vanity outside the small bathroom alcove. She dumped the contents out and grabbed a bottle of rubbing alcohol.

James watched as she darted across the room to the closet. Inside was a small ironing board that the hotel provided for guest use. Nancy pulled it out, and brought it and the alcohol back to where Franklin was lying. Next, she grabbed the floor lamp and pulled it over beside the bed. She removed the shade, flooding the room with a harsh white light. "Did you bring that old surgical kit with you?"

"Yeah, it's in my bag, but I can't use those. They're archaic—I don't even know if they're sharpened."

"I don't think we have a choice."

James took a deep breath and tried to think of anything else they could do but came up with nothing. "Okay. Grab the kit and sterilize the tools as best you can with the alcohol but leave enough for me to clean the wounds with."

Nancy got the kit from his duffel bag and unrolled it on the bedside table. A stack of plastic-wrapped cups was sitting next to the room's ice bucket; she unwrapped one and filled it halfway with alcohol, then placed the business end of each tool into the cup.

"Help me slide the board under him." James gently rolled Franklin to one side, enough for her to slide the ironing board underneath his thigh. "We're going to need thread to sew him up with. Did you bring a sewing kit with you?"

"Do I look like Susie Homemaker to you? No, I didn't bring a sewing kit with me." She looked around the room and grabbed the threadbare, dusty blanket from the floor where they had tossed it the night before.

"No, no, no! We are not going to try and close a stab wound this deep with strings pulled from a hotel blanket. That's disgusting."

"You got a better idea?" Nancy stood over him with her hands on her hips, giving him the same face-melting expression Kellie, the waitress, had given Franklin over breakfast.

"Okay, MacGyver, if you can get some loose, we'll give it a shot."

Less than a minute later, Nancy had managed to pull loose a thread almost three feet long. "Thank God for cheap blankets," she muttered. She picked up one of the suture needles from the kit and began to thread the string into the hole at the top. "Crap! It pricked me." She stuck her finger in her mouth. "It's not like a regular needle—the sides are flat and sharp."

"You okay?"

She checked her finger. "Yeah, I'm okay. Let me try this again. She removed a second needle from the kit, held it flat between her fingers, and slid the thread carefully through the hole. "Got it." The needle and thread were added to the cup of alcohol along with the rest of the tools.

"Okay, here's how we're going to do this. The knife in his thigh is more dangerous than the cut up his arm, so we are going to start there. When I unwrap it, you douse it with alcohol, and I'll pull the knife free. I'll need one of the scalpels to widen the cut enough to try and put a few sutures in the muscle, then we will need to close the skin. Hopefully, he didn't hit an artery." His mind flashed back to Private Duboski, and he shook his head to make the memory go away. "If he did, we'll know the second I take the knife out."

"What if he wakes up?"

"I'm hoping he won't. With as much blood as he's lost, I doubt he would have the strength to raise his head even if he did."

Nancy nodded and positioned the alcohol bottle above Franklin's leg.

James' hands were shaking. He paused to try and calm his nerves.

Nancy put her hand on his shoulder. "You can do this."

He looked up at her and nodded. "On three. One, two, three." He opened the towel and blood immediately welled up around the knife. With one steady movement, he pulled the knife free and dropped it on the bed beside them. Blood flowed freely from the opening, but there was little pressure behind it.

"Now the alcohol."

Nancy poured a generous amount of alcohol over the wound. Franklin's body stiffened, then relaxed. She handed James the scalpel. He leaned in and began to explore the wound.

"Stop!" Nancy shouted from beside him. "Look at this." She held up Franklin's knife so that James could see the blade. The sharpened tip of the knife was missing. A jagged line of broken metal ran across the upper end.

"It must have hit the bone when he stabbed himself."

"If you close the wound around a piece of the blade that big, it could move and do more damage."

"You're right." James pointed at the lamp with a bloody finger. "I'm going to need more light, bring that in closer."

He used the flat side of the scalpel to widen the opening in Franklin's leg, hoping to see a glint off the broken portion of the blade. But between the blood and the indirect light, he soon gave up hope of that working. "Hand me the bullet probe from the kit—the thin metal piece with the wide rounded end."

Nancy pulled the probe from the cup of alcohol and handed it to him.

Even with the tourniquet in place, blood was still welling up inside the wound. James wiped it away as best he could, then pushed the probe into the opening. Applying gentle pressure, he guided it through the swelling fat and muscle of the leg, hoping to feel it touch the tip of the blade. Sweat beaded on his brow as he willed his hands to remain steady.

This was ludicrous. Without an X-ray of the area to work from, trying to find the broken blade was like looking for the proverbial needle in a haystack, but this haystack was full of blood and quickly swelling shut. He stopped, took a deep breath, then removed the probe and went in again at a slightly different angle.

"Anything?" Nancy's voice was soft and worried.

"No." He shook his head, half in answer to her question and half out of frustration. "I can't feel anything. If I don't find it soon, I'll just have to sew it up and let the surgeons at the hospital find it later. That is, if it doesn't slip during transport and cause a massive hematoma to form that could cause him to lose the leg." *Or bleed out in the ambulance like Duboski did on the table.*

"You've got this," Nancy whispered.

James thought he heard doubt in her voice. "Thanks." He removed the probe and tried another angle. "It's no use. We're just wasting time. Get the needle ready, I'm going—" The probe jerked in his hand. "Wait, I think I found something." He moved the probe slightly to the left, then it jerked again, this time hard enough that he lost his grip on it.

He reached for the probe's bone handle. His fingers almost touched it, then the probe moved again.

James hesitated; his heart beating hard in his chest. He tried again to grasp the probe's handle. *It was the blood on my hands, made it slick. Surgical tools don't move by themselves.* This time when he gripped the probe's handle, it didn't move. Relief flooded over him. He tried to pull the probe free, but it wouldn't move. He tugged a little harder. Nothing, no movement.

It's the swelling, it has to be. He used his index finger to push the probe to the left. It slid easily, but when he removed the pressure, it recentered itself and turned. Involuntarily, he snatched his hand away.

"What's wrong?" Nancy leaned in and looked down at the probe sticking out of Franklin's leg.

"Did you...? It just—" he sputtered.

"It just what? Did you find the blade?"

James' mind raced. *It's stress. It's just the stress of the situation causing my mind to play tricks on me.*

"I think so." He nervously rubbed the tips of his fingers together. The drying blood began forming little balls between them. *Pull yourself together, you can do this.* He rubbed his hand on the leg of his pants. "Hand me the forceps. I'll use the probe as a guide."

Nancy took the forceps from the cup and placed them in his outstretched hand.

He closed the forceps and inserted the tip into the wound at the base of the probe. He allowed them to trace its length to the end deep inside the wound, then loosened his grip, allowing the forceps to open. "Fingers crossed?" Nancy nodded and showed him her hand. Sure enough, her slender fingers were actually crossed one over the other.

He applied pressure to the back of the forceps and felt them close around something. He shut his eyes and whispered a prayer to a god he wasn't sure even existed, and pulled back. The tips of the forceps slipped off whatever they had been around and snapped closed.

Chapter Twenty

March 16, 1870

"Damn it, there's dirt and rust inside the wound." Doc Mitchell was sweating, and Constance used her kitchen towel to wipe the sweat away from his eyes. "Constance, I need you to get a small dipper and use it to pour some of that hot water into the opening in his hand. We have to flush it out."

She nodded and rushed into the kitchen.

"Padre," he called to Pastor Jacobs who was standing behind Turk at the end of the table, praying. "I appreciate what you're doing, but you'd be a hell of a lot more helpful over here."

Pastor Jacobs hesitantly moved around Turk to stand beside him.

"I need you to take that cross off from around your neck and loop the leather strap it's on around Edward's arm, just below the elbow. Pull it as tight as you can, then use the cross like a fulcrum and tighten it even more. Understand?"

With shaking hands, Pastor Jacobs did as he had been instructed. The more he tightened the strap, the less blood flowed from Edward's hand.

"That's perfect, now hold it tight." Constance was ready with the dipper of boiling water. "Turk, Ella, be ready to hold him down. This is gonna hurt." He opened Edward's hand as far as he dared, then signaled Constance to pour the boiling water in a steady stream from the dipper directly into the open wound.

The hot water filled, then ran out of the cavity, carrying blood, dirt, and debris with it. Edward screamed and tried to lift himself up off the table. Turk threw himself over Edward's legs, and Ella pressed her weight down on his outstretched arm. Edward fell back on the table, unconscious.

The empty dipper tumbled from Constance's hand and onto the ground. She dropped to her knees next to her husband, stroked his hair, and began to whisper comforting words in his ear.

Doc Mitchell used the scalpel to slice small amounts of shredded flesh from around the edges of the opening in Edward's hand. When that was done, he picked up the forceps. Painstakingly, he picked out each fleck of rust and dirt that remained after the wound had been flushed. Satisfied that he had gotten it as clean as he possibly could, he took the suture needle and thread from the pan.

"Constance," Doc Mitchell said evenly. She looked up at him from her place beside her husband. Her eyes were red, and her cheeks wet with tears. "Give him another shot of that whiskey and make it a big one, then hand me the rest."

Her hand trembled as Constance brought the bottle to Edward's lips and filled his mouth. "My mother taught me this trick when I was child," she muttered and held his nose closed. Edward automatically swallowed the liquid in order to get a breath, then began to cough. "I'm sorry," she whispered and returned to stroking his hair.

Pastor Jacobs took the half-empty liquor bottle from her and handed it to Doc Mitchell.

"Ready?" Doc Mitchell looked from Turk to Ella, then tipped the bottle up and let the whiskey pour into the open wound.

Edward immediately began to convulse on the table.

"Hold him still!" Doc Mitchell yelled and attempted to suture the wound. He had two stiches in when Edward began to shake violently and choke.

"Turn his head, Constance! He's gonna vomit."

Constance turned Edward's head to the side just as he threw up his lunch and a large portion of the whiskey. The room filled with an astringent, sickly-sweet smell. Turk gagged and turned away. He stumbled to the door and managed to get it open, retching as he did so. Edward's convulsions continued, and without the pressure on his legs, his feet kicked and pounded against the table.

Doc Mitchell rounded the table to try and secure Edward's legs, leaving the needle halfway through the skin. He caught a knee to his nose before getting them under control. "Hold him still!" he screamed at the table.

Turk rushed to his side and took back over holding Edward's legs. "Sorry, Doc. I thought I was gonna be sick, too."

Doc Mitchell used the sleeve of his shirt to stanch the flow of blood from his nose. With Edward's convulsions again under control, he crossed the room to the hot water on the stove. He grabbed a rag, soaked it in the water, and pressed it to his face. He held it there for a few seconds, allowing the blood to clot, then returned to the table. His eyes watered, and his nose throbbed with every heartbeat, but he couldn't let that stand in his way.

He looked down at Edward's hand. It was sewn closed. Thirty-five stitches, each one neatly done in a perfect row. The suture needle was swinging gently beneath Edward's outstretched hand. He looked up at the people standing around the table. Still vigilant in their positions, only he could see what had happened. He grasped the needle, intending to tie off the last stitch. It felt warm and vibrated between his fingers. His hand began to quiver as panic started to overtake him.

The needle jumped from between his fingers. He watched in disbelief as it moved up the palm of Edward's hand under its own power. The point of the needle worked its way underneath the last stitch, looped around, did it again, then doubled back on itself, tying a perfect knot. It then used its own sharpened edge to sever the thread. With the job complete, the needle ceased moving and fell to the floor.

Ella released Edward's arm and came around to Doc Mitchell's side. She took his trembling hands in hers and looked down at the closed wound in Edward's hand. "That's beautiful work, Mel. How did you do that so fast?"

He looked up at her but couldn't speak. He had just witnessed the impossible. Overwhelmed with confusion and fear, he couldn't voice all the thoughts that were rushing through his mind.

* * *

Ella saw the blood around Mel's nose and bruises starting to appear around his eyes. Being hit by Edward's knee had done more damage than she had realized.

"It's okay, Mel, you did it. Now let's get *you* taken care of." She took his hand and led him away from the table to a chair next to the stove. Mel leaned his head back. She took the towel he had used to stop his bleeding and resoaked it in the hot water, then wrung it out, folded it neatly, and placed it across his rapidly swelling eyes and nose. "You just sit there and don't move. I'm going to go check on Edward and Constance."

Mel grabbed her hand. His grip was hard, and she winced. "Doctors always make the worst patients, just relax," she whispered in his ear. "I'll bandage Edward's hand and help Constance get him into bed. I promise I'll make *you* feel better later tonight." She lifted one side of the hot cloth and kissed his temple. When he let go of her, she noticed his hands shaking.

Chapter Twenty-One

December 16, 2008

The probe in Franklin's leg moved as if searching the depths of the injury on its own. James stared at it—in total disbelief—unable to move from the shock of what he was seeing. The probe worked itself back and forth, digging deeper into the gash in his leg. It then reversed and pulled out, almost to the point of leaving the wound altogether. A moment later, the tip of the knife appeared at the surface. The probe gave it a nudge and the tip floated out on a trickle of blood. The probe stopped moving and fell onto the mattress.

James reached out with the forceps, grasped the metal fragment, and lifted it from its resting place. His hand shook from nervous tension, and he admitted to himself, a little fear as well.

"You got it!" Nancy exclaimed from behind him.

Frightened by her outburst, he dropped the forceps.

"I didn't—I um..." The words just wouldn't come. How could he tell her that an inanimate object had come to life in front of his eyes and managed to do in a matter of seconds what he, a trained surgeon, had been unable to?

"You better sew that up." Nancy handed him the suture needle and thread. "I'll see what I can dig up to use as a bandage once you're done."

He nodded, still unable to express what he was thinking, and began to sew the wound closed. The first two stitches went in without a problem, but then he was overcome by a wave of crippling anxiety. His hand began to shake uncontrollably, and the suture needle slipped from his fingers. He reflexively grabbed for the needle but missed it because it was floating in midair next to Franklin's leg. Horrified, he watched as the needle turned, and with the speed of a bullet, shot back to the open wound and pierced the skin an eighth of an inch above his last suture. Within seconds, the wound was neatly sewn closed and the tread tied off. The needle dropped to the mattress as if some unseen hand had released it.

* * *

"Mmmmmmgh," Franklin groaned and woke Nancy from a restless slumber. As a nurse, she had watched as patient's family members tossed and turned, trying to sleep in uncomfortable hospital room chairs, but until last night, she had never had to try and sleep in one herself. She made a mental note to try and be more sympathetic.

She looked over at Franklin and noticed that his eyes were open.

"Where am I?" he asked, his voice thick from the anesthetic.

"You are in room 207 of Golden Valley Memorial Hospital." She laid a hand on his arm to soothe him. "You're going to be okay."

Franklin tried to smile, but his eyelids fluttered, and he fell back asleep instead.

"Looks like he's starting to come around." Nancy looked over at James. The poor man had been pacing at the end of the bed for most of the night. "I love how worried you are about him. Guess this first trip together is not really going like you hoped."

"That's an understatement," he said with a smirk before taking a seat on the arm of her chair. "Back at the hotel, did you notice anything strange while I was sewing him up? Like, maybe that I didn't do it?"

"What do you mean, you didn't do it? *I* certainly didn't, and you were the only other person there, unless poor unconscious Franklin did it himself."

"No, that's not it." He ran his fingers through his hair, took a deep breath, then let it out. "Something weird happened. Either that, or I'm losing my mind. You're not going to believe this, but I didn't sew it closed. In fact, I didn't find the piece of the knife that was broken off inside his leg. All that happened while I was *not* touching the instruments. They did it on their own."

Nancy reached up and began gently rubbing his back. "You're tired, and you're just getting mixed up. Of course, *you* found the tip of the knife, and then *you* closed up the wound and did a beautiful job of it as well. Surgical instruments don't move on their own, they need talented hands like yours to move them."

"Then why don't I remember doing it? And why do I clearly remember seeing that probe and suture needle doing what I couldn't do?" He stood and returned to pacing at the end of the bed. "I tell you Nancy, I think I'm losing it!"

"You're not crazy," Franklin mumbled from the bed.

Nancy took a glass of water from the bedside table. She gently raised Franklin's head and helped him take a small sip.

He smacked his lips and made a face. "It's warm."

"Next time you're lying unconscious in a hospital bed, I'll make sure to keep your water cold for you." Nancy rolled her eyes at James and let Franklin's head settle back on his pillow.

"Thank you," he said kindly, oblivious of her sarcasm. "You're not crazy," he said again, this time stronger, and he was looking directly at James.

Franklin picked up the bed control and pushed the up button. A low, mechanical whirling filled the room, and the head of the bed started to slowly rise. "You wouldn't listen to me, so I had to show you."

"Had to show what to me?" James placed his hands on the footboard of the bed and looked down at Franklin. "Show me that you're nuts, that you're suicidal, or that I'm just an idiot for listening to your cock-and-bull story?"

Franklin pushed the button again, and the head of the bed crept even higher, bringing him into a sitting position where he could look James in the eye. "Show you what the tools can do, and prove to you that what I told you was the truth. You are not losing your mind, the tools did for you what they have done for everyone they have ever come to. If you keep them with you, you will go on to make great discoveries and become well respected in your field. If you don't die first."

Nancy got the surgical kit out of her handbag. "Are you saying that all those people from the newspaper clippings were not actually doing the great works they were credited for, but that *these* were actually responsible for their successes?"

Franklin nodded.

"I don't believe it." Nancy dropped the kit back in her purse.

"What more can I do to get you to understand?" He uncovered his leg to expose the line of stitches. The original blanket-thread stitches had been replaced with a synthetic polymer thread that would dissolve as the wound healed, but the holes from the earlier stitches were still visible.

Nancy leaned in and looked closely at the stitches, then motioned for James to look as well. The stitches that had been put in by the hospital's surgeon were unevenly spaced and crooked, but the holes from the stitches that had been done in the hotel room were perfectly aligned and exactly one-eighth of an inch apart.

"Looks like it was done by a sewing machine," James said barely louder than a whisper. "I couldn't have done that well in a surgical suite, much less in a dark room on a worn-out mattress."

The door to the hospital room creaked as it opened, and all three of them looked up to see an older man in a white doctor's coat come in carrying a clipboard.

"Well, Franklin, glad to see you're awake." He made a quick notation on the clipboard. "Which one of you were responsible for that fancy stitchery that young Franklin here brought in with him?" he asked, stopping on the opposite side of the bed from Nancy and James.

"That would be me." James' cheeks blushed red. "I hope I didn't make too much of a mess of it."

"On the contrary. I wanted to see the man with hands steady enough to make those perfect stitches. I hated to remove them, but with that odd thread you used, I'm afraid I didn't have much choice. What was that thread anyway?"

"Would you believe it came from a threadbare blanket?" Nancy asked.

"Not if I hadn't seen it with my own eyes. Just like I wouldn't believe that human hands had done the stitching."

"Thanks." James looked down, and Nancy knew that he hoped the doctor couldn't tell that he was taking credit for something he had not actually done.

"You have a bright future ahead of yourself, young man. A very bright future." He turned his attention to Franklin. "We're going to need to keep an eye on you for a couple of days just to make sure there's no infection. If everything continues to look good, we will release you. It was a pleasure to meet you, Franklin." He shook Franklin's hand, then reached out for James. "You as well, Dr.—"

"Hughes." James took his hand and gave it two quick pumps. "James Hughes."

"Dr. Hughes." He looked over at Nancy. "And are you *Mrs.* Hughes?"

"Not yet, but soon." She showed him her hand and wiggled her fingers. The small diamond in her ring sparkled when it caught the light.

"Then congratulations are in order. I wish you all the best." He started to leave, then stopped at the door and turned back. "Looks like you are in good hands, Franklin. I'll have a nurse check back in on you after shift change. Until then, if your friends here feel like helping you, you can stand up and try to take a few steps. That leg will be sore at first, but it's never too early to start getting back on your feet." With a smile and a nod, he left the room, pulling the door closed behind him.

James looked down at Franklin's leg, then dropped heavily onto the arm of the chair. "I don't understand, how could this be happening? I know what I saw, but my mind refuses to accept it. Civil War era surgical tools don't just move on their own."

A mechanical hum filled the room again, and the head of Franklin's bed made the slow journey back to lying flat. It stopped with a bump. "*These* do."

"Maybe they do." James heaved a great sigh.

Nancy took his hand in hers. "So, what do we do now?"

"Now you have a decision to make." Franklin looked over at them. "You can keep the tools, get rich and famous and most likely die young, or you let me help you to be rid of them and stop the cycle of death by putting an end to this once and for all."

"Oh, is that all?" James closed his eyes and rubbed his forehead with his fingers. "I'm tired, and you need to rest. You're stuck here for a couple more days, and I guess we are stuck here with you, so for now I'm taking my fiancée with me and going back to the hotel. Hopefully, after a few hours of uninterrupted sleep, I'll be able to see things more clearly."

Nancy nodded and pulled James up from the chair. "I think that's for the best. Goodnight, Franklin. We will see you in the morning." They headed for the door.

"James? Nancy?" Franklin called out and stopped them.

"Yes, Franklin?" Nancy answered him as they turned back around.

"Could you stop at that café again tomorrow morning and bring me a cup of coffee, extra cream?"

They looked at each other, then turned and left the room, closing the door behind them.

"Thank you!" Franklin's muffled voice floated to them from the other side of the door.

Chapter Twenty-Two

March 18, 1870

"I don't know how to thank you, Dr. Mitchell." Through the stage window, Constance handed him a cloth bundle filled with bacon and biscuits. "Doesn't seem like enough after you saving Edward's hand and all."

"You think nothing of it, Constance. We owe you a debt as well, seeing that Gene's the one that found us stranded out on the prairie. So, what say we call it even."

She nodded and winked at Ella. "You're a very lucky girl."

With a whistle to the team and slap of the reins on their rumps, Turk got the stage moving. Ella waved goodbye to her as the stage pulled away.

"Make sure to change the bandages daily and keep the stitches clean!" Dr. Mitchell shouted to her over the noise of the stage.

"I will!" Constance watched until the stage had disappeared into the haze of heat rising from the parched prairie soil.

"No, Daddy, you shouldn't be doing that!" Marie's raised voice came from inside the station.

"Leave him alone, he knows what he's doing!" Gene's voice came from the bedroom.

Constance opened the bedroom door and gasped. Edward was sitting on the edge of the bed with Marie on one side and Gene on the other. Edward had his pocketknife in his good hand and an old, gnarled piece of Ponderosa Pine clamped between his knees.

"Edward Turnbull, just exactly what in God's name do you think you are about to do with that?" Constance marched over to the bed and towered over her husband.

"What does it look like I'm about to do? I'm about to start whittling."

"Oh no you are not!" She snatched the wood from between his knees and pointed it at him. "You are supposed to be taking it easy and letting that hand have time to heal."

"I told him that, Momma," Marie said. "I told him that Doc Mitchell said he was to lay still and not risk hurting his hand again, but Gene begged."

"Did not!" Gene stuck his tongue out at Marie.

"That's enough, children," Constance scolded. "Now you two get out of here and leave your daddy alone. I gave you both chores to do, and I expect them done before supper or you'll both go to bed hungry." She pointed a stern finger toward the door. "And close that door behind you when you leave. I need to talk to your father."

Marie and Gene walked slowly toward the door with their heads down. Their distress lasted just long enough for them to get inside the next room when Gene reached out and punched his sister in the arm, then ran outside.

"I'm gonna get you for that!" Marie screamed and slammed the bedroom door.

"Those two are going to be the death of me." Constance heard the tiredness in her own voice as she settled down on the bed beside Edward. "You're no help either. You know what Dr. Mitchell said, you have to take it easy with that hand. What am I supposed to do if you bust those stitches open and bleed to death right here in the bedroom?"

Edward smiled at her. She took a deep breath and laid her head on his shoulder. "It's hard enough out here with just the four of us. Now you're hurt, and I'm going to have to take up the slack till you're better and able to work again."

"I plan to be up and at 'um in no time, until then, Gene can handle a lot of things I do. He's young, but not too young to learn how to work. He's been begging me to whittle him out a pair of six-guns to play with, I just figured that while I'm stove up, I could make those as a thank-you present for all the hard work he's gonna be doing."

"But your hand—"

"You let me worry about my hand. If it gets to smartin' too bad, I'll lay the knife down."

"You *promise*?" She held the gnarled piece of wood up and out of his reach.

"Yes, *I promise,* Now help me out onto the stoop, so I don't get shavings all over your nice clean floor."

"Okay, but it really wouldn't make a difference seeing how much dust has already settled all over everything with all that's been going on this week."

"You and your dust." Edward leaned in and gave her a quick kiss. "You act as if a little dust was the worst thing about living out here on the prairie. Something may come along some day and put an end to us, but I guarantee you, it won't be dust."

Chapter Twenty-Three

March 21, 1870

The stage bumped and shook as it traveled along the well-worn trail between the station and its final stop in Kansas City. Pastor Jacobs snored quietly in one corner as Ella kept up a string of small talk that Doc Mitchell heard very little of. His mind kept going back to that line of perfect sutures in Edward's hand, and the fact that he had not sewn them there.

He'd played the scene over and over in his mind, how he had started the first stich, then had to leave his post to hold down Edward's spasming legs while Turk ran outside to vomit. When he had returned, Edward's hand had been completely sewn up. The needle had moved on its own and tied off the stitches when his trembling hands couldn't do it.

* * *

"So, I'm thinking I'm going to stay in Kansas City for a...Mel, are you listening to me?"

"Hmm? Oh, yes." Mel turned from the window and smiled at her.

"It *is* hot in here, but it should cool down considerably once the sun starts to set."

Ella noticed the lines in his face that had not been there a few days before, the bags that had formed under his eyes, and also that the nails on his hands had been chewed down to the quick. She reached over and placed her hand on top of his.

"I'm sorry," he said. His voice had lost some of its strength, and his fingers moved nervously under hers. "It's just, it's—" He shook his head, and then turned back to look through the open stage window.

She took a deep breath, slowly let it out, closed her eyes, and summoned her inner strength. She had fallen in love with him. It was crazy as they had only known each other for a short time, but she knew it all the same.

* * *

Doc Mitchell had made a decision. He had developed strong feelings for Ella, and he hoped that there was a future for them in Kansas City—or wherever they decided to stop. If he couldn't trust her with what was going on inside his head, then there wasn't much use in leading her on. He would tell her what had happened back at the station and pray to God that she didn't doubt him or think him crazy.

He turned to face her. "Ella, I need to tell you something—"

"Mel, I need to tell you something—" she said at the exact same time.

They both laughed.

She reached up and caressed his cheek. "You first."

"No, what I have to say may take a bit of explaining. You go ahead."

"Okay…" She took a deep breath. "I know it's just been a short time since we met but—what I mean to say is that while I was watching you work. No that's not right, either. I, uh realized that… Well, it's like this—" She groaned and balled her hands into fists. "Okay, I can do this. Mel, the truth is that I—"

"Whoa!" Turk's voice carried from the front of the stage as it came to a jarringly fast stop. It threw Pastor Jacobs forward, and he landed on the floor at their feet.

"Dammit." Ella sighed, sounding frustrated.

"What-what the devil is going on?" Pastor Jacobs, who had been sleeping soundly, pushed himself back up in the seat and looked around the cabin as if trying to get his wits about him.

"Doc, I'm gonna need you up here!" Turk called out from the driver's platform.

"I'm sorry, Ella, can we talk about this later?" He hoped she didn't hear the relief in his voice. "I better get out and see what's going on." Doc Mitchell didn't wait for an answer. He threw open the stage door and stepped out into the hot afternoon sun.

Immediately, he became aware of two things: the scorching heat that made the stuffy inside of the coach seem pleasant by comparison, and a horrible stench of rot and decay.

Ella leaned out of the stage window. "What's going on, Mel?"

"Get a handkerchief to cover your mouth and nose before you come out. Tell the padre to do the same. Something's dead up ahead, and the smell's horrible." He pulled out his handkerchief and used it to cover his mouth and nose as well. He squinted against the sun and saw Turk standing over a large mound in front of the stage. The horses nervously stomped at the hard prairie soil, obviously disturbed by the smell as much as he was.

"You better get up here, Doc." Turk motioned for him. "Hope you don't get sick easy."

Doc Mitchell drew closer and realized that the heap was a dead and bloated horse. Over time, the heat had caused its body to inflate to three times its normal size. Flies loudly buzzed as they swarmed, feasting on its flesh.

"Jesus Christ," he whispered as he looked down at the animal.

"I don't think Jesus had anything to do with this." Turk pointed up the trail about ten feet from where the horse lay. A man's leg was sticking out of the tall grass that lined the trail. The boot and pant leg were still intact, but the leg appeared to stop just below the hip. From the way the grass next to it stood straight and tall, clearly, the leg was no longer attached to a torso.

He heard Ella approaching from behind him. Without turning, he held up his hand. "Stop, Ella. Go back to the stage with Pastor Jacobs. Get your pistol and keep it in hand till we figure out what's going on out here." He stood with his hand raised until he heard her footsteps fade and the stage door close. "You got a spare rifle on the stage?"

Turk nodded.

"Good. Strap on your holster and make sure your pistol is fully loaded. Fetch the rifle for me. We best be prepared for anything when we go up there."

Turk didn't reply. A moment later, he returned with two pistols at the ready, holstered on his hips, and a Sharps Rifle with a handful of shells.

"Careful with that," Turk said, handing the rifle to Doc Mitchell. "There's a round already loaded in the chamber."

Turk took the lead as they rounded the dead horse and cautiously made their way toward the leg.

The oppressive afternoon heat bore down on them. The sweat running down Doc Mitchell's back caused him to shiver. He recalled how his father had called that sensation a ghost tickle. He'd laughed at that as a child, but now it seemed to fit the situation perfectly.

About two feet away from the leg, Turk stopped short and raised his hand, signaling Doc Mitchell to do the same. Across the trail in a nearby growth of Indiangrass and Goldenrod, a large turkey vulture was watching them, partially hidden by the weeds. It ducked its wrinkled red head out of sight and came back up with a shredded piece of flesh in its beak.

"Look up there." Turk motioned skyward with a jerk of his head. More vultures had begun to gather and were circling above them with their wings fully extended, floating on the wind currents. "They're attracted by the smell."

Two of the birds broke formation. They floated down to a spot off in the distance to their right and immediately began to hop about. They made low, guttural hissing noises that caused the hairs on Doc's neck to stand on end. He shuddered again, but this time it had nothing to do with sweat. Finally, the birds settled down and began pecking and ripping at the flesh of whatever they had discovered.

The air became thick with the sound of flapping wings as the other birds took their cue from their less-timid companions and found places at the carrion buffet that had been spread before them. Their greasy black bodies and bobbing red heads now spotted the fields on either side of the trail.

"Mel! Turk!" Ella called out from behind them.

They turned at the sound of her voice and saw that the bloated body of the horse was now teeming with vultures violently pecking at its hide, trying to make a way to the delicacies that waited for them underneath.

"God Almighty, I've never seen anything like that in my life," Turk whispered under his breath. "Get back inside the stage!" he yelled to Ella over the growing din of the vultures. He reached over and took back the Sharps. "Cover your mouth and nose."

Doc Mitchell pulled the handkerchief from his back pocket for the second time since they had stopped and placed it over the lower half of his face. Turk brought the rifle to his shoulder and took aim at the undulating mass of flesh-eaters.

***

In the rising heat, the black mass of vultures and horse shimmered in Turk's sights. With a steady hand born from years of hunting and having to defend himself and his passengers, Turk applied consistent pressure on the trigger and fired a round into the wake of vultures. A muffled boom like the sound of a cannon in the distance followed the sharp crack of the rifle as the bullet punctured the horse's distended midsection and sent the birds flying.

An acrid stench immediately assaulted them. Turk's eyes watered and his throat felt like it had been coated with kerosene. Beside him, Doc Mitchell wretched and turned away.

Turk paid him no mind as he watched the birds scatter, then reform their circle overhead. "I guess if there was anything hanging around here that we needed to be worried about, that surely sent it running for the hills." He looked again at the birds overhead and wondered how long it would take them to get up the nerve to come back down to earth.

Doc Mitchell straightened up and returned to his place beside him.

"You all right?" Turk asked.

The doctor nodded, then spat and wiped his mouth. "I guess we can use the team to pull what's left of that horse off the trail, then those buzzards can have their way with it while we find out who or what's scattered out there in the fields."

Doc Mitchell stood at the edge of the road, looking out over the fields of scrub and prairie grass. Turk assumed he was trying to see anything they might have missed.

"That's everything but the head!" Mrs. Gattis called out.

She was looking down at the pile of body parts that had been rescued and partially reassembled beside the stage. "What could do this, and why?" she asked.

"Not Indians," Turk said. He had found the left hand a few minutes before and had just placed it at the end of the left arm. "An Indian'll scalp a fella to prove that he's a mighty warrior. They hang the scalps around their homes or wear 'em like some kinda prize, but doing something like *this* would just be a waste of time. This just don't make no damn sense." He realized who he was talking to and removed his hat. "Sorry, ma'am, I didn't mean to—"

Mrs. Gattis shook her head and went over to join Doc Mitchell.

Pastor Jacobs was pacing slowly back and forth beside the remains, whispering a prayer. Turk wanted to ask him if he thought he had offended Mrs. Gattis but wasn't exactly sure if it was a sin to interrupt a padre while he was praying. Figuring it was best not to take any chances, he leaned back against the stage and studied the body at his feet.

Doc Mitchell sauntered up beside him, lighting his pipe.

"Sorry about that, Doc, I wasn't thinking when I said that about the scalping. I—"

"Don't let it bother you. Ella's tough, she'll be all right. She's been oddly emotional the last day or so. I think the trip's just getting to her."

Turk nodded, then pointed at the remains. "So, what do you think?"

"I think that one man couldn't do that to another man," Doc said, circling what was left of the body. "Whoever that was, he was ripped apart."

Pastor Jacobs stopped praying.

Turk looked up at him and saw the late afternoon sun glint off the tears running from the padre's eyes.

"There's no sign that a knife, ax, or saw was used," Doc Mitchell went on. "No rope burns on the wrists or ankles that would show that a horse was used to pull them off. It's just not humanly possible for one man to have done this much damage."

"So, you think that an animal might have done this?" Pastor Jacobs knelt next to the limbless torso and laid his hand on its chest.

"I didn't say that." Mrs. Gattis came back and stood next to Doc Mitchell. He took her hand when she reached out for his. "It's too clean. Animals kill for food or to protect themselves. They leave a mess when they kill. Whoever *that* was, he was *not* killed by an animal. It had to have been at least three men, and those three men were in no hurry. He died slowly, and it would have been incredibly painful. When he was finally dead, they took their time and spread the pieces across the fields on either side of the road." He used his handkerchief to wipe the sweat off his face. "This was torture, cold and calculated. Nobody should have to suffer the way this man did."

"Did you see this?" Pastor Jacobs reached into the dead man's coat and pulled out a silk handkerchief.

Turk took it from him "I'll be damned." He unfolded the handkerchief and showed it to Mrs. Gattis and Doc Mitchell.

"Looks like there's a monogram," Mrs. Gattis pointed out and Turk handed her the piece of silk. "JS."

"Jackson Shay." Turk ran his hand over the stubble of whiskers that covered his chin. "The gambler who was on the stage. The gambler who stole one of Turnbull's horses and decided to go off on his own."

They all looked over at the dead horse that was currently being devoured by more than twenty vultures.

"He was a son of a bitch, but he didn't deserve this," Turk muttered.

"Amen," Pastor Jacobs whispered, raising his eyes to heaven.

"Well, he's not going to bury himself." Doc Mitchell put his hands on his hips and looked out at the sun hanging low in the sky. "If we get started now, we *might* get him in the ground before dark."

Turk nodded. "I'm gonna pull the stage a ways down the trail. We can make camp there. Mrs. Gattis, if you don't mind, could you get us a fire started? It's gonna get chilly out here once the sun sets. What's left of the bacon and bread that Turnbull gave us is in a bundle under my seat next to the lock box. *If* anybody's hungry."

"Sure, why don't you help me with that, Pastor?" She reached down and helped the old man get back to his feet. "I think you've done all you can for now."

Turk could see the exhaustion in the pastor's face. This was probably the worst thing he had ever experienced. Slowly, the pastor reached out to Mrs. Gattis with a shaking hand, and she led him back to the stage.

Chapter Twenty-Four

The full moon sat low in the western sky and its light cast a pale, blue glow over Shay's grave. Turk tossed the final shovel full of dirt onto it, then used the back of the shovel to tamp down the loose earth. Pastor Jacobs had fashioned a cross from some sticks Mrs. Gattis had found while gathering kindling for the fire, and she steadied him as he pushed it into the dirt.

"Let us pray." Pastor Jacobs looked over at them as if to make sure that his reluctant congregation had bowed their heads before he began. Doc Mitchell and Mrs. Gattis closed their eyes and let their heads dip down, but Turk refused. Something inside him said that he should keep watch.

"Glorious Lord, we lift the soul of Jackson Shay up to you tonight. He was a gambler, a man taken to drink, and a fornicator, but his sins are not for us to judge, and his soul is not ours to condemn or acquit. We are merely your sheep left to wander this barren world until you, our shepherd, see fit to call us home. As you command in your holy book—"

A frigid gust of wind blasted across the prairie, carrying with it a cloud of dust. The pastor gagged and started coughing. Lightning flashed in the sky, and a deafening peal of thunder shook the ground.

Then all was silent. The temperature dropped dramatically, and Turk saw Doc Mitchell put his arm around Mrs. Gattis who had begun to shiver.

"What the hell was that?" Turk whispered through the sound of his chattering teeth.

"I have no idea," Doc Mitchell whispered in return.

Mrs. Gattis screamed. Turk drew his gun from its holster. "Look!" She pointed past them as a lone figure appeared, silhouetted by the moon's harsh glow. The man moved slowly toward them through the tall prairie grass. He was tall and thin, and walked with a hitched gate that made him appear to be lurching toward them more than walking. In the silence, Turk could hear his spurs jangle with each step he took.

Clouds gathered suddenly behind him, blotting out the moon. Thunder crashed above them. Lightning struck the ground behind the man, setting fire to the dry prairie grass. Another gust of wind, this time burning hot, blew past the man. It pushed the flames forward, setting fire to more of the thirsty prairie and assaulting them with ash, debris, and smoke that reeked of death.

Turk raised his arms to protect his eyes and gagged as the oily smoke filled his lungs.

Something heavy struck his leg as it rolled past. He looked down in time to see Shay's head come to rest against the cross that Pastor Jacobs had placed on the grave. The dead man's eyes were open, wide with terror.

"Christ!" Turk stumbled back in shock, then regained his balance and wheeled around with his gun pointed where he had last seen the mysterious figure. There was no one there.

Flames erupted around Turk, separating him form the others.

It sounded like someone was choking off to his left. He pivoted on his heels and brought his gun around. Doc Mitchell hung in the air illuminated by flames. He was being held there by a cowboy; his gloved hands wrapped around the doctor's neck. Doc Mitchell kicked and slapped at the man, but his grip remained firm.

Turk fired two rounds. The heat rising from the flames made it impossible to tell if the bullets had hit their mark. The cowboy released Doc Mitchell who fell to the ground and lay there motionless.

Thunder crashed directly above him. Turk ducked and dropped to his knees. He looked up and stared into the face of a demon from the depths of hell itself. The cowboy that had so effortlessly held the doc suspended in the air was now reaching for him.

A massive scar ran from under the man's hat across his face to his chin. His mouth, full of black putrid teeth, grinned through its destroyed lips. A long-dead and rotting eye stared out at him from underneath a split eyelid as the reflection of the flames danced in the other.

From somewhere behind him, Mrs. Gattis screamed. The cowboy jerked his head in her direction. Turk used the distraction to scoot back and try to get to his feet.

Mrs. Gattis was throwing fistfuls of dirt and gravel at the cowboy. The dirt struck him in the face and chest, but he paid it no mind as he began to move toward her.

Revulsion flooded through Turk as he saw the corners of the cowboy's shredded lips turn up in a smile. Thick black blood trickled down the cowboy's chin as new fissures opened in the dry dead skin from the pressure of that hideous grin.

* * *

Doc Mitchell groaned and opened his eyes as he regained consciousness. He managed to pull in a ragged breath through the swollen muscles of his throat, then panicked as he saw the flames dancing all around him. *ELLA!* His mind screamed her name, and he forced himself to his feet.

For a split second, he could not comprehend what he was seeing. Ella was throwing rocks at the man that had just tried to kill him. Turk stood a few paces away with his gun pointed at the lumbering figure, and Pastor Jacobs was on his knees with his head bowed in prayer.

"Ella, run!" he screamed, but the pop and crackle of the flames and the howling wind drowned out his voice. He forced himself to take another breath, and the superheated air scorched his already raw throat. He put his handkerchief over his mouth and nose, and ran headlong into the inferno.

* * *

Turk took aim at the cowboy. He was about to pull the trigger, when he saw Doc Mitchell run into the growing wall of flames that separated him from Mrs. Gattis and Pastor Jacobs. He hesitated, waiting to see if the doc would come out into the clearing around Shay's grave. If his shot went wild and hit the doc, he would never be able to forgive himself.

He counted the seconds. The doc should have been clear of the flames by now, but he hadn't appeared in the clearing. Turk's heart sank. He aimed again and fired two more rounds. Both shots found their mark in the center of the cowboy's back. The man stiffened and stopped, then seemed to shake off his wounds and continued lumbering toward Mrs. Gattis.

* * *

Ella's fingers were bleeding, and two of her fingernails had been torn loose as she frantically dug for rocks to throw at the nightmare walking toward her. The very man that had taken her and her husband captive. The man that had scalped her husband with the sword that still hung from his belt had now come back for her.

She thought she heard Mel call out to her, but all she could see were the growing flames. They seemed to follow the cowboy as he lunged toward her. A shot rang out, and then another from somewhere behind the wall of fire. If they hit the cowboy, they did nothing but slow his progress.

Beside her, Pastor Jacobs had fallen to his knees. His eyes were shut, and his lips were moving.

"I could really use your help here, Padre!" The old man didn't move, didn't look at her, never stopped praying.

Her bruised and bloody fingers touched the decapitated head of Jackson Shay. She drew back in horror, then kicked the head aside and grabbed the cross it was resting against. She ripped it out of the ground and held it over her head like a dagger. Screaming at the top of her lungs, she charged toward the man that had brutally tortured her husband. She ran at him full speed, giving voice to all her fear and sadness. His scarred and bloody face turned toward her as she leapt and swung the pointed end of the cross at him with all her strength.

The cowboy struck at her with uncanny speed, but before his hand made contact, she buried the cross deep into the side of his face. She landed hard on her back. All the breath knocked out of her.

The cross impaled the man's cheek and now stuck out of his mouth. Black blood ran down its hilt and dripped on the front of his shirt. Ella watched in horror as he reached up and ripped the cross free. At his touch, it became engulfed in flame.

"Fret not thyself because of evildoers, neither be thou envious against the workers of iniquity." Pastor Jacobs' voice quivered weakly but was still commanding as it cut through the crackling howl of the flames "For they shall soon be cut down like the grass, and wither as the green herb. Trust in the Lord and do good. So shalt thou dwell in the land, and verily thou shalt be fed. Delight thyself also in the Lord, and He shall give thee the desires of thine heart."

Ella scrambled to get away as a percussive sound began rumbling deep inside the cowboy's chest. He threw his head back, and something between a scream and a moan escaped him. She covered her ears and pulled herself into a ball, trying to avert the horrifying sound.

* * *

Pastor Jacobs grasped the silver cross that he wore around his neck—the cross he had used to tighten the tourniquet around Edward Turnbull's arm, the cross that he had been given to him by his elderly mother at his graduation from the seminary—and he held it out toward the evil man. "Commit thy way unto the Lord." He prayed as loud and as strong as his aged lungs and voice would allow. "Trust also in Him, and He shall bring it to pass. And He shall bring forth thy righteousness as the light, and thy judgment as the noonday—"

Abruptly the sound emanating from the cowboy stopped. In one smooth, swift motion, he raised the burning cross over his head and hurled it at Pastor Jacobs. It struck the silver cross in his hand. The force of the impact drove the cross backward, embedding it in the wrinkled, loose skin of his throat. Pastor Jacobs tried to scream, tried to call out to God for help, but could not make a sound. His skin sizzled and blistered, then burst into flames that quickly spread to his thinning hair.

* * *

The instant he heard Mrs. Gattis scream, Turk's already racing heart began to pound even harder, and his once-steady gun hand started to shake.

The sky split open in a blinding stream of lightning. The clouds erupted overhead, and rain poured out of them, dowsing the flames. Billowing steam rose from the earth and formed a cloud that hung low over the prairie. Turk stumbled forward, unsure of his footing but needing to get to Mrs. Gattis before the cowboy did.

Lightning struck again, momentarily blinding him. His foot hit something, and he stumbled. When his vision cleared, he saw that he had tripped over Doc Mitchell. His clothing was singed, and his head had been crushed.

Mrs. Gattis screamed again. Turk jumped to his feet and turned toward the sound just in time to see the cowboy unsheathe his sword.

"NO!" Turk screamed and fired his last two rounds at the cowboy.

Both bullets hit their mark, but not before the sword had cut Mrs. Gattis nearly in half. The cowboy looked back at Turk over his shoulder, smiled, and plunged his free hand into Mrs. Gattis's gaping midsection.

Turk raced toward the cowboy with his gun in the air. *If bullets won't kill him, I'll beat him to death!*

The cowboy pulled his hand free, and Mrs. Gattis fell to the ground, not moving. In his hand was an undulating mass of blood and tissue.

A split-second later, Turk was on him.

The cowboy turned, brought his sword around, and separated Turk's head from his neck. In his last conscious moment, Turk thought he heard a baby's cry.

***

Darkness overtook Doc Mitchell. A bone-chilling cold replaced the heat from the fire. He wrapped his arms around himself to try and hold on to what little warmth his body was producing. Lost in an endless darkness, he was afraid to turn or take a step because he was unable see what lay before him. The silence was maddening, and he realized that he couldn't even hear his own breathing. He tried to speak. His tongue moved, his lips formed words, but he heard no sound. He screamed until his throat ached and his lungs burned, but there was only silence.

A yellow pinpoint of light appeared above him, flowing fluidly in the darkness. He tried to touch it, but it was out of reach. A blinding shaft of brilliant blue light shot out of the pinpoint, creating a perfect circle under his feet. The circle of light began to ripple as waves formed on its surface. The waves crashed against the souls of his shoes. Where they touched, ice formed. The waves grew taller and more powerful. They lashed against his ankles, and they were also encased in ice.

A second light appeared in the darkness and danced playfully around the first. As it passed back and forth through the beam, it seemed to irritate the waves and they grew even larger, like the sea in the midst of a storm. When the waves broke against his legs, they became frozen in place.

He pounded his fists against the ice. He tried to scream again, and like before, he could feel his body making the sound, but still there was only silence.

The second light began to violently streak around inside the darkness above him. It moved so fast that it left streaks in its wake. Within those streaks he could see a face, laughing, then crying — then screaming.

"*It's him,*" a distant voice whispered. "*Who's him? That's him, there. Where? There, the dead man. Is he? Not yet, but yes.*"

The face inside the streaks of light became two. They floated over and around him, alternately laughing and screaming, before they coalesced and melded back together as the face of the one-eyed cowboy.

Fear and revulsion drove him near to the point of madness. He fought desperately against the ice that bound him. His struggling caused the sea of light at his feet to rise up. The waves lapped at his thighs. Slick walls of ice formed and bound him even tighter. He beat on his new restraints with his fists, only to find them soon covered with frozen shackles of their own.

In the darkness before him, the glowing face of the cowboy lazily floated in his direction. Its torn lips parted, revealing the broken and rotted teeth underneath. It drew nearer, the face becoming larger, and its mouth opened even more. He could see its black tongue outlined in glowing white. It drifted ever closer, and he knew that it intended to eat him—to take him inside its mouth and let the frantic muscle that writhed there wrap itself around him and feast on him.

Rotten teeth passed over his head and underneath him. The once storming light under his feet died down, became quiet, then disappeared completely.

The horrid tongue pulled back and quivered as if in anticipation of the morsel dangling in the darkness before it.

His heart was racing and his blood rushed through his system under such pressure that he thought sure his veins would rupture and bring an end to this nightmare.

The demon tongue lashed forward. Doc Mitchell screamed, and this time, the sound cut through the silence. The tongue split down the middle just as it reached him, and his world became as white as it had previously been black.

He stood in the whiteness, unencumbered by the ice that had formerly held him captive.

"*What happened? How'd he do that? I don't know, but—*" The whispers grew faint in the presence of the white.

The sound of his breathing seemed loud after the deafening silence of the darkness. He pulled in a deep breath. Smells of grass, wood, and recent rain washed over him. A gentle breeze ruffled his gray hair and carried on it the soft crunch of a horse's hooves walking through snow.

Something moved within the white, but he felt no fear. Joyous anticipation alone filled him.

A mounted rider came into view. He had seen this man before. He was riding a massive white horse, sitting tall and proud on its back. His face and body, along with that of his horse, were covered with the painted adornments of a warrior, and he wore the skull of a giant wolf on his head. The warrior's horse came to a stop, and the grace with which he dismounted amazed Doc Mitchell and filled him with awe.

The anticipation inside him grew until he could hold it in no longer. "Great warrior, why have you brought me to this place?" he implored. "Tell me, I need to know."

The warrior stepped forward and extended his hand. Between them, a circle of stones appeared, inside of which burned a small fire. The warrior sat and motioned for him to do the same.

Never taking his off the giant, Doc Mitchell settled down on one of the stones opposite the warrior. He watched intently as the warrior brought out a pipe that appeared to have been carved from the horn of a bull or maybe a ram. The warrior pulled a burning twig from the fire and touched it to the opening in the pipe. He drew in deeply, causing the tobacco there to glow brightly, then passed the pipe to him.

His hands shook as he took the pipe and brought it to his lips. When he hesitated before taking a puff of the strong-smelling tobacco, the warrior nodded and motioned with his hand that he should continue. The tobacco's odor was the opposite of its taste. The mellow, fruity-tasting smoke filled his mouth, then his lungs. He exhaled through his nose and closed his eyes as the world around him started to shimmer and bend. He felt compelled to take another draw off the pipe. The warrior vanished, and Doc Mitchell was back in Animas Forks.

A young girl was slumped over the back of a horse as it staggered past the building that used to serve as his office. It managed to reach the center of town before falling and tossing the motionless girl into the street in front of the Sagebrush Saloon. The girl's hair was matted and filthy, her clothes covered in blood and dirt. She rolled to a stop, and her hair fell away from her face. He recognized her. She was little Marie Turnbull.

"Marie!" he cried and rushed to her side, but as he reached for her, the world faded again to white.

* * *

Ella sat quietly rocking in a well-appointed, but not fancy, nursery. The rhythmic squeak of the chair as its runners passed over a loose floorboard had lulled the baby in her arms into a deep, peaceful sleep. Morning sun filtered in through the curtains that partly covered an open window, warming them both and making her feel as sleepy as the child she was holding.

Sounds of a busy street, horses hooves trampling down a dirt road, conversations between groups of men, and the distinct sound of glasses clinking together floated in through the window. The baby began to wiggle and cry. She brought it up to her shoulder and gently patted its back.

The baby belched and calmed. Ella let it rest once again in her lap. It smiled up at her, cooed, and giggled.

There came a great clatter of rustling wings as a massive turkey vulture landed on the windowsill. When its shadow fell over the child, its smile faded, and it lay still.

"Look at the baby, yes look, no don't, yes." Whispered voices came from the direction of the black bird of death.

The child's complexion had turned ashen gray; its limp arms and legs lay awkwardly at its sides.

"It's so still, yes. So cold, yes. What kind of mother would let her baby die? This kind. No not this one, yes"

A tear rolled down her cheek and splashed on the dead infant's forehead.

"Why?" she asked the vulture.

The bird's dead black eyes never shifted from the lifeless child in her arms. It extended its massive wings to their full length and sparks flew from beneath, setting fire to the curtains. The fire streaked across the floor, engulfing everything in the room except for her and the chair she was sitting in. Through the smoke, she heard the vulture cry out, its call initially harsh and guttural, turned into a high-pitched laugh.

I have to save the baby! She tore her eyes from the flames and looked down at her lap. Her abdomen had been torn open, spilling its contents into her hands.

* * *

Turk awoke with a start. The ground beneath him was moving, and a stained, white canvas shook and jostled above him. He tried to sit up but couldn't. The best he could do was turn his head side to side. To his left, boxes and barrels of different sizes were strapped to a low, wooden wall that he immediately recognized as the side of a wagon. The parcels were wet, as if rain had leaked in on them through the wagon's cover. The canvas above him was also wet and covered in brown stains—the color of dried blood.

Someone was lying beside him. Turk's gaze traveled down the person's frame until he saw an old bowler hat sitting on the man's chest. Terror overtook him. He began to frantically struggle against his invisible restraints. His movements stirred up a swarm of flies that had been attracted by the smell of blood. The man lying beside him slowly turned his head. Turk screamed when he saw the long scar, the split lip, and the rotted teeth.

The wagon came to a stop, and the cowboy's mouth widened into a grin. They lay there, side by side, staring at each other. He could smell the cowboy's rancid breath and heard his lungs wheeze and crackle when he drew in air through what remained of his nose.

The sound of boots striking dry earth came from outside the wagon, and a shadow traveled down the side of the canvas covering.

Go away, don't come back here! He tried to warn whoever was outside, but he had no voice, his words only echoed inside his head.

The shadow hesitated, then continued to make its way down the length of the wagon.

NO! STOP! GET AWAY!

The rear covering of the wagon came loose and was caught up in the prairie wind.

Stay away, he's a killer! Do you hear me?

Turk lifted his head and looked out the back. The shadow moved again, then Edward Turnbull appeared in the opening.

No!

Turk's head dropped back against the wagon's floor. The cowboy's grin widened. He winked his one good eye, sat up, and fired a single shot.

Chapter Twenty-Five

May 22, 1870

Ella gasped and sat up, holding her hand against her midsection. Dawn was breaking over the horizon, and in its first rays, she checked her hands for blood. They were clean, except for some dirt under her nails. Mel was asleep and gently snoring beside her. A little farther away, Pastor Jacobs was resting quietly.

For the longest time, she sat and watched as the sun rose over the horizon to take a place of prominence in the morning sky. Her dream kept creeping back to her. The cowboy with the ruined face, Mel burning to death in a wall of flame, Turk's head, the pastor's cross. Tears filled her eyes and spilled down her cheeks at the thought of the baby in her arms, and she didn't try to stop them. Its precious smile and gentle voice, so innocent, so beautiful. Then the vulture...

Her stomach churned, and she knew she was going to be sick. She kicked away her bedroll and managed to make it behind the stage before her empty stomach began to heave.

* * *

Turk opened his eyes and sprang to his feet. The morning sun was blinding bright, and he had to turn away.

"Ella!" Doc Mitchell cried out. "Where are you? Ella!"

Turk turned toward the coach just as Doc Mitchell ran past him. He reached out and grabbed the doctor's arm. "Doc, what's going on?"

"I can't find Ella." Doc Mitchell jerked his arm free. "Now, stop asking stupid questions and help me look." He moved off in the direction of the stage, and Turk made for the horses that were tethered a few yards away.

"I found her! She's back here!" Doc Mitchell's voice called out from behind the stage. By the time Turk got to them, Mrs. Gattis had curled up in Doc Mitchell's arms and she was crying softly.

Turk grabbed the canteen from the driver's area and wet his handkerchief. The doctor applied the cool damp cloth to the back of Mrs. Gattis's neck. After a bit, she was able to regain her composure, and Doc Mitchell helped her to sit up.

"Mrs. Gattis are you—"

"It's silly." She held up her hand and Turk helped her to her feet. "I just had a bad dream."

Doc Mitchell turned, and Turk saw his worried expression.

"What kind of dream?" Doc Mitchell asked her.

"We were attacked by the man that killed my husband. Except this time, his face had been split open, there was a massive—"

"Scar that ran from his forehead, across the bridge of his nose, and split his lip open?" Turk finished her thought. "I had the same dream."

They both looked over at Doc Mitchell who nodded his head.

"How is that even possible?" Mrs. Gattis asked.

"It's not," Doc Mitchell answered.

"But it happened." Turk leaned against the stage. "Where's Pastor Jacobs? I wonder if he had it, too?"

"I don't know," Doc Mitchell admitted. "When I woke up and couldn't find Ella, I panicked." He reached over and placed his hand on Mrs. Gattis's shoulder. "I didn't even think about the padre."

"Maybe he's still asleep," Mrs. Gattis said. "He was exhausted after we got Shay buried. It seemed to take a lot out of him, praying over the grave and all." She put her arm around Doc Mitchell and laid her head against his chest.

Turk could tell that they needed a minute alone. "I'll go check on him."

He headed back around the stage, taking time to store the canteen back where he kept it. Sure enough, Pastor Jacobs was still in his bedroll, lying next to the wooden cross he had made from kindling and placed in the dirt at the head of Shay's grave.

"Padre, you awake?" Turk called as he started toward him. There was no answer and dread began to flow through him. He knelt down and gently shook the old man. "Padre?"

Pastor Jacobs didn't move, so Turk rolled him over, expecting the worst. What he hadn't expected to find was the pastor's silver cross buried deep in the scorched and blistered folds of the old man's neck.

Chapter Twenty-Six

December 17, 2008

James rolled over and let his legs dangle off the side of the bed. His head was pounding, and he was having trouble swallowing back the fear that threatened to spill out of him and into the room.

It was just a dream.

The five little words turned over and over again inside his head, but was it, really? It had seemed so real. He wasn't an idiot; he was a doctor. He knew how dreams worked. Dreams were just the mind's way of cleaning out the dirt and cobwebs that gathered in its dark corners and hard-to-reach recesses. It was like spring cleaning for the sake of sanity. Dreams helped process fears and stressors. They were like the little worker bees of the mind, helping people to get past things that would otherwise get in their way while they were awake.

The toilet flushed, and a moment later, he heard running water. The bathroom door opened, and Nancy stepped out into the room. Her nightshirt was wrinkled, and her eyes were puffy. She yawned and stretched until the vertebrae in her back snapped like little firecrackers, then she dropped down beside him and didn't say anything. She just reached out, took his hand, and squeezed it enough that the knuckle on his index finger popped.

"Rough night?" he asked.

"I didn't sleep well. Nightmares."

"Hmmm..." He removed his hand from hers and put his arm around her shoulders. "I know the feeling."

Nancy looked up at him. "My grandmother told me, when I was a little girl, that the best way to stop a nightmare is to tell it before it disappears from your memory. She said that once you say it, you set it free."

"Did it work?"

"It did when I was six." She smiled and leaned her head against his shoulder.

"Well, I guess it's worth a shot. You go first."

"It was so strange, like I was watching a movie. Not a modern one, but more like an old western. I was looking down at this group of people as they were burying some guy. All of a sudden, all hell broke loose and this dude in an old derby hat showed up and started killing everybody."

James' breath caught in his throat. That had been his dream as well. He had seen the man in the hat—a bowler, not a derby—but Nancy probably didn't know the difference. His face was scarred, and he had a sword hanging off his gun belt.

"I get shivers just thinking about the guy," she continued. "He was tall and thin and had this hideous scar running across his face. It's getting kinda hazy now, but it seems like he was carrying something when he first showed up."

James stood, walked over to the window, and looked out at the deserted hotel parking lot. The sun was just coming up over the horizon, and it cast long shadows off the weeds growing at the edge of the hotel property.

"What's the matter?" Nancy asked, sounding worried. "Did I say something wrong? I know it was a crazy dream and that's not all of it, but—"

"It was a head."

"What?"

"The man was carrying a decapitated head, and he was wearing a bowler hat not a derby." He turned from the window and moved back over to her side. "I think we had the same dream."

"That's impossible." She looked up at him. "How did it end? Your dream—what was the last thing you remember?"

"The man in the hat cut off one guy's head, then all of a sudden, I was in the dark. It's hard to explain, but there was this light, then that cowboy was back, but this time, just his face. He tried to bite me, but not really bite, it was more like he tried to swallow me whole. Then everything just went white, and that's when I woke up and you were gone."

Nancy nodded. "I saw the guy lose his head too, but after that..." She paused, and he thought she must have been having a hard time remembering what had happened next. "I don't know, I was sitting in a rocking chair holding *a baby* when some big bird came in the window. There were these strange voices, then the place was on fire. When I started to get up so that I could get the baby away from the fire, it was dead and, and..." She wiped the back of her hand across her eyes. "I don't know, but I woke up, and I was sick to my stomach and had to throw up."

He sat down next to her. "What do you think it means?" The silence in the room hung heavy about them as James racked his brain, trying to make sense of it all.

"It has to be the tools." James got up, went to Nancy's purse, and pulled out the cloth bundle. "As much as I don't want to believe it, what we saw in the dream works alongside of Franklin's story. One of the men that died must have been Dr. Mitchell, but who were the other people, and why did that man come in and kill them?"

Nancy began nibbling at her thumbnail. It was a nasty habit that she fell into when she was thinking. He had said something to her about it on a few different occasions, and she always said she would stop. She never did. He walked over and set the surgical kit on the mattress, then reached out and took her hand away from her mouth.

"I'm doing it again, aren't I?" she said sheepishly.

He nodded and tried to smile but couldn't force it.

"Sorry." She took her hand out of his and shook it. "Wait, that couldn't have been Dr. Mitchell. It said in one of the articles that came with the tools that he died in Lawrence, Kansas from a head injury. Those people weren't in a city, they were out in the middle of nowhere."

"You're right, everyone in the dream died. The minister died when the cross he was carrying was forced into his throat. The younger cowboy had his head cut off, the older man ran into the flames and never came out."

"Then the lady stabbed the man in the hat with a wooden cross that she took from the grave, and he cut her open with his sword and pulled out—" Nancy slapped her hand to her mouth, ran for the bathroom, and retched.

He waited until she had finished and washed her face, then held out a towel to her. She took it and thanked him with a nod.

"Why don't you lay back down for a few minutes?" he suggested. "I'll run over to the café and get us some coffee and donuts. Maybe that'll help to settle your stomach."

Nancy nodded again, kissed him on the cheek, and returned to the bed. He waited for her to settle in before heading for the door.

"I'll be right back." He opened the door. Franklin was standing outside with his hand raised to knock. He was still dressed in his hospital gown; an IV tube hung from the needle taped in his arm.

"Did you have it, too?" He rushed into the room, giving James a view of his naked backside through the split in the gown.

"Franklin, what are—?"

He dropped down on the bed beside Nancy, cutting her off in mid-sentence.

"The dream, did you have the dream?" He looked frantically from Nancy to James, then back again.

"We did." James sat on the opposite side of the bed from them. "We both dreamed—"

"That a scarred-face cowboy in a bowler hat killed a bunch of people outside a stagecoach."

They nodded in unison.

"After that, did you become a giant warrior and smoke the ram's horn pipe with the old man that ran into the fire?"

They both shook their heads.

"Well, shit," Franklin said, then his eyes rolled back in his head, and he fainted.

Chapter Twenty-Seven

May 22, 1870

Doc Mitchell stood in the shade from the stage as he watched Turk shovel dirt over Pastor Jacobs' grave. He found it very ironic that the pastor would spend eternity lying next to Shay. *The angel and the devil.*

Turk stopped shoveling and stretched.

"You take a break," Doc Mitchell told him, stepping out of the shade and into the blazing sun. Ella had not been able to shake off the sadness she felt after waking up from the dream. The padre's death had only made it worse. The last few hours, she had been in the stage crying off and on. He knew that there was nothing he could do to comfort her and hoped that a little physical activity would help get his mind off her soft cries.

"I've got this." Turk waved him off. "Go see if you can get her calmed down."

"No." He shook his head and looked down at the hole they had just placed the pastor in. "She said she wanted to be alone, and I've got to honor that." He took the shovel from Turk, filled it full of dirt, and tossed it in the grave. "Did I ever tell you why I decided to leave Animas Forks?"

Turk shook his head. "Nope."

"No, I guess I didn't. I was afraid you and Ella would think me insane." He pitched another shovel full of dirt into the hole. "But after the dream I had last night, I think I've got to tell someone or else I *am* going to lose my mind. It's all so odd." He mopped the sweat off his forehead, then went back to filling the grave. If he was going to say what he needed to, he didn't want to look at Turk while he did it.

"I had a whopper of a dream last night too, Doc. At this point, I don't think you could say anything to make me doubt your sanity."

"I guess we will see about that. A few weeks ago, an old Indian medicine man was brought into town. He had been shot, burned, and beaten, but somehow, he was still alive. When the warrior brought him to my office, I tried to save him but could not." He paused and looked up a Turk who was intently watching him. "No, that's not true."

Turk took the shovel from him. "You go back in the shade. I'll finish this."

Chapter Twenty-Eight

December 17, 2008

James and Nancy managed to get Franklin stretched out on the bed, and she started to remove the IV from his arm.

"You sure you don't want me to do that?" James asked.

"No." She could see how tired he was in the way he just stood there with his hands on his hips. "I've got this. You go get that coffee. I know I need it, and I'm guessing Franklin is gonna need some, too, once he comes around."

"Extra cream," they said simultaneously and laughed.

"Okay, if you're sure you're all right."

"We'll be fine." She smiled and gave him a quick wink. "Go on, and hurry back."

When he had gone, she removed the IV and caught the little bit of blood that escaped in a tissue. She folded a second tissue into a neat square and taped it on his arm with two bandages she had found at the bottom of her purse.

"Guess that'll do it," she said to no one in particular.

After washing her hands in the sink outside the bathroom, she leaned in close to the mirror and studied her eyes. Her lids were ringed in red, and small veins had started to creep in from the sides. *Not your best look.*

There was a small bottle of Visine in her purse. She turned to go get it, but caught a glimpse of her profile in the mirror and stopped. She wasn't model thin, but she always had thought that her figure—what her grandmother had called *cornfed*—was attractive. Her hips were well proportioned, and her breasts were still perky—even at twenty-eight. She looked down at her stomach's reflection, then pooched it out and pulled her shirt tight over the little bulge that she'd made there.

"Does he know?"

Franklin? She sucked her gut back in and whipped around, surprised by the sound of his voice. His eyes were open, and he was looking over at her with his head propped up on the pillow.

"I thought you were asleep," she said, trying to straighten out the wrinkles she had caused in her shirt.

"Well, does he?"

She slumped as she walked back over to the bed and sat down.

"No." she said, looking down at the spots on the worn hotel carpet. She quickly turned to Franklin and pointed her finger in his face. "And don't you tell him."

He held up his hands like she was pointing a gun instead of her finger. "It's not mine to tell."

Nancy lowered her hand and frowned. "I know I should, but we just got engaged and this is our first vacation together…"

Franklin let out a little giggle. "How's that working out for you?"

"Very funny. But that's my point. This is all too much, too fast." She breathed in deeply through her nose, then blew the air back out though her lips, making a little whistle. "I love him. I don't want to run him off."

"Do you really think that could happen?"

"Ugh! I don't know." She started pacing at the end of the bed. "No, I don't think so, but then sometimes I do. We haven't even been dating a year, and now, all this." She looked down at the ring on her finger and fought back tears. "No, he wouldn't leave. He's too good, too responsible, too —. He loves me." A single tear traveled down her cheek and around a smile that she couldn't hold back. "He does love me, you know."

The sound of snoring filled the room. She looked over at Franklin, who had fallen back asleep.

Chapter Twenty-Nine

May 23, 1870

Turk couldn't shake his dream from the night before. Mrs. Gattis and Doc Mitchell were sitting together near the burned-out campfire, but he was too keyed up to join them. "I don't know how it could be, but if what you are telling us is true, Doc, then the folks back at the stage station are in a heap of trouble."

"All I know is what the warrior showed me in my dream." Doc Mitchell was using a stick to stir the long-dead coals of their fire from the night before. Little clouds of dust rose out of the ashes and floated out across the prairie. "I don't want to believe it, but seeing as how we all had the same dream about that damned cowboy with the scar, then I don't see how I can call the dream I had after it a coincidence."

Turk dropped to his knee in front of them. "In my dream, after that cowboy lopped my head off, I woke up in the back of a wagon just in time to see him shoot that Turnbull fella in the head. Now, if these dreams are true, then how was I able to see that happen if I was already dead out here by the stage?"

"I didn't say they were true—"

"You didn't say they weren't!" He stood back up. Doc Mitchell got to his feet and in his face.

"I didn't say they were true. I questioned if they could contain some truths, and if they did, I said I thought we should go back and check on the Turnbulls."

"And I said if they didn't, then we were wasting six days of a trip that has already taken too long and caused us to have to bury two men." Turk took a step back, needing to put some distance between them. They were all frustrated and tired, and he didn't want this disagreement to get out of hand. "And what good would it do if we did go back? We'll either scare them folks at the station for no reason, or they will just think we've lost our minds."

"Well, I can't think of any way we will know if those dreams meant anything if we don't go back and see if that renegade demon of a cowboy has been there."

"I'm sorry." Turk took his bandana from his pocket and wiped the sweat off his face. "I need more proof than an *if* before I put these horses through any more hard pullin'. Plus, we barely got enough food for the three of us to make it into Lawrence, much less out to that station and back. So, unless you got something more substantial to show me, then we are moving out in the direction of Kansas City."

"Stop it, you two!" Mrs. Gattis yelled. Turk could see the bags that had developed under her eyes and wet trails running down her face. "They're true."

Doc Mitchell rushed over to help her up.

"Thank you, Mel." She gently touched his face, then slowly dropped her hand.

"What do you mean, Mrs. Gattis?" Turk could see the concern in her face and moved a little closer.

"After our shared dream last night, I dreamt that I was rocking a baby." She looked over at Doc Mitchell. "This isn't how I wanted to tell you." She burst into tears and buried her head against Doc Mitchell's shoulder.

"Ella, are you—are you sure?"

She nodded against his shoulder. "I know it sounds crazy, it's just been a few days since we, but I'm—"

"I better give you two a minute." Turk saw the look in the old man's eyes, and it left no question about where they were heading next. "I'll go get the team hitched up, and we'll head back to the Turnbull's station whenever you're ready." He left them standing next to the cold remains of the fire and made his way toward the horses.

Chapter Thirty

December 17, 2008

"After the cowboy did what he did in the camp," Franklin said, "it was like I was sucked up in the sky by a giant vacuum cleaner. I kept rising higher and higher until I smashed through a cloud, and everything went white. Next thing I knew, I was riding this giant white horse, I had on leather chaps, and I had a giant wolf's skull on my head. Did you get any extra cream?" Franklin looked over at James and held up the cup of coffee he'd brought him.

"I put extra in there."

"Really?" Franklin sipped at the coffee and grimaced. "Still tastes too much like coffee."

Nancy reached over, took the cup from him, and placed it on the bedside table. "Franklin, honey," she said sweetly. "If you don't tell us about your dream, I'm going to dump the rest of that over your head."

He looked up into her stern face and decided that she wasn't bluffing. "Okay. So, I was wearing the wolf skull and chaps. The horse I was on walked out of a cloud and up to the old man from the dream."

"Dr. Mitchell," James said, and Franklin nodded.

"I think so. He was just standing there looking at me. So, I got off the horse and went over to him. He looked scared, like he'd been wrestling with something big and mean. I started to ask him if he was okay, but before I could, he said, *great warrior, why have you brought me to this place, tell me, I need to know*—did you get any donuts?"

"Jesus, Franklin!" James reached into a paper sack, pulled out a cruller, and threw it at him. Franklin tried to catch it but only managed to deflect it onto the floor. "What happened next?"

"What did you do that for?" Franklin looked over the edge of the bed at the ruined pastry. "That was really wasteful—did you get any more?"

"Franklin!" Nancy reached for the cup of coffee on the bedside table.

"Okay, okay." He held up his hands. "I don't know why I knew it would work, but I motioned at the ground with my hand, and a roaring fire appeared out of nowhere surrounded by big rocks. Me and the old man took a seat on either side of it. When I sat down, I felt something poke me in the back. I reached around to see what it was, and there was a calumet sticking out of the waistband of the breechcloth pants I had on under the chaps."

"What's a calumet?" Nancy interrupted him.

"I guess you'd call it a peace pipe. At least that's what they called it in those old movies where we were always the bad guys. The bowl of it was carved from a ram's horn, like the one me and Randy—" He looked over at James who was still holding the paper bag. "Well, did ya?"

"Fine." James reached in the bag, pulled out a glazed donut, and handed it to him. Franklin took a big bite, chewed it thoroughly, and swallowed. He started for a second bite, but Nancy took the donut away from him and laid it to rest on the rim of the coffee cup.

He narrowed his eyes at her. "So that's how it gonna be, huh?"

Nancy nodded and raised her eyebrows.

"The calumet was already packed with tobacco, so I pulled a burning twig out of the fire to light it. I took a puff, then handed it over to him. Whatever was in the pipe went right to my head, and I started seeing things. I saw my ancestor, Floating Feather, hit the cowboy with a rock and split his face open, then I was in the doctor's office when Floating Feather blessed the doctor with his dying breath. Then I saw the cowboy, the surgical tools, Floating Feather, and the doctor all swirling around together. And there was blood, lots and lots of blood."

He stopped talking. His mouth was dry. He wanted a drink of coffee but was afraid if he asked, Nancy would make him wear it. He cut his eyes to the cup and made a show of swallowing with a pitiful dry noise. His plan worked. Nancy must have felt sorry for him because she took the donut off the rim of the cup and let him have a sip of the coffee inside. He smiled and nodded his thanks.

"So," he went on, "after that, I started swooshing from one place to another, moving so fast that I couldn't breathe. Every time I stopped, I saw a doctor with the tools, then that doctor was dead, and the cowboy was always nearby. There were all these weird, whispered voices, but they never made any sense. Anyway, over and over and over again, every doctor that I saw use the tools died. But it wasn't just the doctors, it was anyone that touched the tools. They all died, too. The cowboy killed them all. Then all of a sudden, there was a bright flash of light, and I was back at the fire. I looked over at the old man, and he was crying. I guess he saw the same thing I had—" The donut and coffee that he had wanted so badly suddenly felt like a stone in his stomach. He knew that James and Nancy were waiting for him to finish telling them about his dream, but he wasn't sure he could go on.

Nancy must have seen the concern in his face because she placed her hand on top of his and gave it a gentle squeeze. "It's okay, Franklin. You can tell us. What happened after your vision?"

"Okay, like I said, the old man had his head down in his hands and he was sobbing. I could see his tears running down his arms, but it wasn't tears, it was blood." He looked back at Nancy and shook his head. She squeezed his hand again and nodded. "The old man took his hands away, his face was covered in blood, his eyes had been gouged out, and the side of his skull had been caved in. But it wasn't Dr. Mitchell I was looking at, it was you, James."

Nancy took her hand off his and joined James at the foot of the bed. She was crying. James put his arm around her and pulled her close.

"After that, everything went white, and I woke up in the hospital. I knew that I had to tell you what I'd seen, so I jumped out of the bed and rushed right back here."

* * *

James tossed the bag with the last of the pastries in it to Franklin and was surprised when instead of taking one out and eating it, Franklin just put it on the bedside table next to his coffee. Nancy looked up at him, and he could see how worried and confused she was.

"What do you think this all means?" she asked just above a whisper.

"I don't know what to think." He leaned in and kissed her forehead. "It's 2008, we are way beyond believing that dreams are anything more than our brains just passing gas to get some relief. But I would've also said that we are beyond believing that Civil War era surgical tools could operate all by themselves." He closed his eyes tightly and massaged his right temple where a headache was starting to come on. "I guess at this point, we don't have a choice. We're just going to have to trust Franklin to lead us to where we need to be to get rid of those tools before anyone else gets hurt."

James pulled a chair over and straddled it beside the bed next to Franklin who was staring off into space, evidently still lost in the memory of his dream. "When we first met, you said you had come to help us get rid of those surgical tools before they got us killed."

"Got *you* killed," Franklin corrected him, then looked over at Nancy. "I didn't know that they would get all of us killed, too, until I had that dream last night."

Nancy was leaning against the wall beside the bathroom door. Her hand was on her stomach, she looked frightened and her face was pale.

"So, how do we do it?" he asked, turning his attention back to Franklin. "How do we get rid of the tools and put an end to all this?"

Franklin sat up and looked directly into James' eyes. "I have no idea."

"*WHAT*?" James exploded, shot up from his chair, and started across the bed, intending to beat some sense into Franklin.

Nancy rushed over, grabbed his waistband, and pulled him back into the chair. "Stop it! Getting angry is not going to accomplish anything. Maybe Franklin can tell us what he *does* know."

"If he actually knows any—" James' cellphone rang inside his pants pocket, interrupting him. He stood, pulled it out, and flipped it open. "This is James," he said angrily into the receiver.

* * *

James turned his back on them and began talking in hushed tones. Nancy wondered who he was talking to, but when James opened the door and went outside, she turned her attention to Franklin.

"He's tired and frustrated," she whispered while doing a quick check of Franklin's bandages. "When he gets off the phone, just tell us what you know, and we'll figure out our next move from there. Okay?"

Franklin nodded.

She heard a soft click. James opened the hotel room door, came back inside, and sat down in the chair next to the bed. The anger had left his face and it had been replaced by a look of deep sadness.

"James, what's wrong?" Nancy went around the bed and knelt beside him. He seemed to be on the verge of tears. She placed a comforting hand on his knee, and he covered it with his own and gave it a gentle squeeze.

"He's dead."

Nancy looked over to Franklin who only shrugged and shook his head.

"Who's dead, James?"

He looked up into her eyes, and a tear ran down his cheek. "Dr. Carroll. Someone broke into his house last night and beat him to death with a bottle of scotch."

"Who's Dr. Carroll?" Franklin asked.

"He's the man I was with when the tools were delivered." James took a deep, shuddering breath, then seemed to pull himself together enough to keep going. "That was Calvin Cooledge—"

"The president?" Franklin asked.

Nancy shot him a stern look and motioned for him to stop talking.

James stepped over to the small dresser that sat at the end of the bed and picked up the messenger bag. He reached inside, pulled out the surgical tools, and unrolled them. He stared down at them for a long moment, then pulled out the scalpel and turned it slowly between his fingers, watching as the light reflected on its unblemished surface.

"Dr. Carroll inspected these tools when I first got them." He placed the scalpel back in the kit and rolled it up again. "Now he's dead—just like the people we saw in the dream." He took another trembling breath and looked back down at his hands. "Calvin inspected them, too."

"Oh, my God, James, you're right. We've got to warn him we've got to—"

James shook his head and faced her. "I already did, while I was outside. I told him everything. I also told him that he needed to get out of town and come join us. There's safety in numbers, right?"

All three of them exchanged glances.

"Yes." Nancy nodded, feeling totally unsure but also needing to find something positive to hold onto. "That makes sense."

"I told him to start packing, that I'd call him right back and tell him where to meet us." James looked over at Franklin. "Where should he meet us, Franklin?"

Franklin took a deep breath of his own.

"Lawrence, Kansas."

Chapter Thirty-One

May 23, 1870

Turk and Mel were hooking up the team and making the final preparations for the return to the Turnbull's station when they heard the unmistakable sound of horses pulling a wagon.

"Ella," Mel said, "you better go back and get in the stage until we see who this is and what they want."

She had just placed a hastily made bouquet of wildflowers on Pastor Jacobs' grave. Instead of doing what Mel told her to, she laced her arm in his. She had been through enough on this trip already to know that if something else were to happen, she wanted them to be together when it did. Mel gently placed his hand over hers.

"So that's how it's going to be, huh?"

Ella nodded and gave his hand a gentle squeeze.

"Good enough, then."

A few moments later, a covered wagon pulled by a two-horse team came to a stop beside them. The man riding shotgun jumped down and went straight over to Turk.

"Where the hell you been, boy?"

"Good to see you too, JD," Turk flatly replied.

"There's a running bet back at the office that you're dead. You just cost me a sawbuck."

"Sorry to disappoint. We got held up a bit at the station, then a gambler I was taking to a card game decided to steal one of my horses. That's him under the first pile of dirt over there."

"Serves him right." JD spat a stream of tobacco juice in the direction of Shay's grave. "Who's in the other one?"

"A padre I had on the stage. Hard country got the best of him. Passed last night."

Ella had stood by quietly long enough and decided to break up their little reunion. "I'm Eloise Gattis, and this is Dr. Melvin Mitchell." She walked over to the man with her hand extended. JD looked down at her hand for a second, then cautiously shook it.

"Ma'am," he said with a nod.

"We were on our way to Kansas City, but we now have reason to believe that Mr. and Mrs. Turnbull and their children may be in danger. Are you by chance heading in the direction of the Turnbull's stage station and, if so, would you allow Dr. Mitchell and myself to accompany you?"

JD turned to Turk. "What the hell is she talking about?"

"It's a long story, but I do need to go back and check on the Turnbulls—"

"What do you mean, *you*?" Ella interrupted him. "I think that Mel and I—"

"No." Turk pointed a finger at her. "You're expectin', and the doc needs to see to it that you make it back to Kansas City in one piece and have that baby. Right, Doc?"

"He's right." Mel placed his hand on her shoulder and turned her to face him. "And you know he is."

"I know, but those poor people—"

"Will either be fine when Turk gets there, or they won't be. There's nothing you or I can do to change that."

"It's settled then," Turk said. "JD, I'd appreciate it if you would take charge of the stage and get the doc and Mrs. Gattis back to the city. I'll take shotgun on the supply wagon and meet you all back there in a few days. I'll explain it all to the boss when I get back."

"It's your ass if he ain't happy."

"Understood." Turk shook JD's hand, then climbed up on the seat of the supply wagon.

"Cox, this here is the ghost of Turk Brennan," JD told the wagon's driver. "Watch out for him, he's trouble."

"Good to meet ya, Turk. We best get going. We were already running behind schedule before we stopped. Old man Turnbull's liable to be a mite steamed if we ain't on time."

"I guess I'm ready if you are," Turk told him, then looked back down at Ella and Mel. "It's been an interesting trip, folks. We can talk all about it over a beer at The Gray's House when I see you again, and Doc, you're buying." He gave them a wink and with a slap of leather, the supply wagon pulled away.

"You got it, Turk!" Mel called out. "And Godspeed."

Ella raised a hand to the departing wagon, then wiped away a tear that was clinging to her eyelash. For some reason, she could not shake the feeling that they would never get to have that beer.

Chapter Thirty-Two

December 18, 2008

Under normal circumstances, the drive from Sweet Springs, Missouri, to Kansas City, Kansas, would only take a little over an hour. Riding in a car with Franklin was no normal circumstance. Two stops for food and four smoke breaks had stretched their travel time to almost three hours. They arrived at the Kansas City International Airport with only minutes to spare and pulled into the green, arrival's zone just as Calvin came out of the building.

"James!" Calvin dropped his two duffel bags, rushed over, and shook James' hand.

"Thank God, you made it," James said, as Calvin continued to vigorously pump his hand up and down. "We were worried you might have trouble."

"Oh, I w-w-w-was, too. I was, too!" Calvin still hadn't stopped shaking his hand. "After what happened to p-p-p-poor, poor D-D-D-David, I was concerned I might meet an equally horrible f-f-f-f-fate."

James managed to pull his hand free and stepped back beside Nancy. "Calvin, you remember my fiancée, Nancy."

"Fiancée?" Calvin looked from James over to Nancy, with a huge smile on his face. "Fiancée! Oh, my goodness, th-th-th-that is great news!" He took Nancy's hand, but she pulled him into a hug before he could start his ritual, nonstop hand shaking.

"Thank you, Calvin, I'm so glad you're here." She ended the embrace with a quick kiss to his cheek, then rapidly moved out of reach.

"And Calvin, this is Franklin."

"Oh yes, yes, yes, Franklin. You told me about him on the ph-ph-ph-phone. The Indian boy." Calvin made a beeline for Franklin who had been watching the exchange from the rear of the car, ready to initiate him with the traditional Calvin handshake.

"How!" Franklin raised his hand next to his face with the palm outward, stopping Calvin in his tracks.

"Oh, m-m-m-my." Calvin glanced over at James and Nancy, then turned back to Franklin and raised his hand in a similar manner. "Oh, yes." He cleared his throat. "Uh, uh, uh, how!"

Franklin stood there for a moment with a serious look in his eyes, then burst out laughing. "I'm just messing with you, Calvin!" He reached out, grabbed Calvin's hand, and began to pump it up and down in the same swift manner that Calvin had shaken James' hand.

"Oh, m-m-m-my, yes." Calvin's voice quivered. His pudgy body jiggled with the exchange that only ended when his glasses vibrated off his nose and he had to pull his hand away from Franklin to catch them.

A horn blew from somewhere behind them in the mass of cars waiting to pick up passengers.

"We better get going." James pushed the passenger seat forward and waited for Franklin and Calvin to crawl in before putting it back in place for Nancy.

Once behind the wheel, he put the car in gear, and started to pull away from the curb.

"Stop!" Calvin cried out from the back seat.

James hit the brakes. The front of the car dipped, and a chorus of horns blew from the line behind them.

"What's the matter?" James turned around and looked back over the seat.

"My b-b-b-bags, they are still sitting out there on the walk."

"I'll get them!" Franklin said and started to crawl out the back.

"No, you won't," Nancy told him. "If you pull those stitches loose out here at the airport, we will all be in trouble." Franklin's smile faded, and he slumped back down in the seat like a pouting child.

"I'll get 'em." James ran over and grabbed the two small duffels Calvin had brought with him, then opened the hatch on the rusty old Bronco, and tossed the bags in.

Just as he was about to get back in behind the wheel, a flash of light caught his attention. When the glint came again, he looked over just in time to see what appeared to be a tall man in a bowler hat disappear into the crowd of people rushing into the airport.

Was that man wearing a sword?

The reality of what he had just seen sank in. He dropped into the seat, threw the car into gear, and peeled out of the arrival's lane, nearly clipping the car next to him.

* * *

"Be careful, James! What's gotten into you?" Nancy held onto the door handle with a death grip, having been caught off guard by their sudden departure. James didn't answer. "Franklin, Calvin, are you okay?" She peered back over the seat at their passengers. Both appeared unhurt, but Franklin was cradling his injured arm.

"Oh, oh y-y-y-yes, yes." Calvin pushed his glasses back up on his nose. "K-K-K-Kansas City certainly is an exciting place."

Franklin nodded but didn't say anything. She didn't care for the pale color his skin had turned but had no choice but to accept his answer. Satisfied that they were unhurt, she turned back around and placed her hand on James' leg. He jumped.

"I'm sorry," James said. His breathing was shallow, his face red, and beads of sweat stood out on his forehead.

Nancy switched the Bronco's temperature control to allow some of the cool outside air to flow into the vehicle. "What happened back there?"

"I don't know, maybe nothing." He released his right hand's grip on the steering wheel, ran it through his hair, then rested it on top of hers. His palm was sweaty. "I just—" He swallowed hard enough that Nancy heard it. "As I was getting in, I saw something—some*one*." His eyes never left the road while he was talking.

"It's okay." She gently squeezed his thigh. "What did you see?"

"*Him*," he said just above a whisper.

"Him who?" Franklin asked from the back seat.

James looked over his shoulder at Franklin, then back at the road.

"I think I just saw the cowboy from our dreams."

Chapter Thirty-Three

May 25, 1870

The sun had set by the time the stage pulled up in front of the line office in Lawrence, Kansas. The area was alive with noise from the nearby, crowded saloons. JD jumped down from the driver's area and opened the door of the stage.

"End of the line folks!" he bellowed.

Mel got out first and offered Ella his hand. She took it gladly and followed him into the hustle and bustle of a city for the first time in over four years. The sound of gunshots echoed off the building. Mel grabbed her and pulled her back against him just as two drunks on horseback came perilously close to them while racing down the center of the street.

"You gotta be careful around here this time of night," JD instructed them from the top of the stage. "Folks get a little lit, and all hell's liable to break loose." He dropped their bags off the opposite side of the stage onto what Ella hoped was a sidewalk, then jumped down beside them. "This is where the stage stops, but if you folks still want to get into Kansas City proper, then you should be able to hire a carriage in the morning to get you there. I'm guessing y'all will want to find a place to stay for the night. There's plenty to choose from just over yonder." JD pointed to a side street that ran diagonal to where they currently stood.

"Can you suggest a good hotel, preferably something nice, something new?" Ella asked.

"Hell, lady, they're all new. Quantrill and his Raiders seen to that." He slapped at a mosquito that had landed on the back of his neck. He looked at the dead insect in the palm of his hand, then brushed it off on his pants leg. "Probably the best in town is the Excelsior. It's just up the way a bit."

"That sounds perfect. What do you think, Mel?"

"Any place with a soft bed and strong coffee sounds good to me." Mel fished around in the pocket of his vest, pulled out a dollar bill, and gestured with it toward JD. "Mind hoofing our bags over there once we get checked in?"

"I was planning to do that anyway. But, seeing as you asked so nicely..." He smiled as he stuffed the bill into his shirt pocket, then rounded the stage to get the bags.

Chapter Thirty-Four

December 18, 2008

Franklin watched Calvin pull a handkerchief from the inside pocket of his jacket and began to meticulously clean his glasses. Scrubbing first the center portion of each lens before turning his attention to the outer edges. The sun was pouring in through the side window of the Bronco and he held them up to check his work. He frowned, then started the process all over again.

"Why do you keep doing that?" Franklin asked him.

"I c-c-c-can't seem to get the silly things c-c-c-clean." The frustration was evident in Calvin's voice. "I scrub and scrub b-b-b-but when I hold them up to the sun, they are still d-d-d-dirty." He raised the glasses again to the window. "S-S-S-See?"

He leaned his head out of the way so Franklin could look at the lenses.

"No, they're not."

"W-W-W-What do mean they're n-n-n-not?" He looked back through the glasses. "I can c-c-c-clearly see the dirt, I'm not b-b-b-blind. Maybe you sir, are the one in need of optical c-c-c-correction. If you cannot see the d-d-d-dirt that is obviously lingering on th-th-these—"

"It's the window," Franklin interrupted.

Calvin dropped the glasses onto his lap and shot Franklin a confused look. "*What's* the window?"

"That piece of glass beside you that rolls up and down."

"I kn-kn-kn-know what a window is!" he snapped back. "W-W-W-What does that have to do with the f-f-f-filthy state of my g-g-g-glasses?"

"They're dirty," Franklin answered.

"Yes, they are dirty, young man. Th-Th-That is my p-p-point. My glasses are dirty and I-I-I –"

"No, not your glasses, the windows. *They're* dirty. When you hold your glasses up to the windows to see if they're clean, you're seeing the dirt on the windows, not the dirt on your glasses."

Calvin leaned in close to the window, squinting. He put the glasses on, took them off, and put them on again. "Yes, well."

* * *

Nancy had been listening to the men behind her and forced herself not to laugh. The trip had taken on a different feel after James thought he had seen the cowboy with the scarred face at the airport. An underlying sense of fear and confusion radiated though the car like a low current of electricity. She guessed that Calvin sensed it, too, and it prompted his neurotic need to constantly clean his eyewear.

"Franklin," she said, hoping that some conversation would help lift the mood inside the car. "Back in the hotel, how did you know we needed to go to Lawrence to get rid of the tools?"

Franklin didn't answer, and when she glanced back, she found him looking out the window at the passing landscape.

"Yes, F-F-F-Franklin," Calvin asked, "how d-d-d-do you know that?"

"It was Randy," he answered without taking his eyes off the passing scenery.

"Who is R-R-R-Randy?" Calvin asked. When Franklin didn't say anything, he turned to Nancy for an answer.

"Randy is an old Indian man with a pocket full of peyote that got Franklin stoned one time too many," James sarcastically answered from his position behind the wheel.

Franklin turned from the window. "No man, it was only one time."

"Go ahead, Franklin, tell us what happened," Nancy said, ignoring James.

"Like I said, it was Randy. After we shared in the ancient greeting ritual—"

"W-W-W-What's the ancient g-g-g-greeting ritual?" Calvin interrupted.

"Getting stoned on mescaline sucked through the horn of an old goat," James answered.

"It wasn't from a goat," Franklin corrected him. "It was a ram's horn." He had obviously missed the sarcasm in James' voice once again.

Nancy covered her mouth and pretended to cough as a signal to James to lay off the smart aleck remarks. Doing so, also hid a smile that she couldn't suppress.

"So," Franklin continued, "after we partook in the ancient ritual of greeting, I was righteously gorked. That was some *pretty potent peyote,* so I was just sitting there enjoying the buzz when all of a sudden Randy started to change. One minute, it was Randy sitting across from me on a rock, next minute, it was an iridescent rainbow-colored cockroach in an Indian headdress, and it started telling me about how I had to find James."

"S-S-S-Sorry to interrupt, young man, b-b-b-but I am pretty well versed in entomology, and I f-f-f-feel confident when I s-s-s-say that cockroaches, or P-P-P-Periplaneta Americana if you are referring to the most c-c-c-common form of the insect f-f-f-from the f-f-f-family Blattodea, does not come in a rainbow coloration and certainly n-n-n-not in an iridescent f-f-f-form."

Franklin stared at Calvin for a moment, then leaned in close to him. "*Peyote* man," he whispered, "we were smoking *pe-yo-te*."

"Yes, well." Calvin pulled the handkerchief back out of his pocket and began to scrub at the lenses of his glasses.

"Go ahead, Franklin." Nancy smiled at him across the back of the seat and gave him a quick wink.

"So..." Franklin took a deep breath. "Roach Randy says that once I find the pasty-looking white man in the beat-up old Bronco—"

"What did you just say?" James asked, sounding offended.

Franklin held up his hands. "Those are the words of Randy the Roach. I'm just telling you what he said."

"What did he tell you to do after you found James?" Nancy asked, trying to keep the conversation on track.

"Roach Randy told me that I had to convince the pasty—um James, that he was in danger, then take him to Lawrence, Kansas, and that once we were there, all would be made known. I asked him why I had to be the one to find you, and that was when he told me about my great ancestor, Floating Feather."

Calvin scooted forward in his seat and leaned in close to Nancy. He placed his hand beside his mouth. "Na-Na-Na-Nancy, dear," he whispered. "You are aware that this young man is insane, correct?"

"Hey," Franklin said.

"Oh, oh, oh. N-N-N-No offense intended," Calvin said with a nervous grin.

"Okay." Franklin nodded and went back to staring out the window.

"I know it looks that way." Nancy placed a hand on top of Calvin's. "But everything he has told us so far has been true, and for now, it's all we've got to go on."

"I see." Calvin settled back in his seat. "I-I-I-Interesting. It's all v-v-v-very interesting."

"Franklin," James said, "did Randy tell you anything about what we should do once we are in Lawrence? We should be there in about forty-five minutes."

"Nope, after that he was just plain old Randy again."

"Then I guess we just find a hotel for the night and see what happens next." Nancy reached out and gently massaged James' shoulder. "I think we could all use a good night's sleep."

Chapter Thirty-Five

November 22, 1875
Lawrence, Kansas

Dearest Prudence,

 I hope my letter finds you well and that you will extend my well wishes to your loving Jonathan and my handsome twin nephews, Andrew and Steven.
 Let me begin by expressing my regret that it has taken me so long to write to you. Mel has settled into his work at the Lawrence grange and although he finds working for the betterment of the local farmers fulfilling, I fear it lacks the excitement that being a physician once afforded him. He is a good man, dearest Pru, and I hope someday that you will be able to meet him. I feel secure that you will see in him all the qualities that caused me to fall so desperately in love with him.
 Since my last letter, little Melvin Junior has learned his alphabet and numbers up to one hundred. I wish you could see him, Pru. He is the embodiment of his father, but I truly believe I can see our dear departed mother in his

eyes. I miss Mother and Father deeply. I guess it is the curse of a military wife to be far from home when the hard times come. I am so thankful that you were there for them. The pain would be immeasurable if I had to live with the thought of them being alone in their final hours. I believe that they would have approved of me being with Mel as strongly as Father disapproved of my marriage to Joseph. Father warned me against being a military bride. A part of me deep down in my very soul wishes I had listened to him.

We are still residing in the Excelsior Hotel. The grange has arranged for us to remain here for as long as Mel continues his employment with them. A hotel in the busiest part of a town such as Lawrence is probably not the best environment for raising a rambunctious little boy, but we are making the best of it. Mel says that we should be able to afford a small farm outside of town before long. It can't happen soon enough for me. I'm sure I'm not the—

BAM, BAM, BAM

"Mr. Mitchell, Mr. Mitchell are you in there?"

Ella jumped at the sudden banging on the hotel room door. It took a moment for her to pull herself out of the world of her letter and into the present.

BAM, BAM, BAM

"Mr. Mitchell—"

She crossed the small drawing room and opened the solid oak door. A young man no more than twelve years old stood there with his fist raised, poised to deliver another round of blows. His cheeks were red, and he was out of breath.

"My goodness, young man, what's all the commotion about?"

"I'm sorry, ma'am." The boy reached up and snatched his hat off his head. "I'm looking for Mr. Mitchell from the grange office. Is he here?"

"I'm afraid he's not. He lives here, but he's not here right now."

"*Shit fire!*" The boy stomped his foot, then slapped his hand over his mouth. "I'm sorry, ma'am!"

"No need to apologize, it's nothing I've not heard before. Why are you in such a rush to find my husband?"

"Telegraph come in from Kansas City. There's been a shootin', and a little boy needs doctorin' fast. Doc Collier's out of town seein' to a birthin', so they's bringin' the boy by buckboard this way. They say Mr. Mitchell used to be a doctor—"

"Used to be is right." Mel's voice came from the stairs at the end hallway followed by the sound of hard soles walking on a wooden floor. "When the sheriff gets here, you tell him that I'm out of that business, and if he needs a doctor, he will have to find one somewhere else."

Mel stepped around the boy, entered the hotel room, and kissed Ella's cheek.

"Go on, you heard me!" he barked at the boy and slammed the door.

"Shit fire!" The boys muffled reply came from the other side.

Mel chuckled and crossed the room to a small table. He lit the oil lamp that was sitting on it before settling down in a straight-back chair and opening the daily newspaper. Ella stood silently watching him, and after a moment, he looked over at her. "What?"

"Did you hear what that boy said?"

"Yes, I did. He said the sheriff needs a doctor and told him to come fetch me." He folded the newspaper and laid it on his lap. "I've put that part of my life behind me, and you know full well why. The sheriff will just have to find somebody else."

"There *is* nobody else. The doctor in Kansas City is at an outlying farm delivering a baby." She crossed the room and placed her hand on Mel's shoulder. "A little boy has been shot and may die if he doesn't get help immediately. You are the only chance he has."

Mel placed the paper on the table. He stood and looked down into Ella's eyes. "If the boy has been shot, he is going to need surgery. The only tools I have are in my kit, and if I dare to use them, I could be inviting that monster back into our lives. I'm not willing to risk that, I'm sorry."

"But, Mel—"

"I said no, Ella. I refuse to risk our lives and the life of our son."

"Even if someone else's son dies in the process?"

Mel's face fell as he considered her statement. His breathing grew heavy, and she could tell that the decision pained him.

"Yes, damn it, yes." He turned from her and faced the open window.

She took his arm and leaned her head against his shoulder. The evening sun cast long shadows off the buildings that lined the street as people were going busily about their daily routines. He was a good man; she had known that from the moment she met him. Even now, in this horrible situation, he was trying to protect his family. She loved him for it, but it hurt her to think of a mother losing a son to such a tragedy. She tried to put herself in that woman's place, and the thought of it broke her heart.

"Mommy! Poppa! Mommy! Poppa!" Junior's voice echoed down the hallway outside their rooms over the clatter of his running in his new cowboy boots, his *big-boy* boots. The hotel room door burst open. He pushed between them and pointed out the window. "Wagon's coming! Billy says there's a dead boy in it no bigger'n me!"

"Junior, what have I told you about what Billy says?" Ella sternly asked him. She wished her son would find a better friend than the son of the hotel's bartender. Unfortunately, in a town like Lawrence most families lived on the surrounding farms, so playmates near his age were hard to come by. Billy Hodgkins was just two years older than Junior, but the boy acted like he was already an adult. She assumed this was from his upbringing, having been raised in a bar by a single father.

"You said, don't believe everything Billy tells me." Junior turned from the window and looked up at her. "But this time it's true. *Look*!" He turned and pointed down the street.

Sure enough, the sheriff from Kansas City was riding ahead of an open buckboard as it made its way hurriedly down the street. A crowd had fallen in behind it, likely drawn in by the sound of a woman alternately crying, then screaming, from the back of the wagon.

Ella slapped a hand to her mouth to stifle a sob as the wagon pulled closer. It stopped outside the hotel's front door, and she could clearly see that the woman cradled the limp, blood-covered body of a small boy.

BAM, BAM, BAM

Ella screamed, and Mel rushed across the room. She followed him, leaving Junior looking out the window at the happenings on the street below.

Mel fumed. "I told that boy to leave me out of—"

He snatched the door open so hard that it creaked on it hinges. His face hardened. He faced the sheriff, not the boy.

"Sheriff, I—"

The sheriff silenced him with a raised hand. "Before you say anything to make me madder than I already am, Mr. Mitchell, you listen and listen good."

Mel took a step back and allowed the lawman to come inside the room. The sheriff crossed to the window where Junior still stood watching the goings-on surrounding the wagon below.

The sheriff glanced out, turned, and narrowed his eyes at Mel. "Do you hear that?"

The sound of the woman's cries echoed up from the street below.

"There's a woman down there whose husband has just been shot down dead by a drunk whore, for no reason other than stepping into the Gray's House Saloon to get a beer for himself and a sarsaparilla for his son." He moved away from the window, then pointed back at it.

"You are the only man within fifty miles of here that might, *just might*, be able to keep her from having to bury that boy beside his daddy tomorrow morning in the Kansas City boneyard." The woman screamed again. The sheriff took Junior by the shoulders and turned him from the window. "That little boy down there bleeding all over his momma just turned six. Did you catch that? *Six!*" He looked down at Junior "How old are you, boy?"

"Five," Junior whispered. His lower lip started to quiver, and he pulled out of the sheriff's grasp. He ran to Ella, buried his face in her skirt, and quietly sobbed.

The sheriff got face to face with Mel. "Now. Do you have something you want to say to me?"

"Plenty," Mel grumbled.

Ella noticed the red flush rise in his cheeks, and the unmistakable anger in his voice. She feared he might throw a punch at the man standing in front of him.

"And I *will* have my say," Mel huffed, "and you *will* listen to every word." He moved back, widening the space between him and the sheriff. "But it will have to wait till another time." He turned on his heel and stormed out the door.

"I'm sorry about all this, ma'am." The sheriff gave her a slight nod and followed Mel out.

She dropped to one knee and hugged Junior tightly against her. "Mommy has got to go help Daddy save that little boy." She dried his tears with the tail of her dress. "You be brave and stay here until I get back, understand?"

Junior sniffed and nodded.

"Good boy." She caressed his curly blond locks. He was so handsome.

The woman below let out a cry so full of heartbreak and sadness that Ella pulled Junior back against her and kissed the top of his head. "Mommy loves you."

She stood and started for the door, hesitated, then ran back to their chest of drawers. In the third drawer from the top, buried beneath her underthings, she found what she was searching for. She clutched Mel's surgical kit to her chest and whispered, "God protect us," then dropped it into the pocket of her housedress.

* * *

The woman in the wagon screamed when Doc Mitchell tried to take the injured boy from her arms.

"It's okay, Mrs. Walkins," the man driving the buckboard said in a soft and caring tone. "This is the man I was telling you about. The *doctor*. Let the *doctor* take a look at him."

Mrs. Walkins looked at Doc Mitchell but didn't release her bleeding son. "You have to save him, Doctor. He's all I got left." Tears spilled down her cheeks, and she shuddered, trying to take a breath.

"I have no way of knowing what I can do unless you let me look at him." He could hear how harsh his words sounded, but he had learned long ago that in an emergency, being direct was the only way to make yourself understood. He slipped his arms under the boy and was immediately shocked at how quickly blood soaked through the sleeves of his shirt. After another moment's hesitation, Mrs. Walkins loosened her grip.

"What's his name?" he asked as he lay the boy out flat in the bed of the wagon.

"Jedidiah, after his father." She broke down in tears, and Ella, who had just come through the front doors of the hotel, rushed to her side to give comfort.

"Okay, Jed," Doc Mitchell whispered. He ignored everything else going on around him and began to unbutton the boy's shirt. "I need to see where you got hit. This may hurt a little, but I need you to be strong and—" He looked into the boy's face for the first time and saw that his eyes were closed. His small, delicate chest rose slowly, then settled down deeply before rising again. He used his thumb to push open one of the boy's eyelids, only to discover that his eye was rolled up so far that he could barely see the iris.

With no time to waste, he tore open the boy's shirt and used his own sleeve to wipe away some of the blood from his chest. He counted three entry wounds. He slowly rolled Jedidiah to one side and looked at his back. Two of the bullets had gone all the way through. From the location of the exit wounds, it appeared that one could have nicked the boys left lung. As if he needed more proof, he heard a soft wheezing sound when the boy managed his next breath.

As he began to roll little Jedidiah back over, blood bubbled up from beneath the waistband of the boy's trousers. He wiped away the bright, red liquid, lowered his face toward the wound, and sniffed. The blood carried with it a distinct odor of human waste. He carefully loosened the boy's trousers enough to look inside them. A fourth bullet had hit him just below the navel. It must have nicked his colon, then exited through the meaty part of his lower back. The boy was lucky that it didn't damage his spine.

Lucky?

He looked back down at Jedidiah and realized how ludicrous that thought had been.

If the colon *was* damaged as he suspected, that meant that waste was flowing into the wound and into the body cavity.

Three wounds to the upper body.
Pierced lung.
One wound to the lower abdomen.
Possibly damaged colon.
Massive blood loss.

Doc Mitchell ticked off the list in his head. By all rights and measures little Jedidiah Walkins should already be dead. The fact that he wasn't and that he had managed to stay alive in the jostling back of a buckboard all the way from Kansas City to Lawrence meant he was a fighter. Fighter or not, it would take nothing short of a miracle to save him, and Doc Mitchell didn't believe in miracles.

* * *

"Mel?"

Ella had been holding Mrs. Walkins in her arms as Mel examined the boy. Now, both she and the boy's mother were looking at him, waiting for an answer. The young mother shook against her, and again, Ella's mind slipped back to thinking about Melvin Junior. She glanced up and saw his pale, moon-shaped face looking down at them from the window above. He gave her a little wave, and her heart nearly broke. She pulled Jedidiah's mother in tighter.

"Mel, she needs to know."

He wiped his hands on his pants leg and looked up at them. Ella didn't like what she saw in his face. His lips were pursed tightly together, and his brow was furrowed. She braced herself for what he might say and stood ready to help Mrs. Walkins in any way she could when her husband rendered his verdict.

"Mrs. Walkins..." He paused, and the young mother stiffened against her. Ella gave her upper arm a soft squeeze, then nodded for Mel to continue.

"Mrs. Walkins, little Jed here is barely alive. The bullets appear to have nicked two of his major organs, his lung and colon. Without surgery, there is no way to know how badly they were damaged." Mel took a deep breath. "I feel sure that if he does not have surgery, he will not survive. But I also feel secure that if surgery is attempted, he will die from the further shock and damage to his system." He cleared his throat and looked back down at the boy lying beside him on the wagon. "It's too late, Mrs. Walkins. I'm sorry."

"No!" Mrs. Walkins pulled out of Ella's grip and threw herself on her son.

Ella took Mel's hand and held it for a moment, watching through tear-filled eyes as Mrs. Walkins grieved for her son. Her heart and soul cried out for the woman. To lose a son or a husband was a horrible thing, but to lose them both on the same day, at the same time was unimaginable.

Mel placed his hand on top of hers, then turned to the sheriff. "How the hell did this happen?"

The sheriff motioned for them to follow him. "It was just a stupid accident," he said, once they got inside the hotel and away from the grieving mother. "Today's the boy's sixth birthday, and his daddy promised that he would take him into Gray's Saloon and order him a drink from the bar—sarsaparilla, of course. Seems the boy had developed a keen interest in what went on behind the saloon's swinging doors, and his father decided it was best to show him the truth before he became too taken with his fantasies." The sheriff looked around

Mel at the dying boy and his mother. "Mrs. Walkins didn't think too highly of the idea, but the boy's daddy insisted. So anyway, that's what he did."

"That idiot, a boy that age has no business—"

"I know, and I don't disagree with you." The sheriff raised a hand to stop Mel from going any further and motioned for him to keep his voice down. "I saw them go in and went in to tell him that very thing, but before I could, a ruckus started upstairs where the Gray's whores take their fellas. No telling what happened, but all of a sudden, somebody starts shootin' and this fat old miner comes tumblin' down the stairs with half his face missing. That crazy old whore, Marlene, comes chasing after him—buck naked and holding a pistol in each hand. That woman ain't been right in the head since her daughter, or lady friend, or whatever she was, up and disappeared a few months ago. So, she commences to shooting at anything and anybody that moved. I drew on her, but—"

The sheriff stopped talking and looked down at his feet. He pulled a dirty handkerchief out of his pocket and wiped at the sweat on his brow. "But that was when Mr. Walkins decided to grab his boy and try to get out." He stuffed the handkerchief back in his pocket. "He stepped *between* me and her. I'm surprised I didn't shoot him myself."

The sheriff took a deep breath, closed his eyes, and shook his head as if he were trying to shake away the memory of what he had witnessed. When he opened his eyes again, they were rimmed with red. "The first bullet hit him square in the back, the second took out the top of his head. When he fell, his body twisted, leaving that poor baby unprotected. I don't know how many times that boy got hit before I was able to aim and take her out. I hit her twice, dead center of her chest. She won't do nothing like this again." He took his handkerchief back out, wiped at his eyes, and blew his nose. "Guess Mrs. Walkins was right. It *was* a bad idea. I just wish that—"

"Doctor, come quick!" Mrs. Walkins screamed from behind them.

Mel turned and rushed back to the wagon, and Ella stayed close on his heels. Mrs. Walkins had pulled the boy back up in her lap. His eyes were open, and he was crying.

"He said my name," she whispered. "He said my name! *He SAID MY NAME*!" she screamed. "My boy is alive, Dr. Mitchell. You said he was going to die, but he's alive, and he said my name!"

"Mrs. Walkins, if he said your name, it was just a little rebound before the end. It happens with people that are dyi—"

Jedidiah Walkins lifted his hand and reached out toward Mel.

"*Hurts*," he whispered so quietly that only Ella, Mel, and his mother heard it.

"Jesus, God," Mel whispered in response.

"Mel, you have to—"

"Ella, no. The surgery will kill him. I can't—"

"Maybe not." Ella reached into the pocket of her house dress and removed his surgical kit.

"No." Mel took a step away.

"What's happening?" Mrs. Walkins cried out. "Why aren't you doing something? Why?"

"Mel, you have to." Ella extended the surgical kit toward him.

Mel looked from her to the boy in his mother's arms. "You know what could happen if I do."

Ella nodded. "And I know what *will* happen if you don't."

Mel snatched the kit out of her hand and turned toward the door of the hotel. "Hodgkins!" The hotel bartender was standing just outside the door with his son, Billy, close at his side. "I need a long table. Throw a clean tablecloth over it and get me lots of towels and hot water." Hodgkins nodded and rushed back inside. "Ella, you go in and gather all the oil lamps you can find and set them up around that table. I'm gonna need plenty of light."

"Thank you," she whispered before rushing toward the door. Behind her, Mel instructed the sheriff to keep everyone out of the hotel and called for help to get Jedidiah inside.

Chapter Thirty-Six

December 18, 2008
Lawrence, Kansas

"Now this is more like it!" Nancy moaned as she rolled around on top of the satin duvet that covered the king-size bed in their hotel room.

"What did you say?" James asked from the adjoining bathroom.

He had announced that he needed to take a shower and brush his teeth as soon as they had arrived and checked in. She assumed it was just an excuse to have a few minutes to himself after a long and exhausting drive with Calvin and Franklin.

On the other hand, all *she* wanted to do was luxuriate in the over-the-top splendor of their Hotel Excelsior hotel room. She grinned, recalling the heated, thirty-minute discussion between Franklin and Calvin that prompted James' decision to stay there. The two had been going back and forth over the quality of the complimentary breakfasts, Calvin insisting that only a true *hotel* would offer real eggs as opposed to powdered eggs. Franklin had countered, that although that might be true, he had never been offered the link sausages that he enjoyed when staying at a hotel, but that they were staples of the continental breakfast at most *motels*.

James chose the magnificent Hotel Excelsior the instant he saw the sign on the interstate advertising it. He pronounced that they would stay there for the night and demanded no further discussion on the matter. The pouting from the back seat had been considerable but blissfully *quiet*.

James came out of the bathroom with a towel wrapped around his midsection like a skirt. He had his toothbrush in his hand, a circle of white froth surrounded his mouth. "Did you say something?"

Nancy took one look at him and laughed. "I was going to say that this bed is so comfortable that it would be criminal not to sleep in it naked, but now that I've seen you in all your glory..." She made a show of looking him up and down. "I think I need a pair of footy pajamas."

He smiled, tossed his toothbrush back in the direction of the bathroom, then pulled the towel off and used it to wipe his mouth.

"Would those be the footy PJs with the trap door in the back?" Before she could answer he leapt on the bed and pulled the duvet up over them.

"Wow, this is a comfortable bed," he said from underneath the covers.

"Shut up and kiss me," she giggled.

* * *

James woke up to pitch blackness. He lay quietly in bed listening to Nancy's breathing and took comfort in it. What had he gotten them into, *her* into? Traipsing across the country searching for a way to get rid of those damned surgical tools before it was too late. *If it's not already too late.* No, it wasn't, and he would see to that. He had come this far and was going to put an end to the cycle of fear and death if it was the last thing he did.

The carpet felt soft under his feet as he made his way to the bathroom. The automatic light over the vanity almost blinded him when it came on, and he jerked the door closed behind him so as not to disturb Nancy. A few hard blinks later, he had grown accustomed to it enough to see himself in the mirror. He looked as tired as he felt—even after a few hours of sleep in what had to be the most comfortable bed he had ever laid down on.

The twist of a knob filled his hands with cold water, and he splashed his face and shivered as it trailed down his chest. The towel he had been wearing after his shower was still lying on the floor at the foot of the bed. He grabbed another off the stack supplied by the hotel, and ran the ridiculously soft towel over his face and chest. *Spoils of staying in a hotel that you can't afford.* The thought made him smile. *Thank God for American Express.*

He stopped and stood absolutely still. There were voices coming from the other room. He recognized Nancy's voice immediately. *Who could she be talking to at this hour?* The other voice was higher in pitch. He strained to make out the words but couldn't.

A shiver of fear washed over him. The only people Nancy knew in Lawrence, Kansas were Franklin, Calvin, and himself. The only other person they had spoken to since their arrival had been the old man that checked them in at the front desk. His voice had been low, warm, and full of southern charm. The voice he was hearing from the other side of the door was reed thin and seemed cold, even though he didn't know what it was saying.

This is ridiculous. Nancy's probably just talking in her sleep. That's it. It must be. Usually, the most obvious answer was the correct one.

* * *

"Who are you?" Nancy asked, not sure that she really wanted to know.

"Have you seen Junior?" The woman was facing the hotel window, looking down at the street below. "I sent him to fetch his father. The hour is late, and we all need to be in bed."

"Where's your husband?" Nancy asked.

"He's likely down in the saloon. He's been spending far too much time there since— well the last few days. I told Junior to check there first. If he's not there, I told him to try the outhouse."

"The outhouse?"

"Yes, the outhouse behind the kitchen. Mel has never taken to the idea of using a chamber pot."

"I don't understand. All these rooms have their own bathroom, it's right—" Nancy turned and pointed toward the bathroom, but instead of a door, a small trundle bed sat there against a solid wall.

"You know how men are," the woman continued. "They can get so set in their ways. I tried to explain to him that there was no shame in it, and that it certainly made more sense than traipsing through the hotel in the middle of the night, then crossing the back lawn to that smelly excuse for a toilet. But he would have none of it—said that he never pissed in a pot the whole time he was in Animas Forks, and he wasn't going to start now."

A rattling noise caught Nancy's attention, then a thin shaft of light appeared in the wall to her side. It split the trundle bed in two before taking the shape of a door.

"That must be him now," the woman said.

"Your husband—" Nancy started, then stopped when she realized that she was alone in the room.

She turned back to the mysterious door. A tall, thin man wearing a bowler hat stood there silhouetted in the light. A revolver was holstered on one hip and a sword on the other.

* * *

James opened the bathroom door, allowing the light to spill out around him. In its soft glow he could see Nancy standing at the side of the bed. She was looking right at him. He stepped into the room, and she began to scream.

* * *

Calvin paced nervously around the room, or at least in the space not taken up by two double beds. Franklin was sleeping soundly in the one closest to the window.

Calvin didn't enjoy sharing a sleeping space with *anyone*. He knew that this odd phobia stemmed from being forced as a child to share a bedroom with his two older brothers. Being the youngest had made him the perfect target for their relentless practical jokes. Ever since he had been out on his own, he had never slept well when forced into close confines with another person. He was well aware that if he ever took a wife, he would have to endure years of psychotherapy in order to share, much less enjoy, their marital bed.

Franklin snorted loudly and sat up. A sound somewhere between a car accident and a roaring lion came from deep within him, then he smacked his lips loudly a few times, stretched, and yawned.

"F-F-F-Franklin!" Calvin exclaimed. "You have nearly s-s-s-scared the life out of m-m-m-me!" He placed his hand on his chest to try and still his racing heart.

"Humph." Franklin sniffed and smacked his lips again. "Mouth's dry." He stuck out his tongue, letting his teeth scrape against its dry surface. "Need some water."

"Then g-g-g-go get some." Calvin pointed toward the bathroom door. "There's a p-p-p-plastic cup sitting on the sink."

Franklin bared his teeth like an angry dog and made a retching sound. "Bathroom water, oh no. That's just wrong. There're germs in there."

"D-D-D-Don't be ridiculous. The cup is wr-wr-wr-wrapped in plastic, and the water that comes in is h-h-h-highly chlorinated as required by law. It's p-p-p-perfectly safe."

"Yuck!" Franklin made the retching sound again and covered his mouth.

"Well, if you can't drink the w-w-w-water from the faucet, then your b-b-b-best bet is to go down to the bar and see if they have some b-b-b-bottled water."

"Yeah, bottled water. That's a great idea!" Franklin threw back the covers and slid out of bed, totally naked. "I'll be right back!"

"No!" Calvin turned his back on the naked Indian. "You c-c-c-can't go down to the bar like that."

"Of course not." Franklin chuckled. "I've gotta put some shoes on."

"Yes, yes, yes," Calvin stuttered nervously. "And probably a p-p-p-pair of p-p-p-pants as well."

"Aw, man." Calvin heard him pull the sheet from off the bed and risked turning back around. Franklin was now swaddled in white cloth, looking very much like a Roman nobleman.

"Why don't *I* g-g-g-go get *you* a bottle of water?" Calvin asked, then rushed from the room before Franklin had time enough to answer.

Chapter Thirty-Seven

December 20, 1875
Lawrence, Kansas

Junior Mitchell rushed down the stairs and out into the lobby of the Excelsior Hotel. His momma had sent him to find his daddy because his daddy was late coming home, *again*. The lobby was empty, the door shades had been drawn, and the only light in the room came from a small lamp on the front desk. Mr. Caruthers, the hotel manager, had put out *that* sign. When he had gotten old enough to start venturing out on his own, his momma had told him what *that* sign said and had made him repeat it back to her.

For after-hours service please ring bell.

His momma said when *that* sign was out after dark it meant that Mr. Caruthers had gone to bed and should not be disturbed.

One night when *that* sign had been out, Billy Hodgkins had dared him to ring the bell. Billy said that if he didn't, then he was chicken. He had done it. When Mr. Caruthers told his daddy what he had done, he had gotten a whipping. He wanted to ring the bell and ask

Mr. Caruthers if he had seen his daddy, but he wasn't sure that would be reason enough to risk another whipping. Instead, he gave the desk a wide berth and headed toward the saloon.

Junior peeked in through the swinging doors that separated the saloon from the lobby. Mr. Hodgkins was running a cloth across the top of the dark wood surface of the bar. The room was empty, but the smell of beer, and the vinegar-and-water solution that he used for cleaning stunk, and Junior wrinkled his nose.

"Excuse me, Mr. Hodgkins?" Junior called from outside the door. He'd heeded another one of his momma's warnings. She said that if she ever caught him setting foot in the saloon, she would tan his hide. A spanking from his daddy was bad enough, and he wasn't about to risk getting one from her, too.

Mr. Hodgkins looked up from his cleaning. "Is that you, Junior?"

"Yes, sir," Junior said, making sure to add *sir* because his momma said that was how you were to speak to older folks.

Mr. Hodgkins put his finger to his lips and made a "Shhhhh" sound, then waved for him to come inside.

Junior braved taking a single step inside, so Mr. Hodgkins could see him better.

"What's got you out so late?" the bartender asked, crossing the room. "If old man Caruthers hears you out here, he'll tell your pa and you'll get another tannin' for sure."

"I'm looking for daddy," Junior whispered. "Momma says it's late, and we all need to be getting to bed."

For some reason, Mr. Hodgkins found that funny. He shook his head, chuckling softly. "Your daddy should have gone to bed a couple of hours ago." He went back to the bar, picked up his rag, and plunged it into a small bucket. When he brought it out and started wiping down the bar again, the vinegar smell grew stronger in the room and made Junior's eyes water.

"Last I seen him, he was headed around back toward the outhouse. If I was a bettin' man, I'd say he was out there sleepin' it off."

"Okay." Junior stared at him a moment. *Sleeping what off?* He shrugged off Mr. Hodgkin's remark and decided to make the outhouse his next stop. "Thank you," he whispered over his shoulder as he pushed back through the swinging doors.

He entered a hallway off the lobby that led to the back door of the hotel. He hated the hallway. Even in the middle of the day it was dark, but at night, it felt more like a cave. The door at the end didn't have any windows in it to allow light in, and what little light seeped in from the lobby soon faded, leaving him in total darkness.

He wished he had a candle, but his momma said boys his age couldn't be trusted with fire. Probably because Billy Hodgkins had nearly burned down the outhouse using a candle to try and get a look at Mrs. Kilgore who lived on the third floor. Billy had heard from an older boy that she wore garters, and he figured the best time to see if it was true was while she was doing her business. Billy's father had made him mop the floor in the saloon for three whole weeks to pay for the two boards that had to be replaced, and he had to apologize to Mrs. Kilgore, too. Junior thought he would have rather had a spanking.

The heel of his boot struck a loose board and the thud echoed around him. He stopped walking and listened. Mr. Caruthers' room was somewhere down this hall, and he didn't want to wake him.

A board squeaked in the darkness ahead of him, sending nervous tingles down his back and arms.

"Mr. Caruthers?" he whispered, hoping that no one would answer. "It's just me, Melvin Mitchell Jr. I'm headed to the outhouse."

Silence. He breathed a sigh of relief and moved farther into the dark hallway, this time on tiptoes, hoping to not make any other noises. If Mr. Caruthers were to tell his daddy that he woke him up again, there weren't no telling what kind of whooping he'd get.

The floor squeaked again, this time from behind him. The little hairs on the back of his neck bristled and stood on end. His heart raced so hard it felt like it would burst out of his chest. Junior closed his eyes, took a deep breath, and held it until little red bursts of color began to flood his vision.

The squeak came again, closer this time. *I got two choices. Run to-*

ward the door that's somewhere down there in the dark, or look back over my shoulder and see if anything's there.

He summoned all the courage that was stored in his little body and looked back the way he had come. Someone was there, standing just inside the entrance to the hall. The light from the lobby made it impossible to tell who it was. The figure took a step toward him and raised its hand.

Junior's nerve gave way. He ran deeper into the hall, never taking his eyes off the scary figure behind him. A bright light filled the dark hallway ahead of him.

"What the—"

He ran full speed into the large gut of Mr. Caruthers, who nearly dropped the small lantern he was holding.

"OOF!"

Junior bounced off him and landed flat on his back. His breath knocked out of him. Mr. Caruthers leaned in over him, and the little yarn ball at the point of his night cap bobbed forward and touched the end of his nose.

"Melvin Mitchell Jr., I should have known!" he growled. "You just wait till I tell your father that you have been down here prowling around in the middle of the night disturbing my guests. He'll whale the living—"

"Hold up there a minute, Kenneth." Mr. Hodgkins rushed into the lantern's light from the darkness of the hallway. "The boy was just headed to the outhouse to look for his daddy. Guessin' he got a little scared down here in the dark."

"Yes, sir." Junior nodded.

Mr. Hodgkins reached down and helped Junior to his feet. "I was just comin' down here to check on him when he didn't come back soon enough to suit me."

Mr. Caruthers straightened up and cleared his throat so loudly that the rumble could have been heard all the way back in the lobby. "Very well, then." He leaned in and got eye to eye with Junior. "But next time, bring a candle or lantern with you, so you can keep your wits about you and stay quiet." He turned abruptly, went back in his room, and closed the door, plunging Junior and Mr. Hodgkins into total darkness.

Junior heard the bartender reach in his pocket. A second later, a match flared into life.

"Don't let old thunder britches get to you. He's all blow and no wind. You know how to light a match?"

"Yes, sir." He nodded.

Mr. Hodgkins reached back into his pocket, pulled out a box of long kitchen matches, and handed them to him.

"It's dark out back. Not as dark as this old hallway but dark all the same. Better take these so you don't fall in a rut and break your leg."

"Thank you," Junior said meekly, then smiled.

Mr. Hodgkins chuckled and rustled his hair. "Aww, it ain't nothin'. Hope your daddy's okay. Maybe he didn't fall in."

Junior reached into the box, got out one of the matches, and struck it against the heel of his boot. The familiar smell of sulfur tickled his nose.

"Looks like you got it under control." Mr. Hodgkins tousled his hair again and headed back down the hall toward the light of the lobby.

Chapter Thirty-Eight

December 19, 2008
Lawrence, Kansas

The bar of the Excelsior Hotel was located just off the main lobby. Calvin stepped in through the old-fashioned, swinging saloon doors and took a moment to look around the room. The management had done an excellent job of keeping the feel of an Old West saloon alive in that part of the hotel. From the size of the crowd, it was obviously a big hit with tourists.

Country music blared through the sound system and a few couples were taking advantage of a small dance floor built in the far corner of the room. Tall wooden tables were placed haphazardly around the rest of the space, and a long, hand-carved mahogany bar ran along the wall across from the door.

Most of the tables were filled with people drinking, smoking, and having a generally good time, but the bar area was empty except for an older gentleman sitting hunched over and nursing what appeared to be a rather large glass of whiskey. The man seemed oddly out of place in his heavy wool suit and unkempt gray hair.

Calvin made his way through the clouds of cigarette smoke and took a seat at the bar a few stools down from the old man. A stack of paper napkins had been left on the bar, and Calvin took one and began to clean his glasses. The bartender burst through a door to his right, holding a large tray of appetizers.

"I'm by myself tonight!" he yelled to Calvin over the noise of the crowd. "Be with you as soon as I can."

Calvin started to tell him that he was in no hurry, but the bartender had already disappeared into the crowded room. He looked back over at the old man. Surprisingly, the man was also looking at him. Calvin smiled and nodded, but the man just sat and stared at him.

"B-B-B-Busy night," Calvin said and smiled again, trying to be polite.

The man looked around, then back at Calvin and snorted a laugh. "You must be drunker than I am."

"I d-d-d-don't drink."

"You stayin' at the hotel?"

"Um, yes." He wiped the lenses of his glasses in a fast, circular motion.

"Humph, I thought we were the only ones here." The old man tossed back the remainder of his drink, then reached over and pulled a full bottle from a shelf just below the bar's surface, and refilled his own glass. "I know, I know..." He waved a hand in the air, then he reached into his pocket and produced a gold coin. He held it up as if showing it to someone before using his thumb to flip it toward the other end of the bar.

Calvin watched the trajectory of the coin until he lost sight of it in the lights set into the ceiling above them.

"That ought to cover it," the man grumbled.

Calvin was beginning to feel very uncomfortable and looked around, hoping to catch sight of the bartender.

"Where you from?" the old man asked.

The bartender was waiting on a table near the dance floor. Calvin waved his hand in an attempt to get the man's attention but gave up when he turned to take an order at a different table.

"I said, where are you from?" the old man persisted. He pronounced his words very carefully as if he were talking to an idiot.

"Oh," Calvin said, startled. "M-M-M-Massachusetts originally, but now I run a s-small museum in —"

"*Yankee*. Humph. Well, I guess I can't hold that against you." He refilled his glass from the bottle and drank it down. "Me, I was born in Tennessee but spent the biggest part of my life as a traveling doctor. I was in a hellhole called Animas Forks most recently."

Animas Forks. Animas. Where have I heard that before?

"Did-Did you say you were a d-d-d-doctor?" Calvin asked.

"Yes, sir. Served as camp saw bones for Marmaduke's 18th Arkansas Infantry Division." He raised his glass in salute and nearly toppled off the bar stool. "After Lincoln's signature dried, I hit the road, going wherever I was needed, which was everywhere. Thought I was gonna settle down up there in the Colorado mountains, but..." His words faltered into mumbles as his chin dropped down against his chest and his shoulders slumped.

Calvin thought that he had fallen asleep or passed out. He reached over and gave the man's shoulder a gentle shake and almost screamed when he sat upright on his stool.

"That bastard cowboy killed that—just like he killed all them Indians."

"C-C-C-Cowboy? What cowboy?"

"What do you mean, what cowboy?" He poured himself another shot. "The cowboy that got his head split open by the damned witch doctor. You know the one, I told you all about him."

His words became more slurred with every drink. Calvin stared at him in confusion *Could this drunk old man be talking about the very cowboy we were on the run from? How could he know—?*

"I tried to save him!" the man bellowed at the top of his lungs, then slumped over the bar, resting his head in his hands.

Calvin expected the bartender to come over and take the man back to his room or toss him out the door, but he was still calmly taking orders at the table across the room. It appeared that nobody in the place had heard the old man shouting.

"I should've fought back—should've let that flying Indian demon kill me like he did Curtis." The man looked over at Calvin, took another drink, and wiped his mouth on the arm of his sleeve. "I would have been better off dead and in pieces in the street. But no, I tried to help. Now I'm gonna die. The cowboy's gonna kill me. Maybe Ella and Junior, too. What have I done?" He let his head fall back into his hands and quietly wept.

Calvin's mind raced. James and Nancy needed to talk to the man —needed to find out everything he knew about the cowboy. Maybe he could answer some of their questions. *I have to go get them.* He started to slide off the bar stool but stopped himself. *What if he leaves before I get back?* He needed to find out the man's name. Was he staying in the hotel, and if so, what room?

He looked over at the man and watched the steady rise and fall of his back. *Is he asleep?* The old man began to snore softly as if in answer to his thought. Calvin gently nudged his shoulder.

"I gotta piss!" the old man announced at the top of his lungs and sat up. He stood and started to weave. Calvin reached out to help steady him, but the man pushed his hand away.

"I may be drunk, but I'm not drunk enough to need the help of a Yankee!" He took a step, weaved again, then righted himself by placing a hand on Calvin's leg. "Right, it'll be a cold day in hell before Melvin Mitchell drinks too much to make it to the outhouse." He straightened up, squared his shoulders, cocked his head to the left side, closed his right eye, and managed to walk a straight line out the door.

"But, but—"

The old man waved him off and stepped gingerly out of the bar. Calvin watched him closely as he began to sway near the base of the lobby staircase. He grabbed the rail post for support before heading down the dark hall beside the front desk.

"Sorry for your wait, what can I get you?" the bartender asked.

Calvin flinched and almost slipped off the barstool. While he had been watching the old man, the bartender returned to his place behind the bar.

"Easy there, buddy. You okay?"

"Oh, oh, oh, y-yes." With a shaky hand, he reached for another bar napkin, then began rubbing at the lenses of his glasses. "I-I-I, oh what was it I needed?" He held his glasses up to the light. Satisfied with their cleanliness, he slid them back into place. "Now I remember, I-I-I-I was hoping you could give me a bottle of water for my friend upstairs."

"Sure, no problem." The man reached into the cooler below the bar and pulled out a plastic bottle dripping with condensation. He wiped it off before handing it to Calvin. "That'll be six-fifty."

"H-H-How much did you say?"

"Six-fifty," the man repeated in a slow, clear manner.

"S-S-Six-fifty, yes, well." Calvin reached for his wallet and counted out seven one-dollar bills. "K-K-K-Keep the change." He smiled up at the bartender as the man slid the bills off the bar and stuffed them in his pocket.

"Anything else I can do for you?"

"N-N-N-No – Oh, yes!" He reached for another napkin and removed his glasses. "Do you know if the elderly gentleman I've b-b-b-been sitting here talking to is staying at the hotel?"

The bartender peered up and down at the empty bar. "What elderly gentleman would that be?"

Calvin nervously rubbed at the lenses of his glasses with the napkin. "There was an old m-m-m-man sitting here when I came in. W-W-We talked for a while before he excused himself to the lavatory. I think he might be related to a man that my-my-my companions and I have come here to find out about. He said his name was Melvin M-M-Mitchell, which is the same name as a doctor who was around this area back in the late 1800s." He raised his glasses to the light, frowned, and resumed cleaning them. "My c-c-c-companions and I have come a long way looking for information on D-D-D-Dr. Mitchell, and if that man is a relative, he might could give us some insight into his ancestor."

"Look, I don't know who you think you were talking to, but from what I've seen, you've been sitting here by yourself this whole time. It's late. Maybe you should just go get some rest."

"No," Calvin said and threw the napkin down on the bar. "No, no, no. I-I-I-I was talking to an elderly gentleman with unkempt gray hair and a b-b-b-bushy mustache. He flipped a coin to you to pay for the b-b-b-bottle of whiskey he helped himself to from down there b-b-b-behind the bar." Calvin pointed toward the back side of the bar.

"He got a bottle from back here?" The man indicated the area in front of him. "Down here, where I just got you a bottle of water?"

"Yes, yes, right there." Calvin nodded.

"Look for yourself. Ain't nothing down here but a cooler stocked with ice and sodas. All the whiskey is over there on the backbar." He pointed toward the three rows of bottles arranged neatly behind him against a lighted mirror.

Calvin stood and crawled back up on the barstool. He leaned so far over the bar trying to see what was behind it that the bartender had to place his hands on Calvin's shoulders to steady him.

"Satisfied?" the bartender asked.

Calvin looked up into his face and smiled. "Q-Q-Q-Quite. Perhaps I am a little tired."

"No problem. Why don't you take your water and head off to bed?" The bartender slid the bottle of water over to him. "I'm sure you'll remember things differently in the morning."

"Yes, well..." Calvin took the bottle and turned for the door. "I guess I'll say g-g-g-goodnight then. G-G-G-Goodnight."

"Hey mister!" the bartender called out. "If you're looking for info on the olden days around here, you need to go talk to Cactus Clyde. He runs a tourist trap on the outskirts of town. The place is a dump and kinda corny, but Clyde's the real deal. There should be a brochure for his place in the rack over there next to the vending machine. Tell him Little Willie sent ya."

Calvin looked around the lobby and spotted the vending machine and a wooden rack stuffed with tri-fold pamphlets hanging on the wall next to it. He began to thumb through the rows of tourist literature.

Save 50% on your first round of miniature golf at Goofy Golf!
Buy 2 get 1 free at Millie's Moonshine Manor!
Discover REAL TREASURE at Grumpy's Gold Mine!
(Kids half off – You Dig?)

Then he spotted it. A burnt-orange pamphlet with a picture of two men on the cover, facing off in the sunset for a duel. Calvin set the bottle of water on top of the vending machine before pulling the pamphlet free from the rack.

Cactus Clyde's Old West Museum and Gift Shop.
2722 Woodward Street, Lawrence, Kansas

He quickly scanned the information inside, slipped it into his back pocket, and reached up to get the bottle of water. Condensation forming on the sides of the bottles had made it slick, and it slipped through his fingers. He managed to catch it by using his arm to pin it against the plastic window of the machine. A line of bottles identical to the one he had purchased inside the bar for seven dollars were racked up inside. A small sticker attached below them read *$.50*. Calvin took off his glasses and looked again at the price.

Murmuring his frustrations under his breath, Calvin turned, and started up the stairs.

Calvin opened the hotel room door with one had while carrying the expensive bottle of water in the other. "Here's your w-w-w-water, F-F-F-Franklin, you owe me—"

A loud snore came from Franklin's side of the room. His roommate for the night had fallen back asleep, lying flat on his back. He was still naked.

Calvin was contemplating pouring the water over Franklin's head when the sound of a door closing below their window caught his attention.

He bypassed Franklin's bed, all the while looking away so as not to see him presented there in all his glory, and slipped behind the blackout curtains that covered their window. Their view consisted of an empty lot that separated their hotel from its nearest neighbor, the Claremont Restaurant.

He watched a man step away from the building and walk into the empty lot. Calvin took off his glasses and used the edge of the curtain to clean them. Either his eyes were playing tricks on him, or this was the same man he had met earlier in the bar, and he was carrying a lantern. Calvin twisted the cap off the plastic bottle of water and took a drink, hoping it would settle his nerves.

Earlier in the day, he had looked out the window and noticed that the empty lot was filled with gravel and other construction debris, but now, in the light from the man's lantern, he saw a well-manicured lawn. A thick carpet of grass, slightly brown from the recent frosty nights, lay clearly visible beneath the man's feet as he made his way farther from the hotel.

The man walked with a determined gait until he reached the center of the lot where he stopped and raised the lantern above his head. It revealed the base of a small building a few yards ahead of him. He quickly covered the distance to the building and knocked hard enough that Calvin heard the wooden door rattling in its frame. After a second of waiting, the man opened the door and went inside. Calvin stifled a laugh when the lantern's light illuminated a moon that had been carved in the upper third of the door.

Chapter Thirty-Nine

December 19, 1875
Lawrence, Kansas

The cold wind whistled around the building, and Junior shivered as he started across the yard outside the hotel. He had left his sweater upstairs in his rush to do what his momma had asked.

If it's going to be this cold, I wish it would snow.

He was disappointed that there hadn't been any snow yet that year, and now it seemed even more discouraging because it was getting close to Christmas. His momma had told him to not lose hope and reassured him that either way, St. Nick would find his way to his bedside on Christmas Eve. Billy Hodgkins said that there was no such thing as Santa Claus, but Junior didn't believe him.

He had been holding his hand up beside the match to keep it from going out, but a sudden gust of wind pushed past his hand and extinguished the match, plunging him into darkness. He stopped walking and reached into his pocket for the box of matches. Fumbling in the dark, he managed to get a match out of the box and moved to strike it against his heel.

"Who's out there?"

Junior startled and stopped mid-strike, but immediately recognized his daddy's voice. Even so, it sounded strange. His words were slurred, but they also sounded worried.

"It's just me, Poppa," he answered. "Momma says it's time for bed and you need to come on upstairs."

A hard thumping noise echoed across the yard. It sounded like someone trying to open a locked door or like the sound his daddy made when he tried opening the door to their room at the hotel after a late night out at a grange meeting. Sometimes on those nights, his parents would argue. They thought he was asleep, so he would lie quietly in bed. His momma always said that listening to grownups when they were talking privately was bad. He never wanted his parents to think he was a bad boy.

A loud crash caused him to jump and drop the unlit match he was holding.

"What the hell—?" his poppa grumbled from the outhouse.

Junior picked out another match and slid the box closed. Maybe his daddy had come out without a lantern and had fallen trying to leave the outhouse.

"Stay where you are, Poppa! I'll bring you a light!"

He tried to light the match off his boot heel like he had done inside but its sole had become wet from the dew on the ground, and it didn't fire. He tried again but rubbed it too hard, and the head broke off the match.

The crack of splintering wood followed another loud crash. The door to the outhouse opened sending a dim, yellow light across the yard. Junior could plainly see his daddy seated on the platform inside. He started to call out again, but stopped when the silhouette of a large man extinguished most of the light.

"NO! NO—!"

His daddy's cries were cut short.

Junior heard glass breaking, then the little bit of light that was escaping from the outhouse winked out.

"Poppa!" Junior fought with the box of matches and managed to free one before dropping the box on the damp ground. He raised his foot, intending to strike it on his heel, then thought better of it. Mr. Hodgkins struck matches using his thumbnail. Junior tried it. The match didn't light, but he did smell the sulfur that had been stirred up with his attempt.

The sounds of a struggle followed a deep muffled thud. He started toward the outhouse as fast as he dared in the pitch darkness. Someone shouted behind him—probably old Mr. Caruthers, angry that his sleep had been disturbed. He couldn't worry about that now. His poppa was in trouble and needed him.

He began to run, all fear forgotten. He tried again to light the match, but his thumbnail just slid off the head.

"Popp—" He ran headlong into a wall. The small bone that formed the ridge of his nose snapped, and he tasted copper. He hit the wall so hard that it knocked him off his feet. He landed flat on his back in the wet grass. Something moved beside him. He could hear raw, raspy breathing as it circled him. With every breath came a deep wheezing that ended in a soft crackle. Something grabbed the front of his shirt, and he was lifted upward. The heels of his boots scraped across the grass as his legs dangled below him.

"Hey, what's going on out there?" Mr. Caruthers' voice called out in the darkness, and Junior thought he heard feet running on wet grass.

He started to fall. He landed with his legs tangled painfully underneath him. Without thought, he ran his thumbnail across the head of the match. This time, it fired. A dead eye with a split eyelid, a broken and disfigured nose, and a mouth full of rotted black teeth stared down at him. Dead flesh that had once been lips rose into a sneer so full of hate that Junior thought he was looking into the face of the devil himself. He screamed and continued screaming until Mr. Caruthers grabbed him up and pulled him into his arms.

Through his quickly swelling eyes, he could see people running from the hotel. They carried lanterns and candles and soon the yard was bright as the sunrise on a cloudy morning.

"Junior! Melvin Jr.!" Fear and panic filled his momma's voice.

"He's here!" Mr. Caruthers yelled. "I've got him."

"Oh, thank God!" His momma grabbed him and cradled him against her. His nose hurt, and the world seemed to be spinning around them.

"Get me a light over here!" someone shouted.

The words were muffled, like part of a bad dream. The dream got worse when his momma started to scream.

"Mo—" he tried to ask what was wrong, but she placed her hand on the back of his head and pushed his face down against her shoulder. A flare of pain shot through his broken nose.

"Not now, not now." Her words were firm, but she was sobbing around them.

"Go back inside, Mrs. Mitchell," Mr. Caruthers said. "Take care of the boy. There's nothing you can do here." His voice was low and comforting, and Junior felt someone lay a hand on his back. "Go on now," he said.

"Yes." His momma hesitated, then turned and started to walk away. Her hand slid off his head and down to his back. He managed to lift his face off her shoulder.

Mr. Caruthers and another man were standing on either side of the outhouse. The door lay in pieces at their feet. Mr. Caruthers lifted his lantern high in the air. Its light filled the outhouse and revealed his daddy splayed out on the rough, wooden floor. His coat and shirt were covered in blood and where his handsome face had once been, was now a gaping red hole. Junior screamed, and his momma began to run.

Chapter Forty

December 19, 2008
Lawrence, Kansas

"Well, this place is a dump."

James looked over at Franklin and couldn't suppress a grin. Their Indian companion had succinctly put into words what he imagined they all were thinking. Cactus Clyde's Old West Museum and Gift Shop was in fact, a dump. In all honesty, calling it a dump might be insulting to dumps.

The crumbling adobe building sat on a deserted bit of back road noticeably out of place surrounded by sycamore and black walnut trees. Its exterior was coral pink, and two long, rotten hitching posts separated the parking lot from the building's wooden plank porch. A tin roof had been installed over the porch, and it now leaned severely to the left. It rested on an end section which had fallen long enough ago that scrub brush had grown up around it.

A metal sign hanging on an old piece of baler wire bounced in the breeze against one of the remaining support posts. Nancy stepped up and turned it around. Large, block letters had been stamped into the metal. A little bit of red paint could be seen around their edges.

COME ON IN, WE'RE OPEN!

Below that:

Ice cold Kick sold here!

A caricature of a mule kicking his hind legs up so far that they struck the bottom of the K in Kick filled out the bottom of the sign.

"I hope old Cactus Clyde has held up better than his museum," Nancy said as she dropped the sign back against the post with a clang.

"Well, maybe a mite better, but not much!" A ragged laugh filled the air.

An old man wearing full cowboy regalia pushed through a pair of swinging doors and came onto the porch. The spurs on his boots jangled with each step he took on legs severely bowed from too many days in the saddle. He wore a ten-gallon hat pulled down low on his head, spindly wisps of gray hair and a bushy white mustache flowed out from under it. A faded, red bandana was tied around his neck, its ends tucked into the collar of a mud-brown shirt with silver snaps running up its front. He wore a gun belt slung low around his waist with an ivory-colored handle protruding from each holster. He used his thumb to push the hat back on his head, raised his hand, and stepped down off the porch.

"Welcome, partners to—" The gun belt slipped off his hips, tangled around his feet, and he fell face-first onto the short, dirt walkway that led up to the building. "Carnfoundit! Son of a b—"

"Oh, my God! Are you all right?" Nancy ran over and took his arm to help him up.

"'Scuse my language, missy, it's just—well, I'm embarrassed to say, that weren't the first time that's happened." He stepped out of the gun belt, and after a second's consideration, kicked it underneath the weeds growing along the edge of the porch. He slapped at his shirt and pants, knocking loose some of the dust, then straightened up and raised his hand to them as if nothing had happened.

"Welcome, partners, to Cactus Clyde's Old West Museum and Gift Shop! Just inside these here doors lies the greatest collection of Old West memorabilia this side of the Rio Grande. So, hitch yer horses up to the rails and come on in. The next tour'll be startin' just any minute now." He turned on his heel and sauntered, cowboy-like, back inside, letting the swinging door close behind him.

"I-I-I guess that answers *your* question," Calvin said sarcastically and snickered at his own joke. He cut if off abruptly when no one laughed along with him. "May-May-Maybe we should just go inside."

James let Nancy and Franklin fall in line behind Calvin, then hesitated a moment before bringing up the rear. He had a funny feeling, a kind of dread that he couldn't shake. *If I were to yell for them to turn around, get in the car and leave, would it make any difference?*

"You coming?" Nancy had stopped at the door and was waiting for him.

"Yeah." He took a deep breath and forced himself to smile. "Right behind you!"

* * *

Nancy waited for James to catch up to her. It was bad enough that they had to come to this death trap, but if he thought she was going in without him, he had better think again. He leaned in and gave her a quick kiss on the cheek. She wrapped her arm around his and together they stepped through the swinging doors.

Cactus Clyde's Old West Museum and Gift Shop looked no better on the inside. Plexiglass display cases filled with tacky cowboy gifts and knickknacks lined the walls of the first small room that they entered. Horseshoe puzzles, red felt cowboy hats, pop guns, fake vomit and horse manure *(trick your friends!)*, plastic beer mugs, Indian blankets, rubber tomahawks, and feathered headdresses; it just went on and on.

"Do people actually buy this crap?" she whispered to James.

"You'd be surprised what crap people *will* buy, little missy."

She hadn't noticed Cactus Clyde standing behind the old-timey cash register on the counter beside her.

"I'm sorry, I didn't mean to—"

"Ha!" The old man let out a laugh that echoed around the claustrophobically small room. "Don't let it bother you, honey. I can't believe what some folks will lay out good money for myself. Truth is that *this crap* is what keeps the lights on. You'd be surprised how many city slickers come in here and spend forty bucks to get a headdress lined with plastic feathers and a rubber tommyhawk so their spoiled-brat kid can play Injun, but they won't drop a quarter of that amount to take their kid on the tour to learn what the Old West was really like."

He shook his head, then looked back at them. "Look folks, it's been a slow week. Hell, a slow month's more like it. You seem like good people. If you want to take the tour, usually it's ten bucks a head, but I'll let you all in for twenty-five. If'n you don't want to go through the museum." He shrugged. "But I'd shore appreciate it if you bought a little somethin' to help cover the light bill."

Nancy looked up at James, and he gave her a nod. She reached in her pocket, pulled out two twenties, and handed them to Cactus Clyde.

"Thank you, ma'am. You don't know how much that means to an old cowpoke like me." For a moment, she thought he might tear up.

"Step right this way, folks!" Cactus Clyde the tour guide came back as fast as if somebody had thrown a switch. He motioned grandly for them to make their way into the next room. "This is our first stop."

She took James' arm again, and they followed Calvin and Franklin into the dark, musty-smelling room.

"Now where is that carnfoundit light switch?" Cactus Clyde grumbled.

They all stood there in the dark for a moment, then there was a loud snap, and bright, warm light filled the room. They were standing in a model of a mid-eighteen hundred's living room. Wooden sconces hung on each wall, holding oil lamps that had been converted to electricity, but in a nod to the past, each lamp held a bulb made in the shape of a flame. The filament inside glowed and flickered, giving off a warm, orange light.

"Cozy, ain't it? Now if'n y'all don't mind, just find ya a seat, settle in, and I'll tell you the story of the Old West."

A small loveseat sat against one wall, and she and James settled in there. Calvin opted for a rocking chair, leaving Franklin with a straight-back chair that sat beneath a fake window. She watched as Franklin cautiously reached out and tried to touch the windowpane. He seemed disappointed when his finger passed through the window and touched the faded picture of a barn that hung on the wall behind it. He grunted, brought his hand to his side, and dropped heavily into the chair.

"Now that everyone has found their seat..." Cactus Clyde looked over at Franklin who smiled and gave him a little wave. "Right. Now, what you are sitting in is an exact replica of what a home in the Old West mighta looked like. All the furnishings, including the ones you're sittin' on, were brung here from a home located just outside of Santa Fe, New Mexico, near historic Fort Marcy. Now Fort Marcy was active from 1846 till its de-mise in 1868. Here's a funny story—it seems that after the fort had been abandoned for about twenty years, a group of women pokin' around its walls found Spanish money hidden at the base of one of 'um. Well, you can only imag—"

"Was that barn outside the house?" Franklin interrupted.

While they had all been politely listening to Cactus Clyde, Franklin had quietly turned his chair around and was looking out the glassless window.

"I'm sorry, what?" Cactus Clyde sputtered.

"That farm." Franklin pointed at a faded picture hanging on the wall. "Was *that* farm outside *that* window back when it was in the house in New Mexico?"

"No, son," Cactus Clyde said as if trying to explain algebra to an infant. "That there's just a picture I hung up so's if ya looked out the winder you wouldn't just see the wallpaper. There weren't no farms like that one in New Mexico back then. Probably ain't none there today, neither." He cleared his throat. "So, you see these womenfolk found these Spanish coins," he continued his story, "pert near two thousand dollars' worth buried at the base of one a them there walls. Well, word got around the town of Sante Fe, and next think you know—"

"So, this isn't really an exact replica of what this home in the Old West would have looked like then," Franklin said, still facing the wall.

"Franklin, you're being rude," Nancy hissed.

"What?" He turned back around. She gave him her best *will you please shut up* look. "Oh, sorry," he said and smiled sheepishly.

"Humph, well maybe we should just move on." Cactus Clyde forced a smile and opened the door to the next section of the museum. "Inside here, we have an incredible selection of authentic ropes and barbed wire that the ranchers of the time would have used."

She looked up at James and raised her eyebrows. They needed to be on the road, not talking about rope and wire.

"Ask him about Dr. Mitchell," she whispered.

"Ask me about who?" Cactus Clyde said from directly behind them.

They both jumped and Nancy let out a little squeal.

"Well." Cactus Clyde chuckled. "When you're a cowboy workin' the range, you gotta make sure your hearin's good. Never know when a coyote or rattlesnake's liable to sneak up on ya. Now, who was that you wanted to pick old Cactus Clyde's brain about?"

She elbowed James and motioned with her head toward their host.

"Dr. Melvin Mitchell," James said. "I think he was in this area back in the late eighteen hundreds." James paused, and Nancy knew that he was hoping the man would jump in and say something. They had all agreed on the way over that they didn't want to say too much. They were afraid if they started talking about crazy dreams, odd occurrences, and killer cowboys, folks might think they were nuts and throw them out.

Cactus Clyde just stood there looking back at him, his facial features had tightened, and his lips were now just two thin, pink lines underneath his massive mustache.

"Um…" James continued. "I was given an old surgical kit as a gift at my graduation, and I don't know from whom. We have reason to believe that it might have belonged to a Dr. Mitchell. We are kinda researching the history of those tools, hoping that maybe we can find out who sent them to me."

Cactus Clyde's mustache twitched once to the left, then back to the right. "Yeah, there was a Dr. Mitchell around these parts back then. Him and his family lived in the old Hotel Excelsior. That was till somebody killed him out back in the outhouse."

Nancy noticed that he had dropped the old cowboy accent and thought she saw a look of concern wash over his face. She checked to see if James had noticed the change, but evidently, he hadn't.

"That's a coincidence," James jumped in. "That's the hotel where we're staying."

The troubled look suddenly disappeared, and the old Cactus Clyde returned. "Well, ain't that somethin'. Now back to them there ropes I was telling y'all about." He stepped over to the door and motioned for them to move into the next room. "You know, a cowboy without a good rope is like a snake trying to wear a sweater. It just don't work!"

Nancy looked up at James and shrugged, then took his hand and they walked into the rope room. Franklin and Calvin slid in behind them. "He should have asked about the cowboy with the scarred face," Franklin whispered.

"Shhhh," Calvin hissed, trying to make him be quiet.

Cactus Clyde slammed the door, and they all turned and faced him. He seemed to be standing taller. The bow in his legs had disappeared, and they watched spellbound as he reached up and peeled the mustache off his upper lip. He removed the ten-gallon hat, and with it came the wisps of white hair. Underneath, he had a head full of black hair with just a little gray at the temples. He ran his hand through his hair as he turned toward Franklin. "What did you say?"

"Nothing?" Franklin smiled and shrugged. "It's just, well you see, we all had this dream about a cowboy, one with a scar across his face. He was wearing a bowler hat and had—"

"A sword on one hip and a pistol on the other?" Cactus Clyde's voice was dead serious, his tone flat and foreboding. "Also had a little one-shot pistol in the pocket of his vest."

Franklin nodded and reached for the pack of cigarettes in his shirt pocket with a trembling hand.

"You can't smoke in here." Cactus Clyde walked over and sat on a bale of hay that was part of the room's decorations.

"Okay," Franklin said softly. "I'll just step outside and—"

"No!" Nancy, James, and Calvin all said in unison.

"Okay," he whispered and slid the pack back into his pocket.

"So, he's back?" Cactus Clyde said to no one in particular. "It's been so long, I hoped he was gone for good this time."

Nancy walked over and sat next to him on the bale. "Hoped who was gone?"

"The cowboy."

She looked up at James. He raised his eyebrows and shrugged.

"The cowboy from our dreams?" she asked hesitantly.

"Yep, that's the one." Cactus Clyde looked into her eyes, then across the room at the others. "I'm sorry."

"S-S-S-Sorry for what?" Calvin asked.

"You know for what." Cactus Clyde's voice was cold and direct. "People that see the cowboy don't live very long."

"Look," James said, "if you know something about this cowboy, then speak up and stop with all this bull—"

Cactus Clyde was on his feet and in James' face before he could finish. "Know something? Know something? I know everything, and I know that there is nothing I can say or do that will make your lives last even one day longer once the cowboy is on your trail. It's just a matter of time till he finds you, and you end up like ol' Doc Mitchell, his son, and the others who have crossed his path." He stepped back and took a deep breath. "You're good as dead, boy." His tone had changed to one of sad acceptance—no longer angry. "And if all of you saw the cowboy, you all are as good as dead, too."

Nancy was on the verge of tears; she wiped at her eyes, then hovered her hand for a moment over her midsection. Her mind flashed back to the dream where she was rocking the dead baby. Her tears returned and she rushed over to James, flung her arms around him, and cried heavily on his shoulder. He gently stroked her hair, and his arm encircled her waist.

"Shhhh, it's okay, everything's going to be okay," James whispered.

"Evidence!" Calvin's voice echoed around the room. "Evidence! W-W-W-What evidence do you have to back up w-w-w-what you're telling us?"

Nancy lifted her head off James' shoulder and wiped her eyes dry with her sleeve. Calvin stood face to face with Cactus Clyde, and she thought he almost looked courageous in such a defiant position.

"You want evidence, little man?" Cactus Clyde stared back at Calvin.

"Y-Y-Y-Yes." Calvin shrank back from Cactus Clyde's unblinking stare. "Please?"

Cactus Clyde returned to the bale of hay, but instead of sitting on it, he pushed it aside with his boot, revealing the outline of a trap door. He reached down, stuck his finger in a small hole in one of the planks and pulled it open. Beneath was a wooden stairway leading down into darkness.

"Don't stand there gawkin'! You wanted evidence, come on and get it."

Cactus Clyde disappeared into the hole, and they could hear his boots descending a flight of wooden stairs. A moment later, a light came on, filling the opening with a warm glow.

"What do you think?" James asked Nancy.

"In for a penny, in for a pound, I guess?" she answered but wasn't so sure that she meant it.

The four of them gathered around the hole and peered down into it.

"W-W-W-Well, here goes." Calvin put his foot on the first step and bounced a little like he thought it might break under his weight. When it didn't, he smiled and started down. Nancy went next, followed by Franklin. At first, James hesitated, then followed them down, pulling the trap door closed above him.

Chapter Forty-One

April 22, 1902
Providence, Rhode Island

"Goodbye, Mother."

Melvin Jr. laid a single rose on the loose dirt of his mother's grave, then placed the palm of his right hand on the surface above where he thought her heart might be located six feet below. The soil was warm to the touch, and he thought that was how it should be.

"I'm so sorry for your loss, Junior."

Reverend Thaddeus Thibodeau stood next to him with his hand out. Junior smiled and allowed himself to be helped up. Thad was not just the minister at the local Missionary Baptist church, he was his mother's dearest friend and oftentimes constant companion.

"Death is never an easy thing to accept, but your mother did it gracefully. She was a wonderful woman."

"She loved you, you know." Junior said, looking into the man's sad eyes. Thad had not released his hand and he used that grip to pull the reverend into a hug. "You should have married her," he whispered.

"Don't think I didn't try." Thad let go of Junior's hand and looked down at the grave. "I knew I loved her the first time your Aunt

Prudence brought you two to the church. I don't think I took my eyes off her the entire time I was preaching. She was absolutely radiant sitting there in the pew with the sunlight streaming in on her through the stained-glass windows." Thad smiled and turned back to Junior. "The first time I asked her to marry me was a year later at the Founder's Day picnic. She told me *no* that day and again the next year when I asked her, and then every year after that. It became our special tradition. Every Founder's Day I would propose, and every Founder's Day she would turn me down."

"Did she ever tell you why?"

"Yes, she did, three weeks ago." He reached out and placed his hand on Junior's shoulder. "I was standing next to her sickbed as we watched the Founder's Day parade pass by her window. I asked her to marry me. She took my hand in hers, and in that whisper that was all she had left of her voice, she said no, as I expected her to do. *I've asked you to marry me every Founder's Day for twenty years*, I told her, *and twenty times you've said no*. I had never asked her why before, but this year seemed different, so I asked."

He slid his hand off Junior's shoulder and returned it to his Bible.

"What did she say?"

"She said that she had allowed herself to love two men during her life. Her first husband, and then your father. She went on to tell me how both of the men she loved had died horrible deaths, and that she felt cursed. Then she said the most beautiful words I have ever heard. She said, *Thad, I love you too much to risk your life by allowing you to be my husband*."

Thad brushed away a tear.

"That sounds like something she would say." Junior was well aware that his mother always put others first in her life. His mind drifted back to the time after his father died, and she had made the decision to return home, to where she had grown up. They'd traveled first by stage, then on a train. It had been a long trip from Kansas to Rhode Island for a little boy with a broken heart and a broken nose, but she kept him occupied by reading to him, teaching him card games, and telling him stories about growing up in New England. He could not have asked for a better mother, and as she lay in her bed, wasting away from the disease that was eating her alive, he had made sure to tell her that every chance he could.

"So, what is next for Dr. Melvin Mitchell Jr.?" Thad asked.

"That's a good question—I really don't know. Mother saw to it that I received a good education, and she pushed me toward medicine. I don't mean that badly, I'm glad she did. I had no idea what I wanted to do with my life, and thanks to her, I discovered a love for treating those in need." He paused as a wave of grief passed over him. "There is no need for another doctor around here. You can't swing a dead cat without hitting one kind of doctor or another."

Thad laughed at that, and it gave Junior a moment to collect his thoughts.

"I think once I get Mother's affairs in order, I'm going to head west. She never told me much about my father, other than he was a good man and that he loved me. I think I'm going to go back to Kansas City or Lawrence, Kansas, to be more precise, and see if anyone there remembers my parents. Maybe if I can find a connection to my father there, it will point me in the direction I should go. I know that seems frivolous, but Mother left me well cared for, so I can stand to spend some time finding my way without having to worry over my next meal."

"I think that is a marvelous idea. A boy, or I should say a *man*, needs to know where he came from. Roots are important."

"Thank you. For some reason, hearing you say that makes my decision easier. I've never told you this, but I've always looked up to you. When I was younger, I used to pray that you would marry my mother so that you *could be* my father. Childish dreams I guess, but I have always thought of you that way."

"And I have always looked at you as my son." Thad pulled him into a hug.

He wept openly onto his surrogate father's shoulder until his eyes failed to make any more tears. He had felt so alone leading up to his mother's funeral, and hearing Thad say those things filled his heart with joy and overwhelming sadness at the same time. He dried his cheeks and wiped his nose with his hand, then absentmindedly wiped it on his trousers.

"Thank you." He looked into Thad's red-rimmed eyes. "Thank you for always being there, for Mother, and for me. I—"

"There's no need to thank me. I did it out of love for the both of you." Thad reached up and wiped away a tear from his own eye, then took a deep breath and let it out slowly. "Enough of this. What will people think if they see two grown men standing around crying on each other's shoulders?"

"I guess we do make quite a sight, don't we?"

"We do, we do at that. You mentioned getting your mother's affairs in order. What do you have left to do?"

"I just have to go through a few of her belongings in a closet, and an old trunk. I plan on donating her things to the Women's Aid Society at the church before leaving. Other than that, it's just a matter of closing her account at the bank. I plan to leave the day after tomorrow."

"That soon?" Thad's eyes widened in surprise. "I had hoped we could spend some more time together, but if that's your plan, then you need to stick to it. How about I come over and give you a hand sorting you mother's things, and I can take your donations for the church when I go?"

"I'd appreciate that. I plan to be at the bank in the morning when it opens, so how about noon?"

"Noon it is, and I'll bring us something to eat while we're working."

He could tell that Thad was searching for something else to say.

He understood how Thad was feeling. His mother's death had not come as a surprise, but how do you ever prepare for the loss of someone who had been your guide and protector for your entire life? There were no words to express the loss and no true words of comfort. This all felt very final, very over. He nodded and started to turn away, but Thad grabbed him by his shoulders and pulled him into another embrace.

"I love you, Son."

Chapter Forty-Two

December 19, 2008
Lawrence, Kansas

James stepped off the stairs and into the bunker. *If that's what you call it.* It appeared to run the length of the tourist trap it sat beneath. The walls were lined with stained and faded maps all of which had different markings—in multiple colors—that marred their surfaces.

A computer had been set up in one corner of the room. The large screen above it showed video feeds from six different cameras. Three were focused on the exterior of the building, and a fourth showed the interior of the room directly above them. Cameras five and six showed the parking lot and dirt driveway that led up to the building.

Two glass cases stood waist high in the center of the room. Inside the one closest to James were pistols, knives, arrow heads, bits of clothing, and other relics. He walked around to the second and found it full of wanted posters, telegrams, and newspaper clippings, some of which were identical to the ones he had received in the package with the surgical tools.

"What is all this, Cactus Clyde?" Nancy asked, pulling James' attention away from the cases.

"First off, let's drop the *Cactus Clyde* stuff. My name is actually

Clayton Caruthers. Cactus Clyde is a character my grandfather came up with when he started this place back in the fifties. He's also the one that built this..." He raised his arm and motioned around the room. "I guess you would call it a research and surveillance center."

"So, you're Cactus Clayton!" Franklin exclaimed. "Cool." He stared at the computer's monitor screen, then slowly reached out and touched it with his finger.

"No, you can all call me Clay. And stop that!" Clay took Franklin by the arm and pulled him away from the monitor and back over with the rest of them.

"Okay, Clay," Nancy started again. "What is all this?"

"This is a complete—or as complete as possible—tracking of the cowboy you saw, from his first appearance back in 1870 to the most recent in 1984. The computer that your friend here was so amused by runs twenty-four-seven scouring the internet for any mention of ninety-seven different keywords that my father, grandfather, and myself have come up with over the years to tell when he's been seen. I was standing right here the last time it found anything. Twenty-four years ago, it pinged on a small story in an Estelline, Texas newspaper called the *Estelline Register*."

Clay opened the glass case full of clippings, took out a small section of yellowed paper, and held it up for them to see.

"It reads, *a local drifter known only as Little Cesar was admitted to the Hall County Hospital after he was found wandering through the streets in the area most affected by last night's freak tornado. Although there were no signs of a head injury, Little Cesar insisted that moments before the tornado struck, he had witnessed a zombie cowboy emerge from a column of flame and walk into a local pawn shop.* It goes on to say that the pawn shop that the cowboy allegedly entered was moments later leveled by the tornado, leaving two men dead."

"What would you think if I told you that I saw him yesterday?" James asked.

Clay didn't answer, he just turned his head to the side and gave him a quizzical look.

"He was on the concourse of the Kansas City airport, watching us as we got in a cab to come this way."

"You say that was yesterday?"

James nodded.

"So, he's here." Clay returned the clipping to the glass case and gently closed it. "Our mysterious cowboy has returned to Lawrence, Kansas."

Chapter Forty-Three

April 23, 1902
Providence, Rhode Island

"On behalf of First Union Bank of Providence, please accept our heartfelt condolences." Mr. Wetsdale rushed out of his small office off the lobby of The First Union Bank the instant Junior stepped through the front doors. He was a short, round man prone to aggressive sweating, especially when it came to folks taking their money from his bank.

Junior recalled his mother saying time and time again that she wished she had started her account in The Fidelity Bank of Providence, but since Mr. Wetsdale was a *personal friend* of her sister's, she had started it at First Union and never moved it. Junior had spent all morning working up the nerve to go there. Now that the bank manager was looking up at him with beads of sweat standing on his forehead, he found it hard not to laugh, knowing how upset Mr. Wetsdale would be once he learned what he intended to do.

"And Junior, on a personal note, just let me say that every time your mother set foot into this bank, it was as if a fresh summer breeze flowed in with her."

"Yes, sir, Mr. Wetsdale, you are not the first to tell me something like that. My mother was a very special lady, and she will be missed terribly by all who knew her, especially me."

"Of course." Mr. Wetsdale nervously shuffled his feet and wrung his hands.

It was obvious that the next move would have to be Junior's. He had been running over what he planned to say in his head all morning.

"Mr. Wetsdale, as you know, my mother left all her personal belongings and holdings to me. I have decided to go west, so I will be withdrawing her holdings here at the bank and closing her account. I would appreciate it if you would see to that immediately as I intend to leave first thing in the morning."

Mr. Wetsdale just stared up at him, with his mouth open and eyes glazed over.

"Mr. Wetsdale?"

"Oh, oh yes." The banker removed a silk handkerchief from his coat pocket and dabbed at his forehead with it. "Yes, of course, but might I suggest a different plan? You say you are going west, well that can be very dangerous. I would suggest you leave the bulk of your mother's estate here at the bank for emergencies. I could give you say, *four hundred dollars* to get you on your way, and if you were to run into trouble, a simple wire transfer could be done in just a matter of days. I believe that is a *much better* plan, don't you? So, if you will follow me over to the desk, I will arrange a cash withdrawal for the four hundred." Mr. Wetsdale started toward the teller's desk.

Junior placed his hand on the man's shoulder and stopped him. "I appreciate your concern, but I've made up my mind. Now, if you will, please close out my mother's account and give me her holdings. In cash." He smiled down at the little man and noticed that his complexion had turned a light shade of green.

"But Dr. Mitchell—"

"*Now*, Mr. Wetsdale."

The banker's shoulders drooped, and the smile he had been feigning the whole time turned into a sneer.

"Right this way." Mr. Wetsdale turned his back on him and walked over to the row of teller windows that flanked the rear wall of the bank.

Junior forced himself not to smile as the banker made a show of opening and closing the locked door into the teller area. Mr. Wetsdale then went to a shelf of ledger books behind window number one and pulled out the book marked with an *M* in gold leaf on the spine. He began flipping through the pages and made some notes on a tablet, then motioned for Junior to step up to the first window.

Mr. Wetsdale loudly cleared his throat. "Our records indicate that your mother had a total of fourteen thousand, two hundred and twenty-seven dollars and seventy-two cents in cash in her account plus a small jewelry box and two unnamed items stored in our safe. If you will sign here, I'll have the lead teller fetch your cash as I remove the items from the safe in the back room." He passed a withdrawal slip through the window and watched silently as Junior signed it. "Very good." With that, he walked away, stopping only to hand the slip to an older gentleman sitting behind the third teller window.

A moment later, he disappeared through a heavy wooden door into the back room of the bank.

Fourteen thousand, two hundred and twenty-seven dollars and seventy-two cents. He knew his mother had been frugal with her savings and that she had inherited a small amount when her mother had passed, but he never expected there to be such a substantial amount in her account. Mr. Wetsdale had also mentioned a jewelry box and two other items in the safe. He remembered that on special occasions, his mother would wear pearl earrings and a diamond broach, but he always assumed that they were just nice costume pieces. It never crossed his mind that they might be real. And the other two items, what could those be? She had never said anything to him about any of that.

"Excuse me, sir."

Junior was so deep in thought that he had failed to see the older teller step up to his window. Surprised, he caught his breath, then laughed. "I'm sorry, Mr. Sellers, it's been a hard, few days. I'm afraid I was doing a bit of woolgathering."

"Think nothing of it. I have your mother's savings. If you would please count it, then sign this document stating that you were paid in full and are releasing the bank of any liability toward the safekeeping of the funds." He pushed a small stack of bills and a few coins through the window.

Junior picked them up and went carefully through the bills. There were twenty-eight five-hundred-dollar gold certificates, two one-hundred-dollar gold certificates, a twenty-dollar Liberty Golden eagle, a five-dollar half-eagle gold coin, two silver Morgan dollars, a Barber silver half dollar, two Barber dimes, and two Indian Head pennies. All in all, more money than he had ever seen in his life. The money felt heavy in his hands, so he slid it back to Mr. Sellers and signed the paper.

The teller placed the money in a brown envelope and handed it back to him. "Your mother was a grand lady. It was an honor to know her."

Junior smiled and nodded to him. *Good tidings and fourteen thousand, two hundred and twenty-seven dollars and seventy-two cents. That's all that's left of my mother...*

Mr. Wetsdale reappeared a moment later with a worn, leather messenger's bag, a wooden box about the size of a loaf of bread, and an envelope. "You are welcome to use my office to check your mother's things before you go." His voice was curt, but resigned.

"That won't be necessary." Junior offered the bank manager his hand, and Mr. Wetsdale shook it firmly, leaving it moist. "On behalf of my mother, please accept my thanks for all you have done for her over the years." He fought back the urge to wipe his hand on his pants leg.

"Thank you, Junior. I mean, *Dr. Mitchell*. It has been my pleasure."

The banker gave a slight nod, then went back into his office and closed the door. Junior took another moment to look around the bank. He couldn't remember how many times he had accompanied his mother there to do business. Now that he had her things and was about to leave, it felt as if a chapter of his life was over and a new one was about to begin. He took in a deep breath, enjoying the smell of old wood, coal smoke, and money, then turned and walked out into the midday sun.

* * *

"Hello!" Thad called out. "Junior, are you here?"

Junior's mother, Ella, had been a meticulous housekeeper, a place for everything and everything in its place. Now, the living room of the modest home she had shared with Junior seemed cold and empty. Ella had filled her home with mementos and remembrances of family and friends, and when in season, there would be fresh flowers in glass vases spread around the room. Even though the outside temperature was comfortable, Thad felt a shiver run across his back at the sight of the barren room, now devoid of any sign of the woman he loved. For a moment, he pictured Ella sitting on the settee, her knitting flowing from her lap down onto the upholstered cushions, and a pang of grief filled him.

"I'm in here, Thad!" Junior's voice echoed from the kitchen.

Thad quickly moved that way, his footfalls echoed off the bare walls and came rushing back at him. *Ghosts,* he thought to himself and shivered.

Junior was at the kitchen table surrounded on three sides by empty shelves and cabinets; even the icebox stood open with all its contents removed. Thad set the small bundle of food on the shelf nearest the table and looked over at what Junior was studying.

"What's that you've got there?"

Junior opened an envelope that was sitting on the table next to him. He reached in and removed a single piece of paper.

"Did you know my mother had some items stored in the safe at the bank?"

Thad shook his head. Over the years, he and Ella had become close, but two things she never talked about were her finances and her days before coming back to Providence. He knew that she had been married twice and that both men had died tragically, but that was the extent she had been willing to divulge.

"These were in the safe." Junior again showed him the letter, then opened a wooden box and removed a small, leather messenger bag. Inside the bag was a rolled cloth. He flattened it out on the table, then lifted a flap of material to expose its contents.

"What is that?" Thad asked, moving in for a closer look.

"Surgical tools."

Junior turned the bundle around so he could get a better look at the bone-handled instruments. Each one safely stored in small pockets that had been sewn into the cloth.

"Those must have belonged to your father."

Junior nodded. "They did."

"What's in the letter? If it's not too personal," Thad quickly added.

"Read it for yourself. Maybe it will make more sense to you than it does to me." Junior stood up and stretched. He went over to the back door and looked out at the small back yard.

The letter was filled with Ella's beautifully flowing handwriting, and Thad traced a finger over the first few lines before he began to read.

Dearest Melvin,

If you are reading this, then it means my time here in Providence has finally come to an end and I will soon know if the heaven Thaddeus is so fond of speaking about really exists. I pray that it does.

It also means that you now have in your possession the only thing of your father's that I have kept over the years: his surgical tools.

You are well aware of the secret that they carry, and it's your responsibility to see to it that they never again bring the heartache to any other that they brought to me and your father. I chose to hide them away in a bank safe. The decision is now yours as to their care.

I'm sorry to lay this burden on you, but I could never bring myself to part with them.

I love you, Son. You have grown up to be a man who would have made your father proud. Wear his name with honor.

Mother

Thad read the note over again, then looked on the back of the sheet to see if there was anything else. When he saw that there wasn't, he joined Junior at the back door.

"Before you ask," Junior said flatly, "no, I don't know what the secret was. She never told me."

"She must have thought there would be more time."

"It's just another mystery surrounding my father that I will hopefully find the answer to." He ambled back to the table and tucked the letter into the breast pocket of his coat.

"I don't know much about surgical tools," Thad began, as he walked back over to the table, slipped the scalpel out of its pocket, and studied it in the light from the window, "but it appears that these were well cared for."

"My father must have been very careful with them," Junior said as Thad slid the scalpel back in place and closed the flap. "Who knows? Maybe they will bring me good luck." Junior secured the kit with the leather tie, and slipped it back into his father's bag. "I guess only time will tell."

Chapter Forty-Four

December 19, 2008
Lawrence, Kansas

Clay stepped over to a bookshelf and carefully removed a notebook. "My great-grandfather's name was Clayton Kenneth Caruthers. I'm named after him, as were my grandfather and father."

"So, you're Cactus Clayton the Fourth. Cool," Franklin said from across the room where he was still staring at the video feeds.

"No, I'm not. My family felt that numbering the generations was something only rich folks did, so I'm just Clayton Kenneth Caruthers. Anyway..." Clay placed the notebook on top of one of the display cases and opened it. Inside, it had page after page of old-style photo album inserts, the type with glue on them that held the pictures in place along with the thin sheet of plastic that covered them.

He pointed at one of the photos. "This is my great-grandfather standing outside the Excelsior Hotel in 1873. That's the year he began working there as manager. The little boy beside him is my grandfather, they called him CK. If you look closely at the picture, you can just barely see a man standing in the door of the hotel. That is William Hodgkins, and he's important to the story."

"My great-grandfather was there at the Excelsior the night that the cowboy killed Dr. Melvin Mitchell. He beat him to death while the doctor was taking a crap in the outhouse behind the hotel. Two people witnessed the murder—my great-grandfather and Dr. Mitchell's son, Melvin Mitchell Jr."

"When I received the tools," James interrupted excitedly, "there was also an envelope filled with newspaper clippings. The oldest was the report of Dr. Mitchell's death. It said he was killed in a vacant lot. It doesn't mention an outhouse."

"No, it doesn't. I have a copy of that same article here in the files. Outhouses were a necessity back then but not something that would have seemed fit to print."

"So," Nancy said, "when your great-grandfather saw the cowboy kill Dr. Mitchell, was that when he became interested and started trying to find him?"

"Well, yes and no. Random violence like Dr. Mitchell's murder was not uncommon at that time here in Lawrence. The town was busting at the seams with cowboys either heading west with a herd or just coming in off the trail. Homesteaders and highwaymen were always passing through as well. You mix all those folks together, add alcohol, hunger, and greed into the mix, and violence is what you get."

He pulled their attention back to the photo by tapping it with his finger.

"If you remember, I told you that the Excelsior's bartender, William Hodgkins, played a part in all of this. This is where he comes in. It seems that after Dr. Mitchell saved the life of a little boy who had been shot multiple times, he became quite a drinker. One night after a few too many rounds, Mr. Hodgkins overheard him tell a man at the bar that he was gonna die. Heard him say that *the cowboy with the split face* was gonna kill him. The other man asked him what he was talking about, and that was when Dr. Mitchell told him a long and frankly unbelievable story about Indian demons, medicine men, and a cowboy who had his face split open. Hodgkins put it off as the ramblings of one old drunk talking to another and didn't think anything else about it till the doc was killed later that night."

"That was me," Calvin said softly. "That w-w-w-was me!" he repeated much louder.

"What was you?" Nancy asked.

Calvin took off his glasses and started furiously cleaning them with his handkerchief. "L-L-L-L-Last night, I thought it was a dream, but—" He held his glasses up and looked at them against the light from an overhead fluorescent bulb, then started rubbing again. "But it w-w-w-wasn't. I-I-I went down to the b-b-b-bar to get Franklin a bottle of water—"

"Why didn't you just get it from the vending machine?" Franklin asked. "It's a lot cheaper."

James pointed his finger at him and mouthed, *shut up*.

Franklin nodded, looking confused.

"Go on Calvin," James said.

"Y-Y-Y-Yes, well that's it, I mean, w-w-w-what Clay just said, that story. I don't know how, b-b-b-but I was there. I was the man D-D-D-Dr. Mitchell was talking to. I was going to come g-g-g-get you and Nancy to come talk to him. I thought he was another l-l-l-lodger there at the hotel. Maybe a relative of the original Dr. Mitchell. B-B-B-But before I could get you, he got up and left."

"Let me guess, you are all staying at the Excelsior Hotel, aren't you?"

James nodded.

Clay grunted. "Figures. There have been rumors of that place being haunted for years. I never gave 'um much credit, but—"

"We've all had strange dreams, Clay. Even before we got to the Excelsior, we all shared a dream about that cowboy murdering a group of stagecoach passengers. That's what led us here. Franklin had a dream as well that told him to find us so that he could help us get rid of the tools. He says that if we do, we can put an end to the killings that have been surrounding them for over a hundred years."

"Did you say you all dreamed about the death of a group of stagecoach riders?"

Nancy nodded.

Clay took a deep breath and swallowed hard. "After Mr. Hodgkins told my great-grandfather about what he had overheard, my great-grandfather began asking around town if anyone else knew anything about a disfigured cowboy in the area. He even asked at the local newspaper if there had been any stories or rumors of such a thing. Everywhere he went, he got the same answer—*no*. That was until he ran into a man named Jedidiah Dawson Rose, folks called him JD, he worked for the stage line. When Great-Grandfather asked him about the cowboy, he told him that he had not seen it, but he had overheard Doc Mitchell and Mrs. Gattis talking about someone that fit the description."

"So that was enough for him to start digging deeper," Nancy said, just above a whisper. "Confirmation from a different source."

"It was, but that's not everything. JD also told him that he had picked the doc and Mrs. Gattis up on the trail after they had stopped when they found a dead body. It had been cut into pieces and the parts strewn out along the side of the road. A minister that had been traveling with them had died there as well."

"The dead man's name was Shay. He was a gambler." Nancy's hand trembled as she spoke. "The minister was named Jacobs. There was also a coach driver that they called Turk." James put his arm around her and pulled her close.

"That would be Turk Brennan," Clay said. "He was found dead a week later at a stage relay station run by a family named Turnbull. The men that found him said they'd never seen anything like it. Turk and another driver were found dead inside a wagon full of supplies they were supposed to deliver to the station. Old man Turnbull, or what was left of him after the vultures had gotten to him, was lying in the dirt outside the wagon. They found Mrs. Turnbull beaten to death inside, and their son, Gene, dead with a bullet wound in his back. Their daughter, Marie, was missing. They never found her, but from the amount of dried blood they saw inside the barn they just assumed the worst."

Nancy's knees buckled. James grabbed her before she could fall. Franklin brought the chair from the computer table over and held it as James lowered her into it.

"The authorities chalked it up to an Indian raid, but my great-grandfather didn't believe it, so he set out to find the truth. The day after Dr. Mitchell's funeral, he went to talk to Mrs. Mitchell. When he told her about the death of Turk Brennan and the Turnbull family, she broke down and, through her tears, admitted that everything Mr. Hodgkins had heard her husband say was true. He didn't want to press her any harder in her upset state, so he asked if he could come back the next day, and would she be willing to tell him everything in hopes that he could track down the cowboy and see that justice was served. She agreed. But when he came back the next afternoon, Mr. Hodgkins told him that Mrs. Mitchell and her son had taken the morning stage and hadn't left a forwarding address."

Clay closed the book and replaced it on the shelf. Nancy was crying softly in the chair while James gently rubbed her shoulders.

"W-W-W-Where did she go?" Calvin asked.

"Turns out she went to Providence, Rhode Island, but he didn't discover that till nearly thirty years later. By then, he had set up the first version of this place in an empty storage room in the hotel, and my grandfather was helping him in his search. They sent telegrams out to newspapers across the area weekly, asking if there had been any stories or rumors about a cowboy with a scarred face or anyone named Mitchell that had caught their attention. One week, they got a reply from the editor of the *Silverton Standard* out of Silverton, Colorado. He said that they were hearing rumors that the doctor at the Calvary Mine had been killed mysteriously. The doctor's name was Melvin Mitchell Jr."

"Jesus," James whispered, and Nancy placed a hand on top of his. "We have an article from the mine's newsletter about that as well."

"Really, I'd like to see that. We don't have it in our collection."

"We left the clippings and the tools out in the car. I'll—"

"I'll get it!" Franklin shouted and ran for the stairs, simultaneously pulling a pack of cigarettes out of his shirt pocket.

"Wait!" James called out after him.

Franklin came to an abrupt stop on the bottom stair. "What?" The cigarette trembled between his fingers, and he anxiously shifted his weight from one foot to the other.

"I locked it. You'll need the key to get in the back." James tossed the key across the room, and Franklin snatched it from the air.

"Anything else?"

"Nope, just remember you have to—"

Franklin disappeared up the stairs before he could finish his sentence.

"Anyway," Clay continued. "My grandfather left that afternoon for Silverton, and from there, he went on to the Calvary Mine that you just mentioned. That's where he got these."

He turned back to the same shelf that held the photo albums and pulled down a manila envelope. Sealed inside it was a plastic storage bag of handwritten letters. He broke the seal, and the room immediately filled with the odor of old paper and dust. He gingerly removed the pages, and placed them on top of the display case.

"The general manager of the mine gave these to my grandfather along with a bundle of clothes and an old Bible. We discarded the clothes years ago, and the Bible is on a shelf in one of the displays upstairs. This is how he found out where Mrs. Mitchell and her son went after leaving Lawrence, Kansas, and this is what led to my grandfather buying this place and making it his life's work. These are letters written to Reverend Thaddeus Thibodeau. They, along with the Bible I told you about, were left behind when Dr. Mitchell Jr.'s wife left the area after his death. They did some research on Reverend Thibodeau, and it seems that he was murdered in his office at the Providence East End Missionary Baptist Church approximately two months after Mitchell Jr. left town. The secretary at the church said he considered Mitchell—they called him Junior—to be like a son to him. So, the church sent the letters along with Thibodeau's Bible back to Junior Mitchell along with the news of the reverend's death."

"Did the authorities in Providence find who killed him?" Nancy asked.

"No." Clay grimaced. "All the sheriff said was that the body was so brutally mutilated that it had to be the work of a madman." He looked up at Nancy and James. "And that it appeared from the look of the wounds that the madman must have used a sword."

Chapter Forty-Five

July 4, 1907
Effingham, Illinois

Independence Day celebrations were in full swing as Melvin Mitchell Jr. rode into the small community of Effingham, Illinois. Red, white, and blue bunting hung from the roof of the massive courthouse, showing bright in the midday sun against the building's dark red brick and white stone corner blocks. A small brass band played on the steps of the courthouse as families picnicked on the lawn, their checkered tablecloths covered with plates of fried chicken, biscuits, and potato salad.

A pistol shot rang out, and two men on horseback raced down the street. The crowd that had gathered to watch the day's festivities cheered them on. Junior drew closer and saw that a makeshift grandstand had been constructed along the street next to the courthouse.

It had been over three months since he'd lost his mother and set out from Rhode Island to try and learn more about his father. Thoughts of his mother still crossed his mind on a regular basis, sometimes bringing a smile to his face, sometimes a tear to his eye. The smiles were coming more often than the tears as the days slipped past.

But now, he was hungry, and his horse needed water.

He rode across the street, that just a moment before had been a racetrack, hoping to find a café or bar for him, and a stable or blacksmith shop for his horse.

Someone was playing guitar farther down the street and the music cut through the noise of the crowd. It was an upbeat melody that sounded familiar. A high-pitched voice joined in, and he immediately remembered where he had heard it before.

"Oh, dem golden slippers.
Oh, dem golden slippers.
Golden slippers I's goin' to wear because they look so neat.
Oh, dem golden slippers.
Oh, dem golden slippers.
Golden slippers I's goin' to wear to walk the golden street."

His mother would sing that song while she cleaned the house. It was one of her favorites. She sang it as *them* golden slippers, but it was definitely the same song. He vividly remembered playing in the yard outside the kitchen window, listening to her sing as she moved around doing her daily chores. He loved his mother's voice and would scoot over underneath the window to listen to her. That was a *smile* memory.

A group of people—mostly women—were gathered around the entrance to a small building near the end of the street. As he got closer, he discovered that the source of the music emanated from somewhere in front of them. A row of businesses lined the opposite side of the street: a butcher shop, a barber shop, a dress maker, and a leather goods store which had a hitching post. He tied his horse there. Hopefully, someone inside could direct him to a nearby stable.

"That's a beautiful horse you've got there, mister."

A young lady stepped out of the leather goods store and into the bright sunlight. Her blond hair, and the white apron she was wearing, reflected the sun back at him, giving her an angelic look. She had a patch of freckles scattered across each cheekbone that only added to her angelic appearance.

"He looks tired." She gently ran her hand down his horse's nose. "You look pretty beat yourself."

"Humph, I guess I do at that." He realized that he had been staring at her and forced himself to look away while he knocked the trail dust off his jacket and trousers. "I don't know if that's much better." He smiled. "But it'll have to do." He waited a moment for a response, but it didn't come.

"We just got into town," he went on, "and don't know our way around. Is there someplace where a man could grab a steak, and a horse could get some water and maybe a feed bag?"

"At the same place?"

"I um, well, I mean, no—" The question caught him off guard, and he stumbled for an answer.

"Slow down there, fella." She smiled and laughed. "I'm just messin' with ya. We got a small stable and water trough out back. Cost you two bits to feed and water this big boy."

The horse whinnied and lifted his head against her hand.

"That's right, you're hungry ain't you, sweetheart?" She spoke to the horse like it was a hungry child. It shook its mane and whinnied again, evidently enjoying the attention. "As for you…" She looked up at Junior and smiled again. "Right across the street, where all them folks are gathered around is the Sunshine Diner. They just got a new cook, and there ain't no better place in town to get a bite."

"It must be good to have a line like that waiting to get in."

"That line ain't for the food, it's for the little black boy that sits on the stoop all day long playing and singing. Can't be no more than five years old. His granny's the one doing the cooking, and his daddy's waiting tables. Now, scoot on over there and get a bite while I get— what's your horse's name?"

Junior shrugged. "I just call him *horse*."

"Really?" She looked up into the horse's big brown eyes. "He looks like a Gary to me." The horse snorted and stomped the ground with his front hoof. "Gary, it is! Now, as I was saying, you go on over there and eat, and I'll take Gary here around back and see that he's taken good care of."

"Thanks, I really appreciate it."

"Ain't no bother."

She flashed a quick smile that made her nose wrinkle and the freckles on her cheeks appear to dance, then took the reins and began to lead the horse down the street.

"Wait!" Junior called out.

She stopped, then whispered something into the horse's ear before turning around. "Yes, sir?"

"I'm sorry." He took a few quick steps to catch up to them. "I didn't get your name."

She looked over at the horse. "I told you he was gonna ask my name." Gary whinnied and pawed at the ground. "You think I should tell him?" The horse shook its head, and the girl laughed. "Now, don't be all like that. I think it'd be all right." She turned and extended her hand. "They call me Julia, Julia King."

Junior took her hand in his and shook it.

"I'm Melvin Mitchell Jr. Folks back home just call me Junior."

"It's a pleasure to meet you, Junior. Now, if you'd be kind enough to let go of my hand, I'll get busy seeing to Gary here."

He jerked his hand back and felt the heat of embarrassment rush into his cheeks. She winked and led Gary away. He watched them until they passed behind the building and probably would have continued standing there, but a loud grumble from his stomach got his attention.

The crowd had thinned a little outside the café, and he could just see a little black boy hunkered down on the stoop, holding a guitar that was almost as big as he was. He was smiling up at the women that towered over him while he played the instrument with a zeal and ability that would have been hard to believe from someone three times his age.

"So, it's good-bye, children, I will have to go.
Whar de rain don't fall or de wind don't blow.
And yer ulster coats, why, yer will not need.
When yer ride up in de chariot in de morn."

His voice was high-pitched but on key and he sang like a seasoned professional. Junior thought back to the stories he had heard growing up about dark-skinned folks that would sing in the street for money when they couldn't find work in the fields or mines. His mother said it was in their nature; that while they were slaves, they would sing messages to each other in code so the plantation owners wouldn't know what was going on. For a moment, he was lost in the idea of beautiful voices like this one drifting in from the fields and how that beauty contrasted with the torment and inhumane conditions that so many people like this little boy had been forced to endure in the name of commerce and greed.

"But yer golden slippers must be nice and clean,
and yer age must be just sweet sixteen.
And yer white kid gloves yer will have to wear,
when yer ride up in de chariot in de mornin'."

Junior found a place where he could step in between some of the members of the boy's rapt audience. Julia said she thought the boy was five years old, but he thought that eight or nine might have been a better guess. He was small for his age and scrawny, one skinny arm reached over the top of the guitar to hit the strings as the bony fingers on his other hand worked expertly up and down the neck.

"But yer golden slippers must be nice and clean,
and yer age must be just sweet sixteen.
And yer white kid gloves yer will have to wear,
when yer ride up in de chariot in de mornin'."

A threadbare cap sat on the side of the road at the boy's feet, and the sun twinkled off the few coins resting in it. Junior noticed that the boy was carefully scanning the faces of the folks watching him.

"Howdy, mister! Can you spare a penny?" the boy asked between verses. His smile was bright and contagious.

Junior fished around in his jacket pocket until he found a silver dollar. He flipped it toward the hat, and it landed perfectly in the center of the other coins. Its weight caused them to bounce, and they jingled when they landed.

"Gee whiz, mister, you must be rich!" the boy shouted in surprise, then began to play again.

"Oh, dem golden slippers!
Oh, dem golden slippers!
Golden slippers I'm gwine to wear,
'cause dey look so neat.
Oh, dem golden slippers!
Oh, dem golden slippers!
Golden slippers I's gwine to wear,
To walk de golden street."

He ended with a flourish, then jumped to his feet and gave a deep bow to the people watching before grabbing his hat and ducking into the café. Junior noticed that he walked with a limp, favoring his right foot as he ran. The crowd slowly broke up and began making their way back toward the courthouse and the activities going on there.

Junior looked at his reflection in the glass window of the café. He ran his fingers through his hair. He could use a haircut and a shave, but all in all, he thought he was in good enough shape for the Sunshine Diner.

It was warm inside, but he didn't mind. He was too busy enjoying the mouthwatering smell of cooking meat and baking bread. There was one empty table, so he took a seat and started studying the menu board that hung on the wall opposite the window. The special of the day was bean soup with ham and cornbread. Written in the lower left corner of the board, there was also a list of pies to choose from. Lemon meringue was his favorite, and it was third on the list.

The kitchen door opened with a loud squeal from its hinges. A tall, thin black man wearing a dirty apron came into the room, holding a plate of steaming food in each hand. He set them down on the next table over, then turned to Junior. The man reached into the pocket of his apron and brought out the silver dollar that he had tossed to the boy outside. "My boy say you give him that for playin' his guitar. It's too much." He put the coin on the table. "A silver penny says thank you for playin'. That there dollar is charity, and we don't take charity."

The door squeaked again. Junior looked that way and saw the little boy peek out at his father.

"My apologies." Junior slid the coin off the table and back into his pocket. "That song he was playing reminded me of my recently deceased mother. It touched my heart, and I felt led to give him something special for providing me with the memory."

"A silver penny will do just fine."

"Good enough, then. May I give this to him directly?"

"Elijah!" the man called back over his shoulder. "Hustle out here. This man gots somethin' for ya."

The kitchen door slammed open, and the little boy ran up to the table. Junior dropped a silver penny into his hand.

"Thank ya, sir!" The boy flashed that contagious smile again.

"You're very welcome," he said, smiling along with him. "You play beautifully and sing beautifully as well."

"Thank ya! I lernt from my daddy and my granny."

"They taught you well."

"Get on up outta here." The boy's father reached down, put his hand on the boy's head, and physically turned him back toward the kitchen. "Your granny needs help peeling taters. Do good and I'll let you go outside and play some more when you're done."

"Yessir."

Elijah ran to the kitchen without looking back. Junior saw again the pronounced limp and wondered what was wrong.

"You look hungry," the boy's father said. "Now what can I get ya?"

"I'll take the special and a piece of the lemon p—"

"Make that two!" Julia took the chair across for him. He hadn't even noticed her come in. "You don't mind, do you?" She cocked her head to one side and gave him a shy grin.

"Make it two." Junior held up two fingers to the waiter.

"And Ezra," Julia said, "ask Miss Martha to make one of her special bacon sandwiches for Daddy. He's busy and can't get away to come get it himself."

"Sure thing, Miss Julia." Ezra smiled down at her, and she smiled back.

"How's my horse?" Junior asked her as soon as the man left the table.

"Gary? He's happy as can be. There's a young mare in the stall next to him. I think they're kinda sweet on each other."

"Ah, horse love, it's a beautiful thing."

"It is to the horses." Julia raised her eyebrows and giggled. "Word around town is that you gave little Elijah a whole silver dollar for playing a song. You must be some kind of big spender, huh? I should have charged you four bits to take care of your animal."

He plucked the dollar out of his pocked and showed it to her.

"Word travels fast in Effingham, I'll have to remember that."

That made her laugh, and he noticed that she had dimples to go along with the freckles.

"So, your daddy runs the leather goods store, and you work there with him. What does your husband do?"

Her sly grin returned. "Don't think that I don't see what you're doing. It's not polite to ask a lady if she is spoken for, *but* there's nothing says you can't ask about her husband. You get the same information either way."

"I'm just trying to make civil dinner conversation. If you would rather go back to discussing my horse's love life, we certainly can."

"I'll have you know, sir, that I am not married. Nor am I engaged, spoken for, betrothed, or affianced. I am twenty-three years old and gloriously single. Plus, Daddy has a shotgun and says that any boy that comes sniffing around will get both barrels in the belly."

"Which explains the former."

"Very much so."

Little Elijah came out of the kitchen and brought them a plate stacked high with cornbread. "Daddy says to say that the soup'll be out lickety-split. Y'all want coffee?"

"Coffee sounds good to me," Junior told him. "How about you, Miss Julia?" She nodded.

"Two coffees' comin' right up!" Elijah limped his way back to the kitchen.

"Do you know Ezra and little Elijah very well?" he asked Julia. "I don't like the way he's struggling when he walks."

"I really don't. Daddy just hired them last week. This is only the second time I've been in. Daddy comes over here almost every day for a bacon sandwich. He says they seem to be good people."

"So, your daddy owns the leather goods store *and* the Sunshine Diner? He's quite the entrepreneur."

"He is that," she said, the knowing smile again lighting up her face. "And he owns a lot of other businesses around town, too."

Junior chuckled and looked away a moment to compose himself. There was something about her that tied him up inside and made it hard to concentrate.

"Do you think it would be rude if I asked Ezra about it? Elijah's limp, I mean. I'm a doctor. I might could help."

"You're a doctor?" She pressed herself against the back of the chair and sat up much taller. "Only doctor I've ever known is old Dr. Chester, and he's...well...*old*."

"Doctors do grow old, or at least the good ones do. But we don't start out that way." He grinned. "Relax, I'm on my lunch break."

Julia's shoulders slumped a little, and she leaned over and put her elbows on the table. "You're really a doctor?"

"I am." He placed *his* elbows on the table as well and interlaced his fingers. "I graduated from the Rhode Island School of Medicine about this time last year. I was looking for a place to start a practice, then my mother died, and I decided to come out West and try to solve some of the mysteries of my family history."

"I'm sorry you lost your momma." Julia placed her hand over his. "My ma passed a little over four years ago. It's been pretty hard on Daddy and me. How did your father take it when you told him you were leaving?"

He took a deep breath. Why was he telling this stranger his life history? Was it because she was beautiful? Was it because she seemed so sincere when she asked? He didn't know, but what he did know was that he was very comfortable sitting there with her and wanted nothing more than to go on sitting there and talking to her all afternoon. "My father's dead."

She squeezed his hand tighter.

"He died when I was little," Junior continued. "I don't remember much about him, just the few stories that my mother told over the years. That's why I'm on the road. They lived outside Kansas City when they were first married, so I'm headed there to see what I can learn about him."

"Hrumph." Ezra cleared his throat as he stepped up to the table. "Sorry to interrupt, but I's got your food here, and if I ain't mistaken, that there's Miss Julia's daddy hightailing it across the street. Prolly best you two ain't holdin' hands once he gets here."

Junior had gotten so comfortable talking with her that he didn't realize they were still touching. Julia's eyes grew wide, and they both snatched their hands back into their laps. Ezra set the food down in front of them just as her father came through the door.

"Granny 'bout got that sammich ready for ya, Mr. King," Ezra said. "I'll fetch it right out fer ya!" Ezra glanced back at the table as he was turning to leave.

"Julia King," Mr. King bellowed, "where have you been? I'm just about to starve to death and—" he stopped short when he noticed Junior.

"I'm afraid that's my fault, sir." Junior stood and offered his hand to Mr. King. "Your daughter was kind enough to take care of my horse when I first stopped outside, and when she came in the diner, I figured she would be a good person to ask about Effingham. You see, I'm a doctor, and I'm looking for a place to start a new practice."

"A doctor, huh? You think that makes it all right for you to instigate a conversation with a young lady to whom you have not been formally introduced?" He pushed Junior's hand away. "We are not heathens here in Effingham, Mr. –?"

"Mitchell," Julia offered.

"Mr. Mitchell," Mr. King continued. "So, I will thank you to confine your business with my daughter to matters concerning your horse and only your horse. Do I make myself clear?"

"Absolutely, and I apologize for my forwardness." He turned to Julia who was still seated and had been intently watching them. "And my apologies to you as well, Miss King. I pray I have not offended you." He bowed his head in her direction and was thrilled when he saw her smile return.

"Very well," Mr. King interrupted before Julia could speak. "We will be taking our leave now." He extended his hand to Julia, who took it and allowed herself to be helped up. "Ezra, where's that sandwich?"

Ezra rushed through the door with a small bundle wrapped in butcher paper. "I's got it right here, Mr. King. Granny says she give you extra tomater today."

Mr. King took the sandwich. "Thank you, Ezra." The man led Julia outside and across the street.

"You sho' can pick 'um." Ezra fought back a laugh until Junior smiled.

"I guess I can at that." Junior sat back down. "Take a load off, Ezra." He pointed at the chair opposite him. "Looks like everybody's well taken care of, and I can't eat this much food all by myself."

Ezra looked around at the other customers. They were all eating and happily absorbed in their own conversations.

"Thank you, I think I'll do that, but I best let Granny know that I's taking a break. Elijah can run coffee and tea if anybody's needing it."

Ezra went back into the kitchen and returned a second later carrying a massive piece of lemon meringue pie. He set it next to Junior's plate before sitting across from him and beginning to eat.

"So, you's a doctor?" he asked around a mouthful of soup. "Might lot of work to be a doctor I 'magine."

Junior nodded and crumbled a piece of cornbread into his soup. "A few years at the university, then some time studying under a more experienced doctor in order to learn everything that *they* didn't teach me." He scooped up a spoonful of soup and saturated cornbread and tasted it. The soup was warm, salty, and delicious. It filled his mouth with a greasy, comforting taste. He licked his lips and had to take another bite.

"Tain't bad, huh?" Ezra asked with a smile.

"Not bad at all!" He took a sip of coffee to wash it down. "Ezra, do you mind if I ask why little Elijah is limping? It looks like his foot is hurting."

"Yes, sir." Ezra lifted his bowl and drank down what was left of his soup. "Boy stepped on an old barrel hoop playing out back a few days ago. Cut his foot pretty bad, but it's okay. Granny cooked up some mustard greens in a bunch of vinegar and made him a poultice. She says he oughta be better any day now."

"The vinegar should help to fight off any infection, but a poultice full of wet greens could slow the healing of the cut," Junior said around another bite of cornbread. "Do you think Granny would mind if I took a look at his foot? I could possibly help out what she's already done and maybe reduce the pain a bit."

Ezra looked up at him, and Junior wasn't sure what he was seeing in the man's face. "Not that I think she did anything wrong, mind you," he quickly added, concerned that he may have overstepped. "I would just like to help if I can."

Ezra smiled and nodded. "You'd do that for us?"

"Sure, why not?"

"'Cause you *white*, that's why not." He leaned back in the chair and crossed his arms over his chest. "Granny hollered for old Doc Chester when the boy first done it, but he never come. Found out later that he don't help folks like us."

It had been over forty years since President Lincoln had ended slavery in the United States, but Junior knew full well that it hadn't ended the hatred and distrust between the races. Part of him thought that would never end. "I'm sorry for that. It's not right. I promise, I don't feel that way, and if you'll let me, I'd like to try and help little Elijah."

"We'd like that. Granny was worried that she ain't done enough. After my wife run off a few years back, Granny took over being momma to the boy. She the reason he play and sing like he do. Now, I can pick a little, but Granny, she put me to shame."

"Maybe I'll get a chance to hear it. Tell me where you live, and I'll come by after the café closes and see what I can do."

A worried expression washed over Ezra's face, and he looked down at the empty dishes on the table. "That's prolly not a good idea. We live cross the line in Spookville, at least that's what the folks around here call it. Folks there don't cotton much to folks like you comin' round, know what I mean?"

"I do." Junior nodded. I seemed like every town had their own version of *Spookville*. A place off the beaten path where the dark-skinned folks could live without the whites having to see them. It was okay for them to work in their stores and restaurants, or to dig their ditches and harvest their crops. But when it was time to shut out the lights and go to bed, they wanted to make sure that none of them were left in town. *Out of sight, out of mind*. "Why don't I just come back here after you close up for the night? I'll bring what I need, and we can get him patched up then."

"Yes, sir, *yes, sir*. That'd be just right." Ezra stood and started putting the empty dishes back on the tray. Junior also got to his feet and extended his hand to him. Ezra looked down at it like it was something totally foreign, then began to chuckle and nod.

"Ain't you somethin'!" Ezra grabbed his hand in an iron grip and gave it a hard shake, then released it and picked up the tray. "Ain't you somethin'!" he repeated and walked off carrying the tray of dishes, all the while chuckling and shaking his head.

Chapter Forty-Six

December 19, 2008
Lawrence, Kansas

Franklin burst through the door of Cactus Clyde's Old West Museum and out into the parking lot like he had been blasted out of a cannon. The cigarette he had been wanting so badly jittered around between his trembling lips, and he had to concentrate to hold it still so he could get it lit. He inhaled deeply and held the smoke in his lungs until they started to burn, exhaled, then settled happily into the dull buzz he always enjoyed after going too long without a nicotine fix.

He closed his eyes and leaned against James' old Bronco until his head stopped spinning. The sun warmed his face, and he stayed there enjoying its heat until he finished smoking.

Remembering why he had come outside in the first place; he went to the back of the Bronco to open the hatch but couldn't find a handle. He ran his fingers down the edge of the door, then leaned out and checked the side. *Nothing.* He stood back, scratched his head, then snapped his fingers. The spare tire, it was mounted over the hatch door. If he took off the tire, he bet the latch would be underneath. The spare was draped with a ripped and faded vinyl cover. He reached around the back to try and pull it off. His hand hit a lever and the tire swung forward, nearly knocking him over. If he hadn't wrapped his arms around the tire and ridden it out, he would have been flat on his back in the dust.

With the tire out of the way, he went back to the task of finding the door latch. There was no latch. He pulled the pack of cigarettes from his shirt pocket, flipped open the lid, and placed a cigarette between his lips. He felt of his shirt pocket for the lighter. When he didn't feel it, he stuck his hand in his pants pocket. Instead of the lighter, he found James' keys. He pulled them out, looked at them like he had never seen keys before, then remembered what James had said as he was leaving the basement. *You'll need the key to get in the back.*

Halfway down the hatch door was a keyhole. He stuck the key in, turned it to the left, and nothing happened. He shifted his cigarette to the other side of his mouth and turned the key to the right. There was a quiet hum, and the window lowered.

"Well, that's a stupid way to roll down a window," he mumbled to himself. "And the stupid door still didn't open."

Determined to get the clippings and bring them back with him, he decided to just crawl in through the open window. He put one foot on the bumper and grabbed the top of the tailgate. The latch was there. He pulled it, and the tailgate fell open.

"They must have been drunk the day they designed this." He shook his head and reached inside.

The small messenger bag containing the tools and clippings was wedged between the back seat and the rest of their luggage. He crawled inside the cramped space and reached across for the messenger bag; it was stuck. He pulled at it again with no luck. He got up on his feet and crouched over inside the small compartment. Using the strength in his legs, he tried again. The bag broke free, causing him to tumble out of the cargo area and into the parking lot.

He landed hard, flat on his back on the packed dirt surface. The force of the impact knocked the breath out of his lungs and the messenger bag out of his grip, spilling its contents. In a panic, he grabbed the clippings before they could blow away and stuffed them back into the empty bag. *Empty bag? Where were the tools?* He flipped like a beached fish over onto his stomach and looked underneath the Bronco. The open roll was there with the tools in the dirt all around it.

He peeked around the side of the truck to make sure no one had seen what happened. The coast was clear, so he belly-crawled under the tailgate and gathered up the tools. He made sure to carefully wipe the dust off each shiny surface before he put them back in the roll and secured it closed. He placed the roll of surgical tools back inside the messenger bag. With a sigh of relief, he sat up and slammed the top of his head against the tailgate.

"Shit, shit, shit!" He closed his watering eyes and put his free hand on his head, then used his feet to push himself backward until he was clear of the tailgate. When he opened his eyes again, an Indian maiden was standing in front of him holding a feather.

Franklin leapt to his feet, tossed the bag back into the Bronco, and closed the tailgate. Not for one second did he take his eyes off the woman. He again touched the top of his head and winced when he felt the knot forming there. *I'm seeing things. I hit my head hard, and I'm seeing things.*

He stepped to one side of the Bronco and backed a little farther away from the woman. She had dark brown hair that hung straight down her back till it ended just above her waist. Her eyes were the color of red clay and matched her skin perfectly. She was wearing a buckskin dress painted with black, red, and yellow patterns, and her feet were bare.

"Are you for real?" he asked.

The maiden nodded curtly, glanced to her left down the driveway toward the main road, and held the feather out toward him.

"You want me to have that?"

She nodded again.

"Okay." He reached out and took the feather from her. The instant he touched it, the world exploded into a swirl of colors, his stomach lurched, and he began falling toward its center. Wind rushed past him. It filled his ears with a roar and brought tears to his eyes. He tried to scream, but the sound was ripped from his throat and carried away before it could be heard. He closed his eyes and began to pray to the Great One for salvation. If he were to hit bottom at this speed, he knew he wouldn't survive.

Suddenly, there was *silence*. The ground grew solid under his feet. For a moment, he stood there afraid to open his eyes, afraid to move. Birdsong filled the air around him, and the heat of the sun warmed his face. He slowly risked opening one eye, and then the other.

The maiden was still there, and he was still holding the feather, but their surroundings had changed. They stood on a dirt track that crossed the precipice of a mountain. The maiden motioned to her right, toward the smoldering ruins of an Indian camp, then to her left, toward a small town nestled in a plateau. The dirt track they were standing on originated from the town's only street. The name Animas Forks passed through his mind like a whisper, then was gone.

She led him to the side of the track and positioned him with his back against a rock outcropping. He looked back to where they had been and gasped. A portion of the road was gone. Where it had been was now a shallow grave. A massive Indian warrior stood above it, holding a limp and lifeless body. Franklin recognized the warrior from his dream; but in his dream, *he* had been that warrior. Draped across the warrior's arms was an old man that bore the marking of a shaman, his body crisscrossed by a thousand healed cuts, and multiple puncture wounds riddled his ancient chest.

"Floating Feather," Franklin whispered, and the feather in his hand grew warm to the touch.

The warrior knelt beside the open grave and gently lay the body in it. When the medicine man's flesh touched the earth, steam rose up around it, thick enough to obscure Franklin's view.

The steam dissipated. The giant Indian was again standing beside the grave, but now he held the body of a white man. The man was larger than the old Indian had been and was dressed in old-fashioned brown coat and trousers. He stared in horror at the gaping hole where the white man's face had once been. Again, the warrior knelt and gently placed the body in the grave, and like before, a massive plume of steam rose around it. This time when it cleared, the warrior was gone and the path appeared as it had before, undisturbed.

Franklin looked over at the maiden, hoping for an explanation, but she had changed. Gone was the beautiful girl with the flowing black hair and deep brown eyes. A rotting corpse replaced her. The features were the same, but they had been smashed and broken into a death mask. Cracked and bloody skin wrapped tightly over ridges of broken, protruding bone, turning the beautiful face into a mask of nightmares.

He tried to let go of the feather, but it had woven itself into the skin of his palm and fingers, its shaft becoming one with the flesh. The feather grew hotter and hotter until a white glow engulfed his hand. The dead maiden began to cackle, her laughter like fingernails on slate. Black blood oozed from her eyes and her open mouth showed rows of dark, broken teeth. Her gray withered hand shot out and grabbed his glowing hand. She slammed it against the rock outcropping with unbelievable force, sending pieces of stone flying and lightning bolts of pain up his arm. He screamed and jerked his hand free. Pain rippled through his palm and into his wrist as the pieces of his fingertips that had adhered to the rock were torn away.

The colored swirl returned, and he felt himself lifted off the ground. As his vision blurred, he saw that there was now a carving of a feather in the rock. Both maidens were standing beside it with their hands interlaced. The beautiful maiden openly wept, while the dead maiden laughed. He reached out for them, then began to fall.

* * *

"So," Clay said, "you are telling me that you believe the tools are what the cowboy is following—the surgical tools—not necessarily the bloodline of Dr. Melvin Mitchell? Have I got that right?"

"Actually, it's both," James answered. "Somehow the tools find their way to any male in Dr. Mitchell's bloodline who becomes a doctor. Then, when they are used, that doctor becomes famous, or at least highly respected in his field. Not long after, the doctor dies horribly, and the tools disappear until another doctor comes along in the family line."

"And how did you come to know this?" Clay inquired. "There's nothing in the records to suggest it. I mean the surgical kit is mentioned in a couple of articles, but it has never been shown to be an integral part of the story."

"Franklin told us," Nancy answered. She was growing tired and had begun to feel nauseous again. Her head ached from being down in the closed, damp-smelling cellar for so long, and she wanted to go upstairs for some fresh air.

"Franklin, the Indian. And just how did he come by this revelation?"

"How doesn't matter," James stated.

"I didn't believe it either until he proved it to us." Nancy knew that James didn't want to tell Clay about the ancient ram's horn and peyote thing, but this dancing around the truth was getting them nowhere. "Since then, everything he has told us has shown itself to be true." Her stomach gurgled, and she put her hand over it to try and calm it down.

"Prove it? How did he prove it?"

"Look, this is going to sound ludicrous, but he—"

"S-S-S-Sorry to interrupt," Calvin said from across the room. "But d-d-d-do you see this?" Calvin pointed at one of the camera displays on the computer.

"What the hell?" Clay moved closer to the screen.

Nancy stood in awe, staring at the monitor. Franklin was floating in the air next to James' Bronco, and his left hand was glowing.

* * *

Clay rushed up the ladder and threw open the trap door. James, Nancy, and Calvin followed close behind. They rushed through the museum and out into the parking lot. Clay skidded to a stop and held out his arms to make sure none of the others ran past him.

"We better not get any closer." He hoped he sounded confident and in control because on the inside, he was everything but that. "Has he ever done this before?"

"Nope, this is new," James said stepping up beside him.

"I think we should—" Clay was about suggest that they move closer to see if they could get an idea of what was holding Franklin up, but at that moment Franklin dropped out of the air and landed flat on the hard surface of the parking lot.

Nancy pushed past him and rushed over to Franklin.

"I don't think that's a good idea," Clay said. Before he could say anything else, James and Calvin followed Nancy, leaving him standing alone just outside the museum entrance. It suddenly struck him that although he had followed in his father and grandfather's footsteps tracking the mystery of the cowboy with the scarred face, he had never truly believed in it. Up to now, it had been a spooky ghost story. One that he had loved to hear his father and grandfather tell, but this...this was something completely different. The cowboy was a character of coincidence, a nightmare brought to life through circumstantial evidence from random newspaper clippings.

Could James actually have seen something at the airport? That could have been anything, a reflection, a camera flash, but *he* had seen the Indian floating in midair, *he* had seen his hand glowing so bright in the midafternoon sun that it had left a burn on the camera monitor, *he* had watched him fall and heard him land on the ground.

James and Nancy were helping Franklin to his feet while he cradled his hand against his chest and appeared to be in some pain.

"I think I've got some burn cream in the first-aid kit inside," Clay said.

James looked over at him and nodded.

"I'll be right back."

The first-aid kit was tucked away below the cash register. It had been ages since he had needed it, and it had gotten shifted to the back of the shelf. He had to push rolls of cash register tape and extra advertising pamphlets out of the way, then lean in with his head against the edge of the counter to reach it. His fingers grazed the latch of the red-and-yellow metal box, only managing to push it even farther back. He strained and managed to get the extra half inch of reach he needed. This time, he hooked the thin metal handle with his middle finger. A bright green light appeared in his vision, and a buzzer rang out at that exact moment. He flinched away from the counter and landed flat on his rump with the first-aid kit in his lap.

The buzzer blasted again, accompanied by the flash of green. His father had installed a notification system many years before to let them know upstairs when the computer in the bunker had a hit. In the twenty-four years since the alarm last sounded, he had never once checked to see if it was still working. Evidently, it was.

He used the counter for balance as he pulled himself to his feet and placed the first-aid kit next to the register. Looking out at the parking lot through a window that was coated with dust and grime, he could see the Indian gesturing wildly. Clay grabbed the kit and started for the parking lot when the alarm sounded again.

He stopped and looked back out at his guests. Nancy had pulled Franklin into a hug, and James had a hand on his shoulder. The emergency seemed to have passed. They could do without the burn cream long enough for him to go into the bunker, check the computer, and reset the alarm.

* * *

Franklin's words spilled out in a long and incomprehensible string that James was having trouble following. Something about a grave, an Indian maiden, a zombie, and a feather. He was babbling, crying, and gesturing wildly with his hands, all the while trying to light a cigarette. Every time he managed to place one in his mouth, his tears would drip on it, soaking the paper and making it impossible to light. After his third failed attempt, Nancy took the half-empty pack and the lighter from him. She placed a Marlboro Light between her lips and rolled the lighter with practiced precision, then transferred the cigarette to Franklin before exhaling a plume of gray smoke.

Franklin managed a trembling, "thank you," and threw his arms around her.

James placed a hand on Franklin's shoulder in hopes that he would let Nancy go so they could get to the bottom of what just happened.

"S-S-S-Stop that and let go of her!" Calvin barked and Franklin did just that.

"I'm sorry," Franklin whispered and wiped his nose with the back of his hand.

"That's b-b-b-better. Now pull yourself together and s-s-s-start over. What is that you were saying about a z-z-z-zombie feather?"

"No, man. The feather wasn't a zombie, Nijlon was."

"Wh-Wh-Who is Nijlon?" Calvin looked around at the three of them for an answer.

"It was his great-great aunt," Nancy said.

"Four greats," Franklin corrected her. "I saw Nijlon, and she was in bad shape, but before I saw her, I saw Keegsquaw. She's the one that gave me the feather."

"Wh-Wh-Wh-Who's Keegsquaw?" Calvin asked, sounding something like a broken record.

"She was Franklin's great-great—"

Franklin held up four fingers.

"Four times great-grandmother," Nancy finished.

"Of course she was." Calvin rolled his eyes, then motioned for Franklin to continue.

"Keegsquaw was the one who gave me the feather."

"W-W-W-What feather?" Calvin interrupted again and Nancy shot him a dirty look.

Calvin just shrugged and tried to smile.

"Go on," Nancy said.

"Yeah, Franklin," James jumped in. "What feather are you talking about?"

"The one that did this." He had been keeping his left hand close to his chest, now he slowly took it away. The hand itself it was an angry red and had swollen to almost double its normal size. Burned into the palm was the blistered shape of a feather.

* * *

In the bunker, the alarm was even louder than it had been upstairs. Clay jumped down the last few steps and ran to the printer. Nothing was happening there, so he turned his attention to the computer monitor. The small section of the screen that showed the camera focused on the driveway was a mass of static. The alarm had not sounded because the computer had gotten a hit, it was because it had lost signal from one of the cameras. He tapped a few keys, and the alarm stopped, throwing the bunker into eerie silence. A shiver ran down Clay's back as he accessed the playback controls of the camera recordings and shuttled the driveway camera backward.

* * *

"I d-d-d-don't understand." Calvin was cleaning his glasses furiously with the tail of his shirt. "You say that your ancestors miraculously appeared to you and forced you to watch as a giant ghost warrior buried two men in the middle of a dirt road, then she set your hand on fire with a feather—"

Clay burst out of the museum at a full run. James could see that his arms were full, and he was headed directly for them.

"Get in the car!" he yelled. "Get in the car *now*!"

"Clay, what's—?"

"Get in the freaking car!"

Nancy pulled open the door, pushed the driver's seat forward, and shoved Franklin and Calvin in before jumping in with them.

James scarcely had time to get behind the wheel before Clay tossed everything he was carrying onto the seat and slammed the door. "Drive!" he screamed.

James started the Bronco and threw it into reverse.

"No!" Clay slammed his hands down onto the dash. "Not that way. Around the building and out the access road through the trees."

James put the transmission into drive, then pushed the gas pedal to the floor. The Bronco's wheels spun on the packed gravel, sending a cloud of dust into the air. They careened around the building. He spotted an old set of tracks leading off into the woods. The old Bronco groaned as it fishtailed onto the dirt track. The vehicle bounced around the uneven trail. Small branches slapped against the windshield and rearview mirrors.

"Jesus, James, slow down!" Nancy cried out as a particularly big rut caused her to bounce up and hit her head against the roof.

"*No!*" Clay told him. "Whatever you do, do *not* slow down. In about thirty seconds we are going to come to a road. Turn left and keep your foot on the gas till we get into Lawrence."

Sure enough, a moment later an opening appeared in the tree line. James held his breath and mentally crossed his fingers that no one would be on the road when they got there. "Hold on!"

The Bronco shot out of the trees. It took every ounce of his strength to force the wheel to the left. The tires squealed in protest as the heavy vehicle made the turn.

"What the hell was that all about?" James asked when he managed to breathe again.

"He's here," Clay said. "The cowboy is—"

"You saw him, you saw the cowboy?" James risked taking his eyes off the road long enough to look over at him.

Clay's complexion was a ghostly white and he was staring straight ahead. "The alarm started going off, so I ran down into the bunker and checked the footage from the driveway camera. There was a flash of light, and he was there. I only saw him for a split second before the camera shorted out."

A large explosion rocked the Bronco. James fought to keep it under control as a giant plume of fire and black smoke rose behind them in the afternoon sky.

"Did that come from the museum?" Nancy asked. "Clay, do you think the cowboy—"

"No." Clay shook his head, and his chin dropped to his chest. "I did it. My father said that if the cowboy ever showed up, we were to destroy everything, so he wouldn't know we were tracking him. It was booby trapped, the whole place."

"So, you—?"

Clay made the sound of an explosion and slowly nodded his head.

Chapter Forty-Seven

August 9, 1907
Effingham, Illinois

Junior and Julia had become inseparable over the last few weeks, with Julia often serving as a makeshift nurse when he would see patients in the back room of the café after hours. Word had spread quickly through the community of blacks that worked in Effingham about what he had done for little Elijah. A doctor willing to treat them was one thing, but having a doctor who would treat them for free was something else. What started as a trickle of folks each night, soon turned into a crowd much too large to go unnoticed.

"Folks has figured you out, and they knows they can trust ya," Ezra told him after the last person had been treated. It was two o'clock in the morning, and Junior was exhausted.

Ezra produced a small bottle of clear liquid and offered it to him. "Granny makes this back home. It packs a wallop, but it'll perk you up."

Junior took a small sip and nearly gagged as the thick liquid trickled down his throat.

"You can't do it like that," Ezra told him. "Turn it up and swaller hard before it has a chance to fight back!"

Junior hesitated. Ezra snatched the bottle out of his hand and took a big pull off of it. His eyes turned red and beads of sweat appeared on his forehead.

"Whooo-eee! That's the stuff!" He mopped sweat off his brow with the sleeve of his shirt before handing the bottle back to Junior. "Now you do it jus' like I done it."

"You're still sitting there, so I guess it won't kill me." Junior raised the bottle toward Ezra in a kind of salute, then upended it and let the liquor pour freely into his mouth. Red blooms exploded before his eyes, and his internal temperature rose in a line that started in his stomach and went all the way to the crown of his head. He heard the blood rushing through his veins, and his ears grew uncomfortably hot. He gasped for air. If Ezra hadn't grabbed the bottle out his hand, he surely would have dropped it.

"Smooth," he managed to croak out through his swollen throat.

"That it is!" Ezra agreed and laughed as he took another deep drink. "So, I been thinking, if you keep seeing folks here after work, Mr. King, or worse, the constable, is gonna see, and shut you down. That would be bad for the folks around here, and it wouldn't work out too good for you and Miss Julia, neither. I think folks come to trust you enough that you'd be all right if you was to come out to the house and do some doctoring there. Me and momma'll be there if anybody decides to start somethin'. Maybe you could come out Sunday evening after you and Miss Julia gets out of services."

Junior thought it over, and after another drink of Granny's home brew, decided to do it.

"'At's good, 'at's real good." Ezra finished off the bottle and stuck it in his pocket. "There's a bunch of folks out there too bad off to get in to town, but they can make it over to our house. If you sure you gonna be there, I'll let 'um know."

"I'll be there, Granny can help me. I think it's best that I don't bring Julia along. At least, not the first time."

* * *

Spookville turned out to be a half-mile stretch of rundown shacks, lean-tos, and campsites located about three miles outside of Effingham at the end of a dirt road. A nervous tension ran through Junior as he guided Gary to pull the buckboard into the little settlement. Having Julia sitting on the seat next to him compounded the tension.

"You shouldn't have come," Junior told her for the third time since leaving Effingham. "It could be dangerous, and if your father finds out I brought you out here, he'll put a shell in that shotgun of his with my name on it."

"I told you already that Poppa's gone out courtin' to the widow Gray's farm up in Kemps Mill and won't be back till tomorrow sometime. As far as it being dangerous goes, I'd rather be here with you than sitting at home worrying myself sick that you're laying out here somewhere dead." She reached over and placed her hand on his thigh. In Effingham, that would have been scandalous, but out there in Spookville it comforted him.

"Did Ezra give you his address?" she asked and immediately began to blush.

"Don't be embarrassed. I asked Ezra the same thing." He set one of his hands on top of hers. "You know what he told me?"

Julia shook her head.

"He told me that white folks had addresses, black folks just had homes. Then he said I should just follow the road, and I wouldn't be able to miss them."

The farther they moved into Spookville, the more nervous he became. Julia scooted over closer to him on the seat. At every house and lean-to they approached, some people would come out and walk toward them, staring as they passed, while others kept to their porches or hid in the shadows. Many of the people were older, some leaned on canes for support. He saw people who were obviously blind, while others were missing fingers or had misshaped arms and legs from breaks that had not been set properly and were now permanently disfigured.

"These poor people," Julia whispered.

They rounded a small curve and began to hear music coming from behind a clump of scrub brush.

Elijah ran out into the road. "They's here, they's here!" He motioned for Junior to follow him through a break in the brush. Behind the tangle of sticks and weeds was a small house with a leaning porch. Granny was strumming the guitar that he had grown accustomed to seeing Elijah play outside the cafe. Fifty or more people sat on the ground in front of her, listing to the music. Ezra stepped out from inside the house and waved as Junior pulled the buckboard to a stop beside the porch.

"Well, you did come after all." Ezra jumped down off the porch and held his hand out to an old man leaning there. Junior laughed when the man passed Ezra a dollar bill.

"Pinky there bet me a dollar that you wouldn't show up," Ezra explained. "Good thing you did, 'cause I ain't got no dollar to pay him iffin you didn't."

The music stopped. Granny handed Elijah the guitar and joined them. No sooner had Elijah sat down on the porch stoop than the music started back again.

"Why, Miss Julia, what a surprise." Granny raised her hand and helped Julia down off the buckboard. "I wasn't spectin' you to come. Your daddy would tan your hide iffin he knowed yous was out here."

"Maybe we can just keep my visit between us then," Julia told her with a wink.

The old woman cackled a laugh and led Julia toward the house.

"We gots a table set up for you inside," Ezra said. "I'll help you carry in ya things."

Junior jumped down, and with Ezra's help, they managed to carry in the supplies they had brought with them in one trip.

The table sat just inside the door of the tiny front room. What other furniture they had was piled in the opposite corner. The only light came in through one window that opened onto the porch. The song Elijah was playing drifted and filled the room. Like most poor homes of the time, the floor was dirt that had been wet down and pressed over and over again to produce an almost rock-like consistency. Junior noticed small lines where Granny had swept it in order to try and keep the dust under control. An open door led to the back room of the house where he could just make out the shape of a worn, tick mattress lying directly on the floor. Beyond that, another door led to the area behind the house which he guessed was where Granny did the cooking.

Granny wiped away the dust that had settled on the tabletop. "I hope this'll be all right for ya."

"This is perfect," Julia assured her. "You have a lovely home."

"Well, it ain't much, but we's happy here."

A look of pride lived behind the old woman's smile, and it struck Junior deeply. *Life for these people must be hard if they can find pride in the least of things like this.*

"Would it be possible for us to get a bucket or bowl of water to wash up in between each visit?" he asked.

"I'll fetch ya one." Ezra walked out through the back room and into the yard. He returned a moment later with an old wooden bucket filled with water. "I dipped some out for you to cook dinner with, Granny." He placed the water on the floor next to the chair Junior was sitting in.

"Okay then, let's get started. Who's first?"

He and Julia treated one patient after another over the next six hours, while Elijah and Granny took turns playing and singing for the folks that were waiting. They treated everything from sprains and broken bones, to burns, cuts, and scrapes. Quite a few of the people that came through had already been treated by Granny, and Junior started to recognize the many poultices and herbal treatments that she used.

The room grew even more dimly lit as the sun began to set. Ezra lit a few candles that had been made from pig fat mixed with beeswax. Outside, Granny was playing and singing.

"Steal away, steal away, steal away to Jesus. Steal away, steal away home. I ain't got long to stay here."

Her voice was strong and clear in the quiet of the late afternoon.

Junior thought he could hear all the struggles that she had been through in her life expressed in every note.

"*My Lord he calls me, He calls me by the thunder.*"

Junior had started bandaging a particularly nasty cut on an old man's forearm, and as Granny moved into the verse of the song. Her voice was joined by a high tenor that he recognized as Elijah's.

"*The trumpet sounds within my soul. I ain't got long to stay here. Steal away, steal away, steal away to Jesus. Steal away, steal away home. I ain't got long to stay here.*"

A few drops of hot wax from one of the candles secured the bandage closed. "Try and keep the wound clean for at least a few days to keep it from getting infected," Junior told the old man. The man nodded and ambled back out on to the porch. He gave Granny a quick peck on the cheek, walked away, and disappeared into the long shadows of evening.

Junior stood and stretched, causing the vertebrae in his back to snap in protest.

"I think that's the last 'un," Ezra told him as he peered out the door. "You done a lotta good here today. A whole lotta good."

"I'm glad to help anyway I can, I—"

"We've got one more," Julia said through the window. She had gone out on the porch to get some fresh air while he had been bandaging the cut. "She just came in off the road. Ezra, I think she may need some help."

"Yes'm, Miss Julia." Ezra went out onto the porch, then hurried across the yard.

"*Green trees are bending,*" Granny sang. "*Poor sinners stand a trembling. The trumpet sounds within my soul. I aint got long to stay here.*"

The music stopped. "Sweet Jesus," Granny said.

The chair she had been sitting in squeaked as she got up, and a moment later, she and Julia led in a small, very pregnant young girl. As soon as Junior laid eyes on her, he knew two things: she couldn't be more than twelve years old, and she was in distress.

Ezra grabbed a straight-back chair from the other side of the room. Julia and Granny gently turned the girl around and helped her to sit down. She groaned when her bottom touched the hard surface of the chair.

"*Steal away, steal away, steal away to Jesus.*" Elijah picked up the song where Granny had stopped. "*Steal away, steal away home. I ain't got long to stay here.*" His smooth tenor voice carried out across the yard and was joined by a chorus of crickets and bull frogs, giving the already plaintive song an ominous tone.

"What's you name, girl?" Granny asked before Junior could speak.

"Liza Jane, ma'am."

"Who done this to you, girl?" Granny spoke harsh and direct. The girl flinched. "Don't shy away from me. Now, you ain't got no trouble here, but the man what got you dis way, he need to answer for his sin."

The little girl's eyes grew big as she looked up at Granny. Her lips began to tremble, and she started to speak. Before she could say anything, her eyes rolled back in her head, and she fell forward. Ezra managed to catch her, but the pressure that her forward movement placed on her bulging stomach caused a flood of blood and fluid to pour out from between her legs.

Junior jumped up and grabbed her feet. Ezra was still holding her shoulders, and they started carrying her into the next room.

"Our Father, which art in heaven, hallowed by thy name," Granny began to pray.

"We'll need some light in here!" Junior shouted over his shoulder. "Bring me those candles."

Julia grabbed the candles and followed them into the next room.

* * *

"*My Lord, He calls me,*" Elijah sang. "*He calls me by the lightning. The trumpet sounds within my soul. I ain't got long to stay here. Steal away, steal away, Steal away to Jesus. Steal away, steal away home. I ain't got long to stay here.*"

Drenched in sweat, Junior stepped out onto the porch. His trembling hands were covered in blood.

"Misser Junior, is you all right?" Elijah set the guitar down and started to follow him out into the yard.

"Set yourself back down boy," Granny said from the door. "He don't need you pesterin' him right now."

Junior looked up at the three-quarter moon. It was rimmed in red and encircled by a shimmering glow. Granny came up behind him; he felt her more than heard her.

"T'weren't nothing you coulda done in there," she said. "She was already dead before she even come inside. Her little body just didn't know it yet."

Junior's heart filled with anger. He wanted to hurt someone like they had hurt that little girl.

"Why would someone do that? Why? Why put her through that, that poor little girl. She didn't deserve—"

"Course she didn't. None of 'em do." Granny's face turned red, and tears formed in her eyes. "Did you see her feet? Did you see the cuts and bruises? She been walking a long time. I seen it before, 'taint nothing new. If you was to get that baby outta her, dime to a dollar, it'd be white. Somewhere somebody snatched her up, had his way with her, and tossed her out like garbage. Then, when she caught pregnant and had to tell her daddy what happened, rather than go after the some'bitch he tossed her out, too."

"But why—?"

"'Cause in this world, the only thing worse than a nigger is a half nigger, that's why."

Her words struck him like a slap in the face. He didn't know what to say. He was angry and heartbroken all at the same time. He hurt so much for the scared little girl that had just died in his arms, he had never experienced anything like that before. He realized that his mother had sheltered him from a lot growing up and wondered what else she had never let him see. He loved his mother, but right now, he was angry at her and her overprotective nature.

Ezra came out on the porch. "Granny, Miss Julia needs your help."

Granny looked up at Junior and gently placed her hand on his cheek before she turned and went back in the house.

"Is the little girl dead, Daddy?" Elijah softly asked.

"Yeah, baby, she is."

Elijah picked up the guitar and began to play *Amazing Grace*.

"What happens now?" Junior asked. "Do I need to go into town and get the constable?"

"What fur?" Ezra snorted. "That man ain't never gonna come out here."

"But somebody needs to find out what happened! Find out who's responsible."

"Yeah, right. You dreamin', Junior." Ezra stepped down off the porch and walked over to him. "Here's what's gonna happen. When Granny and Miss Julia done wrapping that little girl's body up in a couple of feed sacks, I'm gonna dig a hole over yonder in that field of scrub and put her and that mattress she died on in it. They's already ten or twelve folks buried out there, one more ain't gonna make a lick of difference. Then I'm gonna come back here and get me a few more sacks and make Granny a new tick to sleep on. Lord willin', I'll be able to get all that done before sunup, so I can get myself a couple minutes sleep before we gotta open the café in the morning to make Mr. King his bacon sammich."

Junior fought for something to say—some question that he could ask that would help him understand the flagrant disregard for a young girl's life.

"This ain't your world, Junior. Don't try and make no sense of it."

Ezra stepped back over to the porch and picked up a short-handled shovel leaning there. He placed it over his shoulder and started off toward the nearby scrub lot. A few seconds later, he began to dig and whistle along with the song Elijah was playing.

* * *

Julia was quiet on the ride back into Effingham. Junior didn't mind as he was still caught up in his own thoughts. He kept seeing little Liza Jane's frightened eyes as she looked up at him in her last moments of life. What could have been going through her mind? Fear, confusion, pain that no human being should ever have to experience, much less a twelve-year-old child?

"Stop, Junior! Stop!" Julia reached over and hauled back on the reins. Gary stopped and snorted his disapproval. "What's that, up ahead in the road?"

Junior didn't see anything at first. The road was lit only by the moon. If it had been a cloudy night, they would have been traveling in pitch darkness, but that night, the surrounding countryside was bathed in a soft blue glow. He sat there for a moment staring straight ahead and seeing nothing, then something moved off to their right. A light bounced along beside the road, seeming to weave in and out of the trees.

"Who's out there?" he yelled at the light. "Show yourself!"

He got no answer, but the light stopped moving, then suddenly winked out.

"I know someone's out there! I saw your light. Make yourself known!" He was acutely aware that he was unarmed. Usually, he kept a pistol on his belt and a rifle strapped to his saddle, but his saddle and rifle were back in his room at the boarding house. Ezra had warned him against wearing a pistol into Spookville. He said that some of the residents might not trust him if he were armed, and others might see it as an easy way to get a gun for themselves, so he had left it in the room as well.

"I have a gun, and I'm not afraid to use it!" he bluffed, hoping that he sounded believable.

"You ain't got no gunnnnnn, no he ain't," a scratchy, high-pitched sing-song voice echoed through the trees to his right. "I said he ain't got no gun. *No!* But he do gots a pretty little woman up there with him, don't he? *Yes!*" A cackling laugh echoed through the trees followed by the sound of someone running through leaves.

"Junior, drive away, drive away now. Please." Julia touched his arm. Her voice quivered in fear, and her body shook.

He slapped the leather reins against Gary's back, but the horse didn't move. It shuffled its feet and fought against the bit. The horse was as scared as they were and was looking for an escape. Junior slapped the reins again. Gary reared up, nearly dumping him and Julia out of the seat and onto the buckboard.

"Whoa! Whoa!" he called out to the frightened horse.

"Whooooa, whooooa," the voice in the woods echoed, then laughed.

"Get away from here!" Junior shouted. "We don't have anything you want!"

Silence.

Gary snorted and pawed at the dirt road, digging little trenches under his hooves.

Junior stood. He kept a tight grip on the reins and surveyed the surrounding area. His heart and mind raced.

"I don't see anything," he whispered to Julia. "I think he's gone." He took one more look around before settling back down into the seat. Julia wrapped her arms around him and buried her face in his shoulder. She was crying.

"Let's go, Gary." Junior made chucking sounds with his tongue, and this time *gently* slapped the horse's rear with the reins.

Gary took a hesitant step, then another, then took off at a slow gait. Junior could still feel the horse fighting the bit, but the animal's nerves seemed to have calmed enough for it to be controlled.

His nerves had started to settle as well, and he took a deep, hitching breath to try and hurry the process. He felt Julia doing the same.

"ARRRRGGGHHHHHH!" A wailing scream came from directly behind them in the buckboard. A lantern's light bloomed bright, casting their shadows ahead of them across the horse's back. "I know you're here! *He* knows you're here! *I knows, he knows!*"

Gary reared up and bolted. Junior dropped the reins to grab Julia just as she was about to spill out of the buckboard.

A little man, dressed in rags, jumped into the seat beside him, grabbed the reins in one hand, and began whipping the horse into a frenzy. With his other hand, he held the lantern high over his head. It swung from side to side.

"It's time to die! He gonna get you! I'm gonna get you! You gonna die!" he shouted over the pounding of the horse's hooves. He slapped the reins again and again against its rump and withers.

Junior made a desperate grab for the reins. The man brought the lantern down, catching him on the side of the face. He drew back as blood poured from a cut over his eye, blinding him.

"You're gonna die just like you daddy did! Ain't he, YES! Aint he? I knows that's right!" The man began screaming like a banshee. "He knows! *He* knows! I know, I know, and we's gonna put an end to it, ain't we?"

Junior kicked out with both feet, sending the man flying from the buckboard. He hit a tree at the side of the road with a sickening wet thud. The oil lamp exploded, engulfing the man and the tree in a ball of flame.

Junior wiped the blood from his eyes and managed to grab the reins. He hauled back on them, forcing Gary's head up. The horse fought back but was forced to stop.

"Take these." He handed the reins to Julia. "If I'm not back in two minutes, or if you hear anything other than my voice, hightail it into town and bring help."

"Junior, don't!" She tried to grab the back of his shirt, but her fingers only grazed the surface of the material. "Don't leave me here! I'm scared!"

"Just do what I say," he barked back at her and ran toward the burning tree. The man had said he was going to *die like his father* had. How did he know about his father and what else did he know? Anger filled him, fueling him to run faster. Within seconds, he was at the tree. The old cedar was long dead. Flames were crawling like worms up its dry trunk, and the lowest branches were starting to catch fire.

Junior stopped and shielded his face against the heat. Where was the crazy man that had attacked them? He couldn't see anything through the smoke and flames. He continued to search, moving in a wide arc around the growing inferno. He had to be there. No one could have walked away from the hit he took against that tree. It was impossible.

Behind the tree, a trail of burning grass led away into the scrub of an overgrown field. Junior ran into the field and soon became entangled in the overgrowth. Briers scratched his legs through his pants, and he nearly fell. He looked out over the field, but the trail was gone.

He fought his way out of the weeds and returned to the buckboard. Julia refused to speak to him. She sat as far away from him as she possibly could, and they rode back in complete silence.

He pulled Gary to a stop outside the leather goods store. Julia jumped down, ran inside, and slammed the door behind her.

Chapter Forty-Eight

December 20, 2008

"We can't stay here, not even for one more night." Clay paced at the end of the bed in James' and Nancy's room at the Excelsior Hotel. "If the cowboy was able to track us to the museum, how long do you think it's going to take him to find us here?"

"So, what are we supposed to do? Just start driving?" James knew Clay was right, but he wanted them to have a plan, a direction. "If we knew where we were going, we could at least be making progress."

"What has Franklin said about where you should go? What did the *Great Spirit* tell him?"

James took a deep breath and tried to prepare himself for Clay's reaction to what he was about to say. "It wasn't the Great Spirit—it was a rainbow-colored cockroach that he saw while he was stoned." He paused, expecting Clay's head to explode or for him to pick up a chair and throw it at him, but he just stood there at the end of the bed, staring at him. "Randy the Roach told him to bring me to Lawrence, Kansas, and all would be made known."

Clay rubbed his face, squinted, and pinched the bridge of his nose. "I have so many questions about what you just said, but I don't think I want to know the answers." He sat down heavily on the bed. "If it weren't for the fact that I saw Franklin floating in my parking lot with my own two eyes, then saw a hundred-and-fifty-year-old cowboy madman appear out of thin air, I would walk out of that door and leave you all to it. But I owe it to my dad and grandfather to see this thing through."

There were three short raps on the door to their room, then the sound of a muffled argument going on in the hall outside.

"I'll get it." James rolled his eyes and walked over to the door. When he opened it, Calvin was standing there with his back to him. He and Franklin were arguing.

"If you d-d-d-don't tell them, then I w-w-w-will," Calvin said.

"But Calviiiinnnnn..." Franklin whined.

"Don't *b-b-b-but Calvin* me." He turned and raised his hand to knock again, almost hitting James in the chin instead. "Oh, oh, oh, my, J-J-J-James, I didn't know you were there."

"It's okay, Calvin. Why don't you two come in here before the neighbors call the management?" James went back and sat down on the bed. Calvin stepped inside, turned, grabbed Franklin by the shirt, and pulled him inside the room.

"What was that all about?" Clay asked.

Franklin just stood there, staring down at the carpet. Calvin elbowed him.

"*What?*" Franklin asked.

"T-T-T-Tell them what you just t-t-t-told me."

Franklin peered around the room at each of them. "Fine." He cleared his throat. "Back at the museum, when I went to get the tools out of the car, I accidently dropped them and spilled them out on the ground..." He shot Calvin a dirty look. "But I picked them all up and cleaned them off before I put them back in the bag."

"That's how he found us," Nancy softly said. "When Franklin touched the tools, the cowboy must have been able to sense their location. Oh, my God." She turned and placed her hand on James' arm. "Back at the hotel in Sweet Springs when you got the call about Dr. Carroll, remember?"

He had no idea what she was talking about and shook his head.

"When you got the call that Dr. Carroll had been killed, you took out the scalpel and looked at it. James, you touched the tools. You used them to sew up Franklin's leg, then before we left, you touched the scalpel again. That's how he found us at the airport. Touching the scalpel was the last thing you did before we left to meet Calvin."

"That settles it, then," Clay said. "That's how he's finding out where we are. So, if none of us touch the tools, then we may have a chance to stay ahead of him till we can figure out where we need to go to get rid of them."

"Animas Forks," Franklin said. "I hit my head on the tailgate of the Bronco right after I dropped the tools. Keegsquaw and Nijlon appeared to me and showed me. We have to go to Animas Forks. Floating Feather and Melvin Mitchell are buried on a mountain pass just above the town. We have to find the feather burned into the rock, then dig them up and return the tools to *them*."

"Animas Forks?" Clay asked. "Where have I heard that name before?" He snapped his fingers and ran across the room to the pile of papers he had saved from the museum. "Here it is. I knew it!" He came back over to them holding Melvin Mitchell Jr.'s letters.

Chapter Forty-Nine

August 15, 1907

Melodic guitar music filled the street as Junior placed the last of his bags on the buckboard. Ezra tied a rope around it and strapped it tight against the rest of his things.

"I sho' do hate to see you go, Junior." Ezra pulled a handkerchief out of his pocket and mopped the sweat off the back of his neck. "Granny says you is to stop by the house on your way out. She's got some goodies packed up for you to take with you."

"Thanks, Ezra, I'll make sure to do that. I wouldn't want to leave without saying goodbye to her." He stepped over and extended his hand. "It's been a true pleasure knowing you these last few weeks, and if you ever find yourself up in the mountains of Colorado, make sure to look me up."

"The pleasure's been all mine." Ezra firmly grasped Junior's hand and shook it. "Nope," he said. "That still don't feel right."

Junior laughed. "Hopefully, one day, you'll get used to it."

"What about me?" Elijah set the guitar down and ran over to Junior with his hand stuck out.

"I think I may miss you the most." He took Elijah's small hand in his and gave it a gentle shake. He pulled the boy into a bear hug. Elijah squealed in surprise, then began laughing and wiggling to get away.

"'Taint none a my business," Ezra said as Elijah picked up the guitar and started playing again. "But did you ever settle things with Miss Julia?"

"I tried, but her father won't let me anywhere near her. She was so upset that night when we came home from your place that she told him all about it *and us*. He says I could have gotten her killed taking her out there, and that if I even try to talk to her again, he'll kill me."

"He'd pro'ly do it, too."

"Yes. So, I think it's best that I take this job at the mine and try to forget her."

"Think you can?"

"Nope." He climbed up on the buckboard. "If you happen to see her, tell her I said goodbye."

"I'll do that." Ezra nodded.

Junior slapped the leather reins against Gary's back and drove away.

After a while, he was back in Spookville and guided Gary off the road and behind the stand of bushes that hid Ezra's house from the road. The last time he had made the trip, Julia had been with him and they had been happily falling in love. Coming there by himself seemed awkward and wrong.

No one stirred around the house which was odd for a Sunday. Usually, the neighborhood kids would be running and laughing in the yard while Granny played guitar on the porch or cooked out back. But today it was quiet. *Too* quiet, and a feeling of unease washed over him.

"Whoa, Gary." The horse stopped next to a small patch of grass. Junior climbed down off the buckboard and left the horse to graze.

"Granny!" he called out.

A second later, the old woman stepped out on the porch and pressed a finger to her lips. She waved him inside, then ducked back in and carefully closed the screen door.

Something wasn't right. The unease he felt when he pulled in grew into apprehension, and a shiver ran down his back. Once on the porch, he looked in through the screen door. The front room was dark, but across the room, a dark shadow passed by a window in the back of the house.

He eased the door open, making sure it wouldn't squeak on its old hinges, then stepped inside and closed it silently. Three paces took him across the front room, a fourth and he was inside the bedroom. Two more and he made it into the room at the rear of the house. It was empty as well. Granny was tending the cook fire in the back yard. A small man wearing a straw hat and old work shirt sat across from her. Granny looked past the man toward Junior. She seemed nervous, and he decided that he better quit hiding inside and find out what was going on. He opened the back door and walked out into the yard.

"Granny, who's this?"

The little man jumped to his feet, rounded the chair, and rushed toward him. Startled, Junior balled his fist and drew back with the intention of hitting the man square in the face. The man's hat flew off his head, and Julia's long hair spilled out from underneath. She lunged, wrapped her arms tightly around his neck, and kissed him deeply.

He lifted her off her feet and returned her kisses until they were out of breath and had to stop. "Julia, what's going—why are you—?"

"Shush," Granny hissed, coming up beside them. "She done run off. If her daddy finds her here, we all good as dead. Now get back through the house and back on that wagon a yours and high tail it outta here."

"She's right," Julia whispered. "We have to go." She took his hand and led him back to the house with Granny following close behind. "I'll explain everything once we're on the road."

"I gotcha a mess of fried chicken and biscuits packed up for you to take wit ya. Lord willin', you'll live long enough to eat 'em."

They rushed through the house and stopped beside the screen door. He cautiously looked out at the empty front yard, then nodded, pushed the door open, and they stepped out onto the porch.

"Be careful," Granny whispered, "and don't never come back." She handed Julia a small basket wrapped in an old dishcloth.

"Thank you." Julia leaned in and gave her a quick kiss on the cheek. "Thank you for everything."

Junior took Julia's hand and pulled her toward the buckboard. They were about halfway across the small yard when a shot rang out. They dropped to the ground just as Granny's neck and shoulder exploded, painting the wall and screen door red.

"No!" Julia buried her head against Junior's shoulder.

"Damn it, I missed," a voice said from behind the bushes.

Julia's father made his way into the yard as he cracked the breech of his shotgun, sending a spent shell tumbling through the air. He reached into his jacket pocket for another, then pushed the shell into place, and closed the gun with a loud snap.

"Daddy, what have you done?"

"Just what I said I would do." He took a few steps closer, placed the butt of the gun against his shoulder, and leveled it at Junior's head. "Now get up from there. This boy's gonna die today, then me and you are going back to the house and pack your things. I've made arrangements for you to go to a school back East where maybe they can teach you what it means to be a lady."

Junior stared into the barrel of the gun. He was about to die and there was not a thing he could do about it. Julia was saying something, but her words seemed distant and garbled.

A shadow appeared over Mr. King's shoulder. Junior grabbed Julia around the waist and, with her in his arms, rolled to the side just as a thick piece of wood came down on her father's back. The shotgun fired. Junior felt the heat of the blast on the back of his neck and dirt exploded not an inch from his side. A split-second later, Mr. King's limp body crashed down next to them.

Ezra stood over them holding a stove-length of wood. Julia pulled away and rolled her father over on his back. She leaned down and placed her ear on his chest. "His heart's still beating." She breathed an audible sigh of relief.

"Don't worry none, Miss Julia," Ezra said. "He ain't the first white man I ever beaned with a piece of poplar. I know how hard to hit 'em."

"Granny!" A high-pitched squeal came from behind them on the porch.

Elijah was trying to pull his grandmother up off the floor. Junior and Ezra ran to them, and Junior began to examine the damage Mr. King's missed shot had done to her. Julia left her father and rushed to try to comfort Elijah.

The round had caught Granny in the shoulder, just below the neck. Blood flowed freely from the wound, but it wasn't spraying out. Luckily, the shot missed her carotid artery, but that only meant that she would bleed to death slower if he didn't repair the wound.

"Run to the buckboard, get my doctor's bag, and bring it back to me," he said, looking over at Julia. "Take Elijah with you." He placed his hands over the wound in Granny's shoulder and pressed down hard. The blood that had been freely flowing began to slow. "Ezra, you better drag Mr. King around back and make sure he can't cause us any more trouble if he wakes up. I've got something in my bag we can give him to keep him out until you can drop him somewhere out in the woods. Hopefully, when he wakes up, he won't remember what happened."

"Is she gonna be all right?"

"I hope so."

Ezra nodded and left to deal with Mr. King as Julia and Elijah returned.

"We got your bag," Julia said from behind him on the porch.

"Inside is a bottle of sodium hypochlorite. Open it and sprinkle some of the powder over the wound and my hands, then pray this doesn't get infected."

"There's no bottles in here," she said. "Just an old, rolled cloth."

He risked looking away from Granny and realized that Julia had not gotten his doctor's bag. She had the old messenger's bag that carried his father's surgical tools.

"That's not my bag—" Blood began to run through his fingers, and he added more pressure to Granny's neck. "We don't have time for you to go back. I'll have to make do with those tools. Come around here. When I take my hands away, I need you to put yours where mine are and press hard until you feel the blood flow slow down. Understand?"

She nodded and moved around to his side; Elijah moved with her.

"Elijah, go around back and help your daddy while I take care of Granny, okay?"

The little boy defiantly shook his head, took his grandmother's hand, and held it in his.

"Okay, but stay out of the way, and if I tell you to do something, you do it."

Elijah nodded.

"Ready, Julia?"

She placed her hands above his.

"On three. One, two, three."

He took his hands off Granny's neck, and a wave of blood flowed down her chest before Julia could get her hands in place. She applied pressure, and the flow returned to a slow trickle.

Junior pulled out his father's surgical kit and unrolled it on the weathered, blood-splattered planks of the porch. He quickly found the suture needle and a twist of white cotton thread. His hands were sticky with blood, but he managed to thread the needle on the second try.

"When I tell you, I want you to move your hands toward her shoulder just enough to uncover the edge of the wound, but don't let up on the pressure. Understand?"

Julia nodded.

"As I begin to sew it closed, we will keep doing that. Move just enough to give me room to make one stich. All right?"

She nodded again.

"Good girl, here we go."

He held the needle between his thumb and index finger, placed it against the skin, and nodded at Julia. As instructed, she shifted her hands a quarter inch to the left. Hot, red blood flowed out of the opening, coating his fingers and the needle. He felt the needle shift in his grip, then slip from between his fingers.

"I dropped the needle," he muttered. "Move your hands back over and hold pressure until I can find it."

Julia did as he told her, and he began searching for the needle and thread in the folds of Granny's blood-soaked shirt. *It couldn't have gone far. It has to be right there.* He pinched a fold of cloth between his fingers, feeling for the hard length of metal. *Nothing.* He pulled up another fold and did the same thing again. Still nothing.

"Junior," Julia whispered, sounding frightened. "Junior, something's happening."

"Hold on, Julia, I've got to find this needle."

"Junior, listen to me."

He stopped and looked up at her.

"The bleeding's stopped. Well, not completely, but it has slowed way down."

He placed his hand against Granny's chest to try and feel her heartbeat. It was weak but still pumping. *Thank God.* But that didn't make any sense. If her heart was still pumping blood, then the injury should still be bleeding. There was no way a wound that deep could have begun to clot so quickly.

"Ouch!" Julia screamed and jerked her hands away.

He looked down at the wound in Granny's neck. The skin was torn apart and ragged, blood pooled up to the edges of the wound, threatening to spill over, but none ran out. Something moved in that pool of dark red. First just a twitch, then a thin line appeared and moved like a snake gliding below the surface of a pond. It twitched again, and a few drops of blood jumped out and landed on her already-saturated shirt.

"What's happening?" Julia asked.

Junior shook his head.

Another little splash, then like that snake swimming in a shallow pond, the point of the needle rose out of the wound. It hung there unmoving as if it were watching them as they were watching it. With a sudden violent burst, it plunged itself into the skin at the edge of the wound, pulling the thread through the flesh behind it. It flipped in the air above Granny's throat and repeated the process in the flesh on the other side. It gained speed with each turn and made its way down the length of the wound, making perfect stitches no more than a sixteenth of an inch apart.

Blood poured down Granny's chest as the quickly closing wound forced it out the open end. Less than ten seconds had passed since it had risen from the surface, and now the skin was tightly sewn shut. With an impossible flourish, the needle doubled back on itself, tied three perfect knots. It used its sharpened side to cleanly cut the thread before falling lifeless onto the old woman's chest.

Granny took a deep shuddering breath and squeezed Elijah's hand.

Elijah began to cry and squeezed her hand in return.

Chapter Fifty

"*Dear Thad,*" Clay read. "*I have accepted employment as company physician at the Calvary Mine located in the mountains above Animas Forks, Colorado. This is a stroke of luck as Animas Forks is where my father lived and practiced prior to meeting my mother. The town is bustling with the Gold Prince Mines Company buying the claims for the Sunnyside extension where they plan to build a mill. The arrival of the railroad a few years back has made Animas Forks a viable town again, and I believe it will be a comfort to Julia knowing that there is a large settlement nearby when we take up residence at the mine. Although, she is none too happy at the number of saloons that have opened along the town's two streets. She counted four as we passed from the train station to the mine office this morning. I hope, once we are settled in, to find time to come into Animas Forks and see what information, if any, I can find about my father.*"

Clay passed the old papers to James. "I knew I had seen that town's name somewhere," Clay said. "It's right there in the letters."

James glanced at the documents. "So, I guess that's that." He handed the pages back to him. "Looks like we are headed to Animas Forks. Wherever that is."

"Well, we know it's in the Colorado mountains—"

"Isn't *everything* in Colorado in the mountains?" Nancy interrupted him.

"I know it seems like it," Clay said, "but only about half the state is in higher elevations. The rest is plains, canyons, and deserts. Back before the Civil War, it was a pretty inhospitable place. The gold rush is what really brought folks into the area. Then came the war, and reconciliation led to it becoming a state in 1876. A lot of the mountainous areas are still pretty hard to navigate, especially in the winter. I'm afraid we've got our work cut out for us."

"There's nothing left but to do it, I guess." James stood and looked around the room at the rag-tag group. "I'm sorry I got you all into this, but there's not another group of folks I'd rather have with me."

"I'll go stand watch at the vehicle." Clay picked up the papers he had brought with him and made his way to the door. "Y'all gather your stuff and meet me there. I'm thinking we've wasted enough time sitting here gabbing. If that cowboy's still around, then we need to make tracks and get some distance between us and him." He walked down the hall without another word.

"C-C-C-Come on, Franklin," Calvin said. "I'm packed, but your stuff is scattered everywhere." Calvin led Franklin from the room, closing the door behind them.

The room was suddenly very quiet. James looked down at Nancy who was still sitting on the edge of the bed. She had her hand on her stomach. In the glow of fluorescent light that was mounted above the headboard, she looked pale.

He knelt in front of her and placed his hand on her knee. "I love ya, you know." She nodded and tried to smile, but he could tell something was bothering her. "This is a lot. Are you having second thoughts on the whole marriage thing?"

She looked in his eyes and touched his cheek. "Never—"

Her eyes grew big. She leapt to her feet, ran to the bathroom, and immediately vomited. Great, loud retching noises echoed around the little bathroom and out to where James now sat on the floor. Her quick exit had knocked him over.

He grimaced at the sounds she made, then got to his feet and went over to the vanity. She must have heard him coming because she slammed the door that separated the toilet and her from the rest of the small bathroom.

James soaked a washcloth with cold water. A moment later, he heard a flush. She opened the door; her face was red from exertion and likely, *embarrassment*. He handed her the cool, wet cloth and gave her a moment to run it across her face before he pulled her to him and held her tight.

"We need to talk," she said into his shoulder, then pulled away and led him back to the bed. They sat side by side, and she took his hands in hers. "I fully intend to marry you, that's not what's going on. I—" Tears filled her eyes, and she used the washcloth to wipe at them.

"Hey, it's okay. Tell me. You can tell me anything." He gave her free hand a gentle squeeze and scooted over closer to her.

She took a deep, shuddering breath and squeezed his hand hard in return. "I'm pregnant!" The words burst out of her. She whipped around, put her back to him, and cried into the washcloth.

He sat there for a moment, not knowing what to say or do. *This changes everything.* He was thrilled and scared to death all at the same time. *I'm going to be a father! That is, if the insane ghost of a murderous cowboy doesn't kill me first.*

"James?"

He wrapped his arms around her and placed his forehead against the back of her head. Her hair smelled like shampoo and coconut body wash, and he pulled her tighter against him.

"How about we name him Nathan after his grandfather?" he gently said.

She lifted her head, turned, and looked into his eyes. "You're not upset?"

"No." He shook his head. "No, I'm not upset. In fact, I'm the opposite of upset. I'm thrilled, overjoyed, ecstatic! But I'm not sure what to do. I don't think you should go with us. It's even more dangerous now, but I can't leave you here. What if—"

She placed two fingers against his lips. "I'm going with you. I've been thinking, and I don't feel there's any other way."

He started to protest, but she held up a hand and stopped him.

"I've made up my mind, James. I've touched the tools as well. Back in the other hotel when we were trying to stitch Franklin up, I prepped the tools for you and put them away when you were done. If the cowboy wants everyone dead that has come in contact with those tools, then he will find me whether I'm with you or not."

She was right and he knew it, but he hated it all the same. Now there were six people whose lives were in danger because of him. Six people that he felt responsible for. "I know you're right, but if there was any other—"

"There's not, so let's not think about it." She wrapped her arms around his neck and kissed him gently on the lips. "I love you." She smiled.

He wiped the single remaining tear off her cheek. "I love you, too."

"Then that's settled." She stood and put her hands on her hips, looking around the hotel room. "I swear, you are as big a slob as Franklin! Look at this mess. You have a lot of packing to do, and Clay's waiting downstairs. You better get busy."

"Me? What about you? Half of this crap is yours."

"Yes, it is." She got back in the bed and reclined with her head on the pillows. "But I am with child and in a most delicate condition." She feigned a broad southern accent and pretended to fan herself.

Chapter Fifty-One

September 3, 1907

Kansas City Star
1025 Grand
William Rockhill Nelson – Publisher

"This must be the place."

Junior and Julia stood outside a tall, brick building as horse-drawn buggies and street cars passed behind them on the busy street. Kansas City was nothing like Effingham, and although she put on a brave face, Julia tightly held his arm. He placed his hand over hers, wanting to be a comfort to her as well as being comforted himself by her touch. Providence had been a busy town when he was growing up, but it was a calm and quiet place compared to Kansas City. He would be glad when their business there was completed, and they could return to the road and be on their way to Animas Forks.

The door in front of them burst open, and a young boy ran out holding an armload of newspapers. He was dressed in brown knickers, a white shirt, and worn leather boots. A tight-fitting hat with a short bill sat firmly on his head.

"'Scuse me folks." The boy stopped and touched the brim of his hat. "Didn't see you standing there."

"It's all right," Junior said. The boy practically bounced from foot to foot, obviously anxious to get back to his deliveries. "Do you know if Mr. Nelson is available?"

"Don't know if he's available, but he's in there up on the third floor."

"Thank you, son." Junior dug in his pocket, pulled out a silver penny, and tossed it to the boy who caught it midair.

"Thank you, sir!" With another touch to the bill of his hat, the boy turned, ran down the street, and around the corner.

"Folks certainly move fast around here," Julia said as they watched him go.

"Probably means that we should, too." He opened the door and ushered her in ahead of him.

They entered a stairwell containing a steep, narrow set of steps rising directly in front of them. To their left was a wooden door with a window of frosted glass.

Distribution

was painted on the glass in perfect, one-inch letters. Next to it on the wall was a plaque that read:

Newsroom 2nd Floor
Executive Offices 3rd Floor

"Looks like we are going up." Junior took Julia's arm, and they began climbing the stairs.

The noises of a busy newspaper office filled the stairwell and bounced off the hard surface of its walls, making it difficult to talk and harder to think. On the second-floor landing, they were met by a young lady wearing a dark-gray tailored suit-dress with a high collar and matching hat. She was carrying a notebook and had a large pencil stuck behind her ear.

"Excuse me, miss—"

"Sorry, can't talk. Gotta get to the mayor's office and find out..." The rest of her words were lost in the echoing racket as she descended the stairs, never having slowed down.

"Well, that was rude." Julia's gaze remained on the woman as she disappeared down the stairwell. "I hope the folks upstairs are more accommodating."

"I guess we're about to find out."

They traveled the length of the stairs and came out on the third-floor landing at a door that looked identical to the one downstairs, except the painted letters there said:

**Executive Offices
by appointment only**

"That doesn't look very promising," Junior said, "but we're here now, so—" He tested the doorknob. When it turned easily, he pushed open the door. They stepped into a claustrophobically small office containing a simple wooden desk behind which sat a scarecrow of a man wearing a white shirt with a starched collar. "Excuse me, sir?"

"Do you have an appointment?" The man looked up from the papers on his desk, revealing his incredibly long neck and distinct lack of chin. His voice was high-pitched and effeminate. Junior thought it fit his look perfectly, and for a split second, a picture of a strutting peacock passed through his mind. He had to stifle a laugh.

"I said, do you have an appointment?" the man persisted.

"Oh, sorry. No, sir, we don't. We are passing through Kansas City, and I was hoping to find out some information about my father, he—"

"If you don't have an appointment, then we can't help you. Good day."

"But..." He felt his temper starting to flare. "The sheriff suggested we come here. He said that if there was anyone in Kansas City that might have some information for me, it would be Mr. Nelson."

"Well, he is correct about that, but he should have also told you that you needed an appointment. Now I suggest you go back to wherever it is that you came from and send a telegram requesting one." He hastily flipped through the pages in the book on his desk. "He should be able to see you three weeks from next Tuesday."

"We won't be here three weeks from next Tuesday," Julia told him, with a soothing and slightly whiny tone, like she hoped that a woman's request might hold some sway with the persnickety man. "Isn't there some way we could have just a *moment* of his time this afternoon?"

"Do you not understand the *definition* of the word appointment, young lady?" He glared at her. "It means that you call ahead to make sure you are expected. It in *no way* means that you should show up unannounced and expect admittance. Now, good day."

"Look here." Junior had had enough and decided to give the man a piece of his mind. "There is no need for you to use that condescending tone of voice with my wife. Now apologize before I come over that desk and kick the living sh—"

The door on their left flew open and a billowing cloud of smoke poured into the small office. Through the cloud stepped a big man smoking an even bigger cigar. "What's all the racket out here, Jefferson?"

"I'm sorry, Mr. Nelson." The effeminate voice now contained a jittery note of fear. "I tried to explain that they needed an appointment, but then this man became enraged and threatened to do me bodily harm. I was just about to call—"

"Sit down and shut up."

"Yes, sir." Jefferson melted back into his office chair and began to wipe at his forehead with a silk handkerchief.

"Mr. Nelson, please accept my apology." Junior stepped forward and extended his hand. "My name is Dr. Melvin Mitchell Jr. My wife and I have come a long way to try and find out some information on my father, Melvin Mitchell Sr. He was a doctor in the area thirty years or so ago."

Mr. Nelson shook his hand, then removed the cigar from his

mouth and expelled a thick plume of gray smoke into the office. Jefferson began to cough into his silk hanky, but the man paid him no attention.

"So, you're the infamous Melvin Mitchell Jr., huh? I've heard about you and your parents. I took over this paper about five years after your father was murdered, and you and your mother disappeared. Back then, that was still a big story—what with your father's grave being robbed a few days later and all."

"My mother moved us to Providence, Rhode Island. We had family there. We left Lawrence the day after my father's funeral. Did you say my father's grave was *robbed*?"

"Yep, torn apart in the middle of the night, then his body was stolen a few days later before the undertaker had a chance to re-bury him. It was a hell of a story."

"I imagine it was," he whispered. Julia's hand slipped into his, and he was thankful for the support.

"Jefferson!" Mr. Nelson barked and wheeled around toward his receptionist.

Jefferson jumped so hard that he almost fell out of his chair.

"Wasn't Mac LaMont a reporter for the *American Citizen* back before he came to work for us?"

"Yes, sir, I believe he was."

"Good. Take these folks downstairs and introduce them to him. He has my permission to tell them anything they need to know, and tell Mac I expect a front-page story about their return for tomorrow's edition."

"Yes, sir, yes, sir, just let me slip—"

"Now!"

Jefferson shot out from behind the desk and motioned for them to follow. This time, Junior did laugh out loud when he saw that Jefferson wore only socks and his big toe was sticking out of a hole in the left one.

***

"Melvin Mitchell Jr., as I live and breathe," Mac LaMont said. "I never thought I would ever lay eyes on you again." He was an older gentleman with an impressive set of whiskers. His long goatee hung almost midway of his chest, and the handlebars of his mustache could have easily wrapped around his head and been tied in the back, except for the prodigious amount of mustache wax that had been applied to keep them standing proud.

"I'm sorry, Mr. LaMont," Junior said. "I don't remember having ever met you. Mr. Nelson said you were a reporter here at the time of my father's death."

"Of course, you don't remember me, but I remember you and your father very well. Back then, I covered the grange for the *American Citizen* newspaper and if you remember, your father—"

"Was a grange representative. Yes sir, that much I do remember."

Mac chuckled and seemed lost in the memory for a moment. Before Junior could say anything else, Mac noticed Julia.

"Is this your wife?" Mac looked over at Junior and raised his eyebrows.

"Oh yes, this is—"

"Julia." She finished his sentence and extended her hand to Mac.

"She's just lovely." Mac took her hand and gave it a gentle shake.

A slight blush rose in her cheeks. Junior smiled at her, then turned his attention back to the man they had come to see. "Mr. LaMont, upstairs, Mr. Nelson said something about my father's grave being robbed, then his body going missing?"

"Yes, it was the talk of the town, along with you and your mother's disappearance. There were even a few rumors floating around that perhaps your mother had hired someone to dig your father up, but those never gained any traction."

"I should hope not," he said with a sigh, and Julia placed her hand on his back. "My mother, rest her soul, would have been mortified if she felt people thought of her in that fashion."

"Of course, and I'm sorry for your loss. As I said, they were just rumors. Anyone that knew your mother knew that something like that was impossible."

Mac leaned back against the edge of an unoccupied desk and folded his arms across his chest. "The whole situation was damn strange. Something changed inside your father after he operated on a little boy that had been shot, Walkins was the child's name, if memory serves. Your father took to heavy drinking. Not to say that your daddy didn't enjoy a little nip now and again before that day, but after, it was different. He was shirking his duties at the grange, he became—antisocial."

Mac ran his fingers through the long hair hanging off his chin. "I remember, one night I noticed him stumbling down the street toward the hotel you lived in back then. I came up behind him and called out his name, and he screamed. I'm not talkin' a little squeal of surprise, but a scream of pure terror. I used to wear an old bowler hat back in those days. I guess I thought it made me look dapper." He chuckled. "But that night when your father turned around and saw me standing there in the shadows, it was like he had seen a ghost. He screamed, like I said, and then began to back away. His foot caught on a tree root, and he tumbled ass-over-tea-kettle and landed on his back. I ran over to try and help him up, but he crawled away from me. I said, *stop it Melvin, it's me, Mac.* I took my hat off so he could see my face, and only then did he stop trying to get away. Instead, he began to cry, sobbing like a little girl lying there in the muck of the street."

Mac dropped his chin to his chest and slowly shook his head.

"Did you ever get a chance to ask my father about what had him so scared?"

"No." He looked up, and Junior noticed that his eyes were rimmed in red. He took a deep breath and stood upright. "No, I did not. In fact, that was the last time I saw him before he died."

"Were there ever any *real* theories about who desecrated his grave?" Julia asked.

"A few. The strongest put a crazy little man at the scene. A few folks remembered seeing this little fella around town the day before it happened. They said he had a high-pitched cackle of a laugh and he talked to himself, real peculiar like, almost like he was having a conversation with somebody that wasn't there. Someone called the law on him, and the sheriff locked him up for the night, figuring he was drunk."

"Then why did folks think he could have done it?" Julia asked. "I mean, seeing as he was in jail when it happened."

"Well, that's the thing, you see. The next morning when the sheriff came in, that little fella was nowhere to be found. The front door of the office was still locked, the cell door was still bolted shut, and there was no sign that anyone had broken in or out. But he was gone all the same."

"So, he could have done it. Did the sheriff get his name?"

"No, the sheriff could get nothing out of him. Here's the problem. When word got to the sheriff that your daddy's grave had been disturbed, he rushed right out there. He told me that the ground looked like it had been torn up by a wild animal. Said there were no signs that a shovel had been used. The lid of your father's casket had been torn off, and it was tipped over beside the grave with your daddy's body still halfway in it."

"My God," Julia whispered and tightened her grip on Junior's hand.

"Now when I say that the fella the sheriff put in jail was little, I ain't kidding. Sheriff said he was barely five feet tall and weighed around a hundred pounds. That there's the rub. There's no way that a fella that small could have done the damage the sheriff saw. Much less pull a pine box with a body in it out of a six-foot-deep grave, rip it open with his bare hands, and dump it out on the ground."

Junior nodded. He was trying very hard to pretend that all of this had happened to someone other than his father. His memories of him were of a gruff but happy man who smelled of cigar smoke, bought him candy as a treat, and loved his mother. He didn't want to think of that man lying on the ground, halfway out of a destroyed coffin next to an empty grave. He pinched the bridge of his nose and closed his eyes.

"Junior," Julia squeezed his hand and leaned in closer, her voice low and comforting. "This is a lot to take in. Maybe we should come back tomorrow."

He looked over at her and tried to give her a confident smile. She was beautiful, and it made him love her even more knowing that she was worried about him.

"It's okay." He put his hand on top of hers. "Mac, I think I understand what happened that night, but Mr. Nelson also said that a few days later, my father's body disappeared before they could re-bury him."

"It did. Darndest thing, too. The doctor in Kansas City came out and bundled him up. They put him in the grange office to give the sheriff time to finish examining the torn-up grave, and for old Bertie, the undertaker, could get a new casket made. When they went to fetch him, he was gone. Weren't nothing left in the grange office but the cloth the doc had wrapped him in. Even stranger than the body being gone was that the cloth was half frozen. I don't know if you remember or not, it was cold that December but not cold enough to freeze anything."

If it's going to be this cold, I wish it would snow. The thought passed through Junior's mind and carried with it a feeling of fear and loss that he had long forgotten.

"So," Mack continued. "How did a cotton cloth, wrapped around a body, *inside* an office, freeze?"

"I have no idea. I guess that's one part of my father's story that's going to stay a mystery."

"I guess so." Mac shrugged.

"I appreciate it all the same. Thanks for telling us about it."

"Glad to. Just sorry I wasn't any more help." Mac shrugged again. "Oh wait, Mr. Nelson wanted me to do a story on the two of you for tomorrow's edition. Can you stay a few minutes more and let me ask *you* a few questions?"

He looked over a Julia who gave him a small shrug of her own.

"That shouldn't be a problem," Junior said and placed his arm around his wife.

"Great! My office is just back this way."

Mac turned and started back into the smoke-filled newsroom. They followed him past desks full of men pecking away at typewriters or talking on the telephone. A young man with a Brownie camera on a strap around his neck was asleep in a chair sitting against the wall. As Mac passed him, he kicked the boy's feet, causing him to jump to attention. Mac whistled, and the boy fell in line behind them.

* * *

Julia was asleep and Junior had just begun to shave when someone knocked on their hotel room door. He quickly wiped the shaving soap off his face, tightened the sash on his dressing gown, and opened the door.

"Morning, mister!"

It was the same young man they had bumped into on the street outside the newspaper office the day before, and just like then, he was holding a stack of papers under his arm.

"Well, this is a surprise," Junior said with a smile. "What brings you around so early this morning?"

"This." The boy whipped a paper off the stack and handed it to him. "Mr. LaMont said you were to get the first one off the press!"

Junior looked down at a picture of Julia and himself taking up the left side of the front page. Next to it in bold print was:

Mystery Man Returns with Blushing Bride!

"Well, what do you know about that." He folded the paper and set it on the dresser beside the door. "Wait right there. I've got something for you."

The night before he had folded his pants and left them on the chest at the foot of the bed. He picked them up and was rummaging through the pockets when Julia began to stir.

"What's going on?" she asked, in a thick, half-asleep voice.

"Nothing much. You're just famous is all." He found a silver penny and went back to the door.

"Here ya go." He held it out to the boy, but the boy didn't seem to notice. He was too busy looking past him into their room. Junior turned to see what he was looking at and shook his head. Julia was sitting up in bed with the blankets gathered around her waist. Her sheer nightgown was cut low in the front—the latest style—and the boy was getting an eyeful.

"All right, that's enough of that!" Junior stepped in front of the boy to block his view.

"Jeez, mister. I thought she was pretty yesterday when I saw you out on the street but—" He let go with a loud wolf whistle.

"Yes, she is." He held up the silver penny. "I was going to give you a tip, but I think you've been tipped enough."

The boy looked as if he might frown, but then a big grin crossed his face, and he wolf-whistled again before heading away down the hall.

"Hey, kid!" Junior called after him.

The boy stopped and turned back. Junior flipped the silver penny high in the air, and the boy caught it.

"Thanks, mister!" He took off and ran the rest of the way down the hall and around the corner.

"What was all that about?" Julia asked from behind him.

He closed the door and took the paper from its resting place on top of the dresser. "Oh, just one of your many fans come by to pay their respects."

"Yeah, sure. Now quit pulling my leg and tell me what's going on. It's too early for foolishness."

"Okay, the newsboy came by to bring us a newspaper and ogle your half-naked body."

"The newsboy did what?" She looked over at the door, then down at herself, screamed, and pulled the covers up to her neck. "Why didn't you tell me to cover up? I'm so embarrassed!"

"You'll forget all about it when you see this." He tossed the newspaper on the bed, and it landed open to their picture.

"What's this?" She picked up the paper. "Now I really am embarrassed. Is this what I really look like?"

He sat on the bed beside her and pushed the paper down in her lap.

"Yes, it is, and you are beautiful." He leaned in, kissed her gently on the lips, and she immediately began to blush. "I guess it's time for us to get back on the road if we are going to make the Colorado mountains before the first major snowstorm of the season."

"Uh-huh," she answered absentmindedly, still staring at their picture.

He smiled and went back to the basin to finish shaving. The lather in the shaving cup had dissolved, so he dribbled a little water over the soap ring at the bottom before taking the stiff-bristled brush and stirring it around. It wasn't long before the brush was covered with enough new lather to cover his cheeks and chin.

A straight razor with a wooden handle was lying beside the bowl. It had been a gift to him from Thad on his thirteenth birthday. His mother was sure that he would somehow manage to slit his own throat before he learned to properly shave, but he had survived. Now, so many years later, as he looked at his adult face in the small mirror over the bowl, he realized how much he missed those days. The carefree days of childhood, of his mother's love, and adventures with friends.

"Be careful, you might fall in." Julia had come up behind him and was looking at his reflection in the mirror over his shoulder.

"Drowning in my memories is more like it." He placed the sharp edge of the razor high on his cheek and slowly pulled it downward, removing the white lather and brown whiskers with it.

"Penny for your thoughts."

"They're not worth it." He smiled at her reflection and removed another layer of lathered beard. "But I did want to ask you something."

Her reflection raised its eyebrows in a questioning manner.

"Yesterday when we were talking to Mac, did the crazy little man he described that was put in jail the night my father was killed sound familiar to you?"

"No, not really. Should it have?"

"Think back to that night in Spookville when that pregnant little girl came in just as we were finishing up. Remember?"

"I remember the girl, but I don't remember any crazy little ma—" Realization washed over her face. "Oh, my God, the man that attacked us on the way home."

"Yep, it dawned on me last night while I was trying to get to sleep."

"Do you really think it could have been the same man? I mean if it was, he would have had to have been better than sixty years old. The man that came after us couldn't have been that old, could he?"

"I don't know." He shrugged and started shaving the other side of his face. "We never did really get a good look at him."

"But why? I mean if it was him, why come after us?"

"I don't know that either, but if I had to guess, I think it might have something to do with my father's surgical tools."

"You said we would never speak of those tools again." Her face reddened, and she took a step away from him. "You promised."

"I know I did, and I'm sorry." He wiped the little bit of remaining lather off his face with a towel, then went to her and took her hands in his. "I just want to make sure that we are not missing anything."

Chapter Fifty-Two

December 21, 2008
Oakley, Kansas

"This is it." Clay pointed to the interstate off-ramp that was quickly approaching on their right.

"This is what?" James asked from behind the steering wheel of the Bronco.

"Our next stop."

They took the exit, and a sign on the ramp said:

Welcome to Oakley, Kansas
The Home of Buffalo Bill Cody

"I thought our next stop was Animas Forks?" Nancy asked. She was sitting in the back seat squished between Calvin—who was cleaning his glasses—and Franklin, who was asleep and unaware they had left the highway.

"We are definitely headed that way, but my Uncle Cletus lives here in Oakley. Last time I heard from him, he said he had something of my grandfather's that he wanted to give me. I thought it might be something that could help us out, maybe fill in some blanks. We can just swing by, pick it up, and get back on the road. It won't take long."

Franklin groaned, then stretched. Nancy had to duck out of the way to keep from getting hit in the head with his elbow.

"Are we there yet?" Franklin leaned forward and looked out the front window. "Is this Colorado? I expected more."

"No Franklin, we're still in Kansas," Nancy informed him.

"Then why did you wake me up?"

* * *

"Whoa, look at that!" Franklin pointed out the side window as they approached a giant bronze statue of a cowboy on horseback, hunting a buffalo.

"That's Buffalo Bill Cody. He was born near here," Clay explained. "Before long, they're going to build a museum next to it. It also means we're close to Cletus's place." He motioned to James. "Once you get to the next cross street, turn left, and it will be on your left."

They had been driving through a flat, dusty industrial area that James had a hard time picturing anyone living in. He approached the turn and saw large storage tanks in the distance. He eased the car onto a side street that ran between a gas station on the right and an unassuming little sign for the Frick's Fossil History Museum on the left. Beyond the sign, there was a row of plain white garages with some small ranch houses behind them. He assumed that one of those houses belonged to Uncle Cletus and began to accelerate.

"Whoa! Whoa, boy, you're gonna miss it." Clay placed his hand on James' arm. "Turn here." He pointed at an aggregate driveway that ran in front of the garages. "It's that first one, right there."

James parked the car outside the door of the unmarked, and seemingly unoccupied, two-car garage. He started to ask if Clay was sure that this was the right place but before he could, Clay threw open the door and got out.

"Maybe you guys should stay here till I see what's going on," he said over his shoulder to everyone in the back seat.

"I think that's a m-m-m-marvelous idea," Calvin agreed.

James started to get out as well, but Nancy reached over the seat and placed her hand on his shoulder.

"It'll be okay," he told her. "I'll never be out of sight. You just hang out here with the boys, and I'll be right back." He gave her hand a gentle squeeze and got out of the car.

Clay was standing outside the garage door, staring up at the corner of the roofline.

"Should we knock?" James asked, stepping up beside him.

"No need. He knows we're here." Clay waved toward the eave of the roof above them. James could just make out a small object mounted there. It looked like a black, number two pencil with a small glass lens where the eraser should be.

"Is that a camera?"

"Yup," Clay answered. "You could say that Cletus is a bit of a—" He wrinkled his nose and rubbed his hand across the beard stubble on his chin, obviously trying to find the right words to describe his uncle. "Conspiracist. Yeah, that's a good word for it. Some folks call them preppers. When Cletus got back from Nam, he was convinced that civilization as we know it was gonna come to an end, and that he needed to be prepared for anything, that way he could be the sole survivor. His theory is that *all* the governments of *all* the major powers on the earth are *all* working together to form a *New World Order*. Says that they have a secret base hidden deep inside Mount Everest where they are in constant contact with beings from a planet inside the Proxima Centauri galaxy, and that those beings are feeding them information and technology that will allow them to one day become immortal. Once they achieve immortality, then they will unleash a super flu or some other type of disease that will kill off everyone living on the surface, leaving them with enough food and water to live..." He shrugged. "Forever, I guess."

"So, what would the beings from the other galaxy get out of it?"

"I don't know." Clay looked at his feet and shook his head. "Cletus is an idiot."

The garage door flew open, startling both of them.

"I may be an idiot, Nephew, but I'll be the only idiot still alive when they poison the air with all them spores they've been growing in that lab in China!"

Cletus was a short, stubby man who appeared even shorter due to the severe bend in his back that James thought could have been caused by scoliosis or long-term arthritis.

He was wearing a trucker hat over long, greasy gray hair that hung limp down the sides of his face, and overalls on top of a black shirt that, from what they could see, had a picture of a giant, green pot leaf on the front.

Inside the garage behind him was a mechanic's lift holding up a dirty, powder-blue Oldsmobile Cutlas Supreme that was missing three tires and had 1 John 2:17 spray-painted across one side of the trunk, and Ps 37:29 across the other. The rest of the garage was littered with various tools as well as empty boxes and other assorted junk.

"Uncle Cletus, this is James Hughes."

Cletus turned his head and looked up at him, revealing that the man only had one eye. Where his left eye should have been, scar tissue had formed over the lid, causing him to perpetually wink. Grease and grime covered the rest of his face and hands, giving his complexion a very alien appearance.

"James and I, along with his friends over there in the car—"

Cletus pushed past them and went over to the Bronco. He walked with a pronounced limp that reminded James of Igor from the old Frankenstein movies.

Cletus placed his hand on the hood and traced it along the body of the vehicle until he came to the back passenger side window. He stood on his tiptoes and looked in.

The muffled sound of Franklin screaming came from inside. It grew to full volume as the driver's side door flew open and Franklin burst out, ran, and hid behind the garage. Calvin and Nancy got out more cautiously, then joined James and Clay at the open garage door.

"Um, who or w-w-w-*what* is that?" Calvin nervously asked. He pulled his glasses off his face and started cleaning them with his shirt tail.

Cletus ambled his way back over to them. "Humph." He went back inside the garage and closed the door.

"That," Clay told them. "Is my *odd* Uncle Cletus."

Clay banged his fist against the metal door three times. It rattled in its tracks. The door opened a moment later, and Cletus stood there, now wearing a red sweater over his overalls. He had pulled his hair back into a ponytail and was scrubbing at the grunge on his face with a wet shop towel.

"Nephew, if you had given me a little heads-up that you was comin' this way, I could have tidied up a bit."

"You don't have a phone, and you won't get a computer. Just how am I supposed to let you know when I'm in town? Besides, I didn't know I was going to be in the area till yesterday."

"Well, maybe so, but you still could've." Cletus took his hat off and turned his attention on Nancy. "Ooh, you're a pretty one. Would you ever consider spending your remaining days on the planet with someone like me?"

"Oh," Nancy flatly said. She looked wide-eyed over his head at James.

"Sorry, Cletus," James said. "But we're engaged."

"Figures." Cletus put his hat on and started back inside.

"Last time we talked," Clay said, "you told me you had something of Grandfather's that you wanted me to have. I figured that while we were passing by, I'd stop and pick it up."

"Did I say that?" Cletus pushed the hat back and scratched his head. "Nope. Don't sound familiar."

"Well, that is what you said."

"Hmmm, maybe it's down in the safe-deposit box." The old man turned and walked back into the garage. "You coming or not?" he yelled over his shoulder.

Clay shrugged, then went inside. They all followed him in, and the door automatically closed behind them.

They circled the powder-blue land yacht, then followed Cletus down a flight of stairs that was hidden behind a pile of trash near the back of the garage. At the foot of the steps was an iron door secured with three locks. Cletus felt around in the front pouch of his overalls until he came out with a key. He inserted it in the padlock and turned it to release the shank. The lock below it was a combination style. He smiled up at them before placing himself between them and the lock. A moment later, James heard the tumblers release. Cletus placed his thumb against a small screen on the front of the third lock. The screen glowed green, then an orange line started at the top of the screen and moved down, reading his thumb print. A short buzz came from inside the lock's casing, and the door swung open.

"Cain't never be too careful!" Cletus pushed the door the rest of the way open, motioned for them to go inside, then closed the door behind them with a heavy thud followed by the snap and clatter of the locks resetting.

Floor-to-ceiling cardboard boxes lined the room they were in. Some were marked *C-rations*, others read: Sterno, gas masks and filters, iodine, hydrogen peroxide, flashlights, batteries, and cat litter. That last box got his attention.

"I get why you have all this stuff stored down here," James said. "Except for the cat litter. What's up with that?"

Cletus walked over and placed his hand on the stack of boxes. "Well, this is very important for two reasons. First of all, when the next global ice age sets in, *and it will*!" He glared around the room at everyone, then smiled and turned back to James. "I'll be prepared to keep the driveway out front from freezing. Secondly, if the beings from Proxima Centauri are cat-like people, which I believe they are, I can place litter boxes around my property, and they will be so grateful that I prepared a clean place for them to do their business that they will leave me alone and go somewhere else."

He stepped over and pulled a tarp off something in the corner.

Under it was a stack of plastic children's play pools. "I figure these should be just right for that," he said proudly and walked back over to Clay. "Now, Nephew, what exactly was it that I'm supposed to have for you? No, wait..." He held up his hand. "Let me guess." He tapped his forehead with a crooked finger. "It has something to do with that cowboy that you all have been so preoccupied with," he said sarcastically and looked over at Calvin. "Can you believe that full-grown, educated, experienced men would be stupid enough to believe that a cowboy from the Civil War could still be roaming around the country wreaking havoc? Might as well believe in fairies or gnomes or such."

"Or g-g-g-giant cat people from a g-g-g-galaxy lightyears away?" Calvin asked.

"Humph." Cletus squinted his good eye at him, then backed a few steps away.

"Uncle Cletus, I know you never believed in the cowboy," Clay said. "But he is real. He showed up at the museum yesterday. I had to destroy it to keep him out, but these folks have some new information that I think can help me put a stop to him once and for all."

"And you call *me* an idiot," Cletus mumbled under his breath. "Well, if it's something important, then it'll be back here in the box." He walked into the shadows at the back of the room.

"You'll want to see this," Clay whispered and motioned for them to follow.

There was the loud screech of metal on metal as Cletus pulled open a thick, heavy door built into the back wall of the basement. A light from inside nearly blinded them, and steam billowed out of the room and collected around their feet.

"Argon gas. Hold your breath till it dissipates," Clay instructed. "He keeps the box filled with low levels of it to keep everything dry and protected."

On the walls of the brightly lit vault hung a massive collection of firearms. Automatics, semi-automatics, machine guns, assault rifles, pistols, shotguns, even crossbows and long bows with quivers full of arrows tipped with brightly colored feathers hanging next to them.

Along the floor were wooden crates marked hand grenades, dynamite, and blasting caps. A long, thin box leaned in one corner; it was stamped: **Man-portable recoilless anti-tank rocket launcher.**

"Jesus," Nancy whispered and took James' hand.

Cletus opened a drawer of a dark-green, metal filing cabinet and started rifling through it.

"If it's in here, I probably filed it under nut case!" He looked back at Clay and snickered.

"What are you guy's doing?"

Everyone in the vault jumped in surprise and turned to look at Franklin standing in the doorway.

"What?" Cletus yelled and rushed over to him. "How did—?" He circled Franklin, looking him up and down, then turned and circled back the way he had come. He ran out of the vault and over to the door at the foot of the stairs.

"What did I do?" Franklin asked.

Cletus came back into the vault, grabbed Franklin by the collar of his shirt, and pulled him down low enough to get eye level with him.

"How did you get in here? That door was locked, and it's still locked. How did you do it?"

Franklin looked around the room, obviously confused by all the sudden attention.

"Answer me!" Cletus barked in his face.

Franklin studied him. "Dude, what's the matter with your eye?"

A sound like an angry pirate who had stepped on a lobster exploded from deep inside Cletus. In a flash, Franklin was flat on his back with Cletus sitting straddle of his chest with his fist raised in the air.

Clay shot across the room and grabbed Cletus before he could throw the first punch.

James pulled Franklin to his feet and pushed him across the room to get some distance between them.

"What?" Franklin shouted. "What, what?"

James forced his nerves to settle down before he said anything.

"The outside garage door was locked, so was the one at the foot of the stairs. Cletus over there is very protective of his privacy. How did you get in here?"

"Oh that. It was easy."

"No, it was not easy!" Cletus yelled across the room and started struggling. Clay had to pick him up and hold his feet off the ground before he began to calm down.

"Go ahead Franklin, tell us how you got in," James urged.

"Well, when I peeked out from behind the building, everybody had disappeared. So, I got to poking around that garage door where I saw you guys last. It *was* locked, but that didn't matter none. Back when I was a kid, we used to go into garages with doors like that all the time to borrow people's bicycles. All of them doors have a sweet spot just over halfway up, and if you whack it just right, that sucker'll pop right open." He looked up triumphantly, but everyone just glared at him. "Anyway," he continued, "when I got inside, I saw that sweet ride up on the rack and I was looking at *it* and not where I was going, and I nearly fell down them steps." He looked around James at Cletus. "You really ought to put up a sign or something, somebody could get hurt."

Cletus growled and started kicking at the air.

"I always say if you see stairs you oughta go down 'em, so I did. That's when I found that big door. The padlock was hanging off it, so I figured that meant it was okay to come in. I tried the handle, but the door was locked and needed a combination. Well, everybody knows that the most-used four-number combinations are 1234, 0000, 1111, and 5555, but I figured that whoever had the class to own a car like that beauty on the rack up there wouldn't be dumb enough to use any of those, so it had to be the next most-used number which is 2580."

Cletus quit wrestling to get loose from Clay and went limp in his arms.

"What about the fingerprint lock?" James asked him.

"Is that what that thing was?" Franklin's head drew back in surprise. "I thought it was a kind of a peephole, so I bent down and looked in. I couldn't see anything, so I figured it was dirty. I spit on it and wiped it off with my thumb. Before I could look through it again, the door just popped open. I heard you guys back here talking, so I came to see what was going on."

Cletus was looking up at Clay with his one good eye. "Put me down, Nephew!"

"Are you gonna behave?"

"Fine, I won't kill him."

Clay put him down.

"Don't mean I won't think about it, though," Cletus murmured. "Did you really see that cowboy at your place yesterday?" he asked in a much louder tone.

"Yeah, we did."

"Humph, y'all go up to that hunk of junk you're driving and wait for me. I'll be there in just a minute."

Cletus opened the door for them and waited till they had all gone through, then closed it again.

"What do you think that's all about?" Nancy asked.

"There's no telling," Clay said from the back of the group. "Knowing Uncle Cletus, it could be anything from a tinfoil hat to a bullet-proof jockstrap."

"Do they make those?" Franklin asked, coming to a sudden stop.

Calvin bumped into him. "S-S-S-Stop talking and s-s-s-start moving before you cause all of us to fall b-b-b-back down these stairs." He gave Franklin a shove, and with a grunt, Franklin began climbing the steps again.

* * *

They made it to the Bronco, and Franklin had just lit a cigarette when Cletus came out of the garage, holding a book in his hand. He waved it high over his head as he waddled toward them.

"What's this?" Clay asked.

"What does it look like?" Cletus grumbled as he handed the book to him.

"It looks like a book." Clay turned the book over in his hands, examining the worn cover and filigreed cloth binding. It was covered in dust. He blew some of it off the front cover to try and read what was embossed there.

Franklin sneezed, expelling a lungful of smoke in the process and immediately began to choke. Nancy repeatedly slapped him on the back until he managed to get his breathing back under control.

"Sorry," he croaked.

Clay turned his attention back to the book. He ran his finger across the dust and grime in the embossed area and uncovered the word *LEDGER,* put there in gold leaf.

"Your grandfather—my daddy—sent that to me just before he died," Cletus said. "I went through it and couldn't figure out why he had it or what I was supposed to do with it, so I've been using it to prop up the short leg on my kitchen table. I didn't want to give it to you 'cause it fits perfectly under that leg. Now it's gonna wobble again. Anyway, seeing how you're going on some fool errand to try and kill something that don't really exist, maybe you can get some use out of it. Daddy was as crazy into that cowboy crap as you are. I always wondered if he meant to send it to your daddy instead of me."

"Thanks, Uncle Cletus." Clay ran his finger around a circular dent in the cover and laughed. "I'll check it out."

"Well, if it turns out to be nothin', then send it back to me. It fits just perfect under that table leg." With that, the old man turned and went back into the garage and closed the door.

Chapter Fifty-Three

December 22, 2008
Durango, Colorado

Nancy crossed her legs in the back seat of the Bronco and glanced at her watch. It was one minute past midnight, and Franklin had now been inside the single bathroom at the Shell station for over fifteen minutes.

James, Clay, and Calvin had gone inside to buy coffee and snacks to help keep them awake for the next part of the drive. She had asked them to bring her some coffee as well, and thinking about that made her bladder shudder. She looked again at the corner of the building, hoping that at any second Franklin would appear carrying the old-fashioned door key that was attached by a length of chain to a short piece of two-by-four.

Chivalry is dead.

James had asked her if she needed to go when they first stopped, but before she could answer, Franklin had shouted, "*I do!*" and made a mad dash for the store to get the key. Now she was stuck waiting, and she needed to find a way to take her mind off the urge growing in her abdomen.

She spotted Melvin Mitchell Jr.'s letters sitting in the back of the Bronco. She had begun reading them earlier but started feeling carsick and set them aside.

This just might be what I need to take my mind off the fact that I'm about to pee my pants.

She picked up the letter on top and started reading where she had left off:

October 15, 1907

Thad,

Julia and I have managed to get settled into our cabin here at the mine. The small building must serve not only as our home, but also my office. One room has a separate entrance and has been designated as my consultation room. This cabin will be sufficient for now, but come spring we will need to find a larger accommodation as Julia has just informed me that we are expecting our first child. She asked if I preferred a boy or a girl, and I told her it did not matter as long as it was healthy and as beautiful as she. We have decided that if the child is a boy, we will name him Melvin Mitchell III, after myself and my father. If it is a girl, her name will be Minnie after Julia's mother.

I spent the morning meeting with the local mine agent as well as the foreman of both the Calvary Mine and Black Cross Mine. Mr. Jerry of the Black Cross Mine has offered me a stipend of five dollars a week to be on call for emergencies at his mine, until they can procure a doctor of their own. That extra income will certainly be a welcome bonus, but I fear the work will have me away from home, and Julia, more than I would prefer in her current condition.

Last night, I heard a noise outside our bedroom window. Nothing unusual for a cabin at the top of a mountain, but in my drowsy state it sounded more like a whispering voice than a passing animal. Fortunately, it had not awakened Julia. I slipped from under the blankets and made my way to the bedroom window. The moon was almost full, and it caused long shadows to spill across the ground from the nearby trees. It was impossible to determine what had made the noise. A movement caught my eye, something just out of sight rounding the corner of the cabin. I grabbed my Colt from its holster and ran across the small living room, headed for the front door. I was almost to it when I heard the noise again, and this time, I was sure that it was no wild animal.

"I know you're here! He knows you're here! I knows, he knows!'"

I can't begin to tell you how those words struck fear in my heart.

I flung the door open and fired a round blindly, hoping to hit the man that I knew would be standing there. But the path was empty.

Julia rushed into the room, having heard the shot, and I assured her it was nothing. I lied and told her I had seen a bear and had fired the shot to scare it away, then I sent her back to bed with the promise that I would be right in. That was my intention, but when I turned and checked the path again, I heard somebody laughing back in the woods. I closed the door and set the bar, then as promised, I went back to our bedroom. Julia was sleeping peacefully, so I placed a chair at her bedside and spent the rest of the night sitting watch with my pistol resting in my lap.

This morning, when Julia began to stir, I left my guard's position and returned to our front door. I took another look at our little path, and I saw boot prints in the snow. They appeared to circle our cabin multiple times before moving away and disappearing into the forest.

Nancy looked up from the letter at the sound of voices and discovered James and Clay laughing as they came out of the small store. They carried three cups of steaming coffee and a brown paper bag that hung low with the weight of the snacks inside.

Heat rushed into her cheeks when she saw Calvin and *Franklin* following behind them, each with their hands full of prepackaged snacks.

She slapped the letters down on the seat and flung the door open. "Franklin, where the hel—" She stopped halfway out of the door, gritted her teeth, and clamped down on her stomach muscles to keep from wetting herself. She breathed through the sensation, then managed to stand the rest of the way up just as they arrived at the car.

"Franklin." She fought to keep her voice under control. "Where is the key to the restroom?"

"Oh, did you need it?"

"Yes, Franklin, I needed it fifteen minutes ago. I've been waiting to see you come back around the building so I could get it from you."

"I went in through the back door. It was closer."

She wanted to scream at him but knew that if she did, she would embarrass herself, so she settled for giving him a dirty look.

"What did I do?" Franklin asked the others while she shuffled toward the store.

* * *

"Can you believe all this snow?" James said to no one in particular.

He had taken over driving duties from Clay when they made a pit stop in Durango, before heading farther up into the mountains toward Silverton. Snow was piled higher than the Bronco's roof on either side of the winding road, but Colorado public works had done an admirable job keeping the surface of the road clear. The plan was to stop in Silverton for the night before making their way up even higher to the ghost town of Animas Forks at first light.

Clay had found a phone number for the Imperial Hotel in Silverton and reserved them rooms for the night. They planned to rent a Jeep in the morning, head up the mountain, and bury the tools on the pass above Animas Forks. James estimated that the drive from Silverton would only take about hour, and they intended to be on the road back home before sundown.

If only it hadn't started snowing. It could ruin all their plans. He was ready to get this part of their trip over with. Hopefully, once they were rid of the tools, he and Nancy could salvage the few remaining days of their vacation.

Nancy reached over and tuned the radio to a local news/talk station to see if they could get a weather report.

"...*that's why the government's response is such a joke.*" A nasally, raspy-sounding voice flowed from the car's speakers. "*You know half of them folks ain't even from earth!*" The man's southern twang sounded strangely out of place in the mountains of Colorado. "*Thanks again for the call, Joe. It's always good to hear from a true believer. Hey, looks like we got another caller. Who's this?*"

"*Hey, Newt, it's Sally. You see the weather report? Storm's a comin'.*"

"*Now, Sally, you know you can't trust them weather folks. That's just another way they get in your head. It's all alien technology designed to—*"

"Well, that's enough of that." Nancy hit the seek button on the radio and started it scanning for another station.

"Since when did talk radio shows become all conspiracy nutjobs?" Clay sarcastically asked from the back seat.

"About the same t-t-t-time millennials decided that instead of f-f-f-finding new questions to ask, they would just come up with d-d-d-different answers to the old ones," Calvin said in a tone equally as sarcastic as Clay's.

"Hey, easy on the millennial-bashing back there," Nancy said with a smile that betrayed her angry tone. "Some of us fall in that category. Tell 'em, Franklin."

"Tell 'em what?" Franklin asked, turning away from the window.

"You're a millennial. Tell them to quit blaming us for everything ridiculous in the world."

"I'm not a millennial." He shook his head. "I'm a Native American."

The car suddenly jolted to the right. Black ice had formed on the surface of the road and James hadn't seen it. He sharply rotated the wheel, forcing the car to turn into the skid. He felt the front tires leave the asphalt and move onto the gravel surface of the shoulder. He held his breath as he snatched the wheel in the opposite direction. The tires returned to the smooth road surface, and he managed to regain control. He pulled the car to a stop fifty yards away, underneath a streetlight that flooded an empty intersection with cold white light.

"Is everybody okay?" His voice trembled.

Nancy took his hand. "We're all right, how about you?"

"A little shook up I guess, but other than needing a change of underwear, I think I'm okay." He laughed nervously at his own joke.

"You handled that like a pro," Clay said. "Do you need me to take back over?"

James shook his head and restarted the car. "I'm good. I'm just going to have to keep a closer eye on the road." He put the Bronco in gear, and they were on their way again.

Chapter Fifty-Four

December 23, 1907
Animas Forks, Colorado

Junior stepped into the cabin, and the smell of fresh-baked biscuits and fried chicken welcomed him. Julia had insisted that their first Christmas together be perfect, and she had told him that she planned to spend the day tidying up and preparing the meal. They would be sharing it with Mr. Peck, the proprietor of the local mercantile, and Pastor Murphy, an itinerant minister from the Methodist church.

Junior watched as his beautiful wife scurried around their small kitchen. The night before at dinner, she had told him her mother's favorite Christmas saying. *December twenty-third should be spent with friends, Christmas Eve with family, and then Christmas Day belonged to the baby Jesus.* Julia had said that she and her father had stuck to the tradition even after her mother passed away. Watching her now, he knew that going forward, this would be their tradition as well.

Junior and his mother had not had any such traditions. Most of their Christmas Eves were spent with Thad at the church, preparing meals for the hungry and others in need. Christmas morning was more silent reflection than Santa Claus, until it was time for services, then a meal of leftovers with Thad from their preparations the night before.

He watched as Julia glided around the woodstove like a ballerina on a stage. She was full of Christmas spirit—made even greater by the ultimate gift that she carried inside her.

"You are amazing."

"Oh!" She jumped and nearly knocked over the pot of beans she was stirring. "You scared the ever-loving wits out of me!"

"I'm sorry." He stomped the snow off his boots, then went over and wrapped his arms around her waist. "I wouldn't scare you for the world." He hugged her to him and kissed her lips. "I love you, you know."

"I know." She kissed him again. "I also know that if you don't let me get back to what I was doing, we are going to be feeding our guests burned beans and dry chicken."

He took off his coat and hat and hung them on a peg near the door.

"Did you find us a tree?" she asked with her back to him.

"It's not hard to find a tree around here, considering that the mountains are covered in them."

"I know that, but we don't need just any tree, we need the perfect tree. One just right for hanging ornaments and strings of popcorn."

He went back over and nuzzled his lips against her ear. "Any tree I bring in here will be perfect, once you're done with it."

The skin behind her ear moistened with the heat of his breath, and he kissed her there. She wiggled her shoulders against him and giggled.

"Stop that." Her voice was low and breathy. "We're expecting guests."

"Not for a few minutes yet," he whispered against the back of her ear, then kissed it again.

"Nooooo," she moaned. He sensed her resistance draining away. "What if they're early?"

"They won't be. That would be rude."

"But—"

He kissed her ear again, then trailed his lips down the length of her neck.

She stepped out of his reach, looked into his eyes, and smiled. Without saying anything else, she moved the beans off the fire and placed the cast-iron cover over the flame.

* * *

Mr. Peck and Pastor Murphy were not early, in fact they were almost half-an-hour late. Not even that spoiled the grand evening they spent breaking bread, talking, and laughing. Julia was thrilled that they enjoyed her cooking. She even allowed Pastor Murphy to sweeten her after-dinner coffee with a taste of Brandy from the flask he kept in the pocket of his suitcoat.

Once the dinner dishes were cleared and washed, Mr. Peck insisted on helping dry them, then they all settled down near the hearth. Pastor Murphy packed his pipe and lit it with a burning twig from the fire, and the smell of pipe smoke filled the room. It reminded Julia of her father, and she fought back a tear.

"It wouldn't be Christmas without gifts!" Mr. Peck announced. He was an older man, and she suspected that he had to be sneaking up on eighty. He used his cane to walk over to his coat by the door and pulled three small packages from its pocket. He returned to the fire, handed one to her, one to Junior, and the third to Pastor Murphy.

"Mr. Peck you shouldn't have," she insisted, feeling a flush grow in her cheeks. "We don't have anything for you."

"Nonsense, young lady. Christmas isn't about getting, it's about giving. Besides, you gifted me with the finest dinner I've had since my Martha passed away over thirty years ago. Now, let's hear nothing else about it."

"I'm too full to argue," Pastor Murphy said from his chair closest to the fire. His nose was red, and Julia suspected that it wasn't all from the heat of the flames. He tore open the brightly colored paper that surrounded his gift and let out a hoot of pleasure when a pouch of Sutliff Tobacco fell out on his lap.

"That's the finest tobacco money can buy," Mr. Peck informed him. "I had it shipped in all the way from San Francisco."

"Well, if that's the case, then I need to give this a try!"

Pastor Murphy leaned out of his chair and knocked the ashes from his pipe out onto the hearth. He opened the pouch and filled it again. This time, when he touched the burning twig to the bowl, the room was filled with the smells of fall leaves, honey, and cinnamon. He puffed hard twice, then settled back into his chair.

"Peck, I can't thank you enough. This is truly the finest tobacco I've ever tasted. I'm afraid you have spoiled other tobaccos for me." He chuckled and took another draw off his pipe.

"You are more than welcome, Pastor. Now, Dr. Mitchell, it's your turn." He smiled and pointed at the thin rectangular gift Junior was holding.

"Okay. Merry Christmas, everyone!" Junior found the corner of the wrapping paper and pulled it loose, allowing the rest of the paper to fall away. Inside was a brown wooden box with a silver latch. He looked up at Mr. Peck with a questioning eye.

"Go ahead, Son. Please."

Julia recognized the pure joy in Mr. Peck's face as he watched Junior flip the latch and slowly open the box. She wondered for a moment if he had ever had children of his own. If he had, she imagined that he would have given *them* a similar look on Christmas morning.

Junior gasped as he opened the box, revealing an ornate glass-tipped pen, a small vial of ink, and a silver Ink Knife. "Mr. Peck, this is too—"

"Shush, shush, shush." Mr. Peck waved his hands at him, smiling ear to ear. "Now you, Miss Julia. We've saved the best for last."

Her hands trembled as she worked the covering loose from around the square box she was holding. Junior's, and Pastor Murphy's gifts had been wrapped in colorful foil paper, but hers was wrapped in a white, silk handkerchief neatly pinned at the sides. She set the dainty cloth to the side and lifted the top off the box. Inside was a second silk piece. A child's rattle lay nestled beneath it atop a third piece of silk. Tears rushed to her eyes as she looked up into the face of kindly Mr. Peck. His eyes glistened in the firelight, and she thought she saw tears forming there as well. With her forefinger and thumb, she carefully removed the crystal rattle from the box and gave it a gentle shake. A thin tinkling sound emerged like snowflakes touching glass.

"How did you know?" she asked.

"When your husband came into the store and inquired about the cost of a crib, I guess I just put two and two together and came up with a baby." He laughed and clapped his hands like a thrilled child.

"I don't know how to thank you." She placed the rattle back into its silken nest, then threw her arms around the old man's neck.

"Well then, this is truly a merry Christmas!" Pastor Murphy stood, saluted them with his pipe, then shook Junior's hand. "Congratulations, my boy. Congratulations!"

The clatter of glass breaking in the next room brought their merriment to a sudden end. Junior let go of Pastor Murphy's hand and rushed into their bedroom.

"Stay here," Mr. Peck told Julia, then he and Pastor Murphy followed Junior into the other room.

She stood nervously next to the fire, waiting for someone to tell her what was going on. Seconds passed like hours, until she couldn't stand to wait any longer. She crossed the room and leaned in the bedroom door. Their clothes and bed things were scattered around the room. The small dresser where she kept her privates stood open. Its drawers had been emptied beneath it next to Junior's traveling case.

"Someone must have come in through the window while we were celebrating." Junior leaned down and righted his case. "Looks like whoever it was found what they were looking for and left the way they came in. They must have broken the window glass getting out."

"Sinful." Pastor Murphy lifted the cross that he wore around his neck, then bowed his head in prayer.

"Let's find something to cover that window," Mr. Peck told Junior. "Then we can help you get things in order."

"Thank you, Mr. Peck, Pastor Murphy, but I think we can handle this ourselves."

Julia could tell in her husband's tone that he was doing all he could to restrain his anger.

"Yes," she added. "We will take care of this. It's late." She motioned for the two men to leave the room and saw them off at the front door. When she returned, Junior was on his knees going through the things that had been scattered about.

"Looks like they took the case containing my mother's things that I brought with me from Providence. There were a few documents in it, and a couple of pieces of her jewelry, but nothing of any worth, and—" He looked up at her. "My father's surgical tools."

Chapter Fifty-Five

December 22, 2008
Silverton, Colorado

"I was starting to think you folks weren't gonna make it," the middle-aged man standing behind the reception desk of the Imperial Hotel said. "What with the snow and all." He was dressed like an Old West bartender, complete with black pants, striped shirt, suspenders, and a bow tie. He wore his salt-and-pepper hair slicked back tight against his scalp, and his handlebar mustache stood proud and erect in front of his rosy cheeks.

"We had a little trouble out on the road coming in, but James here managed to get us here all in one piece." Clay slapped James on the back, and a small avalanche of snow fell off his shoulders.

"We certainly are glad to be here." Nancy placed her bag at the base of the reception desk and stretched. "I'll be even more glad to get settled into a soft, warm bed."

The desk clerk smiled. "Well, let's see just how fast we can make that happen." He shuffled through a few cards he had on the desk, looked back up at them, then back down at the cards. "It says here, three rooms for five guests." He eyed them again. "I only see three of you."

"I said s-s-s-stop it!" Calvin yelled as he rushed in the door. A snowball came flying in after him and hit him in the back. A moment later, Franklin walked in, laughing so hard he could barely breathe.

"Stupid m-m-m-man has never seen snow before, and h-h-h-he is losing his ever-loving m-m-m-mind." Calvin dropped his bag beside Nancy's and started wiping the snow off his glasses with the cuff of his sleeve.

"Now, there's five," James said. "Careful what you ask for." He raised his eyebrows.

"Right." The clerk took one more look at his new guests and sighed. "If you will just kindly follow me, your rooms are ready. They're on the second floor." He headed toward a grand staircase, and with James and Nancy in the lead, they all fell in line behind him.

* * *

"So, this ledger that Cletus gave Clay is basically a day-to-day rundown of what the Kansas City sheriff at the time did," Nancy said. "It lists things like *brawl at Rick's saloon, three arrested*, then it lists their names. Here's another one, *shooting at cockfight, self-defense*."

James leaned out of the small hotel bathroom. "How could a shooting at a cockfight be in self-defense?"

She shrugged and went back to work studying the ledger. She had taken a long, hot shower and changed into her favorite cotton nightshirt once they got into their room. Still warm from her shower, she had sunk into the ridiculously soft king-size bed and pulled the comforter up over her. She had begun to look through the old ledger when James excused himself to the bathroom and started the shower.

Melvin Mitchell Jr.'s letters were on the bedside table. She found the one where he told Thad about visiting the newspaper office in Kansas City. From there, she was able to get an approximate date of his departure from Lawrence, Kansas, when his mother had moved them to Providence. She used that date to try and reconcile events within the ledger.

"Find anything interesting?"

James had a towel wrapped around his midsection and was standing at the foot of the bed, watching her. She looked up at him, and for a split second couldn't think about anything except the drops of water running down his chest.

"Um..." She forced herself to look back down at the ledger. "Do you remember Clay telling us that Doc Mitchell developed a drinking problem after he saved a boy that had been shot? I think I found what he was talking about.

"*November twenty-seventh, 1875. One p.m. gunfight at Gray's House Saloon. Three dead. Marlene Hayes, shooter, Jedidiah Walkins, Mac McGinnis. Three Injured. Jedidiah Walkins Jr., age six, Sally Morton, David Roland. Hayes attacked McGinnis over a pay dispute for services rendered. Hayes chased McGinnis from upstairs room number three, brandishing a pistol in each hand and firing wildly. Both were naked. McGinnis was shot in the back as he tried to run. Hayes then began to fire randomly into the patrons gathered around the bar below. Walkins Sr. shot twice in the back. Walkins Jr. hit four times in upper body. Sally Morton, grazed in upper arm. David Roland shot in hand. Hayes killed by sheriff.*"

"That's awful," James said. "Does it say why a six-year-old kid was in a saloon?"

"Nope it just lists his—" Nancy looked up at him again. He now stood there fully nude, rubbing the towel over his wet hair.

"His what?" He stopped rubbing long enough to peek out at her from underneath the towel.

"His, um— is it warm in here to you?"

"Actually, I thought it was a little bit chilly, but you do have the covers pulled up over you."

"Yeah, I guess I do." She used her feet to push the sheet and comforter down to the end of the bed. "That's better." She smiled up at him and waited for him to start drying his hair again.

"Does the ledger have anything to say about the night Dr. Mitchell was killed?"

"Um—" She tore her eyes away and started flipping through the pages, scanning for mention of the doctor's name. "Yeah, this is it. *December 19, 1875. Ten p.m. Disturbance at the **Excelsior Hotel. Dr. Melvin Mitchell Sr. found dead on site. Head crushed. Witnesses, Melvin Mitchell Jr., age five,** Clayton Caruthers, hotel manager. Caruthers states that he witnessed a tall man leaving the immediate area. Man was possibly wearing a bowler or other style of short-brimmed hat. Undertaker removed body to prepare it for burial."

"That sounds like our cowboy." James headed back toward the bathroom. He stopped at their suitcase and pulled out a pair of sweatpants and a t-shirt.

"Don't you think you're gonna get hot if you wear all that to bed?" She hoped he wouldn't hear the disappointment in her voice.

"Maybe you're right." He tossed the t-shirt back into the bag. "Does it say anything else about that night?" He sat on the edge of the bed and pulled the sweatpants up over his knees, then lay back beside her and arched his back to make it easier to get them over his hips.

"Let me see, the next entry is kinda strange. *December nineteenth, 1875. Eleven forty-five p.m. Returned to office. Door locked, lights off, and jail empty. Prisoner missing, no signs of escape. December twentieth, 1875. Two a.m. No sign of escaped prisoner. Seems odd that he went missing at the same time Dr. Mitchell was killed. Will question Mrs. Mitchell this morning and get statement from Melvin Mitchell Jr.*"

"Does it say if he ever found the missing prisoner?"

"Nope, but I'd say he had his hands full. Check this out. *December twenty-first, 1875. Nine a.m. Funeral for Dr. Melvin Mitchell. December twenty-third, 1875. Eleven-thirty p.m. Disturbance reported at Union Cemetery. Grave of Dr. Melvin Mitchell Sr. desecrated, body removed and discarded. Undertaker moved body to grange office to hold until another casket can be made ready. December twenty-forth, 1875. Nine a.m. Body of Dr. Melvin Mitchell reported missing from grange office. Floor around body was wet from melting ice. No footprints found.*"

Nancy laid the ledger down and looked over at James. "Do you think the missing prisoner dug up the body looking for something?"

"Possibly." James rolled over on his side and skimmed his fingernails across her thigh. "Go back a little way and see if you can find where the guy was arrested. Maybe there's something there that will give us a hint."

"Okay, as long as you keep doing that."

She turned back a page in the ledger and immediately saw the notation on the man's arrest, but she pretended to keep looking because every circle his fingers made sent little waves of energy through her. The feeling was so intense that her toes curled, her fingers balled into fists, and she felt flushed.

"Okay, stop, stop, stop." She scooted sideways, moving out of his reach.

"What's the matter? Did I do something wrong?"

"Not wrong, very not wrong." A shiver passed through her, and she looked back at him over her shoulder. "It's just that I want to show you this bit about the prisoner. If I don't do it now, I'm afraid that after we're through, I'll be way too exhausted and just fall asleep on top of you."

"What do you mean you'll—" His eyes grew large, and he flashed a knowing smile. "Well in that case, you *should* go ahead and show me, but make it quick."

"It's right here." She held the ledger out to him and pointed at the first entry on the page. She read it silently to herself again along with him:

Dec. 19, 1875

6p.m. – Vagrant attempted to steal a ham from Ross Meat Co. When questioned, man was rambling and speaking nonsense. Would only mumble, "He knows he's here, I know he's here, he's coming, he's coming." Sheriff put man under arrest for public drunkenness and placed him in cell #1 to sleep it off. Man was unable to provide name or identification when asked. When offered food, man refused saying,

"No time to eat, must be ready. He knows he's here, I know he's here, he's coming, he's coming." If man is still unable to answer questions in the morning, sheriff will bring in Dr. Collier to examine.

"Well, that doesn't tell us much, does it?" James closed the book and handed it back to her.

"Nope." She placed it on the table beside the bed, slipped the nightshirt she was wearing over her head, giggled, and turned off the light.

Chapter Fifty-Six

December 24, 1907
Animas Forks, Colorado

A loud rapping on the cabin door awakened Julia from a fitful sleep. After the break-in, she had been too nervous to relax. She and Junior had lain in bed until the wee hours of the morning, talking about everything and nothing, but no matter how long they talked, she had not been able to cast away the feeling of dread that buzzed like a hornet's nest in her chest. She slipped out of bed, wrapped a robe around herself, and went to the door.

"Who is it?" she asked through the door.

"It's Constable Mayvery, Mrs. Mitchell. I need to speak to your husband."

"One moment constable, I'll fetch him."

Leaving the door barred, she rushed back into the bedroom. Junior was still asleep and softly snoring.

"Junior, wake up." She began shaking him. "It's the constable, says he needs to see you."

"What?" Junior rolled over and looked up at her, his eyes still puffy with sleep.

"Get up." She pulled the covers off him, letting the cold air get to his bare knees. "The constable is outside. He wants to speak with you."

"What about?"

"How should I know?" She took a step back and placed her hands on her hips. "Now, are you getting up, or should I let him in, and he can just crawl in there with you to talk?"

"Okay, I'm up. Go tell him I'm coming."

Junior stood and stretched, then reached for his trousers. Satisfied that he was really on the way, she returned to the door and removed the bar. "Please come inside, Constable."

"Mighty cold out this morning." Constable Mayvery stomped his feet on the small stone area that served as a porch before stepping into the cabin. "Sorry to bother you folks so early."

"It's no problem, Constable. Junior will be right in, and I'll see what I can do about rustling us all up some hot coffee."

"That would be a true blessing, Mrs. Mitchell. A true blessing." The constable was a big bear of a man with thick red whiskers, a broad chest, and even broader belly. His thick Russian accent was warm and comforting, and it always made her smile.

"My that's a beautiful tree you have there. Expecting old Grandfather Frost, are ya? Er, I mean Santa Claus."

"Not this year." She returned from the cookstove with a cup and saucer in each hand and placed them on the table. "But by this time next year, I suspect we will be placing a few snacks out for the jolly old man." She patted her baby bump and smiled.

"Ah, a *malysh*, I didn't know!" He chuckled joyfully, and his belly bounced in response.

Julia made a mental note that the constable might be perfect to play the jolly old elf for the children in town next year. "That coffee should be ready any minute."

Junior came into the living room. He had combed his hair and tucked his nightshirt into his trousers. "Good morning, Con—"

"Papa!" Constable Mayvery raised his arms and pulled him into a bear hug. "Your beautiful lady just told me the good news!" He let Junior loose, nearly knocking him over in the process. "Congratulations! As my mother used to say, may your ducklings grow to bring you many good eggs!" The constable doubled over, laughing.

Junior gave Julia a confused look and just patted her belly in response. That made him smile as well.

"Coffee's ready!" she chimed. "Pull up a chair and have a seat."

Junior motioned the constable to the chair closest to the fire, then took the seat across the table from him. She filled their cups with hot, black coffee, then poured a cup for herself.

"What brings you by so early on such a cold morning, Constable?" Junior asked once she joined them at the table.

"This." He reached deep inside his coat pocket, and like a magician pulling a rabbit out of a hat, produced the stolen surgical kit. "Ta-da!" He laughed as he laid it between them on the table.

"My father's tools! Where did you find them?"

"Up at the Black Cross Mine. I had gone there for their weekly poker game. There was a new man there who tried to sell them to me for enough money to join the game. Idiot. He had no idea who I was. So, I punched him."

"Why did you hit him?" Julia loved hearing stories like those. Back home, the sheriff only ever talked to the newspaper and usually it had been just to crow about how great he was at his job.

"Huh? I hit him because he deserved it!" He nodded, then smiled across the table at them. "Besides, he wanted twenty dollars for *that*!" He pointed at the stained, white cloth roll sitting in front of him. "Everyone knows it can't be worth more than five."

"Well, it's worth more than that to me." Junior pulled the kit over closer to him on the table. "How about my mother's other things? Did the man have any of those on him?"

"No. I'm sad to say that he did not. But you might check with Mr. Terry. Perhaps the man hid them somewhere near his bunk in the workhouse or where he was working."

"Thanks, I'll do that."

Constable Mayvery lifted his cup of coffee in salute, then drank the entire contents in one big gulp. He smacked his lips and slapped his hand against his chest. "Good coffee!"

"Thank you." She reached for the pot to refill his cup, but the big Russian covered it with his hand.

"No more for me, Mother." He smiled and gave her a quick wink. "Unfortunately, I must go into town and deliver the thief to the federal marshal. If I don't start soon, I'll be too late for the Christmas two-for-one beer special at the Sagebrush." He slapped his hands on the top of the table, stood, and went to the door. "Thank you again for your hospitality!"

He pulled open the door and Julia could see a dog team hitched to a sled outside. Something caught her eye, and she moved to the door for a closer look. The sled was made of cut planks lined with slender limbs that had been attached to the runners with stiff twine. A young man dressed only in torn overalls and a thin cotton shirt was tied to the sled. Ropes were wrapped around each of his wrist's multiple times, then lashed to the runners of the sled. His ankles were trussed up in the same fashion, just above his bare feet. His skin was the color of a clear sky, and his teeth chattered louder than the noises that came from the excited dogs.

Junior joined her in the doorway, and they watched as Mayvery carefully tested each set of knots before stepping behind the sled. He raised his hand as if ready to yell for the dogs to mush, but he stopped short and walked back over to the cabin.

"I forgot to say to you, if you want to talk with Mr. Terry at the Black Cross Mine, you should go soon. He told me he plans to spend Christmas with a *special friend* in Silverton." The constable winked exaggeratedly and poked Junior in the belly with his finger.

He returned to the sled, then gave a deep bow to Julia. "Goodbye, Mother!" He called out to her, then faced forward. "Mush dogs! Mush!" He was off and out of sight within a few seconds.

Chapter Fifty-Seven

December 24, 2008
Silverton, Colorado

"We've got a problem," Clay said, walking up to their table in the restaurant at the Imperial Hotel. He helped himself to a piece of bacon off Franklin's plate.

"Uncool, man!" Franklin gave him a dirty look, then took a piece off Calvin's plate when he wasn't looking.

"There was more snow up on the mountain last night," Clay went on. "The road's closed past Eureka. Evidently, they tried to plow it last night, but the truck lost control and went over a ledge and down into the Animas River. Driver jumped out just in time, but nearly froze to death before he could make it back to town. So, nobody's willing to rent us a Jeep or anything else four-wheel drive. Looks like we're stuck."

Nancy felt herself start to panic. She had never let herself believe that they could come so far and fail. She squeezed James' hand under the table.

"No," James said. "I don't accept that. There *has to* be a way to get up that mountain."

"Look, I want to get to the end of this little adventure as badly as you do, but I'm tellin' ya, it ain't happenin'. At least not for a few days, and then only if they don't get any more snow."

"Excuse me." Franklin slid his chair out and left the room.

"What's with him?" Clay asked.

Nancy shrugged and looked around the table. No one had an answer.

"Guess if he's not going to finish his breakfast, then I best not let it go to waste." Clay sat down and scooted his chair up to the table. He reached for a bottle of syrup, and his sleeve fell into a very full cup of beige-colored coffee. He snatched his arm back but not before managing to spill some of the coffee over the nine, empty creamer containers that were scattered around the cup. "What's this mess?"

"Franklin likes his coffee with extra cream," Nancy told him and had to stifle a laugh.

"S-S-S-So what do we do now?" Calvin asked. "It's all w-w-w-well and good for us to sit here till the spring thaw, but w-w-w-what if the cowboy—"

Franklin burst back into the room. "I got one!" he yelled and raised his hands over his head like a sprinter crossing the finish line. People at the surrounding tables all stopped talking and turned to see what the ruckus was about.

"Not you." Franklin grimaced at them and waited until everyone turned back around. "I got one," he repeated in a whisper.

"One what?" Clay asked as he poured ketchup all over the eggs on the plate.

Franklin walked around the table and leaned in over him. "Those are my eggs."

"No, these *were* your eggs. When you got up and left the table, they became community property. I claimed them, and now the law of squatters' rights says they are mine." He forked a big hunk of scrambled eggs into his mouth and began chewing loudly.

"But—"

"Franklin, honey..." Nancy placed her hand on his arm. "We'll get you some more eggs, but first, tell us what you got."

"Thanks, Nancy." He timidly smiled down at her. "But make 'um fried this time. I don't like scrambled."

She closed her eyes and forced herself not to scream. When the feeling passed, she looked back over at Franklin who was watching Clay eat.

"Franklin, what – did – you - get?" she asked.

"Oh, yeah. I got us a way up the mountain and into the ghost town." He looked back down at the plate in front of Clay and tried to reach for the last piece of bacon. Clay blocked him with a fork.

"Not cool, man." Franklin jumped back away from the table, then moved closer to her and James. "Last night after we got in, I went back out to have a smoke, and I met a guy. Said his name was Fighting Chicken but that I should call him Kareem. He's a Sioux, and his ancestors used to live around here before the white man came and stole their land and killed all the buffalo."

He made a face at Clay who was too busy eating the tall stack of flapjacks to pay any attention.

"Anyway," Franklin continued, "he makes funnel cakes at the shop next door. Last night when he found out that we were both Native American, he said that if I needed anything while I was in town that I should just ask, so I did."

"So, he has a four-wheel drive we can borrow?" she asked, feeling her spirits start to lift.

"No, better."

"What's better to get up a snow-covered mountain than a four-wheel drive vehicle?" James asked him.

"I don't know, man." Franklin shook his head. "But Kareem says we should meet him behind the funnel cake store at noon, and he'll hook us up."

"Don't see that we've got any other choice except to show up and see what this guy's up to." Clay burped, wiped his mouth, then pushed his chair back from the table and stood. "See y'all at eleven forty-five. After a breakfast like that, I need a nap." He belched again and waddled out the door.

"Eleven forty-five then," James said as he stood and offered his hand to Nancy. "I think we could all use a little extra sleep after the last few days."

"I'll head up w-w-w-with you," Calvin said. He slid away from the table and got to his feet. "W-W-W-What about you Franklin? If I lay down and try to n-n-n-nap, do I need to worry about you coming in and waking me up with some of your f-f-f-foolishness?"

"Nope." Franklin pulled out a chair and sat down at the empty table. "I'm still hungry."

"Okay then." Nancy leaned in and kissed him on the cheek. "Thanks for finding us a way."

A waitress passed them as they were leaving the restaurant and Nancy heard her ask Franklin if he needed anything.

"Coffee please, extra cream."

Chapter Fifty-Eight

December 24, 1907
Animas Forks, Colorado

The office of the Black Cross Mine was deserted when Junior arrived. He checked his watch; it was just past noon. Mr. Terry must have headed to Silverton for his special Christmas celebration a little early, and from the look of things, he had taken everyone that worked there with him.

The potbellied stove that sat in the middle of the office was still warm with a big tin coffee pot, half full, sitting on it. He found a clean cup hanging from a nail in the wall behind the stove and poured himself some coffee to try and shake the cold after the long trip up the mountain. The thick, strong coffee burned his throat. It warmed him from the inside out, and after another sip, he felt reinvigorated and ready to search for his mother's things.

His first stop was in the bunkhouse located about fifty yards behind the office. The snow between the two buildings had been trampled into mud, and he fought to keep his balance as he walked through it.

It was murky inside the bunkhouse. Its windows were covered in a dark, yellow film from the coal they burned for heat, and from the pipes and cigarettes the men constantly smoked when they weren't underground. A heavy funk of body odor, stale tobacco, and dirt filled the room.

He looked under the mattress of the first bed he came to, then rifled through the few personal items scattered around the floor and on a small bedside table. Finding nothing, he moved to the next bed, then the next.

It crossed his mind that if one of the miners were to come in and find him going through their things, it could mean trouble—or worse. Miners weren't known for their understanding nature and were often quick to fight first and ask questions later.

When he finished with the last bunk on the right-hand side of the long, narrow room, he had found nothing except for the occasional hidden bottle of rotgut whiskey and a tablet filled with sketches of half-naked showgirls. *I'm wasting my time.* He sat on the bed and took a mental inventory of what had been in his mother's jewelry box.

It had contained her wedding ring, a string of pearls, and a brooch with a small diamond in the center. The pearls had belonged to his grandmother, and the brooch was a gift from his mother's first husband. Junior had taken the wedding ring from her hand the day she passed; he planned to give it to his daughter or future daughter-in-law someday. He couldn't let those things go without having searched everywhere for them. They were just too special, too personal.

The door to the bunkhouse slammed open and banged against the wall. Junior leapt to his feet and drew his pistol. His heart raced, and his finger tingled against the cold steel of the trigger. The sudden rush of adrenaline through his system caused his breath to come in short bursts.

"Who's there?" he called.

No answer. *Probably just the wind.*

All the same, he crossed the room and tried to look out one of the grimy windows to see if anyone was there. It had begun to snow again, and the fat, white flakes made it nearly impossible to see more than a few feet in front of him. From what he could see, the mine camp appeared to be as he had left it. Deserted.

He dropped the pistol back into its holster and took a deep breath of cold air to help calm his nerves. He closed the door and resumed his search at the first bed on the left side. A rat dropped from a hole in the bottom of the mattress and scurried directly toward him. Junior instinctively shrank back from the rodent.

The door slammed open again, this time bringing with it a gust of wind and snow. He turned and saw a small, bent figure in the doorway. "He knows you're here. I know you're here."

A gust of freezing-cold wind and snow blew in around the little man. Junior turned away to protect his eyes. He pulled the pistol again, but when he turned back, the door was empty. He raced outside. Through the falling snow he could just make out a hunched figure sprinting away from camp.

"Hey, you! Stop!" Junior shouted.

The man didn't stop, and he chased after him. The new-fallen snow that rested on top of the mud made running hazardous. His feet threatened to slip out from under him with every step.

He followed the man down the trail toward the nearest mine entrance. The narrow path had a rock wall to one side and a sheer drop on the other. He could see the man's footprints in the snow, even though he couldn't see the man himself on the trail ahead.

Junior rounded a sharp corner in the trail and slid to a stop. The mine entrance was less than twenty yards ahead of him. The little man stood in the mouth of the opening with a lit torch held high over his head. The falling snow sparkled in the torch light as it floated down around him.

"Who are you?" Junior shouted. He pointed his pistol at the dark figure. "I said, who are you?"

The little man began to giggle. The sharp, raspy, high pitch of his voice echoed down the mine behind him, then doubled back, adding to the haunting nature of the sound.

"Who are *you*?" The little man repeated his question back to him.

"Who, who, who?" The maddening giggle came again. "He knows you're here. I know you're here." The man's head jerked to one side like he had heard something speaking to him from deep within the mine. "Oh, yesssssss, yessssss, he *is* going to die. Who's going to kill him? He's going to kill him. Gotta see what's on the inside. Gotta see who comes out!"

The man threw the torch into the mine, then raised both hands in the air. He began to sway, letting his arms move side to side like a tree in the wind. Suddenly, he dropped to his hands and knees like an animal and howled. The sound started low and mournful but quickly became a scream. "He – knows – you're – here!"

Junior pulled the trigger; the gun bucked in his hand. *Missed*. He brought the gun back down and prepared to fire again, but the man was gone.

He waited. There was movement inside the mine, shadows danced on the walls. *He must have picked up the torch.* The light grew darker, then brighter as if the man was pacing up and down inside the passage.

Cautiously, Junior moved toward the gaping hole in the mountain's side. He kept his pistol at the ready, his finger on the trigger. The snow crunched loudly underneath his feet with each step. If the man was waiting for him, he would know that he was getting close.

Junior kept his eyes locked on the entrance to the mine and forced himself to breathe shallow and steady. Only three steps separated him from the opening. His finger tightened on the trigger. Two steps, one. He leapt inside and fired. The bullet ricocheted off the stone wall with a loud smack before burying itself in the handle of the torch. The torch began swinging wildly back and forth at the end of the rope that held it suspended from the roof.

A noise came from behind him. He turned on his heel, raised his gun, and fired. The bullet creased the knuckle of the man whose fist was about to knock him out. The punch landed on the side of Junior's face with the power of a ten-pound sledge, throwing him backward against a pile of rocks. His vision began to fade, yet he saw the face of the man who had hit him. He saw the scar that traveled across it, the dead eye, the broken nose, and the black, decayed teeth behind the curtain of dead flesh that was once his lips.

The darkness overtook him, and Junior's last memory was that of a raspy, giggling voice.

Chapter Fifty-Nine

December 24, 2008
Silverton, Colorado

Clay, James, and Nancy were waiting in the lobby of the Imperial Hotel at eleven forty-five as planned.

"I-I-I-I'm here! I'm coming!" Calvin called to them from the top of the stairs. He was dressed in a bright-green parka, a gray trapper hat with a faux-fur lining, and bright-orange snow pants. The outfit was so cumbersome that he waddled as he descended the steps.

"He looks like a giant lime with stubby little legs," Clay whispered to Nancy who had to turn away to keep from laughing. "Whoo-wee, get a look at you!" He motioned for Calvin to spin around so they could see the whole outfit. "Where in the world did you find that getup?"

"W-W-W-Well Franklin stayed true to his word and let me get some s-s-s-sleep. When I crawled out of bed, I s-s-s-started to get dressed and discovered that I had not packed any winter clothing s-s-s-suitable for the type of weather we are heading into. The hotel has a v-v-v-very nice little gift shop that carries winter outerwear, s-s-s-so I picked the brightest-colored p-p-p-parka and p-p-p-pants that they had. I was thinking that if we s-s-s-separated in the s-s-s-snowstorm, I would be easy to find. This hat was a-a-a-a simple choice. It's the only one they had that f-f-f-fit."

"Well, I think you look amazing," Nancy told him.

"Th-Th-Th-Thank you, Nancy." He smiled at her, then shot Clay a dirty look.

The front door opened, and a man entered carrying a suitcase. He sidestepped when he saw Calvin and passed on the far side of the room. As the door was closing, a snowball came flying in and hit Calvin in the head.

Franklin howled with laughter as he came bounding into the lobby, his gloves covered in melting snow. "I got you, Calvin!" He looked around at the rest of them. No one else laughed. He slouched over and started knocking the snow off Calvin's parka. "It's snowing outside," he said.

Calvin slapped at his hands. "S-S-S-Stop it, s-s-s-stop it!"

"We should get going," Clay said. "Take the lead, Franklin." He opened the door and motioned for Franklin to go first, then stepped in between him and Calvin.

* * *

Snow steadily fell as they stepped out onto the main street in Silverton and followed Franklin to the building next door. Compared to the opulence of the Imperial Hotel, Jake's Funnel Cakes was a bit of a letdown. The sea-foam green building had a neon sign of a steaming funnel cake hung in the front window. James, at first, mistook the neon sign as a steaming pile of dog crap, but he guessed that in context with the giant pastel lettering painted on the window next to it, most people would not make that mistake.

JAKE'S FUNNEL CAKES
Get 'Em While There Hot!

He hoped Jake was better at making funnel cakes than he was at using the English language.

They continued around the building and down an alley that was strewn with trashcans, empty cardboard boxes, and a scroungy-looking mutt that was licking at the bottom of one of the cans.

"Oh, poor baby!" Nancy tried to pet the dog but almost lost a few fingers when the animal snapped at her outstretched hand. She quickly moved behind James, giving the dog a wide berth.

"Brudder!" Kareem shouted when he saw Franklin.

The two men embraced like long-lost siblings, hugging and slapping each other on the back. The lovefest went on so long that Clay cleared his throat to get Franklin's attention.

"Brother Kareem, these are my friends." Franklin motioned to them, doing his best Vanna White imitation.

"Bredren, Sistren, it is most excellent to be makin' your acquaintance, bra."

"I thought he was supposed to be an Indian," Clay whispered. "Sounds like Jamaican to me."

James shrugged.

Kareem was wearing a rainbow-colored rastacap over a head full of dreadlocks. Despite the cold, he had on sandals, board shorts, and a t-shirt that read *Reefer Rules* over a picture of a smoking doobie.

Nancy stared at the man that currently had his arm around Franklin's shoulder. "I thought Franklin said you were Native American?"

"I am, sista, I am! On my mudder's side." Kareem grinned and held his hand out for Franklin to slap him five. "My bruh, Franklin, says you need a righteous ride to get up to yon ghost town. Da road gonna be treacherous, bro. But I've got primo transport awaitin'. Check it out!"

Kareem stepped to the side and James' heart sank. Behind him were two beat-up old Ski-Doo snowmobiles.

"Hoo! Hoo!" Kareem danced his way over to the snowmobiles and ran his hand down the bright-orange hood of the one nearest him. "Vintage 1980s craftsmanship, bra. All original parts and low, low mileage." He jumped into the driver's seat of the glowing, orange monstrosity and pulled the cord that started the engine. The snowmobile groaned, then caught with a loud backfire and a puff of black smoke from the tailpipe. "She's alive!"

James leaned over toward Clay. "What do you think?"

"I think were gonna die halfway up the mountain, but what choice do we have at this point?"

Kareem walked back over to him. "Dees fine beauties can be yours to-day, for de low, low price of just four hunnerd greenbacks." He held out his hand and gave him a wink and a smile.

"Two," James countered.

"Ya hurtin' my feelings, bra. Here you is stuck in town, and I got de only way up yon mountain. What would my babies tink?"

"They'd think you made two hundred dollars renting two snowmobiles for a day that you probably couldn't sell for two hundred dollars total. So, take it or leave it."

"Bra, I'm damaged by what you say, but I'll take it. Cash."

James pulled two, one hundred dollar bills out of his wallet and started to pass them to Kareem, but Nancy stopped him.

"Wait," she said. "There's a problem."

"What is dat, sista girl?" Kareem looked offended.

"Those are two-seaters, and there's five of us."

"She's right." James turned back to Kareem. "If we all can't go, then none of us will."

Kareem's face brightened. "No worries, Fighting Chicken's got you, mon!"

The Native American Rastafarian turned and ran into the back storage room of the funnel cake shop. He returned a second later, pulling a dogsled and carrying a short piece of chain.

"Hoo-hoo, lookie what I gots for you!" He dropped the sled at the rear of the first snowmobile he came to and wrapped the chain around the front support of the sled. The other end of the chain he attached to a small trailer hitch on the back of the snowmobile. "Ta-da!" He spun around and landed like a champion ice skater with his hands raised over his head, then took a deep bow.

Franklin clapped enthusiastically.

"Well, what are we waiting for?" James laid the two bills in Kareem's hand, then escorted Nancy to the closest snowmobile.

Clay helped Calvin aboard the other, then climbed into the driver's seat.

"What about me?" Franklin asked.

"Bruh," Kareem said, shaking his head. "Looks like you gotta sit in da *back* of da bus."

Franklin sulked over to the sled and Kareem secured him in with two ropes that were tied to the runner supports.

"All's clear my brudders!" Kareem pretended to wave a starting flag.

James motioned for Clay to take the lead.

Clay had to pull the cord multiple times, then adjust the choke and pull again to get his snowmobile started. The resulting backfire left Franklin in a cloud of exhaust that didn't clear until they pulled away from the funnel cake shop and out onto the main street. James gave his snowmobile some gas and fell in behind them.

Chapter Sixty

December 24, 1907
Animas Forks, Colorado

An odor worse than any smelling salts irritated Junior's nose and pulled him from his unconscious stupor. He fought to get his eyes open, then wished he had lost that battle. He was suddenly five years old again, running through darkness in the lot behind the Excelsior Hotel. His momma wanted his daddy to come to bed—it was late. His daddy was dead. The cowboy killed him. The cowboy was holding him by his shirt. The cowboy was looking into his eyes. He was scared. The cowboy— *The cowboy*— **The Cowboy**—

The cowboy was less than an inch away, staring at him. His hot, rancid breath spread over him with each crackling exhale. The cowboy smiled. The lips on the undamaged side of his mouth turned up while the other side only quivered as the long-dead muscles there tried to follow suit. The cowboy huffed, spewing more of the death smell from his lungs into Junior's face, then he turned and walked out of the mine.

A thick rope was wrapped multiple times around Junior's upper arms, he tried to lean forward but his arms were somehow attached to the boards behind him. Another rope encircled his midsection and bound him tightly there as well. He was still able to move his arms below the elbows so he reached underneath himself as far as he could in that awkward position. His fingers touched a cold, metal hitch. He turned his head to the right and saw rough boards, the same to his left. They had him tied to a mine cart.

"Let me up from here!" He struggled against the ropes that bound him. The only answer he received was the echo of his own voice ricocheting off the walls of the mine. "Are you still here? You can keep the jewelry. I don't care. Just untie me!"

"Just untie me, just untie me, just—" The little man he had followed into the mine shuffled into view, then suddenly stopped as if frozen in place.

"Please, let me up." The pleading sound of his own voice came back to Junior and it made him sick. He had never begged another man for anything in his life, why should he start now? He would just wait for the right chance and make his move. They would have to untie him sometime, wouldn't they? Then he could—

Julia is waiting for me back home. I told her I'd only be gone a few hours. What if they don't? What if they kill me or leave me to freeze to death tied to this stupid cart? What if—

The little man's head slowly turned toward him. The rest of his body remained stone still.

His beady, little-man's eyes locked with Junior's. Suddenly, he skittered across the distance that separated them and stopped with his nose less than an inch from Junior's.

"Knock, knock," the little man whispered. His voice was low and breathy, and his breath smelled sickly sweet like he had been eating candy. "Who's there?" He answered his own question and snickered. "You don't know, do you? Or do you know? He doesn't know, just look at him. Oh, he might, he might."

The little man stood up and reached over into the cart, pressing his chest against Junior's face. He rummaged around, searching for something. All the while, his body was forcing Junior's head back against the rough wooden boards of the cart. Wood splinters ground their way into his scalp and tore at the flesh there like the claws of an angry cat. He tried to use his head to push the man back but didn't have the strength. In desperation, he opened his mouth and bit the man's soft belly.

The little man screamed and jumped back. "Careful, he bites," he hissed, rubbing at the place where he had been bitten. "Tickles, like a feather." He giggled. "Or maybe a horsefly. Yes, tickles like a horsefly."

He had a coil of rope in his hand. He drew out a few feet of it and swung it over his head. "I'm a cowboy!" he crowed and galloped in a small circle. He threw the rope in Junior's direction. It fell far short of reaching him. "I'm not a cowboy." He dropped the rope and began sulking like a child. His voice was rife with disappointment, and Junior might have felt sorry for him if the situation were different. The man was more child than adult, his mind wasn't right. His constant asking, then answering his own questions, his playfulness and sudden swings from laughing to anger were all signs of a disturbed personality.

"He say, I gotta do it, so I gotta do it."

The man dropped to his hands and knees. He placed one end of the rope between his teeth, then crawled toward Junior. When he got close, he rolled over on his back and began batting Junior's hand like a cat taunting a mouse.

"Stop that!" Junior demanded, thinking that perhaps the voice of authority would get the man's attention.

"Stop that," the little man repeated back to him. "Stop that, stop that, stop that, stop that."

He grabbed Junior's hand with a grip so strong that the small bones located there ground together, sending bolts of electricity shooting up into his elbow. "Stop that," the little man said, and used Junior's arm to pull himself up onto his feet. "Stop that." He wound the rope around Junior's wrists and secured it with a tight knot.

Within seconds, Junior felt his fingertips grow numb.

"Stop that." The little man ran to the opposite side of the mine where a metal fastener with a loop at the end had been drilled into the rock. He threaded the end of the rope through the loop.

"*You* stop it!" the little man bellowed across the tunnel at him with the tone of a belligerent child. He held the end of the rope and marched back toward him, stomping the ground with each step. He grabbed Junior's free arm and tied the rope around it as he had done the other.

"Come out, come out before it's too late," he whispered in Junior's ear.

"I don't understand. What do you want from me?"

"We want who's inside you to come out. No, we don't we, yes, yes, we do, a'fore it's too late, yes."

"But there's no one inside me. There's—"

A shadow passed over them as the cowboy came back inside and stepped up next to the little man.

"Too late," the little man whispered, then gave Junior a quick kiss on the cheek. He scurried back to the cowboy's side, then reached up and tugged at his sleeve. The cowboy reached into his trouser pocket and rewarded the little man with a hunk of clear rock candy.

"We did good, yes we did, no." He popped the sweet sugar rock in his mouth and began to giggle again.

The cowboy ambled forward, bent down, and looked into Junior's face.

"I don't understand." Junior shook his head. Tears rushed to his eyes and spilled down over his cheeks, but he didn't care. "My wife, the baby, please don't, please—"

The cowboy stood and kicked the wooden wall of the cart right beside Junior's face. The immense power in his legs shot the cart backward. The ropes around Junior's wrists snapped tight, ripping his arms from his body at the elbows. The cart rolled to a stop a few feet farther down the mine shaft, leaving two distinct trails of blood marking its path. The cowboy walked up and once again stared deep into Junior's face, until the last of his life blood flowed out onto the ground and the light left his eyes.

Chapter Sixty-One

December 24, 2008
Animas Forks, Colorado

The morning's snowfall tapered off as Nancy and the others passed the abandoned mining settlement of Eureka and headed north toward the ghost town called Animas Forks. The twelve-mile trek was proving to be even more challenging than they expected as they threaded their way between steep mountainsides and the Animas River from which Animas Forks had gotten its name.

Nancy held on tight to James with her arms wrapped around him and her hands clasped across his chest. Their closeness kept her warm and made her feel safe at the same time. The snowmobile carrying Clay and Calvin traveled beside them, except in the areas where the road—or what they could see of it—made it impossible. Occasionally, she looked back to make sure that the dogsled carrying Franklin was still attached. After nearly three hours of heavy snowfall compounded by blowback from the snowmobile, Franklin looked more like a sledding snowbank than a person. They had stopped a half hour or so earlier to refill the snowmobiles' gas tanks, and he had assured her that he was okay, and that the piled-up snow actually protected him from the wind.

Now that the snow had stopped, she could look around and was taken by the beauty of their surroundings. Mountain peaks jutted out above them, and they were close enough to see the new-fallen snow blowing off them. *It looks like angels leaving Earth and flying to Heaven.* She took in a deep breath of cold, crystal-clean air and hugged herself tighter to James' back.

"Everything okay back there?" James raised his voice over the roar of the engine.

"Just perfect," she answered.

"Hopefully, were getting close."

"I'm in no hurry. I could stay like this for a long time." She tightened her grip around his chest, and he wiggled his shoulders against her in response.

* * *

An hour later, as the sun began its descent behind the highest of the nearby peaks, the temperature began to drop dramatically.

"Do we have enough gas?" Nancy asked in James' ear.

He knocked the accumulated snow off the fuel gage. It read less than a quarter of a tank.

"I hope so!" he called back to her. "The map said it was just over twelve miles from Silverton, and from the odometer, it looks like we are nearing ten now."

Her head nodded against his back. At that rate, it would take them over six hours to travel those twelve miles, and it was glaringly obvious that their plan of getting rid of the tools and getting back to town in one day was not going to happen.

Kareem had loaded Franklin's sled with two, five-gallon tanks of gas. They had emptied one and a little bit of the other into their tanks when they stopped a few hours before. That meant that they might not have enough to make the trip back. He didn't want to think of the situation that that would leave them in, instead, he placed his hope in the fact that the trip back was all downhill, so they would need less gas for the ride home. At least, he hoped so.

Clay began waving to get his attention. He looked over and laughed. For most of the trip, Calvin had put up a good fight trying to sit up straight with his hands in his lap behind Clay. Now, he was leaning against Clay with his arms around him, lying in the same position as Nancy.

Clay waved again and pointed to the side of the road ahead. Something was sticking up out of the snow. As they approached, he could see that it was the top of a road sign that had become buried in a snow drift. They glided to a stop across from it. The top of the sign was a painting of mountain ranges, everything below that was unreadable.

Clay took off his helmet and ran his hands through his sweaty hair. Calvin straightened up when Clay moved, and he removed his as well.

"Are w-w-w-we there?"

"Sit tight," Clay told him. "I'm gonna go see what that sign says."

When Clay's feet only pushed through a few inches of snow, James decided it was time for all of them to stretch their legs. He took off his helmet, then helped Nancy with the fastener on hers.

"I figure we could all use a break." He took her hand and helped her off the snowmobile.

"What I could use is a restroom."

"Well, I don't know about any public facilities in the area, but there is a nice-looking bush just over there." He grinned and pointed at a stand of sagebrush they had just passed.

"Any port in a storm." She shrugged and headed for the bush.

"Looks like we made it," Clay announced. He and Calvin joined him at the sign as he brushed away the final bit of snow that had been covering it.

Below the mountainscape was written:

Animas Forks
Historic Site
BUREAU OF LAND MANAGEMENT
GUNNISON FIELD OFFICE

"This must be the p-p-p-place," Calvin said, then looked around himself. "Where's F-F-Franklin?"

James looked back at the dogsled and the mound of snow that had built up on it. "You don't think—"

They ran to the sled and started digging away the snow. Clay was the first to find Franklin beneath it. He undid the fastener on Franklin's helmet and carefully lifted it off him. Underneath, Franklin's eyes were closed. The skin of his face had a strange, pale quality to it, giving his normally dark complexion a touch of gray.

James uncovered his arm and placed two fingers against the bottom side of his wrist. "He's got a pulse." He shook Franklin's shoulder. "Franklin, Franklin! Wake up. Can you hear me?"

For a moment, there was no response, then Franklin wrinkled his nose and smacked his lips. His tongue darted out and back in, and he swallowed hard. He slowly opened his eyes and looked around at them.

"Are we here?" he asked. "Do you think there's any coffee? I'm thirsty."

Clay huffed and walked away without saying anything.

"Why don't you get up and walk around a little?" James said. "It'll do you good."

"Okay." He pushed himself out of the accumulated snow and stood up. "Cold," he said and rubbed at his arms and legs.

"Walking around will help with that, too."

"James!" Clay called out from the side of his snowmobile. "Come look at this."

He left Franklin to his own devices and joined Clay and Calvin who were studying a map of the area. Another gift from Kareem.

"From the looks of this," Clay said, "we've got another half mile or so before we reach what's left of the town. I guess you've figured out that we are stuck here for the night."

"If not for longer," James said with a nod. "We used a little over half our fuel getting up here, so we may not have enough to get back."

"I thought about that, too, but I noticed a ranger station just outside of Eureka. I'm guessing there's a radio there, so if we can get back that far we should be able to radio for help."

A wave of relief washed over James.

Franklin came rushing over to them, grabbed Clay's sleeve, and started pulling at him. "You guys, come over here! I found something!" He tugged at Clay's sleeve and started to walk away. Clay didn't move, and Franklin nearly fell in the snow. "Seriously, it's important!"

Clay took a deep breath and looked over at James, the frustration on his face evident.

"Come on," James said. "Let's go see what he found."

They reluctantly started following Franklin back in the direction of the sign.

"Look, look!" Franklin yelled excitedly, still pulling on Clay's coat.

"Calm down, Franklin. We're right here with you," James said as they stopped next to the road sign.

"I think we're here." Franklin pointed at the sign they had already uncovered. "I found this road sign! We made it, guys. We made it." He jumped over and hugged James' neck, then Calvin's, but when he turned to Clay, the big man just shook his head and walked away.

"What?" Franklin asked.

"Come on, Franklin," James said. "I think you've spent too much time on the sled." He put his arm around Franklin's shoulders and led him back to the snowmobiles.

"We better get moving before it gets any darker," Clay told them. He put the map back in its plastic cover and placed it in the storage under the seat. "Where's Nancy?"

"She went to water a bush," James answered. "Why don't we top off the tanks while we wait?"

* * *

The sweet relief of emptying your bladder after holding it for a long period of time is something so glorious that it can never be described in words, but if I had to try... I might say bliss, joy, ultimate satisfaction.

None of those seemed satisfactory, but they would have to do. Nancy gave her hips a little wiggle and started to stand but stopped short when something moved above her.

About ten feet over her head, a narrow ledge protruded from the sheer rock face. She had picked this particular spot to do her business because of that ledge, and the protection that it seemed to give. Now she wasn't so sure she had made a wise choice. The sound seemed to have come from up there. She waited hesitantly, afraid that if she moved, whatever was up there would notice and jump down.

They have cougars in Colorado, don't they? Do cougars hibernate?

She knew that bears did. She squatted there a while longer with the snow radiating cold against her bare backside. When she had first taken that position, the feeling had brought a little thrill with it, but now, she was getting uncomfortable.

I probably just imagined it. James will laugh when I tell him what happened. I'll think it's funny, too, when I'm not squatting bare-ass in a bush anymore.

She listened again, didn't hear anything, and decided it was okay to move.

She stood and had her pants about halfway up her thighs when the noise came again. She dropped back down and stifled a scream.

"Wass she doin' to dat bush, hidin'I think, don't think so." A scratchy, whispered voice floated down to her, followed by the sound of feet shuffling through snow. A small shower of ice and pebbles rolled off the ledge and hit the snowbank next to her, causing a tiny avalanche.

"I wanna see, see what, just see, no not nice, shaddap you." Shuffle, shuffle, shuffle.

Nancy didn't know what to do. Someone was up there and he had been watching her pee. She was scared, angry, and humiliated all at the same time. She wanted to scream for him to show himself, but what if he wasn't just a perv but dangerous?

I'll scream for James. He'll get here before anything can happen.

Shuffle, shuffle, shuffle.

"Ohhh, pretty like a ma, no not ma, like a ma, no."

The voice was coming from directly above her now. She steeled herself and looked up at the section of the ledge that jutted out over her head. She saw nothing, but then something moved. A shadow passed over the edge, then drew back. She held her breath, waiting for a chance to run, to cry out, to do something, anything other than just squat there.

Shuffle, shuffle, shuffle.

"Scared yes, no, no such thing, shhh, no shh."

The shadow moved again, and a black, misshapen oval inched out over the edge.

She trembled; her legs were cramping, and her hands jittered in response to the fear that raced around inside of her.

Within the blackness, blood-red eyes opened and peered down at her. It was a face, not black, but filthy, covered in scars. A hand appeared and picked at one of the scars near the corner of its eye. Something peeled away, and it flinched. "Ouch! Stop it, no-no-no-no ma not ma."

The head jerked, the eyes widened, and it jerked again, this time more violently.

"Arrrgh!" An angry growl escaped it, and it lunged forward. Now she could see the whole face, blood-red eyes sunk deep into the blackened and scarred skin, a nose almost nonexistent amongst the scar tissue.

"Roollf." A guttural sound rolled out of it, bringing with it a long, pink tongue that lapped out and licked at the side of its mouth. "Roollf."

She screamed and bolted from her hiding place in the bush. She managed three strides. Her pants tangled around her ankles and sent her face-first into the snow.

* * *

James was just topping off the tank of the first snowmobile when he heard Nancy scream. She burst out of the brush and fell. He dropped the gas can and rushed toward her.

"Up there on the ledge!" Clay yelled from behind him.

He dropped down beside Nancy and looked up. There appeared to be a little old man crouching down above where she had just been.

A shot rang out. A portion of the ledge exploded, sending snow and debris into the air. James dropped on top of Nancy to protect her. When he looked back up, the little man was nowhere to be seen.

The others rushed toward them. James helped Nancy to her feet, then stood between her and the other men, making a type of human shield until she could put herself back together.

Clay still had his pistol in his hand as he searched the mountainside with his eyes, trying to catch another glimpse of the intruder.

Nancy's cold hand touched James' hand, and he turned and wrapped his arms around her shaking body. He held her tightly. "You're safe," he whispered. "You're okay. I have you. Whoever was watching you is gone."

She nodded against his chest, and her tremors began to subside. "I'm okay. I'm okay." She placed her hand on his chest and looked up into his eyes, then began to cry and fell back into his arms.

"Get her to the snowmobiles," Clay said. "I'm going to take a closer look at that ledge." He touched Nancy's back. "If he's still up there," he whispered, "I'll find him."

"I'll go with you." Franklin fell in with Clay, and they headed toward the ledge.

James put his arm around Nancy's shoulders. "Let's get you warmed up." She leaned against him as they walked.

Calvin rushed ahead and had blankets ready. James helped her settle down onto the dogsled, and Calvin wrapped her up, making sure to tuck the blankets in tightly around her.

"Thank you." She looked up at them and used the corner of a blanket to dry her eyes. "I feel so silly screaming like that but—"

"D-D-D-Don't," Calvin told her and squatted down beside her. "If it had b-b-b-been me, I would have screamed, too!"

That made her smile.

Clay and Franklin returned a few minutes later.

"All we found were some footprints in the snow," Clay said. "I swear it looks like whoever it was paced around in circles before he knelt to look at you, Nancy. Like he was confused or trying to make a decision. It's crazy."

"Crazy is right," James agreed. "We've got enough crazy going on right now, we don't need this. Let's finish filling the tanks and get into town and see if we can find any shelter for the night. Tomorrow morning, we will get rid of the tools and get the hell out of Animas Forks."

"That might be a problem." Franklin was standing beside the other snowmobile. He picked up the gas can and turned it upside down. It was empty.

"Shit," James muttered under his breath. "When I heard Nancy scream, I panicked and just threw the can down. Now we probably don't even have enough gas to get back to Eureka."

"Let's worry about that in the morning." Clay put a hand on James' shoulder. "I'm more interested in finding shelter and building a fire, so we can get Nancy and the rest of us warm."

"Right." He stood and shook Clay's hand. "And thanks."

"Why don't you ride behind Nancy on the sled? Franklin can drive the other snowmobile into town."

James nodded and stepped behind the sled where two runners extended past the end. He stepped onto the runners, then bent down and whispered to Nancy, "I'll be right back here for the rest of the trip."

She looked back at him and mouthed, *thank you,* then put on her helmet and pulled the blankets up around her.

Chapter Sixty-Two

December 24, 2008
Animas Forks, Colorado

"Looks like our luck may have taken a turn toward the better," Clay said. He got a fire going inside the ancient fireplace in one of the few, fully intact buildings that remained in Animas Forks. "Chimney's pulling the smoke out. That's a good sign."

James hadn't known what to expect, but when they rounded the curve in the road and Animas Forks was laid out in front of them, it didn't take him long to realize that the ghost town was more ghost than town. Seven structures could be seen sticking out of the white blanket of snow. The most prominent of them was a large, two-story home. Its Victorian style stood out from the smaller, cabin-type structures that dotted the hills around it. Clay pointed to the house, and they started making their way down what at one time must have been the main street of the town.

Efforts had begun to restore—or at least *save*—what was left of the old buildings. Modern metal scaffolding stood beside one of them, others were wrapped in caution tape. With the sun fully set, the buildings took on a haunted look as they cast their shadows across the unblemished snow.

Nancy tapped his hand to get his attention and pointed at the sky over the farthest reaches of the town. Birds were flying in a circular pattern there, moving in and out of the dark silhouette of a mountain peak that rose sharply at the edge of town. In the fading sun, he thought he could just make out a cut through the mountains. The road, if that's what it was, climbed steeply before leveling off near the mountain's peak.

James wondered if the others' nerves were as frayed as his, after the encounter earlier on the road. He had taken on the job of lookout, watching for anything strange, while the others concentrated on their driving. Trouble was, everything there was strange. Everywhere he looked seemed to have something hiding in the ever-lengthening shadows. His mind raced with the possibilities of danger waiting around every building, or hiding in the evergreen trees that dotted the sides of the mountains that surrounded them. He breathed a sigh of relief when they made it inside the big house on the hill.

A massive bay window opened out of the wall behind them, giving an incredible view of the moonlit snow and the buildings below. The rest of the house was made of exposed, hand-cut boards. Rough saw marks were still visible in the wood, and large knot-holes made a perfect playground for rats and other critters that might be looking for a warm place to sleep. Strands of material hung down from the overhead boards and cast dancing shadows across the walls in the firelight.

"What's all that hanging down from the ceiling?" Nancy asked as she looked around the big room.

"Probably cloth soaked in sap or some kind of glue," Clay answered. "A lot of the old houses would use that concoction as insulation along with straw and mud." He pulled out his knife and dug at a soft spot in the wall he was leaning against. "This was probably the nicest place in town back in its day. Hard to believe that was over a hundred years ago." He stood and dropped the knife back in his pocket.

"You should all stay put till I have a chance to check things out."

Clay pulled his pistol from the holster he wore draped over his shoulder, then zipped up his parka. "A breath of fresh air will do me good. You two lovebirds enjoy the fire."

A burst of cold air swept through the room when Clay opened the door.

"Brrrr..." Nancy purred and snuggled up tighter against James. "This would be romantic if it weren't for the fact that we could be killed at any minute."

"We're safe enough for now," he reassured her. "Clay's out walking patrol, and Franklin and Calvin are upstairs. I doubt anything could get in here right now without someone noticing."

A board squeaked, and Nancy stiffened against him.

"It's just Franklin or Calvin. Relax, everything's okay."

She smiled up at him, took a deep breath, and closed her eyes. "I love ya, you know."

"I love you, too." He bent down and placed a soft kiss on the tip of her nose.

Whomp!

Something heavy hit the floor above them. Nancy abruptly sat up and slammed into his nose with the top of her head.

"What was that?"

"Oh, my nose," he groaned.

"What?" Nancy looked around at him.

A thin trickle of blood ran out from underneath James' hand and down onto his upper lip.

"Oh my God, James." She scooted around behind him and pulled his head back against her shoulder. "Here, let me see." After gently wiping the blood away with the corner of the blanket, she felt along the bridge of his nose.

"Is it broken?" His voice came out hollow and weak, but he couldn't help himself. "Well, is it?"

"I don't think so. I'm so sorry." Nancy leaned to one side and gently placed a kiss on his nose. "That'll make it better."

"My mother used to do that. I didn't understand it then, and I still don't." He managed a soft laugh, then grimaced when a pain shot through his nose and across beneath his eye.

"Doctors always make the worst patients."

Whomp!

A fine mist of dust rained down on them.

"Cut it out up there, you guys!" Nancy yelled.

"Franklin, quit foolin' around!" James angrily added.

Whomp!

"That's it!" James got to his feet, then stood there for a moment to let the room stop spinning. "I'm gonna go put a stop to whatever's going on up there."

"But—"

"It'll be fine, Nancy. If I need anything, I'll yell, and Clay's just outside if you need him." James pulled a small flashlight from his pack and headed for the stairs. "I'll be right back."

"Promise?"

"I promise." He gave her what he hoped was a confident smile, then headed up the ancient stairs. Six steps up, the staircase took a hard turn. He looked back down at Nancy. He thought she might have been crying, and for a second, he considered turning back and waiting with her till Clay returned.

Whomp!

Something above him in the darkness hit the floor with enough force that the stairwell shook. He braced his free hand against the wall to keep from tumbling down.

With each step, the light from the fire in the room below grew dimmer. He pressed the button on the side of the flashlight, and a weak beam illuminated the steps ahead of him. He shook it and slapped it against his leg, trying to get more power out of the cold batteries. It didn't help.

"Franklin! Calvin! I'm coming up."

The next step brought his eyes level with the floor of the second story. Cobwebs reflected the light from the flashlight back at him as dust particles floated through its beam. Otherwise, nothing moved.

"Where are you guys? This isn't funny."

Another step up and he could see down the length of the narrow hallway. A closed door sat halfway down each side of the hall. The single door at the end was open and a soft glow radiated from inside. He pointed his flashlight in that direction and thought he saw someone cross the beam.

"Calvin, is that you?"

A cold breeze blew down the hallway. He shivered. Something skittered off to his right. He swung his light around and saw the tail of a large rat disappear into a crack between two boards. When he shined his light down the hallway, the door was closed.

"James!" Nancy called out. "Is everything all right up there?" Her voice echoed from the room below him.

"Yeah," he called back, sounding jittery. He didn't want to alarm her, so he forced himself to calm down and tried again. "Yeah, so far so good!"

He continued up onto the landing, keeping his light concentrated on the door at the far end of the hall.

"You guys better not be messing with me. If I get down there and you're not dead, you're gonna wish you were!" He immediately regretted the words.

Cautiously, he made his way down the hall. The skittering came again, this time from behind him, and he stopped. *Stupid rat.* He closed his eyes, took a deep breath, and counted to ten before opening them again.

This part of the house had not seen the restoration work that the lower level had. The floorboards in the hall were warped and uneven. The doors were water-stained and covered in graffiti and initials that past visitors carved on their surface. Lengths of old wallpaper hung loose and flopped in the air currents like the wings of a dying bird. He shined his light on a larger piece and could just make out the old pattern of golden leaves and filigrees now almost too faded and dirty to see.

The door at the end of the hall creaked open—its old hinges

moaning in protest. The flashlight's beam revealed part of something lying just out of sight inside the room.

If this was a horror movie, then a guy in a hockey mask will be waiting for me to go in there with his ax held over his head.

James leaned against the wall and placed his hand on his chest. His heart was beating too hard and too fast, and he took a few deep breaths to try and slow it down.

Great. It's bad enough that I'm up here, but am I really gonna psych myself out thinking about Freddy and Jason? What's next—the wolf man? Just get a grip on yourself and get on with it.

He took one more deep breath, pushed the door fully open, and entered the room. Franklin was lying just inside the door. James dropped to his knee and touched his fingers to the side of Franklin's neck. His pulse was strong.

"J-J-J-James!"

He snapped his light to the side. "Calvin!"

Calvin was sitting in the corner with his legs splayed out in front of him. He had blood on his face and also on the shaking finger that pointed at something behind him.

"Calvin, what—?"

"Hit, hit hard him, no, yes, hit him!"

Something heavy struck James in the back of the head, and the world went dark.

* * *

"James, are you all right? Jesus God, James!" Clay shook James' shoulder, hoping to heaven that he would open his eyes. "James! Can you hear me?"

His eyes fluttered, then sprung open.

"Thank God, you—"

James jumped up and landed on top of Clay with his fist raised over his head. His face was a mask of panic and fear, his eyes darting left and right.

"It's me, it's me! Clay! Calm down buddy, just calm down."

James' arm slowly lowered, and he slumped over to the side. "What happened?"

"That's what I'd like to know." Clay sat up and touched the knot at the back of James' head.

"Ouch!" James ducked away from his touch, then sat up straight. The panic had returned to his eyes. "Franklin, Calvin—?"

"They're okay, but you all have matching lumps. Where's Nancy?" Clay asked.

"She's downstairs, I heard a noise and—"

Clay slowly shook his head. Now *he* was starting to panic.

They both jumped to their feet and ran for the stairs. Calvin and Franklin were standing in the hallway outside the door and were nearly run down as they passed.

* * *

"No!" James cried out when he saw the empty room downstairs. The blanket he and Nancy had been sitting under was torn into pieces, and their bags that had been placed neatly beside the door had been ransacked and were now scattered across the room. Nancy's backpack was missing. He ran for the door, but Clay caught his arm before he could get to it.

"Slow down before you rush out there and get yourself killed!"

He wanted to slug Clay, wanted to tell him what he could do to himself. Nancy was missing, and he had to find her.

"Tell me what happened," Clay said.

"We don't have time for that, we have to find her!"

"We will." Clay's tone was calm and in control. He took him by his shoulders and forced him to look at him. "Wherever she is, she had to leave tracks in the snow. If you go rushing out there all crazy, you are just liable to mess up the one clue we have to help find her. Understand?"

"Shit!" James closed his eyes tightly together and stomped his foot on the hard wooden floor. "Okay, you're right, you're right." He opened his eyes and used his sleeve to wipe away the tears of frustration that threatened to run down his cheeks.

"What's going on?" Franklin asked as he came downstairs. "Where's Nancy?"

"We don't know," Clay said. "But we're going to find her."

"Damn right, we are," James said. "Now let's quit all this standing around and start looking." They needed to get moving. If Clay wasn't going to get them organized, he would. "Franklin, take Clay with you and go back upstairs and check all the other rooms."

"I did that before I came down." Franklin said. "They're all empty."

"Are you sure?" Clay asked.

James could tell from the tone of Clay's voice that he doubted Franklin had actually done it.

"Yup." Franklin nodded.

"Then she's gotta be outside somewhere." James spun on Clay. "You were outside. Did you see anything?"

"I did, but not her. I saw something moving in the shadow of the house across the street. I went to check it out."

"And..." James raised his eyebrows and motioned for him to hurry up.

"It was a racoon. Damn thing nearly tore my arm off." Clay pointed at the tears in the sleeve of his parka. "Get your coats on, we're going to do this systematically, making sure we don't miss anything. I'll take the lead—I've got the strongest flashlight—then you, James, then Calvin, and Franklin. We will go out of the house and turn to the right. Stay in a line, that way we are only leaving one trail. Got it?"

"Yeah." James nodded. "But I think I should take the—"

"No, you shouldn't. You're too upset, and if I'm not there to stop you, you'll take off chasing after the first set of tracks you see."

"Fine, but let's go." James picked up his parka from the mess of things scattered across the floor and headed for the door. "Every minute we stand here talking is a minute farther she could be away."

They stepped out onto the small porch and Clay shined his light out across the snow.

The fear of not knowing Nancy's whereabouts was stronger than any fear James would ever feel coming up against the cowboy. She was his life and was carrying his child. If something were to happen to her—

Don't think that way. You will find her, and she will be safe.

"L-L-L-Look over there!" Calvin pointed at a set of tracks in the snow leading toward the street.

James' heart leapt in his chest. "That's got to be her. Come on! Let's go!"

"Those are mine," Clay said and stretched his arm out, blocking him from leaving the group. "Now stay in line like we talked about. We'll go down the steps and start checking around the house. Franklin, you watch our backs. We don't want anyone or anything getting the drop on us."

Four steps took them off the porch and into the yard. Clay slowly trailed his light across the perfect and seemingly undisturbed snow. If there were any tracks out there, they should stand out clearly.

They made their way down the length of the house, then across the back. James started to fear that they weren't going to find anything. If there were no more tracks, then they would have to go back inside, and he would check the upstairs rooms himself. What were they thinking taking Franklin's word that he had already done it?

"Stop!" Franklin called out as they neared the far corner of the building.

"What's going on?" Clay asked. "Did you see something?"

"Look." Franklin pointed down at a trough in the snow that followed the contour of the house.

"That's just where the roof has kept the snow from accumulating as fast. It'll be like that all the way around the house. We're looking for footprints or some other kind of trail. You're supposed to be watching behind us, so just keep doing that and leave the tracking to me." Clay turned his attention back to the unblemished snow surrounding them.

"You're wrong, dude," Franklin said from behind them.

"Franklin, why don't you just go back inside and wait there in case Nancy comes back?" Clay's tone was harsh, but James thought he understood why. Clay and Franklin had not really hit it off. In fact, Clay had told him just the night before at the hotel that he didn't feel like Franklin could be trusted.

"That's probably a good idea," James added. For Nancy's sake, it might be best to keep Clay and Franklin separated. "If Nancy comes back, then you yell for us."

Franklin's face clouded over. He started toward the house. After a few steps, he stopped and turned back.

"W-W-W-What is it, Franklin?" Calvin asked.

"You all think I'm stupid, but I'm not. My people were trackers long before any of your type ever set foot in this country. I know what I'm seeing."

"I know what I'm seeing, too." Clay got up in Franklin's face. "What I'm seeing is a stoner Indian who is wasting our time—time we should be using to try and find Nancy. Now be a good *boy* and go back in the house like I told you to."

"Screw you, Clay." Their eyes locked for a moment, then Franklin dropped to his knees in the snow. "James, give me your light."

James put himself between them and handed Franklin his flashlight. Franklin shined it on the edge of the trough, then looked up at Clay.

"What?" Clay asked.

"This," Franklin told him.

Clay bent down and looked where the light was shining. "I don't see anything."

"Look again." Franklin pointed at the side of the trough.

Clay leaned in closer, then took the flashlight from Franklin and placed it even nearer to the ground. "I'll be damned." There was a footprint in the snow. Not a whole print but just a fragment of an inch of one side. Clay motioned for all of them to scoot back, and he followed the trough a few more feet and found another one.

Franklin cleared his throat, and they all turned to look at him. He was standing beneath the only window at the back of the house. When he had their attention, he pushed the window open, then closed it again. "Your trough starts right here under this window. Strange, huh?"

"The windows actually work?" James asked, amazed. "I assumed they rusted shut ages ago."

"Whoever took Nancy, took her out this window, on the other side of the house from where you were, Clay." Franklin shot him a hard look. "Whoever it was must have been dragging her. That trough ain't from the roof blocking snow, it's from her feet being dragged through it, and it covered his footprints. My guess is, if we go around that corner, we are gonna see the trail lead off from there."

"Wait," James said. "If she was being dragged, wouldn't there be two marks in the snow instead of one?" He feared he already knew the answer.

"Not if her feet were tied together."

Franklin's answer was the one he didn't what to hear. The very idea that Nancy had been tied up and dragged away was almost more then he could stand.

"I can't believe you saw that," Clay told him.

"I can't believe you didn't." Franklin turned and went around the corner of the building. "Told you so!" he called out.

Sure enough, the trough led away from the house, through the back yard, and up the side of the mountain.

"W-W-W-What do you think is up there?" Calvin asked.

"Rocks, trees, snow," Clay answered. "And a maze of deserted mines that stretch for miles underneath this mountain."

James' heart sank.

Chapter Sixty-Three

"Where's he? Coming, when, coming soon, where, here." The little man paced next to a small campfire repeatedly slamming his fist into his temple.

Nancy's mind raced as she watched his every move. The little man had left her leaning against the side of a rock wall. A quick look around had made it obvious that she was inside an old mine tunnel. Her arms and shoulders ached from being bound for so long. Her feet were freezing, and she feared that it wasn't from the cold, but because of the ropes that bound her ankles, cutting off her circulation. The little man had built the small fire, but her legs were tucked back under her, and she was afraid to try and stretch them out in order to get her feet closer to it.

He had stuffed a filthy piece of rag in her mouth, then tied another around her head to hold it in place. It tasted of sugar and rotted meat. If she vomited with it in her mouth, she could easily aspirate and die, so she fought back the urge. She moistened and manipulated the rag with her tongue until it became saturated to the point she could flatten it out inside her mouth, allowing her to breathe more freely.

"Ummm nice, ugly, no nasty, shaddup, mmmmmm."

The little man plopped down cross-legged beside her and began fumbling with her backpack. He struggled with the clasp, trying to figure out how it worked.

"Got it!" He jumped up and danced a jig of pure joy in a circle around the pack. "No me got it? No," he said in his cracked, almost-whisper voice, proudly showing her the open bag.

He couldn't have been more than five feet tall, and he walked with an exaggerated limp. Old scars covering his face, neck, and arms were visible underneath a thick layer of grime that had turned his skin black in places. He smelled like a horse stall in dire need of mucking.

His stubby arms searched deep inside the bag, and she heard her things being pushed about as he rummaged through it.

"Oush!" He jerked his hands out and kicked the bag away. "Hurt, mmmm, shaddap."

He stuck his finger in his mouth and half turned away from her. She thought he might be crying.

When he kicked the bag, it had turned over and scattered most of its contents out on the stone floor between them. A hairbrush, barrette, bandages, clean shirt, extra underwear, and the roll of surgical tools. James had wanted to carry the tools in the pocket of his parka, but she had insisted on putting them in her bag for safekeeping. In the little man's frantic search, the oilcloth roll had come untied, allowing the blade of the scalpel to stick out one side.

The little man whimpered. She looked back at him but couldn't see his face. He had scooted on around and now had his back to her.

As carefully as she could, she leaned over and managed to extended her legs and put her feet on top of the tools.

"Ommmm, hummmm, oush," the little man moaned.

She froze in place, afraid he would turn and see what she was doing, afraid to move that the sound might attract his attention.

His weeping stopped and his head started to slowly bob up and down. *"Bmmmm bmmm, baaak seeeb, habboo aneeeee wooooo—"*

Is he singing? She couldn't believe what she was hearing. *He's hurt, and he's singing to try and comfort himself.*

"Esss seeer, esss errrr, feee baaaag ferrrr."

She eased her feet back, dragging the tools along with her. They made a soft scuffing sound as they skittered across the stone surface. He must not have been able to hear it over his singing. If he had, she was sure he would have done something to stop her. When the tools were within reach, she pinched the blade of the scalpel between her thumb and forefinger, and eased it out of its holder. She gingerly rotated it in her hand until she had hold of the handle and the blade was pointing back toward her. With a little luck, she could slide the blade of the scalpel between her wrists and saw it back in forth, cutting the rope.

"*Un foo de leeleegeel dats leeevs do de laaaa-* Huh!" The little man stopped his singing and sat up. "Ees heeere, no, ya, naaaaad!"

Nancy panicked. She kicked the remaining tools away from her and back toward the fire, then pulled her legs up underneath her again.

"Wha'!" The little man spun around. "Heeebeeemaddddd, cut you! No, arrrrrrrg." His head snapped back and forth as he looked at the spilled contents of the backpack. He lurched forward and tried to scoop everything back into it. "Hurby, hurby, hurby, cut yaaaaaa, no, no, no."

The last thing he grabbed was the tool kit. He stopped with it in his hand, and his head jerked to the side. He stared, unblinking, at Nancy. His eyes were the color of dried clay, a big, gray cataract covered most of the left one. His breathing was shallow and his nose twitched like an evil, demented rabbit. He closed his hand around the tools and gently shook them, then raised them to his face and sniffed at the cloth.

"Hnnnnnn, hnnnnnnnnn," he wheezed, never breaking eye contact. "Hnnnnnnn, naaaa." His head snapped back around and faced the entrance of the tunnel. "Eeeeeeeeeeee!" he screamed and ran in that direction, stuffing the tools into the backpack.

With the little man out of sight, she began frantically sawing at the rope with the scalpel. There was little space between her wrists, and the blade dug into the tender skin there with each thrust. She made progress, but the rope was becoming saturated in her blood, making it harder to cut.

Please don't let me slit my own wrist before I cut through this freaking rope!

She wasn't the praying type, but she hoped God was listening all the same.

The rope suddenly began to unravel, and with one hard tug her hands were free. She dropped the scalpel, pulled the repulsive rag out of her mouth, and frantically tried to untie the rope around her ankles.

"Eeeeeeeeeeee! Eeeeeeeeee!" The little man's squeal echoed down the tunnel.

She pulled at the rope, only managing to make the knot tighter.

Calm down, you're panicking. Stop and think about what you're doing. She closed her eyes for a second and took a few deep breaths. When she reopened them, she looked at the knot in the rope instead of blindly pulling at it.

It's a ring knot. It's a friggin' ring knot! Her grandfather had shown her how to tie one when she was a little girl. He called it a magic knot, because if you pulled on both ends, you couldn't get it untied, but if you pulled just one—

She pulled one end of the rope, and the knot fell open like magic.

"Eeeeeeeeeeee!"

She scrambled to her feet. Stabbing tingles of electricity ran up her legs, and she nearly fell into the fire. The pain was sharp and intense as the blood rushed back through her veins and arteries. With a herculean effort, she forced one foot in front of the other. Lightning radiated up her legs and into her groin with each step. She wanted to scream, but she had to run, had to get away.

Behind her, the mine tunnel fell into darkness. It was her only chance. If she could get back there and disappear into that darkness, she might just live to see James again, to have their child, and be part of a family. With every step, the tingling lessened and became more tolerable.

"Eeeeeeeeee!"

She looked back over her shoulder. The squeal had sounded closer that time. She had one shot at making it into the darkness. Something glinted in the dirt beside the fire, it was the scalpel. She had dropped it when the rope came loose.

"Eeeeeeeeee!"

Definitely closer now, he *was* coming back. She took another step toward the rear of the cave, reconsidered, turned, and ran toward the fire. She grabbed the scalpel, ran back, and threw herself into the darkness. She landed hard against a rock outcropping, and something in her left arm cracked. Pain shot up into her shoulder, and she bit down on her tongue to keep from screaming.

Pull yourself together, don't make a sound. Do it or you're dead!

Steeling herself for the pain that she knew was coming, she used her good hand to lift her broken arm and placed it bent against her chest. The pain was incredible, and the cave started to blur and fade in her vision.

Oh no you don't! You don't get to pass out. Now move your ass!

Scooting on her rump, she worked her way further around the outcropping, hoping, praying that there was a crevasse behind it big enough for her to slip into. Each time she pushed with her legs, her body jostled, and pain like hot ice shot up through her arm. Pain, panic, and terror like she had never experienced before raced through her.

She pushed out again with her feet and felt her butt slip partly over a ledge. She leaned back far enough for her broken arm to stay in place against her chest, but not so far back as to risk losing her balance and tumbling backward into the unknown. With her good hand, she felt along the tunnel floor until it reached the ledge. She hesitated, took a deep breath, then let her hand continue over it. She felt nothing, just cold air flowing out of the depths of the mine behind her. She awkwardly extended her arm and forced herself to lean back another fraction of an inch. He fingertips grazed a surface.

"Eeeeeeeeee!"

The little man's squeal came from the other side of the rock outcropping and caught her by surprise. She startled, lost her balance, and fell backward over the edge. The floor was only about five inches below her, but she was unprepared for the landing. Her broken arm fell off her chest and forcefully hit the stone floor. Intense pain shot through her arm and shoulder, and darkness overtook her.

Chapter Sixty-Four

James sat behind Clay on the snowmobile, holding the flashlight and fighting to keep the weak beam steady as he moved it across the snow. He was watching in case the trail left by Nancy's dragging feet strayed from the mountain path illuminated by the snowmobile's headlamps. Every now and then, the trail would fade, or a secondary path would branch off in one direction or another. James would worry they had lost her trail, only for it to reappear farther up the path.

Franklin was driving the second snowmobile with Calvin riding behind him. It was their job to stop at each of the branches and double-check for any signs that Nancy could have been taken that way. James heard their engine rev after each stop and imagined Calvin holding on for dear life with each jackrabbit start.

The track they were following faded away, and James started methodically scanning the area in front of them, hoping to pick it up again. Little juts of rock stuck up out of the snow beneath the small evergreens that lined the trail. The snow on their branches glistened when his light passed over them. It made him think of Christmas trees and twinkle lights. It would have been beautiful if the situation were different.

Clay pulled the snowmobile to a stop. "End of the line!"

James slid off the seat, removed his helmet, and set it on the ground. They had stopped in a sort of canyon between two, low rock outcroppings. The rock walls on either side were overgrown with vines and moss and looked like whitewashed stone. The snow was even thinner there, revealing the hard-packed, frozen dirt beneath them. He took a few steps away from the snowmobile, and his feet nearly slid out from under him.

Clay grabbed his arms and pulled him back. "Watch where you're going! We're at the top. Next step's a thousand feet down." He took the light and walked to the crest of the mountain. Placing his back against one of the rocks for support, he leaned out and shined the light over the edge. He leaned farther over, then disappeared.

"Clay!" James ran over to where Clay had been. He stopped beside the rock and, following Clay's example, pressed himself against it for support and leaned out.

A bright light struck him in the eyes. Clay stood on the other side of the rock about three feet below him, shining the flashlight back in his direction. He was standing on a narrow path that began the steep descent down the other side of the mountain.

"Give me a hand." Clay reached upward toward him.

James took Clay's hand and pulled him back up and around the rock.

"I thought you had fallen off the mountain," James said once Clay was safely back on the trail. "I was sure I was going to see you and that flashlight bouncing all the way down to the bottom."

"You almost did. Looks like there was once some kind of road here. Probably a high pass of some kind. Erosion has been eating away at it over the years, causing the part of the road here at the peak to fall apart. Who or whatever has Nancy couldn't have come this way."

"I guess we double back and see if Franklin has—"

"James, Clay, down here!" Franklin's voice echoed off the mountain.

"That idiot," Clay cursed under his breath. "Now the whole mountain knows we are up here."

Chapter Sixty-Five

Nancy awoke into darkness, surrounded by the sounds of dancing footfalls and the little man's senseless chatter. She had no way of knowing how long she had been out, but the cowboy and the little man were now standing next to the fire. She forced herself to take long, slow breaths to try and remain calm. From the relative safety of her hiding place, she was able to watch them through a crack in the rock. It was like watching a father and son, only this father was cold and aloof, and the son starved for his attention and approval. The little man frantically moved around him, jumping up and down, waving the surgical kit in the air. All the while, the cowboy stared blankly into the flames of the fire. He never moved, never blinked.

A cold chill passed through her. He was real. All the stories, all their suspicions were true. And he was there—less than ten feet away.

His tall, lanky figure filled the tunnel to the point that he had to stoop over to keep his head from touching the ceiling. Long, skeletal arms hung off his shoulders, ending in gnarled hands that dangled beside the pistol holstered on his right, and the hilt of his sword on the left. A once-red bandana, now faded and filthy to mud-brown, was tied around his throat and tucked into the collar of a tattered corduroy shirt. Over the shirt was a leather vest, the handle of another gun poked out of a small pocket over his right breast.

"See, see, see," the little man chanted as he waved the oilcloth roll in front of the cowboy's face. "Here, here, see, see."

The cowboy's right hand struck like a snake. He grabbed the little man's arm and shook him till he dropped the tools, then continued to shake him as he lifted the little man off the ground and held him up in the air at eye level. Only then did the cowboy look away from the fire. He turned and stared into the little man's eyes as he used his free hand to unsheathe the sword.

"No, see, she ere, see I did," the little man pleaded, his raspy voice dripping with urgency and need. "I did, you, you, me I did you, fer you."

The cowboy drew the sword across the little man's outstretched armpit, easily slicing through the threadbare cloth and into the delicate skin underneath. Blood flowed out of the wound, soaking the little man's shirt and pants before dripping onto the hard stone floor beneath him.

"Ooooush, aaaaarrrrrrggsh, oush, shad up, no, oush mmmmmmm, shad up she ere, mmmmmmm oush."

The cowboy let him go. He landed awkwardly on the hard stone floor, then scurried over to the fire like a wounded dog looking for a place to lick its wounds.

"*Bmmmm bmmm, baaak seeeb, habboo aneeeee wooooo...*" The little man reached out and picked up a burning stick from the fire. "*Esss seeer, esss errrr, feee baaaa ferrrr.*" He raised his bleeding arm in the air and thrust the burning wood into the wound, then let the arm drop and held it tightly in place with his other. "*EEEEEEEEEEE!*" The sound of bacon frying, and the smell of roasting flesh filled the tunnel.

Nancy held her breath and looked away to keep from retching and giving away her hiding place. When she dared look back, the situation around the fire had changed. The cowboy was now kneeling beside the little man and gently caressing what scant hair was on his head.

The little man openly wept with his head against the cowboy's chest. He had retrieved the oilcloth roll, and it was sitting in his lap.

The surgical kit, the scalpel, where's the scalpel?

Nancy began to panic. If she had dropped it when she threw herself behind the rock it could be sitting out there in the dust like a shiny arrow pointing toward her hiding place. Carefully, she used her good hand to search the floor around her. *Nothing.* She checked the surface of the ledge she had fallen over, all the time keeping a watchful eye on the cowboy and the little man. Dust, dirt, and pebbles, but no scalpel. There was a small gap where the ledge connected with the rock wall. Nancy slipped the side of her hand into it, then jerked it back when the tip of the scalpel's blade poked the end of her little finger.

The cowboy's head snapped around as if he'd sensed an intruder, and he looked directly toward Nancy's hiding place. He roughly pushed the little man aside, stood, and took a step toward the fire. His face had been in shadows, but now the flames illuminated the area underneath the brim of his bowler hat.

Nancy's breath caught in her chest when she actually saw his face for the first time. A jagged scar ran from underneath his hat and into his left eye. A shriveled curtain of the decaying flesh that had once been his eyelid dangled dead against the gray orb that filled the eye socket. The pupil of his other eye glowed red as it reflected the flames. The scar continued across the broken, misshapen bridge of his nose before splitting his upper lip and revealing the rotten black teeth underneath. His nose twitched, pulling his destroyed mouth into a hideous sneer. For a moment, she thought he was trying to smile.

She ducked back behind the rocks and tried to make herself small against them. Her broken arm throbbed against her chest, and she could hear the blood rushing through her veins as her heart pumped hard deep inside her. *Did he see me? Sweet Jesus, God help me! Did he?*

A soft thud, then a rustling sound came from the other side of the rock. She held her breath. *Please God, make him go away. Don't let him find me.*

The cowboy's shadow danced in the firelight as it crossed the entrance to her hiding place. Another thud and rustle, and the shadow grew larger.

She could hear him breathing, slow and steady. Each breath brought with it a wet wheeze followed by a soft crackle. Her nurse's mind immediately went to asthma, and the sound of an untreated lung.

Thud, rustle.

His shadow nearly filled the area beside the rock, blocking most of the flame's light. The blade of his sword suddenly thrust through the crack in the rock she had been using for a peephole. It missed her nose by less than an inch. His hand appeared from behind the rock, slowly opening and closing like it was trying to catch the air itself, searching for something, anything that it could grab and pull out of the darkness and into the light.

A scream began to build up deep inside her, bubbling in her gut and rising. Anytime now, it would burst out of her, the cowboy would hear it, and she would die. But there was no stopping it, no holding it back. The pressure of the scream pushed tears out of her eyes and snot out of nose. Her heart did flips in her chest, threatening to rupture with each one. She opened her mouth, and hot breath poured out of her in short bursts.

The cowboy's hand flattened and slapped against the rock. The scream rose up into her throat.

"James, Clay, down here!"

Franklin's voice echoed down the mine tunnel. The hand jerked back, and the sword was pulled free of the crack with a metallic zing. A moment later, she heard hard footfalls moving away from her, their sound growing softer as they traveled into the distance. A second set of footsteps, lighter and more rapid mixed in with them. Within moments, the mine tunnel fell silent, except for the crack and pop of the fire.

Chapter Sixty-Six

Clay and James didn't want to make any more noise, so they set off down the mountain on foot. Judging by the volume of Franklin's voice, he and Calvin had to be fairly close. They rounded a tight curve in the path and spotted the snowmobile sitting beside a copse of evergreen trees next to one of the offshoot trails.

Clay stuck out his arm, stopping James from running past him.

"What's the matter, why did you stop?"

"Shhhh. I think I hear Calvin."

James stood still and listened; this was a stupid waste of time. If Nancy was close by, they needed to be trying to get to her, not listening for Calvin.

"D-D-D-Do you want to get us k-k-k-killed?"

"That's him," Clay whispered, then motioned for them to continue forward slowly.

They cautiously made their way around the curve. There in a pool of moonlit snow, Calvin was sitting on Franklin's chest with his hand over the young man's mouth. Franklin was struggling, trying to push him off.

James stepped on a dead branch under the snow. The soft snap made both of them stop and look their way.

Calvin jumped up and rushed over to them. Franklin was a little slower to get up.

"There's a cave, just over there!" Franklin said as soon as he was on his feet.

"Shhhhh," Calvin hissed at him and waved his hands in the air.

Clay pointed at Franklin, then pressed his finger against his lips.

"There's a cave, just over there," Franklin whispered when he was standing next to them. "And there's a light coming from inside."

"We heard you the first time," James said just as quietly. "If there's anyone in that cave, they probably heard you, too."

Franklin looked at him, wide eyed. "Dude, you might be right. Aw, man."

"You s-s-s-stupid idiot, that's what I've b-b-b-been trying to tell you." Calvin pulled off his glasses and tried to clean them with the tail of his parka, but the nylon material only smeared the lenses.

"Stop it. Both of you," James said and looked over at Clay. "What do we do now?"

"You stay here with these two and keep them quiet. I'll make my way to the cave entrance and see if I can tell what's going on." Clay handed him the flashlight and started down the path, following the trail of footprints.

"D-D-D-Did you guys find anything?"

James looked down at Calvin and started to shush him but didn't. Behind the smeared lenses of his glasses Calvin's eyes looked worried. James reached out and took them off his face and wiped the lenses clean with his scarf before handing them back.

"No," James whispered. "The trail ends at the crest of the mountain. In a small valley between two big rocks. There's the remnant of an old road up there that leads back down the other side of the mountain but nothing else."

"So, n-n-n-no sign of N-N-N-Nancy then?"

James shook his head.

"Did you say there was a road between two big rocks on the top of the mountain?" Franklin asked. His face looked drawn and serious.

"Yeah, that's where we—"

"Could you see the town from up there, or a wide plateau on the other side?"

"It was dark. I couldn't see anything, but we basically traveled straight up the mountain. So theoretically, if there had been lights on in town, I probably could have seen them. What are you getting at?"

"That's it, it has to be."

"I'm c-c-c-confused. What d-d-d-does it have to be?" Calvin asked.

"That has to be where Floating Feather and Melvin Mitchell are buried. Did you see a feather anywhere? It would have been on one of the rocks."

"I told you it was dark and—"

"*RUN!*" A throaty, guttural voice cried out from behind the trees.

"What w-w-w-was that?" Calvin whispered.

"*For God's sake, RUN!*"

A scream of pain cut through the night, then suddenly stopped.

James motioned for Franklin and Calvin to get behind him. They all started backing slowly toward the snowmobile. Two shadows appeared in the pool of moonlight at the bend of the path. One was small, the other was thick and undefinable in shape.

They made it back to the snowmobile, and James motioned for Franklin and Calvin to get on. *Please let there be room for me on that thing if I need it.*

"G-G-G-Get on James. W-W-W-We need to go!"

He risked a glance over his shoulder. Sure enough, about five inches of the vinyl seat was visible behind Calvin. Franklin was standing up with his hands on the throttle which had allowed Calvin to scoot forward enough to make room for him. *Thank God.*

He started to jump on, then stopped and watched as the shadows grew larger. *What if it's Clay, and he's found Nancy?* The thought brought a spark of hope. He looked again at the smaller shadow and how it lurched forward with each step and knew that there was no way it could be.

"Start it." He heard crunching footsteps in the snow and a low moan coming from the shadows. "Start it *now*!" he screamed at Franklin.

The engine roared to life a second later. At that same moment, the ones who had been casting the shadows stepped out from behind the trees and into the moonlight. First was a little man who was carrying the roll of surgical tools nestled in his arms like he would an infant. Next to him was the cowboy. He was carrying Clay, but not in the same way the little man carried the tools. The cowboy's hand was buried to the wrist in the center of Clay's back. Blood dripping off Clay had left a red trail in the snow behind them. The cowboy carried him like a piece of luggage, and Clay's spine was the handle.

With unimaginable strength, the cowboy brought his arm up, lifting Clay into a standing position. For a moment nothing happened, then Clay's head jerked up, his eyes blinked, and his mouth fell open.

"Uh, James." Franklin's voice came from behind him, but he couldn't move, couldn't look away from the horror moving toward them.

Clay's mouth snapped shut with a loud clack, then slowly opened again.

"This is the end."

The words came from Clay, but it wasn't his voice. It was deep and hoarse, strained like someone who was trying to speak after many years of silence.

"This is the end," the voice rasped. "I have followed you for many lifetimes, now you die the final death. You will die, like she died. I will have my vengeance!" The cowboy lowered his arm. Clay's body dropped back down and hung at his side, just above the growing circle of red snow.

"Where's Nancy?" James yelled.

The cowboy didn't answer, but the little man beside him began to hop up and down, holding the tools tightly against his chest.

"Wherz Nacy, wherz Nacy, don't know, yes I do, pretty, no, no, no pretty." He reached up to take the cowboy's hand. The cowboy slapped him away. The little man dropped into the snow but jumped right back up. Blood poured from his nose and the corner of one eye, yet he was smiling. "Wherz Nacy, wherz Nacy."

"James!" Franklin screamed behind him.

"Jmz, Jmz," the little man repeated.

The cowboy stepped forward, dragging Clay's body along with him. James backed away, stumbled, and fell. That was all it took; the spell was broken. He looked up at Franklin and Calvin on the running snowmobile, then back at the cowboy walking methodically toward them with the little man at his heels. He scrambled to his feet and threw his leg over the seat. Franklin gunned the motor, and the snowmobile shot away like a rocket leaving the earth.

Chapter Sixty-Seven

Nancy held her breath as she reached down to pick up the scalpel. She had found a small twig and used it to work the scalpel out of the crack in the rock, then using her teeth, she pulled her shirtsleeve down over her hand so her skin would not make contact with the instrument. She pinched the scalpel between her thumb and finger and eased it into her shoe, allowing her sock to keep it from touching the skin of her ankle.

The cowboy and the little man were nowhere to be seen. They had left the mine tunnel when they heard Franklin call out and had not come back. She had debated staying put in hopes that James or Clay might find her, but then thought better of it. They had no reason to look in that particular mine tunnel over any other of the probable dozen that dotted the side of the mountain. One thing she knew was that they were close enough that she, and the cowboy and little man, had heard Franklin. If she was lucky, *very lucky*, she might find them before the cowboy did.

She had to keep her broken arm cradled in the other—or the pain might cause her to black out again—but she still managed to get to her feet by pushing back against the rock for support and using her legs to push herself up. It would be hard enough to find James, but almost impossible while protecting her arm. She needed some kind of sling for it to free up her other hand.

My backpack! I can pull the strap over my head and put my arm inside it.

She peered around the small campsite, hoping beyond hope that she would see her backpack lying there. The floor of the tunnel was bare, only sticks and dust remained. Her hope sank.

Something white caught her eye, lying just at the edge of the fire's glow. She went over to get a closer look and giggled. Relief flooded over her.

In the little man's rushed attempt to put all her things back in her bag, he had missed one thing: her spare panties. Not just any panties —her granny panties. Big, white cotton underwear that every woman had and prayed that her man never saw her in. She used her foot to scoot them back over to the rock wall, then in the same way she had gotten to her feet minutes before, she leaned against the rock and let herself slide back down into a seated position. Carefully, she slid down onto her back so her broken arm could lay flat on her chest. With her hand free, she picked up the granny panties and pushed her head through one of the leg openings. Then she pulled them down and slipped the other opening over the hand on her broken arm. The pain was incredible, but she fought through it, and in a matter of seconds, her arm rested on cotton with the elastic waistband across the palm of her hand.

She closed her eyes and offered up a prayer of thanks. *And God, please let the material be strong enough to hold my arm in place till I can get out of here.*

She scooted back around until her back was next to the rock, then used her good arm to push herself into a seated position. Her broken arm shifted. She yelped at the jolt of pain that shot up into her shoulder, but it didn't fall. The panties did the trick and kept her arm resting safely in the makeshift sling. With renewed hope, she pushed herself up, using her good arm for balance, and stood next to the fire.

Now what? She looked around again at the campsite and the cold rock walls that surrounded her. *Now I get the hell out of here before they come back.*

* * *

Nancy guessed that she had walked close to a hundred yards in murky darkness before the outline of the tunnel entrance appeared like a silhouette in the moonlight reflecting off the snow. She flattened herself as much as she could against the cold stone wall as she sidestepped ever closer to what she hoped was going to be her escape.

The light of the moon cast a hard line down the wall ahead of her. Once she reached that line, she would be totally visible. She inched her way forward, stopped, and listened. Something was moving just outside. A bank of evergreens jutted out into the path that led to the tunnel entrance. Someone was walking through the trees on the other side. She held her breath, afraid it was the cowboy coming back to continue searching for her.

She slid a little farther back into the shadows, but not so far that she totally lost sight of the path. If it was the cowboy, she had two options. She could run back to her hiding place behind the rock, or burst out of the shadows and hope that the surprise of seeing her would allow enough of a head start that she could run into the trees and try to lose herself there. The thought of going back into the tunnel was more than she could stand, so she opted for the surprise attack.

The footsteps grew louder, and a dark figure moved along the edge of the trees. She bent her knees, ready to run. She would scream as loud as she could, then burst out of the tunnel. Hopefully, that would add to the surprise and confusion and also alert James to where she was.

Whoever it was coming her way rounded the trees. Her leg muscles tensed, ready to spring at the first sight of that stupid bowler hat.

There was no hat, no vest, no gun, or sword. Clay stepped out into the moonlight.

Relief washed over her like waves on the beach, she was going to be okay! Clay would take her to James, and they could—

The little man burst into the clearing. He must have been hiding behind the outside edge of the entrance. He sprang into the air and landed on Clay, knocking him off his feet and sending him face-first into the snow. Clay started to get up, but the little man was faster and jumped on his back. He had a knife in his hand and began maniacally stabbing it into Clay's back. Blood-stained goose feathers filled the air as the little man brought the knife down again, and again, and again.

The cowboy appeared from inside the bank of evergreens and looked down at the little man and his handiwork. He nodded, then reached in his pocket and brought out another piece of rock candy. The little man dropped his knife and took the candy with his blood-soaked hand. He popped it into his mouth before getting up. The cowboy didn't watch him go, he only stared down at what was left of Clay.

Nancy pushed her fist so hard against her mouth to keep from screaming that her teeth broke the skin over the knuckles. Her knees buckled, and she leaned against the tunnel wall for support. Her mind rejected the inconceivable brutality of what she had just witnessed. She was hallucinating, she had to be. The pain of the broken arm, along with the stress of the cowboy nearly finding her hiding in the dark, was too much. She closed her eyes and began counting to ten. When she was done, she would open her eyes, and she would still be in the dark behind the rock.

One...two...three...

I should stay back here in the safety of my hiding place until James and Clay find me. Clay. Clay, Clay's dead.

Four...five...six....

Clay is not dead, they are all out looking for me, I know that, because I heard Franklin call out to them. James and Clay are looking for me. Franklin and Calvin are looking for me. Everyone is looking for me.

Seven...eight...nine...

They will find me. We will all go together and bury the tools, then all this will be over. James and I will get married, have the baby, and live happily ever after. Yes, that is what's going to happen.

A peaceful calm washed over her. The hallucination was over, and she would be fine.

Ten.

She opened her eyes.

The cowboy plunged his hands into the gaping wound in Clay's back. The sound of fingers tearing material, pulling apart flesh and muscle, filled the clearing. Blood poured out around his hands, over Clay's back, and into the snow. The cowboy stopped suddenly and looked back at the entrance of the tunnel, directly at where she was hiding in the shadows. She could see the steam from his breath. It hung in the air around his face like a cloud. He stood there, unmoving, for what seemed like hours, then Clay's body convulsed.

"Run!" Clay croaked. His voice guttural, throaty, and full of pain. "*For God's sake, RUN!*"

The cowboy placed his boot in the center of Clay's lower back, then pulled up hard. The crack of Clay's spine echoed down the tunnel.

Her guts lurched, but there was nothing there for her to throw up. Burning, hot stomach acid filled her mouth. She turned her face away and gagged on it. She spat into the dust on the mine floor, saliva flooded her mouth, and she spat again. *Did he hear me?* She quickly turned back and saw the cowboy walking away from her and around the bank of trees. He carried Clay's limp body in one hand with the little man close at his heels.

She cautiously stepped out into the moonlight, never taking her eyes off the cowboy's back until he was past the trees and out of sight. Behind her, a tree line ended at the side of the tunnel entrance. *That's where the little man was hiding. That's why Clay didn't see him.*

She moved into the cover of the trees, and her foot caught in something. It was her backpack; the little man must have left it. Inside she found her hairbrush, shirt, and a few other things, but not the tools. She started looking around the ground at her feet, hoping that they had fallen out, praying that they were hidden in the shadows. If they didn't have the tools, they couldn't bury them, they would—

Voices echoed down to her from the trail beyond the trees. They sounded angry, but she could not make out what they were saying. A snowmobile's motor blared to life, the engine gunned, and she heard its treads grab snow and shoot away.

Now the cowboy will come back. If I stay here, I'm as good as dead. Dead like Clay. She turned and ran as fast as she could deep into the woods, holding her backpack out in front of her to keep branches from hitting her broken arm.

Chapter Sixty-Eight

James paced back and forth in the snowmobile's lights, trying to think. He had to decide what they were going to do—how they were going to save Nancy—but he couldn't. All his brain wanted to do was to play back, in an endless loop, the cowboy using Clay's dead body like some kind of horrific ventriloquist dummy, and how they had run like scared chickens back to the crest of the mountain.

"J-J-J-James."

He ran his thumb and forefinger across his closed eyes, then pinched them together around the bridge of his nose. Nancy was somewhere down there, alone. *She has to be the priority, we have to find her, rescue her. Nancy comes first before burying the tools. Nancy has the tools. Nancy has the tools!* That meant that the cowboy could find her. If for some reason she touched the tools, then the cowboy would be led directly to her and—

"J-J-James!"

"What, Calvin? What is so important?"

"Something's wrong with Franklin. Look."

Franklin was frantically pulling at the dead weeds and vines that covered the rocks on either side of the mountain passage. He cleared the vines from a small area, grabbed a flat-edged piece of rock, and started scraping away the brown moss and dirt that clung to the stone.

"What are you doing Franklin?" James asked, but Franklin didn't seem to hear him. "Franklin!" he tried again; this time louder, but still got no response.

Calvin slid off the snowmobile's seat and landed on his feet. "F-F-F-Franklin, are you all right?"

Great. It's not bad enough that Clay's dead and Nancy's missing, now Franklin's gonna wig out on me, too. James took a couple of steps closer and noticed that there was blood on Franklin's hands. His knuckles were scraped raw from clearing the brush and scraping the moss off the rock's rough surface.

"Franklin! Franklin, can you hear me?" He put his hand on Franklin's shoulder.

Franklin spun around. His cheeks were wet with tears, and he was gasping for breath. He just stared at James, like he didn't know who he was, then he dropped to the ground and buried his head in his hands.

"This is my fault, all my fault!" His words were muffled, but James heard him clearly enough. "I should have never tracked you down. I shouldn't have interfered. It might have been years before the cowboy found you. He might *never* have found you. You might have stuck those tools in a drawer and forgot all about them!"

"It's okay, Franklin, it doesn't matter." James knelt beside him and spoke as calmly as he could. "We are here now. We have to settle it. We have to find Nancy and put an end to this once and for all. Calvin and I can't do that without you. Do you understand? We need you."

"Stupid *Dave*. Stupid *roach*. I should have known better than to listen to a shiny bug."

James looked over at Calvin who just shrugged. *No help there.*

"What were you doing?" James pressed. "Why were you digging at that rock?"

"The feather." Franklin looked up at him. "If this is where we are supposed to bury the tools, then the feather should be here. It should be carved somewhere on this rock."

"We can worry about that later. Right now, we need to be out looking for Nancy—"

"No!" Franklin reached up and grabbed the front of his parka with his bloody hands. "No, we have to bury the tools. If we bury the tools, then we get rid of the cowboy, and Nancy will be safe, and all this will be over with."

"B-B-B-But, Franklin." Calvin came over to join them. "W-W-W-We don't have the t-t-t-tools. N-N-N-Nancy has them, remember?"

Franklin turned and looked back at James.

"That's right." James nodded. "She put them in her backpack for safekeeping. We have to find her first before the cowboy fin—"

"You are too late."

James spun around, rising to his feet at the same time. The cowboy stood between the snowmobiles. Clay's lifeless body rested on one of the seats.

James' mind flashed back to an old movie with Edgar Bergen and Charlie McCarthy, but he knew that this act from the depths of hell would not be cracking any jokes. Clay's shoulders were slumped forward, but his head was lifted up at an unnatural angle, his dead eyes stared at them, unmoving. The little man was sitting on the seat of the other snowmobile with his hands on the handlebars.

"Voom, voom, ack."

The cowboy lashed out and struck the little man in the face. The impact rocked him backward on the seat, nearly causing him to drop the oil cloth bundle that was sitting there between his legs.

The tools. James started for them, but Calvin grabbed the back of his parka.

"D-D-D-Don't. He'll kill you b-b-b-before you even get close," he whispered.

For a split second, he considered knocking Calvin out of the way and lunging for them, but he didn't. Calvin was right. If he got himself killed, who would rescue Nancy? He nodded and took a step back. Franklin came up beside him. The three of them stood there like three plastic toy soldiers waiting for the battle to begin.

The muscles in the cowboy's arm flexed, and Clay pivoted on the seat toward them. "Where is he?" Clay's face lifted, his mouth snapped shut, then snapped open again. "Who holds the red-skinned devil? Where is the heathen that killed the mother and ruined my face?"

The cowboy's good eye never left them, never blinked. James began to sweat inside his parka. He looked over at Calvin, then at Franklin whose tears had been replaced by the sweat running out of his hairline and down his face.

"We don't know what you're talking about." James felt as much as heard the nervous tone in his voice. His throat was suddenly dry, and he tried hard to swallow. "Where's Nancy? What have you done with her?"

"Wherz Nacy, wherz Nacy, don't know, pretty."

"Give me the red devil called Floating Feather. Bring him out, or I'll raise the very fires of hell around you till your insides boil and you fall to your knees and beg me to take him from you. I know he cowers within one of you, and I will see him destroyed!" Clay's limp body shook at the end of the cowboy's outstretched arm.

"Who are you looking for?" James shouted. "There's nobody here but us!"

Calvin cried out as his parka burst into flames. Franklin grabbed it, pulled it off him, and stomped it into the snow surrounding their feet.

"Stop it!" James screamed. "Stop it! We can't give you someone we don't have."

"Then you die." The cowboy let go of Clay's spine, and his lifeless body fell off the snowmobile and landed in the snow. The little man jumped down and ran over to it. He pulled Clay's head up by the hair, then used his free hand to start opening and closing the dead man's mouth.

"I know that red devil, Floating Feather, has hidden himself inside one of you, just as he hid himself inside the old fool doctor when I killed him the first time," the body of Clay said as the cowboy slowly advanced on them. "I have searched for three lifetimes seeking my revenge, and I WILL HAVE IT!"

"NO!" Franklin moved to block James and Calvin from the cowboy. "My *ancestor*, Floating Feather, was a brave warrior and mighty medicine man who worshiped at the feet of the Great One. You are a devil! You took his life! You are a demon that needs to be destr—"

With lightning reflexes, the cowboy drew the single-shot revolver from his vest pocket and fired. Franklin's body was lifted off the ground and thrown back against the rocks.

James tried to scream, but a massive heatwave struck him, lifting his, Calvin's, and Franklin's bodies into the air. His vison blurred and became blood-red.

Chapter Sixty-Nine

James' feet met with hard earth, and Franklin groaned. As the red light faded, it took time for James' eyes to adjust to their now-shadowy surroundings. They were inside a cold, dimly lit sod house. The damp, musty smell of the place assaulted his nose and made him want to gag.

His mind fought to make sense of where they were and how they had gotten there. What had the cowboy done to them? Calvin was standing next to him, their backs against a dirt wall, while Franklin leaned against the wall at their feet. Franklin's hands shook as they covered the bullet wound in his chest. Blood had saturated his shirt.

A young woman, no more than seventeen years old was tending to a pot that hung on an iron spit over an open fire. The fire's smoke gathered like clouds against the thatched roof until it could make its way out of a small hole cut in one corner. A little boy, maybe four years old, played at her feet. He was filthy, and the cloth diaper that he wore was soiled and yellow with age.

The door to the sod house swung open, and another boy—this one looked to be around ten—came in carrying two sickly looking ears of corn and a handful of greens. He handed them to the woman.

"Is this all that's left?" she asked.

The boy nodded.

"That's not good." She pulled a small knife out of her apron pocket and cut the husks off the corn. The cobs underneath were mostly bare, a few dry kernels spotting their surfaces. She tossed them into the pot along with the greens and stirred them around. "Maybe he'll be too tired to eat when he gets home."

The older boy took the knife from her and made a stabbing motion with it.

"Don't be stupid. He'll kill both of us and toss our bodies out for the buzzards. Then who would take care of Elliot?" She took the knife from him and motioned with it toward the little boy playing on the dirt floor. "It might be months before he finds someone else to drag out to this God-forsaken hole."

Elliot reached out toward the fire. His little fingers touched a hot coal, and he wailed in pain. She dropped to her knees and pulled him into her arms.

"Owwws, owwws!" the boy wailed, sounding more like an old barn owl than a child.

"Shhhhhhhh," she whispered in his ear. "Hush now." She began rocking him.

"Sssssss, ush ow," he repeated back to her.

"*Baa baa black sheep have you any wool? Yes sir, yes sir, three bags full,*" she sang as she held him close. The little boy shut his eyes and laid his head against her chest. "*One for the master, one for the dame, one for the little boy that lives down the lane.*"

The door burst open and an old man stormed in. His stringy, gray hair hung limp beneath an old bowler hat, and his chin was covered with a spotty salt-and-pepper beard. He stopped, surveyed the situation, and kicked the woman in the shoulder with his worn boot. She toppled over, losing her grip on Elliot. If not for the fast reflexes of the older boy, they both would have rolled into the fire.

"Look at the little hero." The old man burst out laughing. "Saved the mother and the baby! Brother, you might turn out to be worth something yet."

The old man was carrying a burlap bag. He tossed it on the small table that sat against the wall underneath the room's only window. When it landed, the bag fell open, and a few pieces of turquoise jewelry spilled out.

James watched as the old man emptied the rest of the bag's contents. More jewelry tumbled out along with some brightly colored stones and feathers. The last thing to tumble out was a human hand.

Calvin elbowed James to get his attention, then pointed toward the older boy who had made his way unnoticed back to the fire and was secreting the girl's knife away behind his back.

"Hell of a haul today," the old man said as he began sorting through the items on the table. "Ought to bring a dollar or two next time I'm in town. Stupid squaw that makes this crap never saw me coming." He picked up the hand, then brayed a mule-like laugh as he turned to show it to the children. "Guess she won't be making any more without this—"

The boy lunged at him with the knife, but the old man was too quick. He dropped the hand, side-stepped the attack, and grabbed the boy's wrist all in one fluid move. Within seconds, the boy was trapped with his back against the old man's chest and the knife against his own throat.

"Do you really think you're ready to take me on, Brother?"

The boy didn't move, didn't try to answer.

"That's what I thought." He turned the knife so that the sharpened tip pushed into the soft flesh of the boy's neck. A small trickle of blood escaped around it and ran down into his shirt. "What have I told you, boy, since the first day?" The knife went in deeper, and the blood ran more freely. "I am god, and you are nothing. You do only what god tells you, you don't think, you don't act, you don't speak, unless god wills it." He chuckled. "Guess god ain't got to worry about that last one, seeing as you're too stupid to talk. I should have left you with those stinkin' gypsies. What the hell was I thinking paying that good-for-nothin' lot four hard-earned dollars for a mute? They should have paid me for taking you off their hands."

He took the knife away from the boy's throat, pushed him down on the ground, and spat on him. "It'll be a cold day in hell before the likes of you can take on god. Now get up off your ass and go help the mother make my dinner."

The boy went and stood next to the girl. She was up, standing by the fire and stirring the pot. She tried to press a dirty piece of cloth against the cut in his neck to stop the bleeding, but he slapped her hand away and turned to face the fire.

Elliot reached up and took the older boy's hand. "Owwws?"

"James." Franklin's voice was weak and strained.

With all that was happening inside the house, James had not been paying any attention to Franklin or Calvin.

He dropped to his knee and took Franklin's still-trembling hand away from the bullet wound in his chest. The bleeding had slowed but not stopped. On one hand, that was good. It meant that the bullet had missed his heart, but it was still a dangerous injury that needed treatment in a hospital.

"Calvin, give me your handkerchief." James held his breath, realizing that by speaking he might be calling attention to himself and his friends. He slowly turned his head and looked back over into the room; the man had returned to digging through his loot while the others were huddled closely to the fire. Obviously, the people could neither hear nor see them.

Calvin was nervously cleaning his glasses. He looked down at his handkerchief, then handed it over. James twisted one end of it and inserted it into the wound. Franklin arched his back and moaned loudly from the pain.

"I'm so sorry." James took Franklin's hand and placed it over the handkerchief. "I know it hurts, but we have to stop the bleeding."

"This is the prize of the crop!" the old man announced.

He held the amputated hand high in the air. A gold band wound around its middle finger like a snake encircling a tree branch. He grasped the ring and tried to pull it free. When it didn't budge, he tried again, this time groaning with the effort, but it remained where it was.

Shock and revulsion passed through James as he watched the old man take the knife the boy had tried to kill him with and used it to cut the finger loose from the rest of the hand.

The old man held the finger in one hand and tried to push, then pull the ring off with the other. It was still stuck. He took a hammer and nail from an old wooden bucket beside the door and nailed the finger to the door post. He ran the knife up inside the finger, coring out the center until he could easily remove the ring.

He laughed and did a little jig, then walked over to the sod house's only window and looked at his prize in what little sun managed to seep in through all the dirt and dust.

"I got you, you triflin' bit—"

The windowpane shattered, and an arrow lodged in the old man's shoulder. He cried out in pain and turned from the window. A split second later, another arrow entered his back between the shoulder blades.

"Help me!" He reached out toward the children.

The oldest boy walked over to him and spat in his face.

"You little shit! I'll kill you for that!"

The boy picked up the knife from the floor where the old man had dropped it. He raised it above his head, but before he could wield the blow that would end the old man's life, the door exploded inward. Three Indian warriors rushed into the room. The first man grabbed the knife from the boy, then kicked him out of the way. The second warrior crossed the room and grabbed the woman—*the mother*—by her hair and forced her to kneel on the floor. The final warrior notched an arrow in his bow and aimed it at the old man's head.

"No, no don't kill me," the old man begged. "Take your stuff and go. Take the kids, take the girl. She's good, really good, and she don't fight back none. Take whatever you want. Just don't kill me!"

A fourth Indian stepped through the door. In his arms, he carried the dead body of an Indian maiden. A headdress of raven's feathers sat impressively upon his head, and his face was painted white. His chest bore a latticework of scars that had been painted white as well. From the leather strip around his waist hung numerous pouches and carved totems. He walked over to the groveling old man and gently laid the woman's body beside him.

"Floating Feather," the old man's voice trembled in fear. "I didn't know she was one of yours. I didn't know. I'm sorry, if I had I— Take the girl!" He pointed at the girl still on her knees in front of the warrior. "Take her. I know she ain't a Native, but she'll do, she'll keep you—"

Floating Feather slapped the old man so hard that his head rocked back. Blood and spit flew from his mouth, and his hat flew off his head and tumbled across the floor. He grabbed the old man by his greasy hair and snatched his head back up. He forced him to look at the dead woman lying beside him. Floating Feather lifted her arm and showed him the bloody stump where her hand had once been, then slapped him again. The old man began blubbering like a scared infant and pleading for his life.

Floating Feather motioned for the warrior holding the girl to bring her to him.

"Your white man's God says if a man should cause a blemish in his neighbor, as he hath done, so shall it be done to him. Breach for breach, eye for eye, tooth for tooth." His voice was low and threatening. His English strong and clear.

The old man stopped crying and looked up at Floating Feather, then over at the girl who was on her knees, sobbing. "I don't—"

Floating Feather pulled a knife from his belt. The warrior lifted the girl's arm, and with one strike, Floating Feather separated the girl's hand from her wrist. He took a step back, and the warrior with the bow and arrow let his arrow fly, striking the old man between the eyes.

Elliot and the older boy rushed to the screaming girl's side. The older boy ripped off his shirt and wrapped it around her wrist, but it did nothing to stop the blood that poured from it.

Floating Feather nodded. One of the warriors picked up the body of the Indian maiden and carried her from the room. The others followed him out.

Floating Feather looked at the old man's body, then over at the two boys who were desperately trying to save the girl. The older boy looked up at him, and their eyes locked. Floating Feather nodded once, then left the house, closing the door behind him.

James' heart raced. He had never witnessed such brutality in his life. A soft noise came from his side, and he looked over to see Calvin crying as he held his glasses in his trembling hands.

The hot, red mist began to form around them again. As he felt his feet leave the ground, James saw the older boy pick up the old man's bowler hat and place it on his own head.

Chapter Seventy

Nancy pushed blindly through the evergreen trees and brush that covered the side of the mountain. She was freezing. She thought back to how she had been sitting by the *warm* fire in the house when the little man had come running down the stairs, swinging a piece of wood over his head. If only her feet hadn't gotten tangled in the blanket when she screamed and tried to get away, she wouldn't have been knocked unconscious by the little beast. It still terrified her to think how she woke up bound next to the fire in the mine tunnel. Fear and adrenaline had kept her from noticing the cold and the throbbing pain on the side of her head, but now, both were making themselves known in a big way.

Her panties were working okay as a sling, but it was far from the protection her broken arm needed. It throbbed with each step, sending shooting pains up into her shoulder. Still, she *had* to keep moving. Stopping meant dying, and she was not going to let that happen without a fight.

The decision to travel up toward the crest of the mountain had not been a conscious one, it had just been the easiest way to go after leaving the mine. Initially, she had followed an old animal trail, and when it disappeared, she just continued on in the same direction. Now, she was lost.

The sun would be rising soon, and hopefully, that would make the going easier. Traveling by filtered moonlight was a slow process. *Where am I rushing off to?* For all she knew, she might be getting farther away from James and safety, rather than closer. She was just running blindly in the dark up the side of a mountain, hoping for a miracle, and she could just as easily have run into the cowboy and the little man as she could James, Franklin, or Calvin.

She knew they had been searching for her; she had heard Franklin call out, but now that Clay was dead, they might have gone back to the house to reorganize. *Who knows?* Franklin may have taken one of the snowmobiles and tried to go for help.

The crack of a gunshot came from her left, and she dropped to the ground. Her broken arm struck a rock, and she clamped her good hand over her mouth to keep from screaming. She scooted back behind a large juniper tree and tried to be as quiet as she could in fear that any noise could cause bullets to come flying in her direction.

There were voices in the distance. She strained to hear what they were saying. Though far away, she recognized one as James, the other was unfamiliar.

When no more shots were fired, she struggled to her feet and started moving slowly toward the voices. She made sure to plant her feet carefully so as not to step on a fallen branch or any loose rocks. Until she could see who was talking to James, she wanted her presence to remain a secret.

The first thing she saw through the cover of the trees was an area between two large rock outcroppings illuminated by the snowmobile's lights. The voices were clearer now, but she still couldn't identify the second one.

"Stop it!" someone screamed. *Was that James?* "Stop it! We can't give you someone we don't have." It *was* James, but his voice was so full of fear that she hardly recognized it.

"Then you die," the other voice said.

NO! Her mind screamed, and she lunged forward. Her foot

landed in a patch of mud and her feet slid out from under her. She reached for a branch of a nearby tree, missed, and began tumbling down the steep slope. She grabbed for anything she could reach to try and slow her descent but didn't stop until she struck another juniper tree, broken arm first. Pain flared throughout her upper body, black spots formed in her vision, then overtook her.

* * *

Nancy's eyes fluttered open. For a moment, she didn't know where she was. A dark, cloudless sky floated above her filled with stars that seemed too close to the ground. She shivered, and her body ached all over. *Then you die,* the stranger's voice came back to her. She sat up, sending a bolt of pain into her shoulder and down her back. She gasped and held her breath until the pain started to subside.

How long had she been out? Was James dead above her on the side of the mountain?

She began looking around for something to use for balance. A limb about five feet long and as big around as her arm was lying within reach beside the juniper tree. She braced herself for the inevitable pain to come, used the branch, and pushed herself up.

The trip back up the mountain was one of the hardest things she had ever done. Snow had made the way muddy and slick. More than once, the limb was all that kept her from rolling back down. She angled her climb in the direction of where she thought the voices had come from earlier, and soon she came to a trail cut through the trees. Cautiously, she stepped out onto it, and tried to get her bearings. The path had been recently traveled. In the moonlight, she could just make out the treads of a snowmobile, but there were footprints there as well traveling upward toward the summit.

Back inside the tree line, she began climbing again. After about twenty-five yards, she spotted the rock outcroppings; two elongated shadows were cast across them by the snowmobile's headlights. She moved even more cautiously as she drew closer to them, afraid that with each step she might find James, Calvin, or Franklin dead. The voice had stopped and that only heightened her fear.

A giant fernbush blocked her from staying close to the path, so she ventured deeper in the trees to get around it. By the time she made it back to the edge of the trail, she was standing just out of sight beside the snowmobiles. She couldn't make sense of what she was seeing. The little man was squatting over Clay's dead body next to the snowmobiles. James and Calvin were standing perfectly still; their eyes were rolled up in their sockets, their heads leaned back, and their mouths open. Franklin lay against one of the rock outcroppings. He was bleeding from a wound high on the left side of his chest, but his eyes were the same as the others, and he wasn't moving.

This is my chance.

Quietly as she could, she moved a few feet farther up the path until she was able to look back at the cowboy. He had his chin lifted and his good eye closed.

It's now or never. If I don't make my move, we could all end up dead.

She eased out closer to the edge of the path. The little man stopped playing with Clay's head, looked directly at her, and smiled.

She stopped and held her breath, waiting for the little man to do something to get the cowboy's attention. He would tap his leg, pull at his sleeve, or touch his hand like he had inside the mine, then they would all die.

Instead, the little man raised his hand and wiggled his fingers at her. "Pretty, no yes, no pretty, yes," he whispered in his ragged, little-boy way of speaking.

She put a finger to her lips and shook her head.

"Shhhh," the little man said and pressed his finger to his own lips.

She nodded. *Could this really be happening?* A cold sweat formed under her arms and on the back of her neck. The sad little man-child was actually listening to her and doing what she told him to do. She needed him out of the way. She needed a clear path to the cowboy.

"Shhhh," the little man whispered again, then gave her another wiggly-fingered wave.

In return, she smiled and blew him a kiss.

The little man blushed so hard that she could see his cheeks turning red through the layers of dirt and scars that covered them.

Her smile grew larger, and she gave him a little nod, then motioned for him to move to the side.

The little man let go of Clay's head. It fell face-first against the muddy path with a sickening thud. The little man stood and started to reach for the cowboy.

She shook her head and waved her finger back and forth in the air.

The little man stopped and dropped his hand back to his side.

"No, say no?" he whispered.

She shook her head and again motioned for him to move to the side. *Come on, just do it!* She screamed at him inside her head.

The little man stepped over Clay's body and inched closer to the trees.

Yes! She continued to wave him on as he sidestepped getting ever nearer to the trees. With her other hand, she reached to her ankle and rolled back her pants leg, exposing the handle of the scalpel hidden in her shoe.

Three, two, one.

The little man stepped into the trees. Nancy grabbed the scalpel and lunged for the cowboy. His eyes opened, Clay's dead body began to convulse, and a mighty roar came from deep within it. James, Calvin, and Franklin all fell to the ground.

Chapter Seventy-One

Franklin was floating inside the hot red mist that had taken them from the sod house. He had been trying to understand what he had seen. His ancestor, Floating Feather, had ordered an innocent woman's death. Why? He had the old man where he wanted him. Killing him was completely understandable, but why torture her? Why not let her live? She had done nothing to them—

A sudden bolt of pain shot through him.

He cried out and opened his eyes. James and Calvin were lying on the ground beside him and Nancy—Nancy was sailing through the air toward the cowboy. The whole scene seemed to be moving in slow motion: the cowboy turning toward her, his hand raised as if to slap her away, Nancy's mouth open, screaming, the little man running toward them from the trees, screaming as well with his arms raised.

The cowboy's hand came down hard and crashed into Nancy's shoulder. Her arm slipped out of some kind of sling, and her expression changed from aggression to pain. Her other arm thrust out, stabbing something into the cowboy's chest.

A blinding, yellow light exploded from the cowboy's chest, then suddenly, everything was silent.

When Franklin's vision cleared. Keegsquaw and Nijlon were standing beside him.

* * *

He knew the second my hand touched the scalpel.
It didn't matter if he was awake, it was too late. Nancy knew she had the drop on the cowboy.
I'm going to end this. Right here, right now.
She ran out of the woods, planted her foot on the path, and pushed off, sending herself flying directly at him. He started turning toward her. *Bring it on!* If he was facing her, she would have a better shot at driving the scalpel deeper into him.

A bomb exploded against her shoulder. White-hot pain filled her chest and shot across her back. She began to rotate in the air. With what little strength she had left, she lunged the scalpel forward. It punctured the cowboy's rotted vest and shirt, then embedded itself into his chest.

She became engulfed in hot yellow light. Heat, dust, and debris rushed up the length of her arm and overtook her. The smell of death and rot accosted her. She struck the frozen dirt of the path and began to roll. Her broken arm flopped uselessly until she came to a stop with it underneath her body. Pain worse than she could have ever imagined rushed over her, and she vomited into the snow. She began to choke on the material that had emptied from her stomach. Tears flowed from her eyes and her bladder let go.

God help me! I don't want to die, not here, not now!

Small hands grabbed her shoulders and rolled her over onto her back. Through blurry, tear-filled eyes she saw the little man looking down at her. He shoved his filthy fingers into her mouth and cleared away the vomit remaining there.

"Pretty. Bad. No pretty, no pretty, yes." He was crying as well. He reached over, took her broken arm, and placed it on her chest. She screamed and he skittered away, but then eased back and sat cross legged beside her. He lifted her shoulders, and she moaned. This time, he didn't even flinch as he cautiously placed her head in his lap.

"*Bmmmm bmmm, baaak seeeb, habboo aneeeee wooooo—*" He gently rocked her back and forth in his lap. "*Esss seeer, esss errrr, feee baaaa ferrrr—*"

She looked up into his face and smiled. "Thank you," she whispered.

The little man nodded and began to laugh, causing her head to bounce in his lap. He threw his head back and howled with happiness.

A long blade cut through the cold night air and separated the little man's head from his neck. His body toppled over, and she was drenched in his blood before being dumped out of his lap and back onto the frozen ground.

* * *

Something struck James' legs and startled him awake. He looked down and saw the little man's head resting against his ankle. It was smiling. He scrambled frantically away from it, pushing himself up against the rock wall next to Franklin.

For a moment, he became caught up in the chaos going on in the little clearing at the top of the mountain. A beam of yellow light streamed from the cowboy's chest, painting the nearby rocks in a sickly jaundiced glow. His arms were flailing wildly like one of those tube men he'd seen outside businesses that when filled with air from a fan below flounced around in an attempt to get attention. It would have been humorous except that the cowboy's version of the tube man wielded a long, sharp sword in one hand.

Someone screamed. It was Nancy. She was lying next to the little man's headless body, covered in blood. James leapt to his feet, rushed over and grabbed her shoulders, intending to pull her away from the cowboy and his sword.

She screamed again and slapped at his hands.

"It's me, Nancy! It's James!"

"James! James!" she reached out for him. "Is the cowboy dead? Did I kill him? I stabbed him with the scalpel, right in his chest."

"I don't know, but I've got to get you away from here." He used his hands to try and wipe away some of the blood from around her eyes.

She nodded, but when his hands touched her shoulders, she began desperately shaking her head.

"What?" he asked. "What's wrong?"

"My left arm's broken, bad." She started crying and clutched at his shirt with her right hand.

"Shit!" He looked around for something he could slide under her to move her more gently, but there was nothing.

"I love you, and I'm sorry!" He grabbed her good arm and dragged her back beside Calvin. "I'm sorry. I'm so sorry. I know that hurt but—"

Nancy was unconscious.

Clay's body cried out and filled the clearing with a deafening yowl of anger and aggression. A massive thunderclap shook the top of the mountain, and a bolt of lightning shot out of the cowboy's chest and into the night sky. The yellow light extinguished with a loud electrical snap, leaving in its place a glowing yellow sphere. It undulated in the air above them, stretching out, then pulling itself back in, appearing to become more solid with each movement.

Something grabbed James' arm. He yelled and pulled away. It grabbed him again, and he realized it was Calvin. His glasses hung off one ear and his mouth gaped open as he looked up at what had become of the storm.

"W-What the h-h-h-hell is th-th-th-that?" he yelled pointing up at the pulsing yellow orb.

"I have no idea." James shook his head. "Nancy stabbed the cowboy with the scalpel from the surgical kit and all hell broke loose."

Calvin's head jerked around. "Did you say N-N-N-Nancy did that?" He noticed her lying unconscious beside them. "Dear God, is sh-sh-sh-she—?"

"No, no." James placed his hand on Calvin's shoulder. "Not dead, just unconscious. But she's hurt, and I don't know how bad."

"But the b-b-b-blood?"

"Not hers." He pointed over at the little man's grinning skull.

"Oh, m-m-m-my."

Nancy began to stir, and Calvin jumped away, startled by the movement.

"Help me get her up," James said, "but be careful. Before she passed out, she said her arm was broken."

"Y-Y-Yes, yes."

James sat down beside Nancy, and with Calvin's help, managed to get her up and leaning back against him.

"Nancy? Nancy, can you hear me?"

She began to choke and turned her face away from him.

"Nancy—"

She shook her head and started pulling frantically at the panty sling that had tightened around her neck when he had pulled her against him.

He leaned her forward, releasing the pressure on her throat.

Nancy took a deep, ragged breath, looked into his eyes, and began to cry.

* * *

Keegsquaw and Nijlon stood side by side, their hands entwined, just as they had been the last time Franklin had seen them. The twins, one beautiful and the other a decaying corpse, didn't move. They just stood there looking down at him.

"Why?" he whispered up at them, hoping to find an answer. "Why did Floating Feather have to kill that woman?"

They didn't respond.

"I don't understand, he—"

Keegsquaw pointed at him, then balled her hand into a fist and brought it back against her chest. Nijlon reached over and grasped Keegsquaw's fist with her rotted fingers.

"Are you telling me to stay strong no matter what I saw in the dream?"

In unison the twins let their hands drop back to their sides and their chins to their chests. Without looking up, Nijlon reached out and placed her hand against the rock Franklin was leaning against. The dead moss and weeds that covered it liquified, flowed over its surface, and down onto Nijlon's decayed fingers, weaving in and out of the ruined flesh of her hand.

Keegsquaw pointed again. This time not at him but at the carving of a feather an arm's length above his head.

* * *

Clay's dead body growled and writhed in the snow. It reached out and slapped its hands flat on the frozen ground, then pushed itself up. For a split-second, James pictured a seal performing in a circus, but that image was forced from his mind when it snarled and gnashed its teeth together so hard that some of them shattered.

The cowboy's rotten mouth was open as if he were screaming. He swung his sword at the yellow sphere. It jerked to one side, avoiding the attack. The cowboy balled his other hand into a fist and shook it toward the orb that pulsed and contorted in the air just out of his reach.

"Oush."

Nancy screamed and buried her face against James' side. When he saw who had spoken, he wanted to scream right along with her. The little man's eyes were open, and he was looking up at them.

James kicked out and his heel connected with the little man's forehead, sending the head rolling back toward its decapitated body.

"It's okay Nancy, I got rid of it. We've got to get you out of here. We've—"

"L-L-L-Look!" Calvin gasped.

The little man's body had managed to get up onto its hands and knees and was feeling around the icy ground, searching first with one hand, then the other.

"Ieee, oush!" the little man cried out. His head was lying on its side no more than a foot from where its body was searching. Tears trickled from his eyes, snot ran from his nose, and his lips dug little furrows in the muddy snow when he spoke. "IEEE!" he screamed, and his body turned toward the sound. "Oush, hurtzz, yes? Yes? Hurtzz!" His right hand swept in the head's direction. "Yes, oush, yes!" The headless body's fingers grazed its head, it opened its hand wide as if surprised, then reached out and gently began caressing the face. "Yes, yesssss." The little man sighed and kissed at the fingers. The hand traveled over the little man's head until it felt his thinning hair. It curled its fingers into the greasy mass and lifted the head off the ground. The body twisted around until it was sitting cross legged in the snow cradling its head in its lap.

"N-N-No," Calvin whispered. "That's impo—I d-d-d-don't accept this. This is another dream, a nightma—"

The body lifted its head with both hands and forced it down against the ragged remains of its neck. Blinding light exploded from the wound, flames leapt out from its torn edges, immediately cauterizing the skin and filling the air with the smell of burning, rotted meat. The little man cried out joyfully, fell back, and waved his arms over his head like a child making snow angels.

"Enough!" the voice speaking through Clay screamed, and the sounds of the little man's celebration immediately stopped.

What remained of Clay stood next to the cowboy. It was bent awkwardly forward. Strings of blood dripped from between its broken teeth. Its head was turned at an unnatural angle, and its eyes were focused on the yellow orb. The cowboy had returned his sword to its scabbard and now stood perfectly still. Smoke drifted up from around the scalpel in his chest, but he paid it no mind. He stared directly at the pulsating orb. The restored little man got to his feet and joined the cowboy. Never taking his eye off the orb, the cowboy reached into his vest pocket, pulled out a piece of rock candy, and handed it to the little man who took it and popped it into his mouth. He reached up, took the cowboy's hand, then turned and looked up at the orb.

"What's happening?" Nancy whispered. James could only shake his head.

Under the weight of their stares, the orb's movements became more spastic. Its pulses quickened and a sound like heavy breathing emanated from deep within it.

"It's afraid," Nancy said. "I don't know how I know that, but I do."

James reached over to take her hand, but Calvin was already holding it.

The scalpel in the cowboy's chest began to glow bright white. The light pulsed, then the scalpel shot from his chest, propelled on a red-hot stream of flame.

Nancy screamed. Calvin leapt to his feet and pressed himself flat against the rock wall with his arm wrapped around his head. James' hands trembled, and his heart pounded inside his chest, but he could not look away.

The scalpel and the flames struck the orb, cracking its surface and setting it alight. Yellow smoke belched from the opening, filling the little clearing with a thick fog that reeked of burnt charcoal and disease.

Nancy began to cough and choke.

James frantically tried to use his free hand to fan the yellow steam away from her. His own eyes were burning. He tried not to breathe, but still the inside of his mouth and nose became coated with an oily film.

A burning-hot wind blew down from the night sky above them, quickly becoming a whirlwind, then building into a cyclone. All the yellow smoke was pulled to its center, then with a loud *whoosh* it was sucked back into the open hole in the cowboy's chest.

"*Bmmmm bmmm, baaak seeeb, habboo aneeeee wooooo—*"

Clay's legs buckled, and he seemed to fall apart. His body tumbled into itself, then into a heap at the cowboy's feet.

Silence filled the clearing.

James could hear his own breathing. Nancy was praying beside him, a constant stream of *Our Fathers* and *Hail Marys*. Someone began to laugh. It was a dry, raspy sound that caused the hairs on his arms to stand erect and his ears to twitch.

"Floating Feather," Franklin's cracked voice whispered. His face was pale; blood from the bullet wound had saturated his shirt and pooled in his lap. With a shaking hand, he pointed up at where the orb had been.

Floating Feather looked around at them and continued to laugh.

* * *

Franklin could feel his heartbeat slowing down. It was getting harder and harder to draw each breath. Keegsquaw and Nijlon were kneeling beside him as he watched his ancestor, Floating Feather, laugh as he floated above the circle made up of his closest friends and most-feared enemies.

"He is not who he once was."

Two voices filled his head in unison. One lilting and beautiful, the other cracked and discordant.

"He has remained too long in this world and angered the Great Spirit. His time must come to an end."

"No." Franklin looked over at them and shook his head. "No, he is a powerful shaman who serves the will of the Great Spirit. He is to be honored and revered."

Keegsquaw and Nijlon closed their eyes, and Franklin was engulfed in a sea of white. He was floating over an Indian village that lay in ruin. Mutilated bodies littered the ground between burning tents. The cowboy was kneeling, encased in ice as a giant warrior lifted Floating Feather's burned and bloody body from the remains of a campfire.

"The Great Spirit was one with him when his tribe was attacked and sent the cloud warrior to him when Floating Father called for help."

His vision shifted, and he was looking down at the shaman's body as Doc Mitchell tried to save him.

"The Great Spirit was again one with him at the time of his death. He sent two winged spirits to escort Floating Feather's soul to the promised land. When Floating Feather saw them approach, he was filled with fear, and he cried out the words of transfiguration. The winged spirits were dispelled, and Floating Feather's soul flowed into the white man's hand and tools, binding them together for all time."

Another shift, and Franklin watched as the cloud warrior sealed the grave in the high mountain pass, then mounted his horse. The animal became agitated. It fought the reins, pawed at the ground over the grave, and foamed at the mouth.

A bright light surrounded the warrior. A moment later, it disappeared as quickly as it had come. The warrior dug his heels into the horse's side, gave a mighty war cry, and galloped full speed into the setting sun.

"The Great Spirit told the cloud warrior of Floating Feather's actions and set him to the task of delivering the tools into the hands of any son of the white man's blood that practiced his medicine up until the one could be found with the strength to reject Floating Feathers gifts and send him to his eternal reward."

"James," Franklin whispered. He was back sitting against the rock, looking at Keegsquaw and Nijlon. "Before, when you showed me your fist and brought it to your breast, you weren't telling me to remain strong in my faith, were you?"

The twins shook their heads in unison.

"You were telling me to be strong when the time comes to put an end to this."

The twins nodded.

"And is it that time now?"

The twins nodded again.

With what little strength he had left, Franklin reached up, slapped his burned hand against the carving of the feather, and screamed.

* * *

Franklin screamed and the spirit of Floating Feather stopped laughing.

"What have you done!" he bellowed.

Lightning streaked across the sky, thunder shook the ground, and hail rained down on them. A freezing-cold wind swept up the trail, bringing with it heavy wet snow.

James grabbed Nancy, pulled her to him, and wrapped his arms around her. He motioned for Calvin to move over next to them.

The cry of a mighty eagle sounded across the top of the mountain.

"No!" Floating Feather cried out in anger.

The morning sun crested the edge of the mountain, carrying with it billowing white clouds. Churning in the dawn's light, the clouds rose higher into the air, growing thicker and more tumultuous with each passing second.

The cowboy took that moment to make his move. He unsheathed his sword and lunged toward Floating Feather.

A blinding bolt of blue lightning shot out of the clouds, striking the ground where he stood. Instantly, the cowboy's feet were frozen in place.

"Noooooo!" A choked and garbled cry came out from deep within Clay's remains. The body twisted and shook, joints popped like firecrackers as his bones snapped back in place. Like a phoenix rising from the ashes, Clay's broken body reformed. He lunged forward, grabbed Floating Feather's ankle, and dashed him to the ground.

The cowboy used his sword like an ice pick, chopping away the ice that coated his feet. Some blows landed high and cut into the flesh of his legs. Black blood flowed from the wounds. Where it touched the ice, the ice melted.

James motioned for Calvin to stand up. He did the same, and as gently as they could, they got Nancy to her feet. They had to get farther away before they wound up in the middle of whatever was about to happen. They gathered around Franklin and stood in the small area near the ledge at the back of the passageway.

The cowboy brought the sword down in a final powerful strike, and the ice that had held him shattered. He turned and leapt on Floating Feather. His strong hands encircled the shaman's throat and began to squeeze.

"Stop it!" Franklin cried out breathlessly and tried to get up, but he was too weak. "Stop." He pointed a shaking finger at the cowboy. "Stop it!"

Thunder rattled the top of the mountain. The clouds separated like curtains on a stage, letting the sun's rays pour down on the clearing. A dark figure riding a white horse appeared and galloped toward them. The horse's hooves threw clumps of dirt and snow into the air behind him as it rushed into their midst.

The cowboy looked up just as the rider lashed out with a long staff and knocked him off Floating Feather. He tumbled over, barely able to avoid the horse's hooves.

Clay's body lashed out, grabbed the horse's tail, and was dragged a few feet away before having to let go.

James watched, transfixed, as the warrior hauled back on the reins, forcing the horse into a hard turn. He raised the staff above his head and flung it at Clay's body. The staff entered its midsection and exited through his lower back before burying its tip in the earth. Clay's hands grabbed the staff and tried to pull itself off. It roared as it inched its way forward, leaving shreds of its insides dangling from the rough wood behind it.

The warrior sat silently watching him, then raised his hand. Lightning shot from the sky, enclosing Clay's body and the staff in a solid block of ice. Thunder clapped above them and the ice, and Clay's body inside of it, shattered like glass.

The warrior dismounted and offered his hand to Floating Feather. "You have lingered too long." His voice was deep and resonate. "The Great One grows weary of your foolishness."

"Behind you!" James shouted.

The warrior turned just as the cowboy drew his pistol and fired two shots. Both slugs entered his side. He didn't flinch or react in any way. The cowboy fired again, this bullet struck the warrior in the center of his chest, he stood defiant.

The cowboy drew his sword, but before he could swing it, the warrior lunged forward and backhanded him in the side of the head, knocking him away.

"I grow tired of this foolishness," the warrior told Floating Feather. "Join me of your own free will, or I will take you to the Great One in chains." He held out his hand. Water bubbled up in his palm and spilled over the sides. As it ran from his hand, it froze, forming a heavy chain that dangled to the ground.

Floating Feather stood and backed away from the warrior. "I cannot."

The chain in the warrior's hand came to life. Like a serpent striking at an intruder, it struck out at the shaman. At the same moment, the little man who had remained silent watching all that was going on around him, jumped on the warrior's arm, causing the chain to miss its intended target.

"No, ourz, redskinz bad. Redskinz kill the mother, redskinz—"

A jerk of the warrior's arm sent the little man flying. He landed next to the cowboy and began to cry.

"Stay back, warrior!" Floating Feather shouted. "I will decide when it's my time, not you and not the Great One." He backed farther up the path toward James, Nancy, and Calvin. "I served him well. I did my service to him without question. I have earned the right to have my way." Floating Feather leapt at Franklin. In midair he dissolved into a mass of black insects. The swarm flew in Franklin's face.

Nancy screamed. James and Calvin fell on their knees next to Franklin and began swatting at the black gnats, trying to kill them or chase them away.

"Hold your b-b-b-breath, Franklin!" Calvin cried. "D-D-D-Don't breathe!"

Franklin's eyes grew big, and his cheeks reddened under the effort of trying to keep the gnats at bay. The swarm grew heavier and began biting at the flesh of Franklin's face and neck. They burrowed at the corners of his eyes and filled his nose. Despite James' and Calvin's best efforts, the insects encased Franklin's head in a rippling, buzzing mask. Franklin screamed. The sound echoed around the little clearing at the top of the mountain, then was cut short as millions of black gnats filled his mouth and entered his lungs.

Franklin's eyes opened, he looked at James, then at Calvin, and he smiled.

* * *

"Ancestor," Franklin said. "Why are you here?"

"Because you serve the Great One as I do," Floating Feather answered.

The world around Franklin had come to a stop. He could see James and Calvin staring down at him. He could see Nancy standing behind James with her eyes closed and cradling her broken arm. The warrior towered over them all, an icy chain hanging from his outstretched hand. The cowboy and the little man stood behind him. The little man held the cowboy's hand, and the cowboy had drawn his pistol.

"Now we will serve the Great One together." Floating Feather's voice echoed through his mind.

Franklin could see black shapes begin moving around the edges of his vision.

"But Keegsquaw and Nijlon said I had to be strong, that it was time for you to move on. That I had to put an end to this, that—"

His vison started to fail under the growing darkness of the gnats flowing out from behind his eyes. They crawled across his tongue and over his teeth until his mouth was full. He felt them filling his lungs.

He couldn't breathe.

"Yes," the voice echoed through his fading thoughts. "We *will* serve the Great One together. My soul in your body."

With that, Franklin ceased to exist, and Floating Feather took full control.

He told Franklin's eyes to look at the white man that Franklin's thoughts called James, then at the older man called Calvin. If he could convince them that their friend, Franklin, needed their help, they might prove useful in his escape from the cloud warrior. He told Franklin's mouth to smile.

* * *

Franklin reached up and grabbed James' arm.

"James, help me up. Help me."

"I think you better lay still, buddy." James pushed Franklin's arm away, then stood and took a step back.

Franklin looked over at Calvin. Calvin just shook his head and moved away as well.

"Come on guy's, you've got to get me out of here before one of these freaks tries to kill me." He stood and turned to Nancy.

"Nancy, please—"

"No!" She screamed and buried her face against James' chest.

The crack of a pistol filled the air. A small hole appeared in Franklin's forehead, then blood painted the rock behind him red. His body lurched, and he reached out for James.

James pulled Nancy with him as he moved out of reach. He looked over at the cowboy. Smoke was rising from the barrel of his gun, then a burst of flame leapt out as a bullet spun from the barrel, followed a split second later by another.

Two more holes appeared in Franklin's chest.

"Do something!" James yelled at the warrior. "They're killing him."

The warrior stood without moving or speaking as the cowboy rushed past him. He had holstered his gun and drawn his sword.

James moved to try and intercept him, but Nancy grabbed him and pulled him back.

The cowboy's attack was vicious. His first blow cut through Franklin's parka, severing his arm from his torso. He turned and slashed across Franklin's chest, then back again, leaving a bloody *X*.

He brought the sword around in a horizontal strike that cut halfway through Franklin's throat. No one moved. Franklin tried to speak, but instead, his head fell backward, and Floating Feather exploded out of the opening and into the light of dawn.

The warrior cracked his ice chain like a whip. It wrapped itself around Floating Feather's waist before coiling out farther and encircling his wrists like frozen handcuffs. The warrior jerked back on the chain, and Floating Feather's arms became bound to his sides.

"You can't do this to me, I have served him well! I—"

A patch of ice formed across Floating Feather's mouth, and he fell silent.

The warrior mounted his horse and pulled Floating Feather onto the saddle in front of him.

"Wait," James said. "What about Franklin?"

The warrior seemed not to hear him and turned the horse to face the rising sun.

The cowboy appeared in front of the warrior's horse. He took off his hat and threw it on the ground at the horse's feet. Flames shot up out of it. He pointed his sword at the warrior and slashed it through the air.

"Do you dare threaten me?" the warrior asked.

The cowboy again carved the air with his blade.

"See what you hold in your hand?" The warrior raised his hand and lightning struck the cowboy's blade, turning it to ice. "The Great One fears not your folly." The blade shattered into a million pieces. "Because you are of the other, you fear not. He has given you false hope. When he speaks, he lies. When he speaks, you listen and live that lie." The warrior nudged his horse forward and started past him.

The cowboy raised his hands. A wall of flame surrounded the horse and its rider, but the warrior walked his horse through it unsinged.

"Return to your master and tell him you have failed to bring Floating Feather to the flames. Tell him that Floating Feather will rest tonight in the arms of the Great One where he belongs."

The cowboy opened his mouth as if to scream, but instead of sound, flames shot from his mouth and eyes. The heat was so hot that the snow on top of the mountain melted, and the remains of Franklin's body burst into flames.

The warrior stretched out his hand. A beam of pure ice shot from it and met the cowboy's fire. Great billows of steam rose into the air. Boiling hot water fell like rain, burning James, Nancy, and Calvin's exposed skin. They huddled together and moved as far away as they could from the battle.

The cowboy stumbled under the pressure of the warrior's ice. The little man rushed over and tried to help him keep to his feet. He stumbled, fell into the cowboy's flame, and was carried by it into the warrior's ice. He hung there for a moment, trapped between them. His skin began to melt. His features ran together, then broke apart into ice crystals that were caught up in the steam and carried away.

The cowboy's flame stopped abruptly, his shoulders sagged forward, and his head dropped till his chin touched his chest.

"When he speaks, he lies," the warrior said again. "Were his lies worth the loss of the only thing you ever loved?"

The warrior dug his heels into his horse's ribs and galloped off into the morning sun.

James had been watching all of it from the safety of the rocks at the end of the path.

"Is it over?" Nancy asked.

"Not for me, it's not." James pulled away from her and stepped out to the middle of the path. "Hey you!" he yelled at the cowboy. He was angry, he wanted to see an end to this cowboy once and for all. He needed to make sure that this demon from another time would not show up again on his doorstep, or his son's, or grandson's doorstep. He grabbed a rock and threw it at the cowboy.

"James! Stop it!" Nancy yelled from behind him.

The rock struck the cowboy in the top of the head. A small fissure opened, and black blood ran down and across his scarred face. The cowboy looked up at him, their eyes locked, and James started to perspire. His mouth became dry, he swallowed hard, trying to force moisture into his throat. His eyes started to burn. He blinked, and it felt like his eyeballs had turned to sandpaper.

Another rock smashed into the cowboy's head. He pivoted away from James to face Calvin.

"G-G-G-Go away," Calvin stuttered. "You've d-d-d-done enough d-d-d-damage!" He had another rock behind his back, and he threw it at the cowboy. His aim was true, and the rock smashed into the cowboy's rotten mouth.

Calvin's shirt burst into flame. James turned his back on the cowboy, ran and tackled Calvin, smothering the flames with his body.

"Tsk, tsk, tsk," a voice said from behind them. "What is this world coming to? Two grown-ass men rolling around in the mud like little piggies while that nasty old cowboy kills their woman?"

James and Calvin jumped to their feet just as the cowboy pulled the single shot revolver from his vest pocket and placed the barrel against Nancy's temple. His skeletal hand, full of her hair, held her tight against him.

"Whatcha gonna do now, hero?" Smoke billowed up from behind a rock outcropping as a red monolith of a being stepped out into the clearing. It stood at least eight feet tall; its naked body was the color of hot coals, and it was covered head to foot in course black hair. A giant cigar stuck out from the corner of its mouth, the smoke encircling its head before drifting off on the morning air.

"Hmmm, what to do? What to do?" it mumbled rhythmically.

"Let her go," James said emphatically. "Just let her go. You can take me if you have to, but just don't hurt her."

"Or m-m-m-me," Calvin interjected.

The giant demon started to laugh, its red body rippling as it raised its face to the morning sun and howled with laughter. "Do you hear that, cowboy? We can take one of them, *if* we have to!" It reached out and put its arm around James' neck. Its skin was hot, and James' skin prickled and itched where it touched him, like he had been rolling in poison ivy. "Let's get something straight here, Doc."

James cut his eyes toward the demon.

"Yeah, that's right, I know you're a doc. Just like I know that pretty little girl that's preggers with your kid is a nurse, and this roly-poly bowl of jelly here," it pointed at Calvin, "runs a medical museum because he could never pass his medical school boards."

It reached over and threw its other arm around Calvin's neck and pulled him in close, too. "Let's get something straight here," it whispered. "Me and the cowboy over there, we work for a fella that could use a few folks like you on his team. It's not such a bad gig. You do what you want, whenever you want, wherever you want, and for as long as you want. When the boss has a job for you, you do it, then get to go about your business."

It let them go and sauntered over to the cowboy and Nancy. "We don't need the girl, so if you agree to join our happy little band of gypsies, we'll let her go." It nodded at the cowboy who lowered the pistol. "On the other hand."

The cowboy raised the pistol to the side of Nancy's head again and pulled the hammer back till it locked in place. "What do you think boys, have we got a deal?"

Thunder rumbled and a massive cloud formed in the sky. The demon looked up. When it turned back to them, James thought it looked worried.

"What do you say boys? It's now or nev—"

Lightning burst from the clouds and struck the demon's back. It bellowed in pain and threw itself to the ground. It writhed in the mud; its skin began to blister and boil.

A second bolt of lightning struck the cowboy, knocking him away from Nancy. She ran for cover. The cowboy started after her, but a chain of ice flew out of the clouds and wrapped itself around his ankles, tripping him and causing him to fall face-first into the mud next to the demon.

The warrior appeared atop his horse. When its hooves touched the ground, a wave of ice shot out from under them, traveling in the direction of the demon and the cowboy. Before it could reach them, the ground opened, and a giant flaming hand reached out and pulled them under. The ground closed above them and immediately froze in place.

Nancy ran to James and threw her arm around him. He held her tight and kissed her cheeks and lips, then remembered her broken arm and loosened his grip.

"Th-Th-Th-Thank you," Calvin said as the warrior walked past him toward the burned remains of Franklin's body.

James walked over to where the warrior had knelt and was holding his hands over Franklin's remains.

"Can you do anything, for Franklin?" James asked. "I mean, he was a good man and a good friend."

The warrior never acknowledged him, only continued passing his hands in a circular motion above Franklin's still smoldering remains.

A crack appeared in the surface, and steam rose around what was left of Franklin. Nancy moved back next to Calvin and pulled James with her.

The warrior began to chant under his breath. His call became louder with each pass of his hand, as did the crevasse in the mountaintop. The steam surrounded them, and a moment later, the warrior rose from within it with Franklin's restored body in his arms.

"Franklin!" Nancy cried. Tears filled her eyes.

James held her close. Calvin reached out and took her hand in his.

They watched silently as the warrior raised Franklin's limp body skyward. The warrior gave a loud cry and lightening filled the sky above him. He knelt, and with great reverence, laid Franklin's body in the grave. Steam rose up around them. When it cleared, the warrior had disappeared, the surface was again solid, and Franklin stood there flanked by two Indians. Their skin was an iridescent white as were the feathers in the headdresses, their leather breeches, and the moccasins on their feet.

A cold wind rushed up the mountain, bringing with it a new round of fat, wet snowflakes and carrying Franklin and his Indians guides up and into the dissipating clouds.

Nancy shivered as they watched them go.

The heavy snow began accumulating around their feet.

Calvin held up his hand. "Wait!" he shouted and scurried away.

James helped Nancy to the snowmobiles, then lifted her onto the seat and climbed on behind her.

"I'm going to miss him," Nancy said, looking up into the rapidly clearing sky.

Calvin picked up something off the ground and hurried back.

"What is that?" James asked.

Calvin laid a dirty, white oiled-cloth bundle on the seat of his snowmobile.

"Is that the surgical kit?" Nancy asked. "The last time I saw it, the little man was holding it."

Calvin untied the leather strap, unrolled the kit, and chuckled.

"What is it, what's so funny?" James asked.

Calvin lifted the kit and shook it above the seat of the snowmobile. Rust flakes and broken metal shards poured out of it. He bent down and blew them off the seat. The fragments mixed with the snow, turning it a dingy orange.

"What are we w-w-w-we going to do now?"

"Well," James said and started his snowmobile. "We don't have enough gas to get back to town. So, I guess we head back to that house and try and make the best of it until someone else is fool enough to come up here."

Calvin nodded, started the other snowmobile, dropped it into gear, and after a jack-rabbit start, made his way down the side of the mountain.

With his arms around Nancy, James revved the throttle, then followed in Calvin's tracks.

The End

Epilogue

December 25, 2008
Skykomish, Washington

Jerry inserted his ID card into the scanner mounted on the wall outside a nondescript metal door at the back of Jenny's Cash and Grab Market. There was a series of low tones, then the metal tumblers in the lock turned, and the door opened. He stepped inside an elevator that was just big enough to hold him and pulled the door closed. He stood in the pitch black of the elevator shaft and waited patiently for the small bell to ring that would signal his descent.

Ding.

The elevator shuddered, then began making the five-minute drop that would place him more than a mile underneath the Mt. Baker-Snoqualmie National Forest.

He had dreaded this trip when he first arrived there at the lab seventeen years ago. A fairly severe case of claustrophobia along with his childhood fears of the dark had almost caused him to walk away from his work. But he had soldiered on, and in time, he came to look forward to his *daily dive* as he called it. He used it as a time to gather his thoughts and prepare for his day.

The elevator made a soft landing. A metal door unlatched in front of him, spilling a shaft of light into the elevator from the hallway outside.

The light in the hallway always felt harsh after his daily dive, and he hesitated a moment outside the elevator door to let his eyes adjust. Satisfied that he could see well enough to find the way to his lab, he made his way down a short hallway, then around the corner to the check-in station.

Corporal Harry Henson was sitting in a small, metal cubicle behind a wall of metal fencing. He smiled as Jerry approached. "Merry Christmas, Dr. Whitworth! What's it like topside today?"

"It's a white Christmas, Harry. I would have been here sooner, but I about had an accident on the way in. I almost hit a sleigh, if you can believe that. It was being pulled by eight reindeer, and it dropped out of the sky right in front of me. I thought I was gonna have to fight the fat old man that was driving it, but instead, he just reached into a big bag on the back seat and gave me this." Jerry reached into the pocket of his overcoat and brought out a baggie full of Christmas cookies tied with a silver ribbon. "Merry Christmas, Harry." He handed the corporal the cookies through a little window, along with his ID.

"That's a good one, Doc." Harry took his ID and scanned it, then pointed to a small notebook on a chain hanging on Jerry's side of the barrier. "You know the drill. Sign in, date and time."

Jerry lifted the notebook and signed his name on the first available line followed by 830A /12242008. He let the book drop back on its chain.

"Come on in!" Harry said around a mouthful of cookie.

There was a buzz, then the sound of metal tumblers turning as a door in the fencing rolled open. He stepped through and took his ID back from Harry.

"See you tonight, Harry."

"Not tonight, you won't. As soon as my replacement shows up, I'm off to Yakima to see my folks. Mom's got a turkey in the oven and mashed potatoes and gravy cooking on top!"

"That sounds amazing, Harry. Have a serving for me."

"You got it, Doc, and Merry Christmas!"

Jerry raised his hand as he walked down the long hallway that led to the computer research and development department. He got lost in the echo of his own steps as he passed the doors to some of the other top-secret labs that were part of Carracorp's underground facility.

He seldom, if ever, saw anyone else in the halls and had on more than one occasion speculated that he was Carracorp's only real working scientist. He raised his ID and placed it against the scanner outside the lab door. There was a low whirling noise, then a door at eye level popped open, and he pressed his right eye to the small contraption inside it. He felt as much as saw the thin blue line that traveled over his pupil, confirming his identity. His lab door opened with a hiss. The overhead fixtures automatically came on when he stepped inside, filling the large room with soft white light.

"Good morning, Anthony," he called out as he took off his overcoat and draped it over his office chair.

"Good morning, Jerry," a soft voice answered from the back of the room. A large computer screen mounted on the back wall of the lab came to life, first blue, then after a few seconds of black, a man's face appeared on the screen.

Jerry walked over to a Mr. Coffee that was programmed to brew a fresh pot every morning at 8:20 a.m. He poured himself a cup, then added a pack of sugar.

"And how are you this morning, Anthony?" he asked and took a sip of the hot coffee.

He had begun working on the Anthony computer model shortly after he first arrived at Carracorp. It was designed to mimic human thought, responses, and reasoning. The bigwigs had been looking for a fast track to creating an affordable computerized home assistant; something that could do a person's daily grunt work as well as balance their checkbook, cook their meals, and make the small decisions that seemed to tie up people's free time. With his background in advanced robotics and computer learning, Jerry had been Carracorp's first choice to head the department. Initially, he had a crew of ten geniuses working under him, but over the years that had dwindled to just two: himself and his assistant, Carl. He had given Carl the day off. It was Christmas after all.

Anthony gave no response.

"I said, how are you this morning, Anthony?" Jerry asked again.

"I am," came the soft-spoken response. The face on the computer monitor smiled, then the monitors at the ten other stations around the room came to life, filling it with Anthony's smiling face. "I am," they all repeated. "I am."

The End

Vince Pinkerton
August 2nd, 2023

A portion of this book was written in the Benson Lodge, located in Silverton Colorado. Six miles south of the Animas Forks ghost town.

Milton Keynes UK
Ingram Content Group UK Ltd.
UKHW040716050824
446355UK00013B/4